Additional Praise for *The Drifter*

"A page-turner with a shout-out to vets everywhere, *The Drifter* is a first-class crime novel set in a second-tier city with plenty of third-rate lowlifes." —*Shelf Awareness*

"Superb . . . A tautly written thriller . . . with a convincing plot, mean and nasty and full of real character. Edgy and slowly boiling to a thrilling climax, this book will hold your interest long after a late night of reading."
—Examiner.com

"A powerful, empathetic, and entertaining tale about the plight many combat veterans face when they come home from Iraq and Afghanistan. Top-notch storytelling." —*Kirkus Reviews* (starred)

"Nicholas Petrie's *The Drifter* has one of the most thrilling openings I've ever read, involving a dank crawlspace, the nastiest, smelliest dog in creation, and a former Marine lieutenant still suffering from the trauma of his war. It can't get better than this, I figured, but it does. Petrie's novel keeps accelerating even as it burrows ever deeper into the dark heart of the new American dream. It is a sterling debut. And yes, the dog is a star."
—William Lashner, *New York Times*–bestselling author of *The Barkeep*

"[Ash's] sharply intelligent, witty voice strikes the right tone for an honest exploration of the challenges returning veterans face, and while this wandering veteran will remind some of Jack Reacher, Peter's struggle to overcome PTSD sets him apart. An absorbing thriller debut with heart." —*Booklist*

"Petrie's expertly paced plot sets a colorful array of characters on a collision course. Readers will look forward to seeing more of the resourceful Ash." —*Publishers Weekly*

"Petrie's impressive debut thriller is fine tuned, the action gripping, and through Ash offers a well-drawn portrait of a vet who can't escape his combat experience. Like Raymond Chandler's Philip Marlowe, Ash's philosophy of detection is to poke a stick into something and see what happens. His discoveries will keep the reader on edge and whet the appetite for more from this author." —*Library Journal*

"Nicholas Petrie's debut novel follows the compelling story of one former Marine's struggle to reacclimate himself to civilian life while honoring his commitment to a fallen soldier. That alone is reason to keep reading, but Petrie amps up the stakes in surprising fashion, creating a story that is moving, thrilling and satisfying on every level. . . . [An] intimate story of personal discovery as well as an obsessive pageturner of a book."

—*BookPage*

"Gritty and engaging, this debut novel will capture readers from the first word. Edge-of-your-seat action keeps the plot racing to a stunning conclusion. . . . This is a fantastic first novel and a captivating thriller."

—*RT Book Reviews* (4 ½ stars)

Titles by Nick Petrie

Light It Up

Burning Bright

The Drifter

THE DRIFTER

Nick Petrie

G. P. PUTNAM'S SONS
NEW YORK

PUTNAM

G. P. PUTNAM'S SONS
Publishers Since 1838
An imprint of Penguin Random House LLC
375 Hudson Street
New York, New York 10014

The Library of Congress has catalogued the G. P. Putnam's Sons hardcover edition as follows:

Petrie, Nicholas.
The drifter / Nicholas Petrie.
p. cm.
ISBN 9780399174568
1. Veterans—Fiction. 2. Retribution—Fiction. 3. Wisconsin—Fiction. I. Title.
PS3616.E86645D75 2015 2015007436
813'.6—dc23

First G. P. Putnam's Sons hardcover edition / January 2016
First G. P. Putnam's Sons trade paperback edition / August 2016
First G. P. Putnam's Sons premium edition / March 2017
G. P. Putnam's Sons premium edition ISBN: 9780735215207

Printed in the United States of America
10

Caminante, no hay camino.
Se hace el camino al andar.

—Antonio Machado

Traveler, there is no path.
The path is made by walking.

THE DRIFTER

PROLOGUE

The Man in the Black Canvas Chore Coat

He walked into Harder's Grange, announced by a chrome-plated bell mounted to the doorjamb. The faded black barn coat made him look bulky. It was mostly the coat. He wore a John Deere hat pulled down low, but there were no cameras. It was a farm-supply store in the middle of nowhere, like they all were.

He saw a chipped Formica service counter, a pot of overcooked coffee, and a few chairs for waiting customers and old-timers looking for company. He understood that most of these places served as a kind of social center for local farmers, whose lives were pretty solitary. He'd grown up on a farm himself, although not in this state.

Behind the counter was a weather-beaten sixtysomething guy in a red plaid dress shirt. He looked up at his only customer, then tucked the USDA brochure he was using as a bookmark into his paperback vampire novel.

The man in the coat set a pleasant expression on his face. "Morning," he said.

"It definitely is," said the counterman, a wide, cheerful smile stretching his wrinkles into a new topography. "And not a bad one at that. What can I do you for?"

"My mom just bought some property this side of Monroe," said the man in the coat. "Off Highway Eleven. And she needs some fertilizer for her garden."

"Son, you come to the right place. We got all kinds. What do you need?"

"I've been trying to get her to use manure, but she says she can't stand the smell. She's looking to plant a half-acre."

The counterman whistled. "A half-acre? That's some garden."

"Well, she and my dad had six hundred acres of soybeans and corn in Bureau County, Illinois, so a half-acre isn't much to her." He shrugged. "She likes to keep busy since my dad died."

The counterman nodded in sympathy.

"Anyway, with the farm she was using Prairie King, the 64-0-0. I believe two sacks would cover a half-acre, right?"

The counterman looked at him. He was on the far side of sixty, but his brown eyes were clear and focused.

This was always the moment, thought the man in the coat.

He'd told a good story.

He looked right. He sounded right.

But farming and the farm-supply business was local, and the counterman didn't know his face, which counted for a lot.

Especially since 1995. And again since 2001.

Finally the counterman spoke. "Son, that's ammonium nitrate," he said. "I cain't sell to just anyone, even if it is only a hundred pounds. We got rules about that kind of stuff. You got your yellow card?"

"Oh, yeah," said the man in the coat, putting a sheepish look on his face. "Hang on, I got it right here." He pulled out his wallet, a worn-down ballistic nylon item with a camouflage pattern. Even the wallet had been carefully assembled to make a certain impression.

He pulled out a driver's license and a laminated yellow ID showing that he was registered with the state to buy certain kinds of fertilizers and pesticides. The form was a single page. The application fee was $44. The counterfeit driver's license had cost a lot more than that.

The counterman scrutinized both cards, looking from one to the other and back again.

"Looks good," he said. "Nothing personal. And you're only getting a hundred pounds, I know. But the state's dead serious about it." He pushed the cards across the counter to the man in the coat, then flashed a grin. "Wouldn't want any of them goddamned socialists to get hold of this stuff."

The man in the coat smiled.

"No, sir," he said. "We surely wouldn't."

The counterman pecked the order into an antique computer and took payment in cash. He directed his customer around to the loading dock to pick up his fertilizer.

Ten minutes later, the man in the black canvas chore

coat turned the old blue Ford pickup onto the county highway, headed northeast.

It was his second stop that day.

Three more before nightfall.

Right on schedule.

PART 1

1

There was a pit bull under the front porch and it didn't want to come out.

Young Charlie Johnson said, "That dang dog's been there for weeks, sir. It already ate up all the cats and dogs around here. I can't even let my dang little brother out the front door no more."

The hundred-year-old house sat on a narrow lot on the edge of a battered Milwaukee neighborhood that, like the house, had seen better days. It was early November, not warm, not even by Wisconsin standards. The leaves had already fallen from the skeletal trees that towered overhead.

But the sun was out, which counted for something. And the sky was a high, pale morning blue. Not a morning for static. Not at all.

Peter Ash said, "Just how big is this dog?"

Charlie shook his head. "Never seen it up close, sir,

and never in daylight. But it's awfully dang big, I can tell you that."

"Didn't you call animal control?"

"Oh, my mama called," said Charlie. "Two men came, took one look under there, got right back in their truck and drove away."

Charlie wore a school uniform, a light-blue permanent-press dress shirt, dark-blue polyester dress pants, and giant polished black shoes on his oversized feet. He was the kind of skinny, big-eared, twelve-year-old kid who could eat six meals a day and still be hungry.

But his eyes were older than his years. They didn't miss a thing.

He was watching Peter Ash now.

Peter sat on the closed lid of a wooden toolbox, his wide, knuckly hands on the work-worn knees of his carpenter's jeans, peering through the narrow access hatch cut into the rotted pine slats enclosing the space under the porch. He had to admit the dog sounded big. He could hear it growling back there in the darkness. Like a tank engine on idle, only louder.

He had a .45 under the seat of his pickup, but he didn't want to use it. It wasn't the dog's fault, not really. It was hungry and scared and alone, and all it had was its teeth.

On the other hand, Peter had told Charlie's mother, Dinah, that he would fix the rotting supports beneath her ancient porch.

She hadn't mentioned the dog.

Peter really couldn't blame her.

Her husband had killed himself.

And it was Peter's fault.

Peter was lean and rangy, muscle and bone, nothing extra. His long face was angular, the tips of his ears slightly pointed, his dark hair the unruly shag of a buzz cut grown wild. He had the thoughtful eyes of a werewolf a week before the change.

Some part of him was always in motion—even now, sitting on that toolbox, peering under that porch, his knee bobbed in time to some interior metronome that never ceased.

He'd fought two wars over eight years, with more deployments than he cared to remember. The tip of the spear. He'd be thirty-one in January.

As he bent to look through the narrow access hatch under the porch, he could feel the white static fizz and pop at the base of his skull. That was his name for the fine-grained sensation he lived with now, the white static. A vague crackling unease, a dissonant noise at the edge of hearing. It wasn't quite uncomfortable, not yet. The static was just reminding him that it didn't want him to go inside.

Peter knew it would get worse before he was done.

So he might as well get to it.

The space under the porch was about three feet high. Maybe twelve feet wide and twelve deep, with a dirt floor. About the size of four freshly dug graves, laid sideways. The smell was rank, worse than a sergeant's feet after two months in a combat outpost. But not as bad as a two-week-old corpse.

Light trickled in through the slatted sides of the porch, but shadows shrouded the far corner, some kind of cast-off crap back there. And that growl he could just about feel through the soles of his boots.

It would be good to do this without being chewed on too much.

He went out to his truck and found a cordless trouble light, some good rope, and a length of old handrail. White oak, an inch and three-quarters thick, maybe eighteen inches long. Nice and solid in the hand. Which was a help when you were contemplating something spectacularly stupid.

Serenaded by the growls from the crawl space, he sat down on the toolbox and took out his knife while young Charlie Johnson watched.

Not that Peter wanted an audience. This certainly could get ugly.

"Don't you have someplace to go, Charlie? School or something?"

Charlie glanced at a cheap black digital watch strapped to his skinny wrist. "No, sir," he said. "Not yet I don't."

Peter just shook his head. He didn't like it, but he understood. He figured he wasn't that far from twelve years old himself.

He cut three short lengths from his rope and left the

remainder long, ten or twelve feet. Tied one end of a short piece of rope tight to each end of the oak rail. Looped the last short rope and the remainder through his belt a single time, so he could get at it quickly.

Then he looked up at Charlie again. "You better get out of here, kid. If this goes bad, you don't want to be around."

Charlie said, "I'm not a dang kid. *Sir.* I'm the man of the family." He reached inside the door, brought out an aluminum baseball bat, and demonstrated his swing. "That's my dang porch. My little brother, too. I ain't going nowhere."

Charlie's dad always had the same look behind the Humvee's .50 turret gun. Eyes wide open and ready for trouble. Daring any motherfucker to pop up with an RPG or Kalashnikov or whatever. But when his wife, Dinah, sent cookies, Big Jimmy Johnson—known inevitably to the platoon's jokers as Big Johnson, or just plain Big—was always the last to eat one.

Peter missed him.

He missed them all. The dead and the living.

He said, "Okay, Charlie. I can respect that." He put his eyes on the boy and held them there. "But if that dog gets loose you get your butt in that house, you hear me? And if you hit me with that bat I'm going to be seriously pissed."

"Yessir." Charlie nodded. "Can't promise anything, sir. But I'll do my best."

Peter smiled to himself. At least the kid was honest.

After that there was nothing more to do but lean back

and kick out the slats on one side of the porch, letting in more daylight. The space was still small. The tank engine in the shadows got louder. But no sign of the dog. Must be lurking in that trash pile in the far corner.

Not that it mattered. He wasn't turning away from the challenge. He was just planning how to succeed.

The familiar taste filled his mouth, a coppery flavor, like blood. He felt the adrenaline lift and carry him forward. It was similar to the static, rising. The body's preparation for fight or flight. It was useful.

He peered under the porch, and the static rose higher still. The static didn't care about the snarling dog. It cared about the enclosure. It jangled his nerves, raced his heart, tightened his chest, and generally clamored for his attention. It wanted him to stay outside in the open air, in the daylight.

Breathing deeply, Peter took the piece of oak and banged it on the wood frame of the porch. It rang like a primitive musical instrument.

Despite everything, he was smiling.

"Hey, dog," he called into the darkness. "Watch your ass, I'm coming in!"

And in he went, headfirst on his elbows and knees, the stick in one hand and the trouble light in the other.

What, you want to live forever?

It was dark and musty under the porch, the smell of weeds and forgotten things, with an animal stink on top. Not a dog smell, but something wilder. Something feral. The smell of the monsters in the oldest of fairy tales, the ones where the monsters sometimes won.

Narrow bars of late-autumn sunshine slanted through the gaps and made it hard to read the space. The dim yellow pool cast by his trouble light wasn't much help. The debris pile in the back corner looked more substantial from this vantage point. There was all kinds of crap in there. Carpet scraps, boxes, old lumber. The splintered bones of missing mailmen.

The growl might have come from anywhere. It seemed to vibrate up through the soil. Peter's little piece of handrail and a few thin ropes didn't seem like much. It would be smart to beat a tactical retreat, get the hell out of there, and return with a shotgun. Or a grenade launcher.

But he didn't.

He kept moving forward on his elbows and knees, white sparks flaring high. Stick in one hand, light in the other. Alive, alive. I am alive.

"Here, doggy. Who's a good doggy?"

The animal waited until Peter was most of the way inside.

Then it came out of hiding in a snarling hurry, teeth flashing white in the darkness. It was big.

Fuck, it was huge and fast and coming right for Peter's head.

When those big jaws opened to tear his face off, Peter reached forward at speed and got that piece of hard oak jammed in there tight, ropes trailing. Now the jaws couldn't snap shut, and couldn't open farther.

The dog, confused, reversed course and tried to spit out the stick. It would use its paws in a moment. Peter went sideways quick and crablike, releasing the stick with one hand long enough to get his arm wrapped around the dog's heavy neck. Caught up the other end of the stick again and trapped it hard in the dog's jaw. Then with the stick as a lever and his arm as the fulcrum, he threw the dog onto its side and laid his weight on its chest, holding the animal to the ground.

Big dang dog is right, Charlie.

Hundred and forty, hundred and fifty pounds. At least.

The dog went silent. Conserving its energy to escape, to get rid of this weight, white eyes rolled back, thrashing and fighting with all of its considerable muscle and will.

But Peter weighed almost two hundred pounds himself, and he was smarter than the dog. He hoped.

His initial plan, if you want to call it that, had been to tie the ropes around the dog's neck to keep the stick in place while holding the dog down with his body.

Not much of a plan, he had to admit now. The dog didn't seem to care much for it, either, still throwing around its big bullet-shaped head, lips curled in a silent snarl, spit flying everywhere.

And it stank like holy hell. Like fear and rage and shit

and death, all wrapped up into one horrible reek that made Peter's eyes water and his sinuses clear.

The stink wouldn't eat his face the way this dog wanted to.

What Peter needed was a third hand.

But Charlie was just twelve. And he was wearing his school clothes. And he was Jimmy's oldest boy. That family had enough damage done.

So Peter was on his own under that porch.

He moved his leg up slowly, carefully, until his knee was on the dog's shoulder, then its neck. He bore down. He didn't want to hurt the animal, but he sure as hell didn't want those bone-cracking teeth to get free, either. The dog's back legs scrabbled in the dirt, trying to get itself out of the situation, but Peter was too heavy.

"Hey, dog," said Peter in a calm voice. "What's your name?"

The dog scrabbled with its long nails, but its big bullet-shaped head was caught now between the pressure of the stick and the weight of the man's knee.

"Somebody probably called you Fang or Spike or something, didn't they?" asked Peter gently, remembering how his father had talked to the horses. A nice calm, conversational tone. The way Jimmy had talked to any in-country local who didn't speak English. "But you're not a mean dog, are you? No, you're a nice puppy. A good puppy. Your name should be Daisy. Or Cupcake."

The dog's eyes showed white in the semidark of the crawl space, and it was panting hard, its great chest heaving. Its legs slowed their scrabbling in the dirt as the man's deep voice worked its way through the fury and panic. Finally it stopped struggling, and the long tongue lolled out between the murderous teeth. Man and beast lay in the dirt together and caught their breath.

"Uh, sir, you okay in there?" Charlie's voice floated under the porch.

"Never better," said Peter, keeping his voice low and even. The dog panted, but the eye was staring at Peter's face.

"So . . ." said Charlie.

"Kid. Give me a minute, okay?"

Peter still held the ends of the stick in his hands. Focused despite the static. He had a few minutes, no more. He worked his hands out to the ropes and slid the knots in close to the dog's jaws.

The dog began to growl again.

Peter could feel the vibrations in his own chest, that tank engine revving slow. It was like lying on a vibrating bed in a cheap motel, but with teeth.

The eye stared at him, waiting.

Waiting for the man to make a mistake.

With the ropes in his hands, Peter carefully crossed them over the bone-crushing jaws, then wrapped them under, over and under, again and again. Snug but not tight, trapping that stick in there like some kind of hillbilly art project. Then he carefully tied the ends in a series of half hitches, ending in a square knot. Super-duper-double-extra-secure.

The remaining long and short ropes were still tucked

into his belt. He tied the long rope around the dog's neck as a collar and leash. He shifted his weight, turned to the hind end with the short rope, and tied its back legs together.

Without allowing himself to think about it, he rolled off the dog and grabbed the rope at the hind legs, then reversed out of the crawl space, pulling the scrabbling dog behind him.

"Sweet holy Jesus," said Charlie, dancing backward in his polished shoes as Peter and the snarling hog-tied animal emerged from the crawl space and into the light. "That's one damn Jesus big goddamn dog."

Peter felt the open air and high blue sky like a balm.

It took a few minutes to get Charlie to put down the baseball bat, but he was fine by the time Peter tied the leash off to a tree, double-checking the knots, then checking them again. Finally he cut the rope from the rear legs and stood away while the dog leaped, trembling, to its feet, ran to the ten-foot limit of the leash, and turned to growl at the humans.

"He sure is ugly," said Charlie. "And he smells real bad, too."

Peter had to agree.

It wasn't a pit bull, actually. Those dogs bred for fighting were beautiful, in their own way. Like cruise missiles were beautiful, or a combat knife, if you didn't stop to consider what they were made to do.

This dog, on the other hand, was a mix of so many breeds you'd have to go back to the caveman era to sort it out.

The result was an animal of unsurpassed hideousness.

It had the bullet-shaped head of a pit bull, but the lean muscled body and long legs of an animal built for chasing down its prey over long distances. Tall upright ears, a long wolfish muzzle. Its matted fur was mostly a kind of deep orange, with brown polka dots.

And the animal was enormous.

Like a timber wolf run through the wash with a pit bull, a Great Dane, and a fuzzy orange sweatshirt.

Seen out in the open like that, even at a hundred and fifty-plus pounds with murderous teeth, it was hard to take the animal too seriously.

What would you name a dog like that?

Maybe Daisy. Or Cupcake.

The thought made him smile.

He got out his water bottle and walked the growling dog down to the end of its rope. Taking hold of the stick, he poured a little water into that deadly mouth. The dog glared at him, the intelligence vivid in those pale blue eyes. But after a moment, its throat began to work as it swallowed. Peter poured until the bottle was empty.

"Sir, what the heck are you doing?" asked Charlie.

Peter shrugged. "Dog's thirsty."

Charlie just looked at him. It was a good look. It said the kid had thought he'd seen all the crazy there was in the world until that very moment, but he had been very, very wrong.

All he said was, "I got to go, sir. I miss first period, Father Lehane says I'm on the bench on Friday." Then he left.

And with the dog growling behind him, Peter went to the truck to unpack his tools and get to work.

2

The porch was sinking into the ground. The bottoms of the original pine posts were turning to mush, and there were no concrete pilings underneath, just a few bricks stacked in the dirt. Fairly typical back in the day. But now the only thing holding up the structure was habit. The porch was used to being there, so it hadn't collapsed.

It wasn't the kind of work Peter had imagined while he was studying econ at Northwestern. Or when he turned down Goldman Sachs for the Marines' Officer Candidates School. It had seemed like a higher calling then, and it still did. Everything else was entirely too theoretical.

But he liked fixing old houses. He'd done it with his dad in northern Wisconsin since he was eight. The job today was simple, a battle he could win using only his mind, his muscles, and a few basic tools. Nobody was likely to die. He could get lost in the challenge and let the war years fade. And at the end of the day, he could see what he'd accomplished, in wood and concrete, right there in front of him.

He braced up the main beam with some two-by-fours he'd brought, removed the rotted posts, and set about digging holes for new footings. The holes had to be at least forty-two inches deep to get below the frost line, so they wouldn't move every winter. In that hard Milwaukee clay, forty-two inches seemed deeper than it ought to be. But Peter's shoulders didn't mind the effort. He liked the fight, how the wood-handled shovel became an extension of his hands. And the white static faded back to a pale hush.

After cutting the rebar and placing it in the bottom of the hole, Peter mixed concrete in a wheelbarrow and poured it into the forms. The dog sat watching, ears up and alert, looking ridiculous with the stick tied into its mouth. When Peter walked past, it fled to the end of its leash and growled at him, that tank engine rumbling as strong as ever. When Peter returned to work, the dog sat down to watch again.

It was like a foreman who didn't make small talk.

But uglier than any foreman Peter had ever met.

Not as ugly as some sergeants, though. Sergeants had the ugly all over that dog.

Lunch was last night's beef stew, reheated on the little backpacking stove and eaten with crusty wheat bread and cold coffee left over from breakfast. Peter sat in his camp chair on the sidewalk, knee bobbing unconsciously to that ceaseless interior metronome, wondering how he'd feed the dog without offering up a piece of himself. No way he was going to take out that stick.

But the animal had to be hungry. Peter left some of the thick stew broth in the pan to cool. He'd pour it past those teeth in another hour.

After lunch, with the concrete hardened but not yet cured, he started cutting out the rotten sections of the deck. When he was done, there was almost nothing left. The supporting joists were sagging, half of them rotted or cracked, and all of them undersized to begin with. It would be easier to replace everything. The only wood worth saving was the main beam and the porch roof overhead. And he might as well replace the beam with something rot-proof, anyway.

It was never simple.

But wasn't that part of the fun?

When it was time for a trip to the lumberyard, Peter put his tools back in the truck. Valuable stuff had a way of walking away when you weren't around, in a working-class neighborhood and every other kind.

He considered the dog for a minute, and decided to leave it where it was.

Who'd want to steal a dog that ugly?

Maybe he'd get lucky and it would escape while he was gone.

But when Peter pulled up in his truck an hour later, there was the dog, as ugly as ever, and smelling just as bad. He chased the growling animal to the end of its rope to check the knots, and found that the rope had frayed a little on one side. He found the spot on the tree where faint blue strands showed on the bark, and smiled.

"Good luck, dog," he said. "That's climbing rope. Kevlar core."

When he reached out to pat the dog's head, the dog shied away. Peter shrugged and went back to work.

He supported the porch roof with long two-by-sixes braced against the ground, then cut out the rest of the deck frame with a Sawzall and hauled the pieces to the street. The dog had taken to rubbing its rope-wrapped chin on the front walk. A pretty good strategy, actually. It kept its eyes on Peter the whole time. He could feel the weight of its stare, a hundred and fifty pounds of dog planning to tear his throat out.

It was better than all those Iraqi freedom fighters. Hell, this was just one dog.

What Peter didn't want to admit was that he almost liked the feeling.

It kept him on his toes. Like old times.

Like the white static was there for a reason.

He unloaded the lumber and stacked it on sawhorses. But before he started putting things together again, he had to clear out all the crap that had accumulated under the porch. He stuffed disintegrating cardboard boxes and trash into construction-grade garbage bags. Broken bricks and scrap lumber he carried to the street. At the very back, tucked against the house, behind a stinking dog bed, was an old black hard-sided suitcase. It was heavier than it looked.

There was a little white mold growing on the side, but it didn't look too bad. There might be some use left in it. Peter didn't believe in throwing stuff away just because it had a little wear.

He set the suitcase by the side door and turned away to finish cleaning up. The stoop was cracked, and the suitcase fell over, then bounced down the four steps to the concrete walk. When it hit bottom, it popped open.

And money fell out.

Crisp hundred-dollar bills. In plain banded ten-thousand-dollar packets. Forty packets, each about a half-inch tall.

Four hundred thousand dollars.

Under Jimmy's broken-down porch.

Peter went back to the suitcase.

It was a smaller Samsonite, about the size of a modern airline carry-on, probably expensive when it was new. But it definitely wasn't new. They didn't make suitcases like this anymore.

Despite its time under that porch, it was in decent shape. Hard to tell if it had been there for thirty years or was bought at Goodwill the month before. Peter picked up one of the stacks of hundreds he'd found inside and flipped through the bills. Mostly newer, with the big Ben Franklin head.

So the suitcase hadn't been there too long.

There were no identifying marks on the Samsonite's outside shell, nothing inside to tell where it had come from. But there were four little elastic pockets on the interior.

Inside each pocket was a small brown paper bag, wrinkled and worn with handling. Peter opened one bag and shook the contents out into his hand. A pale rectangular slab stared up at him. A bit smaller than a paperback book, soft and pliable like modeling clay, smelling slightly of chemicals, with clear plastic sheeting adhered to its faces.

Interesting.

He was pretty sure it wasn't modeling clay.

3

Peter sat on Dinah Johnson's back stoop, waiting for her to come home from work. The suitcase stood closed in the shadow of the steps. On his leg, his restless fingertips kept time to that endless interior metronome. Charlie and his little brother, Miles, were inside, doing whatever boys did in the odd, lonely freedom before their mothers came home from work.

The wind blew hard, another big autumn storm system moving across the continent. No rain, not yet. Early November in Wisconsin, Veterans Day next week. It was dark before suppertime, and getting colder. Frost on the windshield at night. Charlie had already offered Peter hot chocolate twice. He was a good kid. Both concerned and maybe a little relieved that Lieutenant Ash the crazy dog tamer wouldn't come inside.

Peter preferred the outdoors.

After mustering out at Pendleton sixteen months before, he drove north to Washington, where Manny Martinez, another of his former sergeants, was roofing houses outside of Seattle. He left his truck in Manny's driveway, dropped the keys and a note into his mailbox, then hitched a ride northeast, past Marblemount, into the North Cascades. Shouldered the heavy pack and headed uphill alone into the open. Staying off the main trails, above the tree line, away from people, away from everything. He planned to be out for twelve months.

It was an experiment.

He was fine overseas. No, not fine. The war sucked, especially for the infantry. A lot of people were trying to kill him and most of his friends. But it was also exhilarating, a series of challenges to overcome, and Peter was very good at it. Did his job, did it well, took care of his people. Even if it cost. And it did.

Leaving aside the dead, the injured. There were plenty of those. Peter's friends among them.

But the guys still walking around, the guys still in the fight—it wasn't easy for them, either. Some of them had trouble falling asleep, or had nightmares when they did. Overwhelming emotion, fits of tears or fury. A few guys really went off their nut, wanted to kill everyone. Peter had his ups and downs, but stayed pretty steady. His captain called him a natural war fighter. He spent eight years at it, two tours with very little time between deployments. The unit had essential skills, that's what the brass had said.

So, the war aside, he was fine until he got off the plane at Camp Pendleton for the last time.

Approaching the officers' quarters, that was when he first felt it. A fine-grained fizzing sensation as he jogged up the barracks steps. A vague feeling of unease somewhere in the bottom of his brain.

As he walked down the hall, opened the door to his quarters, and stepped inside, it flared into a jittery feeling, a quadruple espresso on an empty stomach. Unpacking his ruck, he felt the muscles in his shoulders and back begin to cramp up. He thought he might be getting the flu.

He showered and changed his clothes, sat at the little desk to do paperwork, but the sparks in his head were rising with a panicky feeling that was impossible to ignore. He couldn't stay in the chair, and he couldn't focus on the pages in front of him. His shirt felt too close at the neck.

Then his chest began to tighten. He had trouble catching his breath. The walls got closer, the ceiling lower. His heart a sledgehammer in his chest.

He didn't even bother to put on his socks and boots, just carried them down the hall and out the main door into the open air, where he could begin to breathe. He told himself he needed some exercise, and walked around the base for a few hours. It helped.

When he went to the mess for supper, it happened again. The mess hall was too loud, too crowded, and the fluorescent lights flickered like those in a horror movie.

He cut in line, grabbed a burger, and fled. He ate outside, walking around, wondering what was wrong with him.

When he went back to his quarters, the pressure in his head grew faster than ever. He knew after five minutes he'd never manage to sleep in there. So he pulled a blanket from the bed and found an empty hilltop out in the scrubland that made up most of the base.

How he survived through the final days of mustering out he didn't know. Drinking helped, but it wasn't a long-term solution.

He called it the white static. His very own war souvenir.

Which was why he came up with the experiment.

The hypothesis was simple. If the white static came when he went inside a building or in a crowd of people, Peter would spend a year outside, alone. Living out of a backpack, up above the tree line when possible, with only the mountains for company.

Maybe give the static a chance to get used to civilian life and fade out completely.

The first days were fine, hiking steeply up through the ancient evergreen forest. As he got tired of listening to nothing but his own thoughts, it got harder. He had no phone, no music player. But after two weeks, his head felt transparent to the world, his thoughts blown from his mind. The static was replaced by the sound of the wind. It occurred to him that he might never go down to the so-called civilized world.

After what he'd seen, he wasn't that impressed with humanity, anyway.

Up in the high country, he lived mostly on lentils and rice, wild greens, and trout caught with his fly rod. Gourmet living. Coffee and hot chocolate were his luxuries. He started with several big caches of food hung from trees in bear-proof cans. He thrived up in the granite and heather for four months without needing to resupply. He walked a vast loop through the North Cascades, keeping off the marked trails. Usually off any trail at all. It made him feel wild and pure and clean. He thought it might cure him.

He made those first supplies last as long as he could before going back to the populated world. Roads and houses. Commerce and government. He hitched a ride on the tailgate of a logger's pickup and, at the outskirts of town, found a small grocery store.

It was the first test of his hypothesis.

But walking through the parking lot, he already knew. The closer he got to the door, the louder the static sounded in his head. He still needed supplies, so he clenched his teeth in the narrow, crowded aisles under the fluorescent lights, trying to get what he needed and into the open air before the white static turned to sparks and began to rise up inside him.

He climbed up into the empty mountains again, where the wind washed him clean. South for the winter, north for the summer. Every time he came down for supplies, the static was still there. After a year, he extended the experiment. Give it another four months. Or forever.

Then Jimmy killed himself.

Peter was deep in the backcountry of the Klamath Mountains in northern California when Manny Martinez heard about Jimmy's suicide and got on the horn. The informal sergeants' network had a long reach. Four days later, an off-duty fireman from Klamath Falls walked up to Peter's campsite with a sorrowful look on his face, and that was the end of that.

From his perch on Dinah's back steps, he saw headlights in the alley, then heard her garage door rolling up. So he was prepared when he saw her. He stood as she walked the cracked concrete path from the garage. The motion light came on, brightening the yard only a little.

"Oh," she said, slowing. She looked him up and down, seeing a lean, rangy man in worn carpenter's jeans and combat boots. The big restless hands at the end of long bony wrists that stuck out past the sleeves of his brown canvas work coat. Her eyes lingered on his angular face, wolfish and unshaven.

Her expression was neutral. It occurred to Peter that maybe he wasn't quite what she expected in a Marine officer.

She said, "You must be Lieutenant Ash."

"Yes, ma'am," he said. "I appreciate your letting me get started without meeting in person. You said that the front porch was your most pressing repair, and you were correct." He tried a smile. He wasn't used to people yet. "Please," he said. "Call me Peter. Jimmy talked about you so much I feel like I know you."

She didn't answer. She was tall, almost as tall as Peter, and wrapped in a long wool coat that went past her knees. She carried her keys spiked out from her fist, something Jimmy would have taught her for self-defense. It looked natural.

She measured him with cool eyes, reserving judgment. But polite.

"Please, come in," she said. "You must be hungry. I'm making supper, if you'd care to stay."

"I'll wait outside," he said. "It's a nice night."

"Don't be silly," she said. "It's cold. Please, come in."

Peter pointed at the back door, the bottom panel covered with a piece of bare plywood. "Something happen here?" he asked. It looked like a quick repair after someone had kicked in the door.

"We had a break-in," she said. "Not long after James." She blinked. "Died."

"I'm sorry," said Peter. "I can replace that when I'm done with your porch."

She turned her key in the lock. "Come inside," she said. "Get out of the cold."

He hesitated, but picked up the suitcase and followed her inside.

He had questions.

4

She sat him down at the big kitchen table, where the static prickled at the base of his brain. Peter took long, slow breaths. His knee bounced to the time of his internal metronome. In a few minutes his shoulders would start to get tight.

Dinah set her large canvas handbag on a wooden chair, then went deeper into the house to hang up her coat and check on her boys. The bag was big enough to carry a complete change of clothes, including shoes. Maybe two or three pairs of shoes.

He heard the front door open, then her sharp intake of air. And the growl of the ugly dog at the far end of its rope.

She came back into the kitchen. "Lieutenant Ash." She raised her eyebrows in an expression that was half surprise and half reproach. "You're doing more than a few repairs. My porch is gone."

She didn't comment on the dog.

"Please, call me Peter," he said. "And yes, I took some liberties. But once I started to take it apart, I could tell it wasn't safe. Don't worry, I'll have it together again tomorrow or the day after. And it's all on the U.S. Marine Corps."

Peter had seen her picture in Iraq, Dinah with the two boys. Jimmy carried it in his shirt pocket on every mission. Said they were his good-luck charm.

He'd clutched it tight waiting for the medevac, eyes locked on the faces of his family while the corpsman was putting the tourniquet on his leg. "I'm such a lucky bastard," he said, his grin widening as the morphine kicked in. "You got to come visit when you get stateside."

Peter had gone to the mountains instead.

In the picture with her kids, Dinah had seemed fragile, like fine china kept high on a shelf.

In person, she was anything but.

He knew she was an ER nurse, so he was expecting the air of calm competence. But he wasn't prepared for how the green hospital scrubs showed her shape, or the way she carried herself, fluid, capable motion with her head held high, her back straight as an iron rod.

And the picture definitely hadn't captured her eyes.

They were the pale blue of deep glacier ice, and filled with knowledge and sadness. And no small amount of concern.

Dinah Johnson clearly hadn't made up her mind about him quite yet.

Jimmy came home damaged in body and soul. Peter hadn't done a very good job taking care of Jimmy over there, and he'd never come to visit when he got stateside. Jimmy had recovered from his physical injuries, after multiple surgeries and months of physical therapy. But his other injuries, the ones not visible to the eye, must have been beyond healing.

Less than a month ago, Jimmy had killed himself.

The least Peter could do was fix the porch on Jimmy's house.

Even if he had to lie to Jimmy's widow to do it.

He'd called her from Manny's house, less than a week after he'd heard the news. He wanted to help.

If he was honest with himself, he'd say he *needed* to help.

So he invented a Marine Corps program that provided free home repairs for the families of veterans. Dinah was the only client, and funding came from Peter's back pay.

From Jimmy's description of the house, there would be no shortage of projects.

And from Jimmy's description of his wife, Peter knew Dinah wouldn't take the help unless he showed up at her doorstep and got to work.

Peter had known women like her all his life. Women who worked long, hard days. Women for whom, even when there was no extra money, even with bills left unpaid, charity was what you did for others.

For yourself, you worked harder. You made do.

But maybe he was wrong. There were new facts to be considered.

A suitcase full of money, for example.

He wouldn't mention the four pale plastic-wrapped rectangles. For the moment, he'd tucked them under the seat of his truck.

Peter hadn't quite made up his mind about Dinah Johnson, either.

When she returned to the kitchen and began to rummage in the cabinets, Peter picked up the little suitcase and set it on the table. The static was rising, and he could feel the muscles starting to clamp up in his shoulders. He didn't know how much time he had before he'd need to go back outside.

"I found this under the porch," he said. "It might have some use left, if you want it. Or maybe you know someone who wants it."

She swiveled the suitcase this way and that, half smiling. "I can scrub that mildew right off." She turned to Peter, her face open and curious. "How is it on the inside?"

Nobody could be that good a liar.

She'd never seen that suitcase before in her life.

"You'll never believe it," said Peter.

Dinah popped the latch and her eyes grew wide. The hundred-dollar bills were crisp and new. She covered her mouth with her hand. Then reached out and slammed the lid shut. Glaring at Peter, she said, "You take that out of here right now."

That wasn't what Peter had expected.

"You're telling me this isn't your money?" he said.

Hands on her hips, she glared at him. "Lieutenant, do you think my home would be in this condition if it was? You think I'd keep *that* in a suitcase under my porch?"

"Maybe you're holding it for somebody," said Peter.

She shook her head, those clear blue eyes locked on his face. "No."

"You know whose it is?"

"No," she said again, but her eyes went sliding off to the side. "I haven't the slightest idea." Abruptly she stood up and began to take things out of the refrigerator. "I really haven't."

She hadn't been lying before, about not having seen the suitcase.

But she was definitely lying now.

She stood at the stove, stirring something that smelled wonderful. Peter's shoulders were clamping up in the small kitchen, sweat beginning to pop on the back of his neck. The fact that three dark doorways opened to unseen parts of the house didn't help. The static turning into sparks. His breath felt trapped in his chest.

This was Jimmy's house, he told himself, breathing deep. Jimmy's kitchen. The long, slow breaths helped stall the static as he watched Dinah's graceful dance from fridge to sink to stove, and it calmed him. Bought him a few minutes, anyway.

He said, "You could do a lot of good with that money, ma'am."

She wore her dark hair short and simple. No makeup that he could see. But there was something formal about her, a guarded perimeter that did not invite intimacy. Maybe it was her grief. Maybe it was something else. But he couldn't quite bring himself to call her Dinah.

She didn't call him Peter, either.

"Lieutenant Ash, I don't want that money. And I don't wish to talk about it. Have you eaten supper?"

"No, ma'am."

"Please let me feed you before you go," she said. "I don't keep alcohol in the house, but would you care for a glass of milk?"

"Yes, ma'am. Thank you."

She set down a tall glass of milk and a big china plate loaded with eggs scrambled with onions and peppers and cheese, buttered wheat toast and spicy refried beans on the side, then carried out two more loaded plates to the bedroom for Charlie and Miles. The smell of the food was like a drug. The static subsided, just a little.

She served herself and sat at the table.

"This was James's favorite meal. I hope you like it. I made it every Sunday night when we first got married. When he was home on leave, he wanted it every day for a week. That man surely could eat."

Peter took a bite of the eggs. They were rich and spicy. He took another bite, with some of the beans on the fork, too. It was easy to see why this would be anybody's favorite meal. "It's delicious," he said. "Thank you."

But Dinah hadn't taken a bite yet. She said, "Tell me something I don't know about my husband."

Peter set down his fork and thought for a minute. "He was good at his job—"

"You mean killing people." Her stare was bleak.

"No, ma'am," said Peter softly.

The static crackled and climbed, distracting him. He cleared his throat.

"Jimmy was a very good Marine. When there was fighting, you were glad he was there. But for Jimmy, that wasn't a sergeant's real job. His real job was to understand the men he commanded. To protect them. To keep everybody alive while they did their job. He was my second in command for two long deployments. I only knew him for a few years, but he was my best friend in the Corps." He blinked. "In the world."

She was quiet for a moment. Then she said, "James and I didn't talk about the war after he came home. Maybe he was afraid of what I would think of him. He joined up after Nine-Eleven, to fight the Taliban. He wanted to defend our country. But he ended up in Iraq, fighting the wrong war."

She looked at Peter. "Maybe you don't agree with that," she said. "But he loved the men he worked with.

He talked about returning to school so he could get a job at the VA. He wanted to help his men after they got home, too."

"He would have been good at it," said Peter. "He was smart. And Jimmy—well, you know what a big guy he was, and with body armor, a helmet and an M4, he was huge. He was intimidating as hell, is what he was."

Peter stared into the darkness, remembering.

"Until he smiled. When he cracked that wide, goofy smile at a checkpoint or a neighborhood meeting, everybody else would smile, too. The civilians, the soldiers. Hell, the whole Mahdi Army. That smile was contagious. You just knew, seeing it, that he would be a good friend if you let him. Everybody liked him. Which made all of us safer. The platoon. The civilians. The women and children down the street."

Peter looked over at Dinah Johnson. She sat very still in her green hospital scrubs, her back straight and proud, her untouched plate steaming on the table, while the tears slid slowly down her cheeks.

After a moment she stood and went to fill the coffeemaker.

Peter finished his meal while the static rose and the room got smaller and his chest felt like it was wrapped in steel bands.

She came over with two white china mugs and the coffeepot. "Do you take cream or sugar?"

Then she looked at him. Her eyes on his face, his posture. The way he twitched in his chair.

"Did I say something?"

"It's nothing." He shook his head, and the simple motion made his vision blur, just for a moment. It was like sparks were coming out of his ears. Part of him was surprised they didn't light up the room. "I should go." He stood and took his jacket off the chairback and walked to the door.

"Lieutenant? Is something the matter?"

He opened the ruined door and walked down the steps as the cool night air washed over him. The stars were dim in the ambient light of the city, but still they shone overhead. His shoulders dropped and his chest began to open.

She watched him from the doorway for a long moment. Peter was ready to leave when she said, "Stay right there."

She disappeared inside, but left the door open. Peter took deep breaths.

When she returned, she wore her long wool coat and carried the two mugs steaming in the night air. "It's decaf," she said.

She sat on the steps, her mug on her knee. Peter stood in the yard, listening to the wind in the trees, feeling his breath come more easily.

"Thank you," he said.

For the food, for the kindness. For not asking questions.

"You're welcome." She lifted her mug. "Drink up before it gets cold."

They drank their coffee in silence.

"Listen," Peter finally said. "About that suitcase."

"No." She shook her head sharply. "Take it with you, or give it away. I don't care what you do with it. But I don't want it in this house."

Peter nodded. "I understand that," he said. "But what happens if the person who left it under your porch comes back for it?"

Again, he didn't mention the plastic-wrapped rectangles. He didn't want to worry her more than she already was.

She watched the steam rise from her cup. Peter could see the wheels turning behind her eyes. She was the kind of person who wore her thoughts on her face, if you paid attention.

He said, "If that person sees the porch has been fixed, won't he wonder about his money? And won't you want to have it here, to return to him?"

She warmed her hands on her mug and took a sip before looking up at him. The pale blue of her eyes was startling.

"It must have been James's money," she said. "I can't think of how else it might have gotten there." She shook her head, looking down at her coffee. "That's not honest money. All those crisp, new hundred-dollar bills."

If it truly was Jimmy's money. But Jimmy was the most honest man Peter had ever met.

He said, "So I should turn it over to the police?"

Dinah didn't say anything.

"Why shouldn't that money be yours?" said Peter. "Think of it like winning the lottery. Pay off your house. Pay for college for your boys. Save the rest for a rainy day."

"No," she said. She took a breath and let it out. "It would be noticed."

Peter felt the muscles bunch involuntarily in his arms and shoulders.

Now he understood why someone had broken into her house. The thieves hadn't found what they were looking for. But maybe they were still looking.

He said, "Is someone watching the house?"

"Leave the money here tonight," she said. "I believe I know where it came from. Tomorrow we'll go make certain."

"Dinah, wait."

She stood with her coffee and stepped up to the badly repaired doorway. "I work an early shift tomorrow," she said. "I'll be home about three. We'll go then."

The skin around her eyes was tight, the wide and generous mouth set hard, but she stood tall and proud. No, there was nothing fragile about her. She was a military wife, a strong mother of boys. A queen in green hospital scrubs. Jimmy always said he was a lucky man.

She said, "Thank you for all your work today. It will be so nice when I can have my morning coffee on the front porch."

Peter could take a hint.

He also could tell a lost cause when he saw one. He turned to go.

She called after him, "And will you please take that awful dog to the pound?"

Peter smiled.

He'd wondered when she would bring up the dog.

5

Peter woke at first light and checked the clock stuck to the dashboard. He put the Army .45 back under the bench seat and stretched in his sleeping bag. He could see his breath in the air, and Dinah Johnson's half-built porch on its temporary supports, just across the parking strip.

He found that he liked the neighborhood. It was in the heart of the city, old houses built close together, and more than a little funky. There was a bungalow on the way to the lumberyard that had planted the tail end of a pink Cadillac in its yard as sculpture. The locals were a mix of black, white, and all shades of brown. College students and working-class people, freshly minted hipsters over their heads in old fixer-uppers, and artists and hippie holdouts turning their homes into giant art projects.

Nobody bothered a guy sleeping in his truck.

He'd tried to rent a hotel room on his first night on the road. It was a test of the experiment. The static, not even a hum when he was on foot in the Cascades, and barely a whisper when driving on narrow back roads, began to fizz in the back of his head as he rolled into the parking lot.

The sparks flared in the lobby, and turned to lightning bolts as he walked the long mazelike hallway to his room. It was the enclosure of the walls, but also the fluorescent lights and the chemical smell of the cheap carpet. The room's tiny window didn't even open. He managed a quick shower with his heart racing, his whole body clenched like a fist, somehow resisting the urge to hurl the TV out the window and burn the place down. He got outside fast, still dripping, barely dressed, head aching like it was split open.

Maybe he was just allergic to the modern world.

After that, he slept in the truck.

It was the big glass of the windshield, he thought, that kept the static low. Not as good as a canopy of stars in the Cascades, but he didn't mind it, even as autumn slid downhill toward winter. And he could roll down his window whenever he wanted.

He was used to waking up cold and hungry in the mountains.

In fact, he liked it.

It made him feel strong, ready. Like his motor was running.

Like he could do almost anything.

* * *

The big dog whined softly in the back. When it changed position the whole vehicle rocked on its springs. Even after Peter had poured the cooled broth into its mouth the night before, it hadn't wanted to get into that dark, unfamiliar box full of strange smells. He had to knock it over and climb inside carrying the damn thing in his arms like a giant growling baby.

What would it cost to feed a dog like that?

When he bought the truck in California on an early stateside rotation, the pickup bed was rusted out. He'd replaced it with a mahogany cargo box, five feet wide, nine feet long, with a marine plywood roof high enough for Peter to walk under, as long as he hunched over a little. It was also, Peter had to admit, sort of an art project. There were windows on both sides of the cargo box, and a skylight in the roof, all salvaged from a wrecked sailboat. The interior was finished with custom maple cabinets, neatly organized. Places for his tools, a cooler for groceries, a hook for a lantern, room to roll out his sleeping bag if he had to. Home for a wandering jack-of-all-trades.

Of course, as it turned out, he couldn't actually sleep back there. The walls were too close.

The dog whined again.

His jeans were stuffed into the bottom of his sleeping bag to keep them warm. He pulled them up before shucking the sleeping bag. The last thing he needed was a neighbor calling the police because of the naked guy. With bare feet stuffed into his unlaced combat boots, he got out of the truck and walked around back in a cold November wind.

He opened the cargo-box door carefully, in case the dog had gotten loose. It shied away from him, but at least it wasn't growling. Peter stepped up and checked the rope holding the stick in its jaws. The rope was fine, but the dog had chewed the shit out of the stick. White oak, one of the hardest woods out there. Almost two inches thick yesterday, there was a lot less of it today where those teeth had done their work.

It was hard to tie the leash to a tree while the hundred-fifty-pound animal was trying like hell to get away from him.

He was going to have to do something about the dog, and soon.

But first, coffee.

He pulled out the backpacking stove, set it on the parking strip with his camp chair, and fired up the old tin percolator. With real cream from his cooler, it tasted pretty good. Real cream was a luxury he didn't have in the mountains, where he'd stirred instant cocoa into instant Folgers, although he'd learned to love the sugary rush. Anything would be better than battlefield coffee, made by pouring a single-serve packet of instant in your mouth dry, then chasing it with plastic-tasting water from a sun-heated bottle. He wasn't ever going to drink that again.

He wasn't going to eat another MRE, either. Only real food.

After cooking up eggs scrambled with sausage and

sliced jalapeños and leftover rice in his battered frypan, he set aside half the food to cool and wrapped the rest in a tortilla. Then sat and ate and watched Dinah's house and thought about the four hundred thousand dollars and pale pliable rectangles found in a suitcase.

It wasn't modeling clay. It was plastic explosive. Peter could tell by the chemical smell. His platoon had used it for everything from breaching doors to blowing up enemy ordnance. Four bricks wasn't a huge amount. But he was hard-pressed to think of a good reason for having it in Milwaukee. When it got dark, he'd hide it under the frame of the truck.

When the coffee was gone, he cleaned up his temporary kitchen, then cornered the dog with the pan of cooled eggs and sausage. He'd picked out the jalapeños. The animal calmed down when Peter started pushing the food past the stick and those outrageous teeth into the side of the dog's mouth with his finger. The dog worked its tongue to swallow, not really resisting, and not growling at all.

Hard to growl while you're eating, Peter figured.

Then he took the dog for a walk, trying not to feel too silly as the dog pulled him down the sidewalk, sniffing at every tree and bush. He was a little worried that someone would confront him and complain about the stick in the dog's mouth, but everyone they approached crossed the street to avoid them. The dog hadn't gotten any better looking overnight. It hadn't gotten any smaller, either. And it still stank.

Maybe Dinah had a hose.

Maybe later. It was seven thirty and time for work.

The wood posts went in quickly on the concrete footings he'd poured the day before. Charlie and Miles left for school, waving cautiously but giving the dog a wide berth. Dinah went out the side door toward the garage on the back alley, avoiding conversation. She waved, then lifted her wrist to tap her watch, reminding him of their afternoon appointment.

By late morning the new beam and floor joists were in and the frame was pleasingly square and straight and true. Peter stopped to reheat the coffee. He was sitting on a sawhorse with the cup warming his hands when a black SUV drove past. It was a Ford, one of the big ones, and fairly new.

A few minutes later it drove past again, this time more slowly, the driver peering out the window. He paused a few houses down, then backed up and stopped in front of the house. The window rolled down. A wide-shouldered black guy peered out at Peter, the porch, and the dog, tied again to the tree in the yard.

Peter waited.

The driver got out, left his door open and the SUV still running, and sauntered over. He wore a gleaming hip-length black leather coat and a black Kangol cap backward on his bald head. In his late thirties or early forties, he was a big guy and he thought that meant something, walking with a distinct strut. A starburst of scars marked the right side of his face, and his right earlobe was missing.

He stopped on the sidewalk, well away from the dog, which was suddenly growling again. "What's with that crazy-looking dog, mouth all tied up?"

Dinah had thought her house was being watched. She hadn't said it, but she was scared.

"You must be from the pound," said Peter, "come for the dog. It was living under the old porch. Hang on a minute and let me get that rope."

"Naw, man, that's not me," said the scarred man, taking a step back. "I'm just a friend of the lady lives here."

Peter kept talking as he stood and walked to the tree. "I'll tell you, that dog's been nothing but trouble. I'll be glad when it's gone." The dog still shied away from him but no longer ran to the end of its leash. "Creeps me out," said Peter, "that animal staring at me all day." He untied the rope and held it out to the man. "You wouldn't believe what I had to do to get that stick in there." The dog stood behind the protection of Peter's legs, peering out at the man and growling louder.

It hadn't growled at young Charlie or his brother when they left for school.

It hadn't growled when Peter took it for a walk.

All morning, it had watched people walking down the street, and it hadn't growled at any of them.

The scarred man took another step back, unbuttoning his leather coat, saying, "I told you, that's not my fuckin' dog." The scars flushed pink on his face as he pulled his coat open and put his hand on the butt of the shiny chrome automatic pistol tucked into the front of his pants. "Now tie that ugly motherfucker up again before I got to do something."

The pistol was smaller, maybe a .32, and sized for concealment. Big Jimmy Johnson, artist of the swivel-mounted .50, would have called it a girlie gun. But it would still put a hole in you.

Clearly this guy was not worried about the cops. The newer gun laws sometimes made it hard to distinguish between armed thugs and citizens exercising their rights, but Peter had some idea which of the two he was talking to.

"Okay, sure," said Peter, nodding. "Hey, it's not your dog." He went to tie it up again.

The scarred man made a show of closing his coat and adjusting it on his shoulders. Not what Peter would have done. It just made the gun harder for the man to get at.

"So. Where'd you find that dog, Mister Fixit Man?"

The tone always changed when someone showed a weapon, thought Peter. This was no longer a friendly conversation. The Army .45 was inside Peter's tool bag, three steps away. But taking it out wouldn't get him any new information.

"It was under the old porch," said Peter, watching the scarred man from the corner of his eye. "I'm just doing some work on the house. I guess the husband died."

The man shook his head. "Damn shame," he said

without any feeling at all. He pointed at the porch with his chin. "How much you charge for this? Must be expensive, huh?"

Now we're getting to it, thought Peter. "No charge," he said. "U.S. Marine Corps is picking up the tab. Death benefit."

"No shit?" said the man. "I always thought the lady was rich."

"Can't tell by me," Peter said. "She didn't even offer me a glass of water."

"You find anything else under there?" asked the man.

"Sure," said Peter. "Scrap lumber, garbage, old carpet. It's all on the curb."

"That all? Nothing worth anything?"

"In this neighborhood?" Peter laughed. "Most of these people are just trying to stay ahead of their bills. They're not hiding gold bars under the front porch. Especially not with this ugly dog living there."

"No shit?" said the man. "Dog was living there? Under the porch? Not no owner?"

"Yeah," said Peter. "Eating all the neighborhood cats. They were afraid it was going to start on the kids. What'd you say your name was?"

"I didn't," said the man. "And I wasn't here. You never saw me. Understand?" He patted the coat at his waistband, where the chrome .32 menaced his nuts.

"Sure," said Peter. "I have to get back to work. I need to get on to my next project."

"You just fuckin' do that," said the scarred man.

And he climbed into the big black SUV and left.

The man hadn't told Peter much. But Peter had learned a few things anyway.

A man with a gun was watching the house.

A man who knew about the money. Probably knew about the plastic explosive. But didn't know where they might be.

And the dog didn't like him.

It would be interesting to see where this thing went next.

6

The porch floor was laid and Peter was packing up his tools when Dinah came home from work, right on time.

Peter got the feeling she was the kind of woman who was always on time. Had her bills in a little accordion folder, kept her checkbook balanced, and flossed her teeth every night. But not uptight about it. Just organized. Knew what she wanted. Working to make it happen.

She parked her old Toyota on the street and went up the front steps with her enormous handbag, bouncing a little on her toes, testing the strength of the deck. She peered at the skirting, at the dog-proof padlock on the sturdy new hatch cover.

She looked at Peter. "Thank you, Lieutenant."

"Please," he said. "Call me Peter. Have you changed your mind about the money?"

She sighed. "No. But I'll need a few minutes to change. I won't be long."

When she came out, she wore tailored black pants and a severe, elegant cream-colored blouse under a gorgeous long black wool coat. The nurse's scrubs had made her seem capable and strong. The change of clothes made her look entirely different. Full of authority, but also slightly removed. Like the VP at Goldman Sachs who had met the interns on their first day.

He had the dog in his arms, carrying it to the truck. It was struggling, but at least he didn't have to tie its legs this time.

Dinah watched silently, an unreadable look on her face.

"What?" he said. It wasn't easy to carry a hundred and fifty pounds of unhappy dog. It tossed its head back and forth, bashing Peter in the head with the stick still tied in its mouth. "Argh. Stop it." The dog definitely needed a bath. Another night and Peter wouldn't be able to get the stink out of his truck. Or his clothes.

The ugly, unfortunately, was permanent.

She smiled at him for the first time. It was a small smile, like a patch of sun on an overcast day, but it was a smile. "For some reason," she said, "I can't quite believe you will take that dog to the pound."

Peter put the dog down in the truck and had to give it a push to get it away from the door. It stood looking at him, whining softly, when he closed the door.

"Sure I am," he said. "A big, smelly, mean, ugly dog will always find a good home."

She laughed softly, a brief musical sound. "I can see why James liked you, Lieutenant."

Peter walked around and opened her door. An officer and a gentleman. It wasn't that she expected it, but something about her seemed to encourage that kind of behavior in Peter. In all men, he suspected.

She was tall enough that she didn't have to hitch herself up onto the bench seat. She'd left her enormous purse inside, but had put the money in a brown paper grocery sack, folded the top, and tied it up with string. The money filled less than half the bag. She held it on her lap with both hands.

"Are you sure you want to bring that along?" Peter asked. "We can always come back and get it."

Dinah shook her head. "I'll leave it in the truck until I'm certain. But I don't want to have to make a second trip." There was something there she didn't want to talk about, and he didn't push her.

He turned the key and let the engine warm up for a minute. She sat with her spine perfectly straight, looking around. "This truck is an antique, isn't it?"

Peter gave her a look of mock outrage. "The word is 'classic,'" he said. "Nineteen sixty-eight Chevy C20 pickup, at your service. Very few original parts."

She looked at the polished green metal door covers and instrument panel. The floor mats were clean and the seat covers new. The slot for the old AM radio was filled with a piece of fine-grained walnut carefully fitted in place and varnished to a high gloss. The shifter knob was a glass ball with a hula dancer trapped inside. Peter couldn't take credit for the shifter knob. The hula dancer had come with the truck.

"I didn't think it would be so orderly," she said. "Or quite so clean."

"It's easier to get stuff done if you know where your tools are." Although Peter had to admit it had been a few days since he'd showered. And he was starting to smell of dog. With Dinah sitting beside him, he was acutely aware of it.

Now she was looking at him with those glacier-blue eyes.

"How did you become a Marine? Jimmy said you studied economics in college."

"When I was in high school, my dad was building a giant vacation house for a bond trader from Chicago. He told me that economics explained how the world really worked. I liked that idea, that I could learn how the world really worked."

He laughed softly at himself.

"It seems pretty naïve now. Anyway, I got a scholarship to Northwestern, and dove into economic theory headfirst. But after a summer internship on Wall Street, I got to see modern finance in practice and didn't like what I saw. Everybody was out to make as much money as possible, and it didn't matter how they did it."

He shrugged.

"I wanted to do some good in the world. Be a part of something bigger. Maybe learn something else about how the world worked. So I joined the Marines."

"Was it a good choice?" She seemed genuinely interested.

"It was a long time ago." He put the truck in gear. "Where are we going?"

"Can you get to Martin Luther King Drive?" He nodded. It was the quickest way to the worst part of town. She said, "Head south on MLK and I'll give you directions from there."

He pulled smoothly into traffic, drove to the end of the block, and turned the corner.

Looking in the rearview mirror, he said, "I'm guessing you're the jazz fan of the family. Maybe you caught it from your parents?"

Dinah looked at Peter sideways. "What was your clue?"

"Not many Dinahs out there," he said. "I'm figuring you were named for Dinah Washington. And your boys, maybe Charlie Parker and Miles Davis?"

"I'm impressed," she said. "Yes, my father loved jazz. There was always music in the house when I was growing up. I suppose I caught it from him."

She smiled to herself. "James, though. James was more of an old-time R-and-B guy. Ray Charles, Sam and Dave, the Staple Singers. Maybe that was why I fell in love with him in tenth grade. He loved to sing. We were in the church choir together."

Peter thought of Jimmy in Iraq. He wasn't singing. He was doing push-ups, or checking his gear, or studying maps. Mostly he was talking to his guys. Getting their heads straight. Keeping them right.

Dinah said, "When the boys were little, and James was home on leave, he'd sing them to sleep. He'd lie on the couch with them on his chest, his big arms around them, and sing so softly I could barely hear him. But that deep voice of his, it would go right through them. 'Swing low, sweet chariot, coming for to carry me hooome . . .'" Her voice was smoky and low.

Peter didn't even know that Jimmy had a music player. Some guys were like that, especially when they were fire team or squad leaders. They sort of put themselves aside. Submerged themselves in the squad. The war wasn't about them. It was about the men they were charged with leading. With protecting, as much as possible, from the war. While still doing their best to win it.

Maybe if Jimmy had kept singing, he wouldn't have killed himself.

Peter checked the mirror again. There was a black SUV a half-block behind them. A big Ford. Peter couldn't see the driver's face. But he thought there would be a starburst of scars marking the right side of his face, and his right earlobe would be missing.

He said, "So what happened? With Jimmy, I mean."

Dinah said, "We got married out of high school. Perhaps it wasn't the best idea, but we just couldn't wait. We wanted to eat each other up." She gave Peter a sly look. "Do you know what I mean? Have you ever felt like that for someone, that kind of hunger?"

Peter looked at Dinah, at her cool blue eyes. He knew what she meant.

Dinah said, "Well, that's how it was for us. James went to work as an apprentice plumber, and I went to nursing school. We had a plan. When I graduated and got a job, it would be his turn for college. Then the towers fell."

She looked out the window. "Once they had him, they wouldn't let him go. They said he had essential expertise. He did three tours and kept getting extended. Can you believe that?" She shook her head. "He had to get blown up to get sent home."

Peter nodded. That's how it was for a lot of guys. If you didn't take the re-up bonus, they would keep you anyway. And maybe that was the story Jimmy told his wife. But Peter knew the real deal. They had talked about it. Jimmy stayed in for the same reason Peter did. He was good at war. And someone had to take care of his guys. To get them out alive.

The truck bumped along. The roads were getting worse as the neighborhood changed. More storefronts were vacant on each block. On the side streets, house after house with the shingles slipping from their roofs. Broken car windows covered with plastic sheeting and duct tape. The black Ford bounced in their wake.

"His physical injuries healed well enough," she said. "But once he came home from the hospital, he seemed like a different person. He became angry at the slightest thing. Sometimes at nothing at all, as if he were looking for an excuse to explode. Then he was just angry all the time."

Peter nodded. All those years of war had changed

him, too. It was the white static, but also something else. He had become a vast reserve of energy kept at bay only with exercise and work. It was a physical need to keep moving, keep doing, to solve whatever problem he had set for himself. If he let his engine idle too long, the white static would rise up inside him until he stood and got back to the job at hand. Maybe it was the war. Maybe it was just who he was now.

Dinah kept talking. "He couldn't find work because the economy had crashed. He was a Marine Corps veteran with an honorable discharge and years of service, but he only had a high school degree, and he couldn't find a job. I tried to get him to start his own business, fixing people's plumbing. But James just couldn't get started. I'd nag him and he'd kick a hole in the wall."

She glared out the windshield like she was angry at the world. "He had veterans' benefits, and they were good benefits. There was money for college. But he wouldn't even apply. He said he didn't want to spend his life sitting at a desk." She shook her head. "James never had trouble with motivation in his life. There was something wrong with him. I wanted him to talk to the VA, but he wouldn't do that, either. He *definitely* wouldn't talk to a therapist. He wouldn't do anything. He slept all the time. I'd get home after working a double shift to find James asleep on the couch, a sink full of dirty dishes, and the boys glued to the Xbox without their supper. It went on for almost a year."

Fatigue, anger, depression. These were classic symptoms of post-traumatic stress. And a traumatic brain injury, too. Peter knew it. Dinah knew it. Jimmy probably knew it, too. But that didn't mean she could help him, or that he could help himself.

If Peter had been there, instead of up in the mountains, could he have helped?

Maybe that was just ego, Peter thinking he would have made the crucial difference. But he wasn't there. He'd never know. He'd let Jimmy down. And now the man was dead.

Something in Dinah had deflated. The breath just gone out of her. Peter didn't say anything. He knew she wasn't really talking to him. She was talking to the empty air, to the cold world outside the glass.

She took a breath and straightened up again.

"Finally, I sat him down. I told him that I loved him, but I wasn't going to carry him. It was hard enough to live without him when he was away. But I couldn't live without him in our own house. I just couldn't, not like that. I told him that he had to go to school, get a job, or get out of the house. I gave him a month to develop a plan and get himself together. I thought it would work. I really did."

Peter knew what had happened after that.

Peter wasn't the only one living with guilt.

He waited while Dinah collected herself. "Two days later," she said, "I came home from work and he was gone. That was four months ago." She shook her head. "I asked him over and over to show me where he was staying, but he wouldn't tell me. He said he'd invite me over when he got a better place. I never did see it." She kept shaking her head as she talked, as if it would undo the past. "He found a job, tending bar. He came to the boys' games, and to the last teacher conferences. He never missed an event. He came over for dinner once a week. I thought he was getting better."

She took a long breath and let it carefully out.

"Then the police knocked on my door."

She didn't cry.

But Peter could see what it cost her not to.

Her voice like wood.

"They found him in an alley."

Peter knew the rest. He had called the Milwaukee Police Department for the details when he came down from the mountains. The cheap street pistol that Jimmy had pressed into the soft flesh beneath his chin. The back of his head blown clean off. There was no autopsy. The city was too broke for autopsies on open-and-shut suicides.

Peter checked the mirror again. The SUV was still there, peeking out from behind a utility truck.

"Dinah," he said, "I have to ask. How could he have come up with that kind of money?"

Dinah shook her head. "I don't know," she said. "I just don't." She turned the paper bag in her hands. "But I can tell you it surely wasn't from tending bar three afternoons a week."

Following Dinah's directions, Peter turned left, then right. She kept them off the main roads, and Peter watched while the tough neighborhood turned to true ghetto. Abandoned cars, shops boarded up, holes in the streetscape where houses had burned down or been torn down by the city. Out the side window he saw two little kids without coats, the soles falling off their laceless shoes, running around in the cold when they should have been in school. Dinah watched them, the smile fallen from her face.

"Dinah?" said Peter. "Where are we going?"

"To see a man I knew once," she said. "A long time ago."

7

Expensive condos lined the river two miles away, but development had stalled out at MLK Drive and hadn't even been imagined on Center Street, where the blocks of peeling-frame storefronts leaned on one another like worn-out drunks sharing a skin disease.

Dinah pointed at a three-story corner building, maybe ninety years old but in better shape than the rest of the block with freshly painted trim and new tuckpointing on the brick. "There," she said. "That's Lewis's place."

Apartments filled the top floors. The ground floor was divided in half. The front had a tavern called Shorty's, the name spelled out in dim neon letters over a faded Pabst Blue Ribbon logo. The big tavern windows were covered with heavy steel security grates. The rear was a storefront with a sign, black with flaking white letters, reading CENTER CITY REAL ESTATE. It looked vacant now, the storefront windows replaced with neatly painted plywood. Except for the small modern security camera mounted high with a view of the whole street.

A gleaming black Escalade was parked on the side street, ahead of a crisp silver Jeep with polished chrome trim and an older but immaculate tan GMC Yukon with a tubular steel bumper.

Nice cars for the neighborhood, he thought. Nobody was out there watching them. Just the security camera.

"This Lewis guy—do you know what he drives?" asked Peter.

"I haven't spoken with him in years," she said. "But I have seen him in that tan truck with the big bumper."

Peter cruised past without slowing. The black Ford was two cars back.

"You missed it," said Dinah.

"Just checking out the area," said Peter, his head on a swivel as he took in the building layout, the alleys and exits. "Old habit." One that he wasn't going to break. Especially not when a man with a gun was watching Dinah's house.

He drove in an outward spiral, checking the surrounding area. The neighborhood was seriously beaten down. More businesses were closed than open. Graffiti was everywhere, from basic tags on the crumbling houses and bullet-pocked road signs to elaborate multicolor displays on boarded-up corner stores. But Lewis's building, whose neat brick and clean paint should have been prime canvas, was oddly pristine.

He looked in the rearview. The Ford had disappeared.

Peter swung around the block and parked at the curb.

Before Dinah could open the door, Peter put a hand on her arm.

"Wait," he said. "Tell me about this Lewis."

"We were friends once," she said. "Lewis and James and I. But things ended badly." She didn't elaborate.

"Okay," said Peter. "But why do you think the money is his?"

"Lewis has his fingers in a lot of things," said Dinah. "They're all about money." She angled her head toward Shorty's. "And James worked at his bar."

She pulled her arm away, set the paper bag on the floor, and slipped out of the truck. She walked not toward the bar entrance but toward the side door, the boarded-up section with the security camera.

Peter took the Army .45 from under the seat, tucked it into the back of his pants where his coat would hide it, and jogged after her. The heavy steel door was already closing behind her when he got there.

He felt the flare of the white static as he reached for the knob.

The space inside was bigger than Peter had expected, a big rectangular room. The outer walls were brick, probably a foot thick, and still showed pale patches where stubborn plaster remained. It looked like someone had taken out most of the interior walls. The oak floor was patched in places, the old finish turned orange with age. Once it had been an office. Now it was something else that wasn't quite clear.

The jittery pressure of the static reminded him to look for the exits. The windows were covered with plywood, so that was no help. There was a door in the back that likely led to another way out, along with a bathroom and maybe stairs to the basement.

In the center of the room stood a walnut trestle table, at least ten feet long and probably custom-made, but only three rickety mismatched chairs. At the head of the table, atop an oil-stained towel, a shotgun lay in its component pieces, broken down for cleaning. It looked like a 10-gauge autoloader, with a fat bore and a shortened barrel. It would clear a room like a hand grenade.

Behind the table was a secondhand bar, worn smooth by thousands of hands. Peter could see the severed end where it had been torn from the wall of some defunct tavern or hotel. A bank of four small security monitors was set on top, and a stainless-steel fridge stood in the corner. At the far end of the room, a U-shaped formation of black leather couches faced an enormous television tuned to ESPN with the sound off.

Two men sat on the couches, feet up, newspapers spread open in their hands, staring at Dinah like they'd never seen a woman before. Dinah fixed them with a regal look that carried all the natural authority of an ER nurse and the mother of willful boys. Now Peter understood why she had changed her clothes.

"Where is Lewis?" she said.

They stared at her for a moment before they saw Peter, who was standing right beside her.

That got them off the couch.

They were big men in worn T-shirts and faded jeans. Their hair was cropped short, their faces lined from sun and wind. Peter watched them come around the couch, flanking him automatically.

They moved like they knew what they were doing and had been doing it together for a while.

The static flared up higher, tension now in his shoulders and arms. This was useful static, making him ready.

The men glanced at Dinah from time to time—they probably couldn't help themselves; Peter had the same problem—but mostly they watched Peter. He was a big man, too, in worn work clothes and sand-colored combat boots, with the same air of semi-domestication.

Peter figured they had all been to the same finishing school. The one where the dress code called for camouflage, desert brown.

"Lewis ain't here," said the first man. He had plump cheeks and fair skin, like he'd been raised on milk and cheese. His red T-shirt advertised Miller High Life, which suited him, because he was built like a beer keg. But he walked lightly, almost on his toes, as if approaching a tango partner. He had a large eagle tattoo wrapping one arm, and a Green Bay Packers tattoo on the other.

The second man had a long, angular face in a deep, gleaming black. "And who might y'all be?" The slow drawl sounded like Texas, or maybe Oklahoma. His T-shirt was blue and read MAXIE'S SOUTHERN COMFORT. His skin seemed a little too tight on his body, every muscle group clearly defined. He wore no shoes or socks, and Peter could see the hard calluses on his feet that came from kicking a heavy bag very hard over a long period of time.

Dinah didn't seem to notice any of those things. She put her hands on her hips, back straight and strong. A formidable woman.

"Gentlemen," she said. "I know he's here. His truck is parked right outside."

Behind the salvaged bar, the door opened and a man walked through carrying a can of Remington gun oil. His skin was coffee-brown, his head shaved. His ancestors could have been from anywhere and everywhere.

He stopped moving when he saw Dinah.

It was not a voluntary pause.

It was total stillness, abrupt and automatic. As if his sensory system had overloaded.

He wore crisp black jeans, a starched white dress shirt with the cuffs rolled exactly twice, and a carefully blank expression that did nothing to hide the hollow eyes of a man who was just punched hard in the stomach.

Dinah said, "Hello, Lewis."

Only two quiet words, but in them Peter could guess their entire history.

It lasted for only a moment, the space of a breath. Then Lewis closed his eyes and opened them again, somehow a different person. Older, maybe, and harder.

"Hey, Dee," he said. "Been a long time, girl." His voice was like heating oil, slippery and dark. The heat and combustion latent within.

Watching Lewis cross the room, Peter thought of a mountain lion he had once seen in the North Cascades. Lewis had the same elemental precision and economy of motion. A predatory indifference. Peter was sure the two men in T-shirts were strong and capable. But compared to Lewis, they were bunny rabbits.

Lewis didn't acknowledge Peter in any way, as if he weren't even there. But Peter knew that if he did anything unexpected, Lewis would be ready. Because Lewis was always ready.

Peter was the same way.

Lewis stopped at the table and looked down at the disassembled shotgun. His hands twitched restlessly at the ends of corded arms. He said, "What you doing here, Dee?"

She tapped her toe twice. It was loud on the hard oak floor. "It's about James," she said. "You know he's dead."

Lewis didn't look up. "Yeah," he said. He contemplated the shotgun's component parts, laid out neatly on the cloth. "I was real sorry to hear."

Dinah said, "I need to know what he was doing for you."

A faint smile tilted the side of Lewis's mouth. "You always was direct." He picked up the barrel and peered down the bore. "I used to like that about you."

"Lewis," she said. "I need to know. Was he working for you?"

Lewis didn't look at her. "I don't run the day-to-day," he said. He put some gun oil on a bore swab and ran it through the barrel. "I went in one night and there was Jimmy, washing glasses." He sprayed a hand swab and wiped down the action, the stock, and the barrel. The simple movements carried the grace of long practice. His shoulders lifted in a shrug. "Man did his job. I let him be."

Dinah said, "I don't know what else you're doing, but I know you. What was James involved with? Was he handling money for you?"

Lewis looked at her now. The force of his full attention was tangible, like a hot desert wind. Dinah didn't waver.

He said, "First place, girl, you don't know me. Could be you never really did." He began to reassemble the shotgun without looking at his hands. There was no trick to it, just practice. Sometimes, to calm himself when the static was particularly bad, Peter would close his eyes and field-strip his 1911.

"Second place," said Lewis, "all the man did was tend bar. The only money he moved went in the till. I wouldn't have asked him to do anything else. And he wouldn't have done it." He locked the barrel assembly into the stock, then thumbed massive shells into the magazine. "You knew anything about either of us, you'd have known that."

Dinah stared him full in the face, deciding for herself.

"All right," she said finally. "If James wasn't carrying or keeping anything for you, then I have a problem. Someone left some money under my porch."

The slight smile tilted Lewis's mouth again. He spun the shotgun in one hand like a majorette's baton. It was a show-off move. His hand wasn't in full contact with the weapon. Of course, Peter was six long steps away, and Lewis could finish the spin and shoot Peter in the chest twice in the time it took him to close the distance. If it was loaded with buckshot, it would literally cut Peter in half.

Lewis turned to the man in the Miller High Life shirt. "Nino. Can you think of anything?"

"It ain't from Shorty's. That place is squared up and nailed down. I know everything comes in and goes out." He assessed Dinah from under raised eyebrows. The beer keg might be smarter than he looked. "How much we talking about?"

Time to step in. The static was rising, although he wasn't sweating yet. Peter said, "Dinah, it's not their money. We should go."

Lewis moved just slightly.

Just enough to change the geometry between himself and Peter. Like that mountain lion getting its hind feet set right in the dirt before leaping on the deer.

He didn't look like a show-off anymore.

Peter was grateful for the .45 shoved into the back of his pants.

He put his hands on his hips to get them closer to the butt. Not that it would be helpful to take out a gun right then. Nor was there any guarantee that he would be fast enough to be useful. Lewis's trick with the shotgun had allowed him to see how very quick Lewis was with his hands. Maybe that was the point.

Lewis tilted his chin at Peter while looking at Dinah. “Who’s this?”

“This is Lieutenant Ash,” she said. “A friend of James’s from the Marines. He’s part of a government program, doing some repairs on the house.”

Appearing to notice Peter for the first time, Lewis looked him up and down, taking in the sawdust on his pants, the scuffed boots, the brown work jacket.

“Jarhead,” he said.

It was a term of pride for some Marines. From anyone else it was an insult. Especially the way Lewis said it.

Peter smiled pleasantly and leaned toward Dinah. “Some guys get jealous,” he explained. “Not everybody makes the grade.”

Nino said, “It sounds like he might want the money for himself.”

Dinah said, “Lieutenant Ash found the money. I wasn’t home. He could have kept it. Instead he brought it to me.”

Nino raised one hand, as if asking permission to speak. “The money,” he said. “How much was it again?”

Now Peter knew why Dinah wanted to leave the money in the truck. He shifted his hands under the waistband of his work jacket. He was left-handed. He mentally rehearsed the movement he would have to make to clear the .45. But he kept his eyes on Lewis.

"I didn't say," said Dinah, cool as a cucumber. "Nor will I. Perhaps it's time for us to leave."

"Perhaps y'all should give the money to us," said the lean barefoot man from Texas, or maybe Oklahoma. He flexed his feet on the floorboards. "We could invest it for you. For your retirement. Is it in your pocket or in your car?"

If they thought it might be in her pocket, they really didn't know how much money it was. The four hundred K took up a good part of that grocery bag, even neatly banded.

Lewis didn't weigh in. Maybe he was waiting to see what happened. Peter began to slide his left hand toward his back. He'd flip the safety as he raised the pistol.

Nino's weight was on his toes, but he was a few steps away. The barefoot man was no closer, but if he led with his feet he'd have a longer reach and get there first. Regardless of how it happened, there would be no confusion between Nino and the barefoot man. They'd done this before.

Peter said, "Hey. Your accent is driving me nuts. I can't pin it down. Where the hell are you from? Texas or Oklahoma?"

The lean man looked at Peter like he'd grown a third eye. "I'm from Norman, originally. But I grew up near Midland."

Nino said, "Jarhead, shut the fuck up. Ray, stay focused. Honey, give us the money. Or else we take it."

"I beg your goddamn pardon," said Dinah, "but you may not."

Nino laughed. Barefoot Ray from Oklahoma smiled slightly and began to bend his knees. Peter put his hand on the .45.

"No," said Lewis.

He spoke clearly, but not loudly.

Nino and Ray turned their heads to look at him.

"This is not who we are," said Lewis. His voice cut through the room like a Randall knife. "We do a lot. But not this. Not taking money from the widow of a U.S. Marine."

Nino made a face like he smelled sour milk, but he took a step back. Ray from Oklahoma unbent his knees.

Dinah looked at Lewis standing across the room. If something passed between them, Peter couldn't see it. She said, "Thank you, Lewis." Then put her hand on Peter's arm. "It's time to leave."

Peter didn't move. He wanted to get outside. After only a few minutes, he was sweating under his coat as the rising sparks heated him up. But he wasn't done.

"Actually," he said. "There's one other thing."

Lewis watched Peter without speaking. Even in stillness he had that lethal grace.

Nino snorted. "Oh, I can't wait for this," he said.

"It's not your money," said Peter, talking only to

Lewis. "We know that now. But it's somebody's money. Odds are he wants it back."

Lewis produced an elaborate shrug. "Not my problem."

Peter smiled pleasantly. "Do you know a guy with a kind of starburst of scars on his right cheek?" He drew the marks with his fingers on his own cheek. "Right earlobe missing? Big black guy, late thirties to early forties, a lot of self-confidence? Carries a chrome .32? Watching Dinah's house?"

Peter kept his eyes on their faces. Not a flicker from Lewis or Nino or barefoot Ray from Oklahoma.

Dinah just stared at him.

"Nobody I know," said Lewis. "Still not my problem. Call the cops."

"This guy stopped at Dinah's house this morning," said Peter. "In a big black Ford SUV. He wanted to know how she was paying for the porch." He looked at Lewis. "He followed us here."

Lewis frowned. "You brought him to my place of business?"

"I didn't bring him anywhere," said Peter. "He followed me. What does it matter? It's not your money, right?"

Lewis shook his head. "You brought him, jarhead. Now get rid of him."

It was Peter's turn to shrug. He made it elaborate, too. "Not my problem," he said. "Besides, what if he's a cop?"

"Get rid of him," said Lewis again. Each word crisp and clear.

"I tried," said Peter. "But he showed me his gun and I got scared."

Lewis gave him a look. Peter raised his hands in a show of helplessness.

"Hey, I'm only one guy. And I'm just a carpenter now. This guy knows my truck. You have this crack team of trained killers. Maybe Nino and Ray could discourage the guy a little."

Lewis didn't like that. But he couldn't see an acceptable way out of it, so he said, "Fine. They'll keep an eye out. Right, guys?"

Nino made the sour face again. "Sure."

Ray from Oklahoma actually seemed to cheer up at the prospect. Maybe he'd get to kick somebody after all.

"Short-term only," warned Lewis. "A few days. We got business coming up."

"I'll take what I can get," said Peter. "You want to trade cell numbers?" Peter didn't even have a phone.

"Get the fuck out of here." Lewis turned away. Over his shoulder, he said, "Nino, next time make sure you lock the fucking door."

Outside, Dinah hissed, "Peter, are you crazy?"

Peter smiled. "Only a little."

It was the first time she'd called him Peter, not Lieutenant Ash. He liked it. He was starting to think she'd let him help her.

They walked across the sidewalk and the cold autumn

wind filled his lungs and blew through his coat, washing away the tension and cooling the sparks back to a pale hum.

Across the street, a black Ford SUV pulled away from the curb and disappeared into the traffic.

Dinah said, “We need to talk.”

“Yes,” said Peter. “We do.”

8

It's not your friend Lewis," said Peter. "Whatever he is, I don't think he knew about the money." He drove a roundabout path toward her house, the big pickup rumbling through the streets.

"I know that now," said Dinah. "And he's not my friend. Who is this man with the scars on his face?"

"Showed up this morning, when I was putting your porch back together. He asked if you were rich."

Her eyebrows climbed skyward. "He asked if I was rich?"

Peter nodded. "He started by asking where the dog came from. I wondered if the dog knew him. It sure didn't like him. It wouldn't stop growling."

She opened her mouth, then shut it again. He watched her hand close on the door handle, looking for something solid, anything, to hang on to. Of course, the truck was still moving, so even that solidity was an illusion.

"You're done now," she said. "The porch is finished, you're going to your next project."

He waited for her to ask, knowing already that she wouldn't. Dinah was so much like the women he had known growing up. His mother, his mother's friends. She would ask a relative for help. She'd ask her husband, her brother, or her father. That's what family was for. But Dinah's husband was dead. Her sons were far too young. And she would never ask a stranger.

He didn't make her wait long. He swung the truck to the curb in front of her house. "If you don't mind," he said, "I'll stick around. The house could use a few more repairs. The Marines aren't expecting me for a few weeks."

Not ever, actually. But he didn't say that.

He waited for her to say something. The dog shifted in the back and the truck rocked on its springs. He hadn't been this close to such a vivid, lovely woman for a long time. He suddenly wanted to touch her. But he wouldn't, of course. She was Jimmy's wife. Even if Jimmy was dead.

He kept his hands on the steering wheel, feeling the faint vibration from the big V-8, a slow, gentle thrum as it idled, perfectly tuned. You'd never know the power in that engine until you stepped on the gas.

Peter felt his own heart beat, slow and patient.

He said, "Dinah, this is serious. Four hundred thousand dollars' worth of serious. Let me help. Jimmy would do the same, if it was me who died over there. You know he would."

She looked at him then, her eyes suddenly direct. He was aware of the grace in her long neck, the strength of her capable hands. The curves of the lines bracketing her mouth. She nodded once. "All right," she said. "Thank you, Peter."

"It's my pleasure," he said. The truck rocked again as the dog moved restlessly. "I need to let the dog out."

The beast was waiting for him at the door, gently nosing his face, then bonking his head with the piece of wood still tied into its mouth. It whined softly and pushed against his shoulder. The wood was chewed down even farther now. He let the leash go and stepped away to see what would happen.

The dog jumped down and made a leisurely tour of the neighboring yards, peeing on the stunted trees and a chain-link fence, trailing the rope behind. Peter took a cured sausage from the cooler, then sat on Dinah's new porch steps with a knife and cut pieces into a small paper bag. He made sure they were small enough for the dog to swallow without having to chew.

Dinah sat beside him, their shoulders almost touching. Peter could feel her proximity like something tangible.

She said, "Are you trying to rehabilitate that ugly dog?"

Peter shrugged. "He's not that bad."

She said, "Maybe some things are too bad to save."

He looked at her. "We're not still talking about the dog," he said. "Are we?"

She looked at the ground for a moment, then right back at him.

"My mama was the steady one," she said. "She taught fourth grade for thirty years, and ran her life like a Swiss watch. My dad was the opposite." A thin smile. "He never seemed to have a job, but he always had money in his pocket. He came and went without warning. He taught me to ride a bike and throw a baseball. One night, just after my thirteenth birthday, he went on an errand and came home covered with blood that wasn't his. He burned his clothes in a barrel in the backyard. Then he left. We waited, but he never came home again. Finally we just gave up. And I knew that I would not marry a man like my father."

She wiped her face. "James was different. A good man. Maybe the war did something to him. Damaged him. But at least he was a working man, not a crook, not a killer. Then I find that he's left a suitcase full of money under my porch. And I don't know what to think."

Peter watched the dog water a tree.

People changed, he thought. Made mistakes. Did things they weren't proud of, maybe things they were ashamed of. Peter certainly had. Jimmy had been one of the best people he had ever known. A better person than Peter, that's for sure. He didn't know what to think, either.

"Dinah," he said, "you're a nurse, raising two great kids and working your way forward. You have nothing to be ashamed of."

She shook her head. "We shouldn't have bought this house," she said. "Do you know what an adjustable-rate mortgage is?"

Peter nodded. He'd studied economics, and even if he hadn't, the financial crisis had given everyone a crash course in mortgage basics.

Dinah kept talking. "We got one seven years ago, and now it's coming due. I have to pay the house off or refinance. Everyone thought their houses would be worth more, so it wouldn't be a problem. Well, now it's worth half what I owe on it. I can't pay the house off. And I can't qualify for a new loan, not without James's income. If they'd even give me a loan. I have a good job, but it's not enough. Do you know how much those boys eat?" She shook her head again. "We should not have bought this house."

"You've got a bag full of money," said Peter. "Why not start over somewhere else? Move to Chicago. Or Seattle."

"I can't just leave," she said. "I have obligations. My grandmother lives eight blocks from here."

Peter nodded. He understood that. The dog ranged around, following its nose.

"So stay," he said, "and be careful with it. Don't attract attention. Anybody shows up, you say, What money? Do I look like I found four hundred grand?"

"I can't—" She stood up and walked three steps, spun on her heel, and walked back. "I can't take that money," she said. "It's bad money."

Peter smiled gently. “No such thing as bad money. It’s just money. Comes in handy sometimes.”

“It’s not the money,” said Dinah. “It’s crossing that line.” She shook her head. “It was better when I didn’t know about it. But now I do, and I can’t have that money sitting around. Or I’ll spend it. Because I damn well do need it. And then where will I be?”

“Okay,” said Peter. “So we’ll find out whose money it is. And give it back, if that’s what you need to do. Maybe we can get a finders’ fee. Maybe get your house refinanced.”

“You would do that,” she said. “Wouldn’t you?”

Her shoulder was almost touching his. Almost, but not quite. He could feel it anyway, the way the earth feels the sun.

“Sure.” He said it casually, with a shrug.

As if he didn’t need it as badly as she did.

As if the ghost of Jimmy wasn’t standing right there staring at him.

The dog trotted over and knocked the bag of cut sausage from Peter’s hands. It tried to stick its nose into the bag, but with the length of oak in its mouth, the dog just pushed the bag across the sidewalk. Peter got up to help.

Dinah said, “I don’t want to be around when you take that stick out of its mouth.”

Peter pushed sausage bits past the fangs with the tips of his fingers while the beast’s throat worked. “Jeez, lady. Where’s your sense of adventure?”

9

It was late afternoon and starting to get dark. The wind blew hard through the bare trees. Thin plastic shopping bags caught in the branches rattled like distant machine-gun fire. Along the streets and sidewalks, paper trash skittered and danced as if alive and in a hurry.

"So what happens next?" she said.

Peter wiped his hands on his pants and collected the dog's leash. "I'll start with Jimmy. Look at his life. Talk to his friends. See what stands out."

"I have a box," she volunteered. "With some of his things."

Peter put the dog in the truck and followed Dinah inside the house. He felt the walls and ceiling with jangled nerves, the static reminding him of all the time he'd spent inside already that day.

Because she was next of kin, the police had given Dinah the things Jimmy was carrying with him when he died. She'd put them into a cardboard box with things

Jimmy left at the house and pushed the box under the bed. She pulled it out now and set it on the kitchen table with the lid still folded shut. As if she was afraid of reopening those memories.

Peter put his hand on the lid. "May I?"

Dinah nodded and Peter opened the flaps.

There was a musty smell, like time itself had been shut away. The box was too big for the contents, as if whoever had packed it was expecting more life to fill it.

Peter had a box like this in his parents' house, and another from the war years tucked away in the back of his truck. The catchall box for things you wanted to remember, or couldn't bring yourself to forget.

The house was getting to him. His chest was tight, his breath coming harder. The hairs prickled on the back of his neck.

"I'm going to do this outside," he said. Dinah gave him a look as he picked up the box, but followed him out the door into the cool November air.

At the picnic table in the backyard, Peter excavated Jimmy's box and laid out the things he found, attempting some sort of chronology. There was a scattering of old photographs. Jimmy and Dinah impossibly young. Jimmy in purple choir robes, looking like some kind of prince. Jimmy in his wedding suit with a thousand-watt smile. Jimmy with his boys at various ages, a baseball mitt on his hand or basketball under his arm. The family at a picnic, paper plates on a blanket.

The wind came up and tried to take the photos. Peter held them in place.

Jimmy trying to look cool on Manny Martinez's motorcycle. Jimmy in uniform, looking deadly serious. Jimmy with the platoon, with his squad, with the other sergeants. Jimmy with an Iraqi goat, goofing for the camera. Jimmy trying to get a baseball out of the mouth of the stray dog he'd adopted in Baghdad. The dog got killed when someone shelled the compound. Jimmy was broken up for weeks.

A high school graduation tassel. A tall stack of letters in their envelopes, tied up with string. An expired military ID, an old watch with a cracked face, a small wooden box. Inside were Jimmy's medals.

Peter set the box atop the pictures to keep them from blowing away.

"His military paperwork? VA paperwork?"

"In the file cabinet," said Dinah. She had her arms wrapped around herself because of the cold. The wind smelled like rain. The bare trees waved overhead. "It takes up a whole drawer."

Peter didn't know what the paperwork might tell him. He certainly wasn't going to go through it out here in the wind.

The last item was a bulky manila envelope with JOHNSON, JAMES written on it in neat black marker. A business card stapled onto the corner, with the Milwaukee police logo on it. A detective. Peter looked at Dinah, asking for permission. She nodded. Peter upended the envelope and slid the contents out on the table.

Keys, a wallet, a rolled leather belt. Nothing else.

Was this all Jimmy had with him when he died?

Peter picked up the keys. Four of them, on a plain ring. A Toyota key with a black plastic grip, a key printed with the Green Bay Packers logo, and two others, maybe for a padlock or a cheap door lock. He looked at Dinah.

"The black key is for the car," she said. "The Packers key is for this house. I don't know about the other two."

The wallet was leather but cheap, the seams torn and peeling. It held a driver's license, a library card with bent corners, six dollars in cash, a folded grocery-store receipt for canned soup and instant coffee, and a scrap of torn paper with words written in Jimmy's easy hand: *worth more dead than alive.*

Peter looked at the paper. It fluttered in the wind. Something about it was familiar, but he couldn't grab on to it. He held it up for Dinah.

"Yes," said Dinah. "The police thought it was a suicide note."

Something there didn't sound quite right to Peter, but he couldn't figure out why. He filed it in his mind for further thought.

He tapped the driver's license. "This has your address. Where was Jimmy staying?"

Dinah shook her head. "I don't know."

"You don't know?"

"Jimmy never told me. He kept saying he wouldn't be

there long. He said he'd let the boys visit when he found a better place."

"Didn't the police look?"

"They didn't find anything. I asked that detective. He was actually pretty helpful. The tavern where he worked didn't have a different address for him, and the VA didn't, either. He wasn't listed with the phone or cable companies, or the power company. The detective couldn't even find a bank account."

Peter was surprised the man had tried that hard. "But you must have had some idea, right?"

"If there was an event with the kids, he'd meet me at the school, or come here and I'd drive." She scratched her chin. "Once, maybe a month before he died, he called to say he was running late. He asked me to pick him up on the corner of Twentieth and Center. He must have lived nearby. It's not the best neighborhood. I told the police, but they never did find it." She shook her head. "I kept telling myself I'd go over there and look. You know, go knock on doors. But I just couldn't bring myself to do it. I think I was afraid of what I'd find."

"Well," said Peter. "It's a good idea. And now there's a better reason."

Not that the man's things were likely to be there anymore. But maybe Peter would find somebody who knew him.

He just had to find a crack, a fingerhold.

* * *

The last item in the police evidence envelope was a leather belt. Peter ran it through his hands and smiled.

Jimmy called it his traveling belt. It looked like nothing more than a sturdy leather belt, but a hidden flap on the inside opened to reveal a long, narrow compartment. It was a pickpocket-proof way to carry money, and very useful if you were a Marine on furlough intent on getting seriously drunk. He was willing to bet the police hadn't realized what it was.

Peter opened the flap.

Inside were five crisp new hundreds, folded to fit.

Peter held up the bills. "This is how you knew the money came from Jimmy."

Dinah nodded. "I knew when I saw it that something wrong was going on. He never kept that kind of money. If he had ten dollars extra when he came over for dinner, he'd sneak it into my desk drawer."

Peter dug deeper into the belt. Past the hundreds was an accordioned piece of yellow paper. Peter opened it up. It was a flier for a missing person, the corners torn away like it had once been stapled to a telephone pole. It had a young man's photo on it. HAVE YOU SEEN THIS MAN? PLEASE CALL, with a phone number.

Peter didn't understand why Jimmy would stash the flier in the belt. Hiding the money made sense, but some flier from a telephone pole?

Peter ran the belt through his hands again. One section was still too stiff. He dug a long finger inside.

It was a folded business card for something called the

Riverside Veterans' Center. Green lettering, cream-colored card stock. The address put it near Dinah's neighborhood. No name on the card, but on the back, written in a faded spidery black hand, was a phone number.

Who was Jimmy hiding this stuff from?

Peter thought for a moment. The coroner had turned over the belt with the wallet. "Dinah, did they give you anything else? Any clothing?"

Dinah nodded. "His pants and shirt were ruined. But they gave me his boots and his old field jacket. He didn't like them, but they were warm, and he wouldn't buy new stuff when we had so little money to spare. I'll get them."

She went inside returned with the jacket and a pair of sand-colored desert boots. The boots were completely clapped out, the seams separating, one sole peeling loose. The field jacket was worn but holding. It had been a lot of places. There was a faint spray of dark stains across the front. Blood from when he'd shot himself, maybe. Peter found the hole in the upper-left sleeve where a bullet had barely missed Jimmy's arm. He'd kept the jacket. He'd said it was good luck, like lightning not striking twice.

Some luck.

Peter dipped his hands into the pockets, looking for anything Jimmy had left behind. Something the police didn't bother to look for.

A few things. A small spiral notebook in the sleeve pocket with half the pages torn out. A pair of beat-up cold-weather combat gloves in the side pocket. And beneath the gloves, a fat stainless-steel pen, a nice one. On the side of the pen were the words LAKE CAPITAL FUNDS. And a Web address.

Peter figured it was some kind of investment house. Jimmy could have borrowed the pen from someone and stuck it in his own pocket when he was done. Jimmy was a notorious pen thief.

Peter held up the pen. "Do you know this place? Lake Capital Funds?"

Dinah shook her head. "We don't have any investments, Peter. We never had enough extra money to invest."

Peter looked at his watch. Lake Capital would be closed for the day.

He repacked the box and walked back to his truck, thinking he'd try to find the place where Jimmy was staying. He'd taken a single photo to show around the neighborhood. While the truck warmed up, he pulled it from his shirt pocket to look at it again.

Jimmy wore dusty desert camo and carried a beat-up M4. He stood in front of a half-demolished mud-brick house with Manny Martinez and Bert Coswell, the platoon's two other squad leaders. Although Jimmy's broad shoulders were slumped and his face was lined with fatigue, his eyes were lively and the smile was genuine. It was a photo of a happy warrior. But now Peter could also see the man who had sung his young sons to sleep.

Peter remembered the day clearly, because he had been there.

Peter had taken the picture.

But that was then.

Who was Big Jimmy in the weeks before he died?

What had he been doing that involved four hundred thousand dollars and four slabs of plastic explosive in a Samsonite suitcase?

The Man in the Black Canvas Chore Coat

He turned the old blue Ford pickup from the two-lane onto a gravel side road not found on maps. The wind had stripped the trees bare of leaves, and their branches mingled overhead like long, bony fingers. There were no houses in sight.

Past the first curve, a clean white Dodge cargo van idled at a wide spot in the road. The driver leaned against the fender, smoking a cigarette, nodding in time to the music coming through his earbuds. He wore jeans torn at the knees and a gray hooded sweatshirt with a plumbing company's logo on the chest.

The van itself had no markings other than the make, model, and license plates.

The man in the black canvas chore coat parked the pickup next to the cargo van and killed the engine. The van driver pulled out his earbuds and hung them around his neck, then pushed himself off the fender and walked toward the back of the Dodge. He pinched out the cherry of his cigarette with a callused thumb and forefinger and tucked the butt in his pocket before opening the van's rear doors.

There were no seats or toolboxes.

Just an old canvas tarp draped over the cargo.

The man in the black coat dropped the pickup's tailgate and hoisted up one of the white fifty-pound bags of fertilizer into his arms. Fifty pounds wasn't heavy, he thought. About as much as a small box of books, or a healthy six-year-old boy. He handled the weight easily enough. He'd carried heavier loads for far longer distances before this.

He carried the bag to the van, then held it momentarily in one arm while he threw back the canvas tarp with the other. Then laid the bag down carefully. The bags would be moved multiple times, and it helped to keep the plastic intact. The van driver came behind him with the second bag and threw it beside the first.

"Careful with those," said the man in the coat. "I've told you before."

"Dude," said the van driver. "They ain't gonna go off on their own."

The man in the coat allowed himself a small sigh.

"One more stop," he said, looking up through the bare tree branches. "You have the rendezvous for tonight?"

"Yup." The van driver nodded. Thrash rock came through the dangling earbuds, spoiling the quiet. "Hey, we're about out of food. Definitely out of beer. Okay if I find a gas station or something?"

"Sure," said the man in the coat. "Don't make any new friends. I'll be an hour or so." He walked to the pickup.

The van driver leaned into the back of his vehicle to grab the corner of the tarp. The fading light shone weakly on the growing stacks of white fifty-pound bags.

Until the tarp covered them up again, and the doors slammed shut, and the van looked like any other white Dodge van in fifty states.

10

Twentieth and Center was an easy walk from Shorty's, the bar where Jimmy had worked. Dinah didn't know which building, or even which block. Peter thought he could narrow it down by knocking on doors.

Jimmy was a friendly guy. Someone would remember him.

Or so Peter hoped.

Driving, he continued to check his mirrors, but saw no sign of the black Ford SUV or anything else. Although, in the dark, one set of headlights looked a lot like the rest.

Vacant lots gaped like black holes where the city had torn down derelict housing. The remaining buildings were duplexes built in the twenties, when factory jobs were plentiful. Once they were tall and proud. Now, even with half the streetlights dark, Peter could see the crumbling chimneys, asbestos siding cracked and falling, roof shingles slipping downhill, revealing the worn layers beneath.

Peter understood why Jimmy didn't want Dinah to see where he lived.

He circled the block twice before finally parking. Getting out of the truck, he thought about taking the .45 with him. It was a Colt 1911. This one had the serial numbers filed off, which under the current circumstances he didn't mind. He'd bought it in the parking lot of a gun show in Washington State, not because he thought he would ever need it, but because for a soldier who'd spent eight years at war, not owning a weapon was like a writer emptying his house of pens.

As handguns went, the 1911 was big and heavy, but it was very similar to the sidearm he'd had in the service, and he was used to it. It felt like an extension of his hand. He didn't have a holster for it, though, and the gun tucked into the back of his pants was awkward. He didn't want to have to do a lot of walking like that, always adjusting, making sure it didn't fall out. So he left it under the seat. How bad could the neighborhood be?

It was full dark now, and getting colder. The wind murmured in the leafless maples and locusts. One thing about Milwaukee, the streets were lined with trees.

Three young men stood on the far corner, talking in low voices and passing a skinny hand-rolled cigarette. They watched Peter get out of the truck but didn't stop the conversation or the progress of the joint. One of them pulled out a phone and poked at it. In Iraq, this would have made Peter worry about an ambush or an IED. He told himself this wasn't Iraq.

The dog whined in the cargo box, so he let it out and took the rope in his hand. The animal was excited, ears up and tugging at the leash.

Peter figured he'd let the dog pee, then put it back in the truck before starting to knock on doors. Nobody would talk with this ugly monster beside him. But rather than sniff the bushes, the dog pulled him eagerly down the darkened street.

"Mingus!" Ahead, a woman stumped along the sidewalk, bent with age. She had a furled umbrella in one hand, using it like a cane, and a plastic grocery sack in the other. Her hair was tied up in a tribal scarf, the bright colors muted by the night. The dog pulled harder, a hundred and fifty pounds of determination. "Charles Mingus, that you?" Her voice was a scratchy shout. She was two houses away.

"Ma'am?" Peter called. He had never been mistaken for a dead black jazz musician before.

"Not you, fool," said the woman scornfully as the dog launched itself forward at her. Peter was pulled nearly off his feet before the rope leash slid, burning, from his grasp.

Shit shit shit. He dove after the dog, thankful for the stick occupying those murderous teeth, trying for a grip on the wood or the rope while the dog lunged at the woman and blows from the umbrella rained about

Peter's head. The old woman was stronger than she looked. Most of them are.

Finally he had the dog in a headlock, down on his knees with the leash wrapped around his hand, but she was still swinging the umbrella like a samurai on acid.

"Who the fuck are you?" said the old woman, not even breathing hard as Peter wrestled with the dog. "And what have you done to poor Charles Mingus?"

Oh, thought Peter. She wasn't crazy.

Charles Mingus was the dog. She knew the dog.

She knew the dog.

He caught the umbrella in one hand and held it still. It was harder than he expected.

"Ma'am? How do you know the dog?"

She turned toward a small duplex house. "I need a goddamn drink."

She didn't look to see if he was following.

Her name was Miss Rosetta Phelps, and housekeeping clearly wasn't a priority. Her kitchen was a narrow blue clutter of unwashed pots and empty bottles.

The white static foamed up and the smell of the dog filled the room, although Peter couldn't entirely fault the dog. He stuck his head through doorways to see the layout and find the exits, the static always looking for more ways to get outside.

Miss Rosetta didn't leave the kitchen. The grocery

sack she'd been carrying held a plastic half-gallon of Early Times, undamaged in the scuffle. At a small corner table crowded with dirty dishes, she poured a long, dark splash into a stained water glass and drained it in a gulp.

She smacked her lips. "Oh, that's nice."

Four fingers of cheap whiskey and she drank it down like iced tea. Peter made a mental note: don't fuck with old ladies.

She reached for a boning knife. "C'mere, Mingus, you poor bastard."

The dog sat at her feet, wagging his tail. "I'm glad he has a name," said Peter. "I was thinking of calling him Cupcake."

"Huh," said Miss Rosetta, looking sideways at Peter. "You don't *look* like no retard," she said. "But I been wrong before." She took hold of the dog by the upper jaw, ignoring the snorts and the inch-long teeth, and started sawing at the Kevlar rope holding the stick in place. "Hold still, dummy."

"You sure you want to do that? This dog tried to kill me once."

Miss Rosetta ignored him. The knife was very sharp. She was already unwinding the rope. The dog dropped the chewed length of handrail on the cracked linoleum with a surprising delicacy, licked his chops experimentally, then put his paws up on the woman's lap and licked her chin.

"Mingus, behave yourself," she said, rapping him on the nose.

When he slurped her right ear, she leaned in and wrapped her arms around his neck, giggling like a schoolgirl. "Dog, you ain't even bought me dinner."

Eventually the dog came to Peter and nosed his hands.

Peter pushed the nose away.

The dog came back.

Peter pushed him away again.

When the dog returned a third time, he moved so fast that he had Peter's wrist between his jaws before Peter knew he had done it.

The pressure of the teeth was perfectly calibrated. The hardest grip possible without quite puncturing the skin. The hot, wet tongue like a rare steak fresh from the pan. The wolfish eyes locked on his face.

The dog wasn't letting go.

Peter sighed. "Okay, Mingus," he said, and rubbed the massive head with his free hand. The stink rose up like a poison cloud. He really had to wash this damn dog. "You win. I'm yours."

The dog released his wrist and licked up his arm to the inside of his elbow. Peter stood and rinsed a cereal bowl, filled it with water, and set it on the floor. The dog drank noisily.

As if on cue, Miss Rosetta reached for the Early Times again, this time filling half the glass and pouring it down her throat without seeming to swallow. He'd better get some answers before she fell off her chair.

Peter said, "Ma'am, how do you know this dog?"

"Poor Mingus," she said. She didn't seem drunk at all. Maybe she was like one of those experimental cars that ran on alcohol. Just topping up her tank. She looked at Peter hard. "Where'd you find him?"

"Hiding under a porch a couple miles from here. The family was afraid he was going to hurt one of the kids. I think he was just hungry."

On cue, the dog looked up, long tongue hanging out, dripping water on the linoleum. "Don't look at me, Mingus," she said. "I ain't feeding you. That Jim might have something upstairs, if the rats ain't got it."

"Miss Rosetta," said Peter. "How do you know the dog?"

But he already knew.

She rested her chin on her hand, her elbow on the table. "My tenant," she said dreamily. "Lives upstairs. Mingus's his dog. Been gone awhile. Went on a trip, took the dog with him. Paid rent three months in advance, cash money. Can you beat that?"

Cash money. "What's your tenant's name?"

"Jim," she said. "Handsome Jim. Big, tall man." The bourbon was catching up. Her speech was still clear, but her face was starting to look a little blurred. "Real sweetheart, that boy. Was a time I'da showed him something. . . ." Her voice crackled and faded, a radio losing reception.

Every Marine knows not to drink on an empty stomach. "Miss Rosetta? Can I make you some dinner?"

She blinked at him slowly. Then smacked her lips, her

head sinking down toward the table and onto her folded arms. After a minute, she started snoring. Peter looked in the fridge. Bread, eggs, hamburger. TV dinners in the freezer. She'd be okay.

She seemed to have some practice at this.

The static was flaring in the small cluttered space. Peter endured the tightness in his chest long enough to neaten the kitchen and wash the dishes, which took some scrubbing. Making sure the door locked behind him, he left with Mingus bounding ahead.

11

The entrance to the upstairs apartment was at the side of Miss Rosetta's duplex. The lamp outside was dark, so trying Jimmy's keys in the lock was difficult until Peter pulled out his penlight.

After a little jiggling, the tarnished old lock turned just fine.

The steps were steep and narrow and complained underfoot. He pushed down the cramped, jittery feeling and climbed.

The dog galloped up ahead of him.

At the top, two doors. The original upper apartment was subdivided into two smaller units. The dog nosed at the right-hand door. Peter tried his keys again. The latch opened without fuss, as if waiting to be unlocked.

The white static rose up. One deep breath after another. He told himself he'd be out of there in ten minutes.

Jimmy had lived in one room tucked into the eaves at the back of the house. The cracked plaster ceiling angled down to the floor, following the rafters. A rag rug covered most of the battered pine floor. The small bed was neatly made with a green wool Army surplus blanket. Jimmy's feet must have hung off the end.

A small television sat atop a small bookshelf filled with war memoirs—Erich Maria Remarque, Ernie Pyle, Philip Caputo, Tim O'Brien, Nathaniel Fick. Facing it was an ugly plaid armchair that was wide enough for Jimmy and looked pretty comfortable. In the corner, a small maple desk.

There was a closet with wash-worn shirts and pants on plastic hangers. A bathroom was shared with the neighboring apartment. The window looked out to the backyard and alley. No lights to be seen. It was dark as death out there.

For a kitchen, Jimmy had a short counter, a bar sink, and an old chrome single-coil hot plate that belonged in a museum. Atop a clean dish towel stood a shining plate and bowl, a mason jar doing duty as a glass, a green ceramic mug with U.S. MARINE CORPS on the side, and a fork, knife, and spoon. No piece matched any other, but each was clean and at rest in orderly progression.

Peter thought of Dinah's description of Jimmy asleep on the couch with the dishes still dirty from breakfast.

Maybe he didn't want his wife to see how he was living. But the man had nothing to be ashamed of.

Shelves held cans of soup, spaghetti, pork and beans.

Store-brand coffee in a half-pound tin, nearly empty. Salt and pepper shakers. Under the counter, a mini-fridge with a folded dish towel laid over the door to keep it from closing. It was empty, clean, and unplugged.

This wasn't how Jimmy had lived every day, not with his fridge unplugged. He was preparing for something.

He'd told his landlady he would be gone for a while.

He'd paid his rent three months in advance.

Peter thought about how Jimmy had made a point of saying please and thank you. Thanks for the coffee, brother. Please pass the hand grenades. It was funny, and Jimmy knew it, but he was serious about it, too, schooling the younger guys. A real man treats others with respect, and demands respect in return. It was an odd habit in a war zone, but because of Jimmy's natural authority, it was also contagious. They had the politest platoon in the war.

Maybe Jimmy was the polite kind of suicide.

The kind who cleaned his apartment and paid his rent first.

Because he didn't want to inconvenience anyone.

Oh, Jimmy.

The dog nosed at the kitchen cabinet. It was still disconcerting to see him without the stick tied into his mouth, but Peter was getting used to it. He opened the door and found a few pans and an old coffee percolator, and two big metal bowls stacked atop a sealed plastic bin with a few cups of dog food scattered on the bottom. Peter set out the bin for the dog, who immediately hoovered out the contents, licked his sizable chops, looked at Peter, and whined.

"It's okay, Mingus," he said. "We'll figure it out."

Mingus went to a worn corner of the carpet, turned around twice, and lay down, nose to tail, watching as Peter went through the closet. There was nothing in the pockets of the hanging shirts or pants; nothing slid between the jeans and sweaters folded on the shelf. Nothing was hidden in the old black suit that Jimmy would have worn to weddings and funerals. Underwear folded neatly in a shoebox, socks paired up in another. Peter emptied the boxes but found nothing but clothes.

The static had begun to crackle and rise, and his shoulders were getting tight, but Peter put each item back the way he'd found it. The man was dead, but it was still his home. And Peter wanted Dinah to see it the way Jimmy had left it.

There was nothing hidden under the bed or under the carpet. Jimmy had taped snapshots of Dinah, Charlie, and Miles to the wall by the bed, but there was nothing hidden behind them. There was no access to the attic or the knee walls where the roof slanted down.

He went through the desk last. It was small and its finish was peeling, but it was made of actual wood, from the days before particleboard turned furniture into disposable objects. The top was empty. There were three drawers down the left side. The bottom drawer was empty. The middle drawer held pens, a scattering of plain envelopes, a half-sheet of stamps. The top drawer held a big manila envelope from the VA, with a thick sheaf of papers. Peter pulled the envelope out to take with him.

Under the manila envelope was a yellow paper flier. HAVE YOU SEEN THIS MAN? Looking at it, Peter thought it was the same as the flier folded up in Jimmy's belt when he died. The photo showed a very young man with cropped black hair, smiling for the camera. He wore a striped button-down shirt. It might have been a high school graduation photo.

This time, Peter read the smaller print. "Felix Castellano, decorated Marine, missing. Please contact his grandmother, Aurelia Castellano." It gave a phone number and date, just a few weeks before Jimmy's death.

There was something about this flier. Peter felt it in the pit of his stomach. The urgent growl of pursuit.

But he didn't know why.

He was down the stairs and out the door with the VA papers and the flier in a paper bag, the key in the lock, the dog crowding him on the stoop, the white static dissolving in the relief of the open air, before he realized it.

It was more than a flier. Jimmy was trying to find the missing Marine.

It was part of Marine culture, part of the lore.

You pick up your wounded.

You carry the dead.

You never leave a man behind.

And here was Peter, doing the same damn thing.

Trying to find the real Jimmy. To carry him home.

Jimmy, with his suitcase full of money and four slabs of plastic explosive.

Oh, Jimmy. What did you do?

12

Stepping out into the darkened street toward his truck, with the bag of Jimmy's papers swinging at his side and Mingus ranging ahead, Peter felt the puff of wind on his neck and heard the unmistakable *zhip* of the bullet passing before the flat crack of the gunshots reached him.

It was familiar, the loose rattle of an AK-47, the way the world slowed down while his mind sped up. The granular glow from the few functional streetlights. The damp autumn breeze on his exposed skin. The coppery flavor of adrenaline in his mouth. He didn't want to like it. But there was something unavoidably delicious about that taste.

Automatically, he turned his head to look for the muzzle flash and saw the man in a Bulls jacket standing beside the open rear door of a sedan stopped at the intersection fifty yards away. The long gun was at his shoulder, but his eye wasn't down to the sight.

With the crystal clarity of stopped time, Peter thought the guy should be ashamed for missing at that distance. Even with an AK, which was notoriously inaccurate. It was like the early days of the insurgency, deposed Baathists full of the false confidence that came from running a dictatorship, walking into the street like action heroes, firing from the hip. This was before they learned to hide, and aim, and blow shit up.

The world popped back into motion when the gunman fired again. The AK clattered and a window broke behind Peter. A car alarm howled. Out in the darkness, Mingus started barking like something out of a caveman's nightmare.

Stepping behind the cover of his truck, Peter couldn't see the dog, but he didn't have time to look. The gunman paused, probably changing clips. Peter fished his keys from his coat pocket, opened the passenger door, reached under the seat and found the .45. Shoved the bag of Jimmy's papers where the gun had been. Mingus kept barking, now from somewhere above him.

Above him? He looked up. Mingus had somehow climbed up on the roof of the truck, sounding like a demon dog.

Then the flat slap of a round punching through forty-year-old truck glass, the asshole shooting Peter's truck, and the *thunk thunk thunk* of punctured sheet metal right in front of him.

It's one thing to shoot at a guy and another thing entirely to shoot a guy's truck. Peter looked at the cracks spiderwebbed around the ragged hole in his window, listened to holes being punched in the mahogany box and the driver's-side door, the door he'd scoured every junkyard in southern California to find, and how the hell did Mingus get on the roof of the truck?

Peter surely must have pissed off somebody, to get a shooter out here so fast.

Thinking all of this while he strode to the back of the truck and peered around the edge of the mahogany box. Lifted the .45 in a two-handed grip, left forefinger on the trigger. Pistol butt solid in the palm of his right hand, shoulder braced, knees slightly bent. Arms strong, line up the notch with the reticule, take a breath, exhale, and squeeeeeeze.

The gun bucked in his hand. The man with the AK dropped to the blacktop.

The sedan lurched forward, squealing its tires, the rear door slamming closed with the sudden motion. It was an eighties Chevy Impala, jacked up high, with gleaming chrome rims. The light was dim, but Peter just caught the plate number. He put a round through the rear windshield and the rear passenger quarter-panel, aiming for the tire, then held his fire as Mingus leaped off the roof of the truck and hauled ass down the street after the car, a ferocious orange blur disappearing into the night.

The dog had heart, there was no denying it.

Peter walked to the fallen man and kicked the AK away, but it was clear already from the crumpled way he had fallen that the man was dead. Peter rolled the man fully to his back and saw the red hole in the center of his forehead.

Just like a paper target at the firing range.

But paper targets didn't fall down.

Didn't erupt in a pool of blood on the cracked asphalt.

Paper targets didn't die.

He looked around for another car, a spotter, anyone. But there was nobody else. The neighbors had gone to ground, turned out their lights. It wasn't their first neighborhood shooting.

Peter sighed.

The dead man had dark skin, late teens or early twenties. His face without lines of care or woe.

Peter had never seen him before.

A stranger had tried to kill him.

Just like old times.

Peter found his shell casings in a pothole big enough to swallow a Honda. He picked up the brass, put the .45 in his coat pocket, and set out after the dog at a fast jog.

He hadn't known the shooter. Which meant that someone had sent him.

Only two candidates came to mind.

The scarred man in the black SUV. And Lewis.

13

The gun banged against his hip as he ran.

The gun was a problem. In addition to the fact that it was annoying, the ballistics would connect him to the dead man in the Bulls jacket. Peter knew from long experience how slowly the wheels of government turned, and how finely a man could get ground up beneath them.

The white static couldn't handle Peter getting locked up.

Not for an hour, let alone overnight.

It didn't matter that he had killed the man in self-defense. The gun wasn't legal, he had no permit for it. If they didn't get him for the killing, they'd get him for the gun. And all the while, the man with the scars prowled around Dinah's house and Lewis's goons lay awake at night wondering how much money she had.

It wasn't just the white static.

Peter had shit to do.

Someone had sent that kid with the AK. Peter needed to know who.

Five blocks from the shooting, he ducked down an alley to eject the remaining rounds, wiping his fingerprints from each with his shirttail, then dropping them through the sewer grate.

On the next block he did the same with the clip, and on the next block, the slide, and on the block after that, the frame.

He stopped to wet his hands with the dew on an unmowed lawn, and rubbed them together to help clean off the gunshot residue. He didn't know if it would help if they wanted to test him, but maybe it would. He shook off the water and wiped them dry on his socks. He'd worn those socks for three days now. He wasn't worried about gunshot residue.

He ran for another hour, looking for a big ugly orange dog. His breath came easily as he methodically quartered the neighborhood, waving coolly at the patrol cars when they roared by. They didn't stop to ask him questions.

He didn't find Mingus. He tried not to worry about the dog. He told himself Mingus was the kind of animal who could find his way home.

He was more worried about the Chevy Impala sedan with bullet holes in the rear windshield and quarter-panel.

And the black SUV driven by a man with scars on his cheeks.

And Lewis and Nino and Ray.

And Dinah, with a man watching her house, and four hundred thousand dollars in a paper bag tied up with string.

Peter really didn't want to get locked up.

But if he went back to his truck, maybe he could learn something.

The police had set up a perimeter. Yellow plastic tape stretched around trees and lampposts and knockdown sawhorses. It contained the dead shooter, the intersection, and part of Jimmy's street with half a dozen shot-up cars and Peter's perforated truck.

Uniformed policemen and other crime-scene people wandered around in the weird glare of portable lights. A few neighborhood onlookers stood in whispering knots on the sidewalk.

Peter stopped at the tape. CRIME SCENE, DO NOT CROSS.

When a police officer came up to see what he wanted, Peter nodded at his pickup. "That's my truck."

The cop was older than Peter, with arms like bridge cables and a face made of stone. He asked for Peter's ID. "My wallet's in the glove box," said Peter. "Or it was before some asshole broke my window."

The cop nodded. "Wait for the detective."

"What happened?" asked Peter. "Somebody get hurt?"

The cop's face didn't change. "Wait for the detective."

Peter waited while the cop went to a group of men standing around the body. Uniformed cops paced around, eyes down, examining the ground.

After ten minutes, a tall, narrow guy in a tall, narrow suit under a long, dark coat came up to the tape line. In his late forties, he had the measured stride of a marathoner and the distant stare of a sniper. He opened a notebook, licked the tip of a pencil, and looked at Peter like he knew every time Peter had crossed against the light.

It was a little disconcerting. The white static fizzed down low.

"Name."

Peter told him. The detective didn't write it down.

"Address."

Peter gave the man his parents' house up north, although he hadn't been back since he mustered out. The detective didn't look surprised. It was the same address on the driver's license. He didn't write that down, either.

"Phone?"

"I don't have one."

That raised his eyebrows. "You don't have one?"

Peter shook his head. Although he was thinking he should get one. One of those smartphones, if he could get one without a credit card. He didn't have a credit card, either. Neither one had mattered when he was up in the mountains.

"What's your business here?"

Peter had the answer ready. "I was working on a

friend's house a few blocks away. I finished for the day, was headed to Speed Queen for barbecue, and stopped to let my dog out. He took off after something. I went after him."

"You stopped in this neighborhood? To let your dog out?" The detective wasn't buying it.

"I'm not from around here," said Peter. "It didn't look so bad compared to where I've been."

The detective's eyes were a mild gray in the crime-scene lights, and utterly without illusions. "I bet," he said. "So where's the dog?"

"I don't know," said Peter. "I never found him. But I did see a black Ford SUV chasing a Chevy Impala going north on Twentieth about an hour ago, going really fast. The Ford almost ran me over. I got the license plates."

The detective raised his eyebrows, an understated disbelieving will-wonders-never-cease? kind of look. "Oh, really."

Peter gave him the plate numbers from the Impala and the black SUV that had followed him from Dinah's house.

The detective licked his pencil again, and this time he wrote down the numbers. And some other things, too, because he kept writing.

Peter said, "You mind my asking what happened?"

"Shoot-out in the big city," said the tall detective, pencil still moving on his notebook. He tilted his head toward the man Peter had killed, who had tried to kill him. "Young man over there, now deceased. Appeared to be armed with an AK-47. Probably not on his way to church."

He closed the notebook and tucked it into his jacket pocket, lifted the yellow tape. "C'mon in," he said. Then strolled through the crime scene like it was his backyard. Peter walked beside him.

"Guy hosed down half the block," said the detective. "Most of two clips, fifty or sixty rounds. Really a fine American. Didn't hit any people I know of yet, although the night is young. Put a bunch of holes in cars and houses. Most of those holes in your truck, unfortunately," he said, pointing at it with his chin. But he stopped short of the pickup, beside a patrol car parked blocking the street.

"No official suspects on the killer. Whoever did it drilled him dead center, right in the forehead. Single shot. That's marksmanship."

Then the tall detective opened the rear door of the patrol car.

"Get inside," he said.

"What for?" asked Peter, keeping his voice mild although the static sparked inside him. His heart thumped harder in his chest. Goddamn it. "I wasn't here. I just want to get my truck and find my dog, and get some dinner. I've been working all day. I'm hungry."

"I'm not taking you in," said the detective. "I'm just going to run your record."

"Because I parked on the wrong block?"

"Because, looking at you, I'm guessing you're a vet."

"I'm a carpenter."

The detective gave him a look. "Don't be an asshole. You were over there. Am I right?"

Reluctantly, Peter nodded. "Marines. Recon."

The detective filed it away. "Iraq or Afghanistan?"

"Both," said Peter.

"Welcome home, son," said the detective, not unkindly. "But you're the only guy I've got with practice shooting at people. So get in the car."

"Goddamn it, I'm trying to be helpful," said Peter.

"So you say," said the detective. "So keep being helpful. Get in the fucking car before I have four cops put you in. With handcuffs."

Peter felt his muscles tense, his pulse rising. He turned and bent and sat, leaving his legs out. It was awkward. The plastic seats were formed to fit a person with his hands cuffed behind him. He could still hear the wind in the trees. It helped, a little. But the back of a police car was just one step removed from a holding cell. And the white static didn't like it.

He shifted on the seat, heart going hard, knee bobbing faster as his interior metronome went into overdrive. The tall detective was looking at him. Peter's shoulders rose and his neck tightened up. An error in judgment. He should have kept going. He should have come back tomorrow. The space got smaller around him. He took deep breaths, in and out, in and out, trying to keep the oxygen moving. The headache would come soon.

The detective leaned on the open door. "You okay there, pal?"

Peter shook his head. "I'm really hungry," he said. "My blood sugar gets low."

The detective eyed him skeptically. "Uh-huh. Listen, when they go through your truck, are they going to find anything? Weapons? Drugs? Pills? Needles? I don't care about a little weed, because, hey, it's practically medicine now. But anything else, you better tell me, because they're going to find it."

The detective leaned over him and Peter felt the disadvantage. Which was why the detective did it. The white static was just a fringe benefit. But the police were unlikely to find where he'd hidden the plastic explosive without putting the truck up on a lift.

"No," he said. "No drugs. Just tools. Some food, camping gear." He was glad he had gotten rid of the gun.

"So," said the detective. "You're living out of your truck." But he seemed sympathetic.

Peter really didn't want to have this conversation. But it was manifestly true, down to the sleeping bag and coffeepot. And it put Peter in a certain category for the man. Maybe that would be helpful.

So he nodded. "Just for a few days," he said.

"The address on your driver's license: that's your parents' house, right?"

Peter nodded again.

"So why aren't you there? Why are you here, living out of your truck?"

"I'm working," said Peter. "Helping out a friend. I don't have a lot of money."

The detective's gray eyes looked right through him.

"You get panic attacks? Nightmares, maybe? Or it takes a pint of bourbon to get to sleep?"

"I sleep fine," said Peter. Which was true, as long as he could see the sky before he closed his eyes. And hear the wind in the trees. Goddamn it. He kept breathing. Maybe it was getting easier.

The detective's face softened a little. "The VA's just a few miles from here. They have some pretty good people. Sometimes it just helps to talk."

Peter opened his mouth and closed it again. How had this cop put him so off-balance?

"No offense," he said, looking up at the detective, "but you don't look like my mother. So what the fuck is it to you?"

The tall detective's face was carefully calm. "Let's just say I've had my share of nightmares." He stuck out his hand. "Sam Lipsky. Rangers, Somalia '89, Iraq '91."

The Rangers were the Army equivalent of the Marines' Force Recon, Peter's group. Somalia was an ugly little war. Mogadishu warlords shot down a Black Hawk helicopter, dropping Rangers in the middle of a hostile city. Then the rescue went bad.

Peter shook the detective's hand. It was lean and hard, like the man.

"So tell me," said Lipsky. His eyes like X-rays, looking under the skin. "Do I gotta worry about you? Like that poor schmuck shot up that recruiting office last week?"

Peter shook his head. "No," he said. "That's not me."

"You're not pissed off, frustrated, unemployed, maybe got something going that's not quite legal?"

"All of that, yeah, except the last one." Peter spread his hands. They were shaking slightly. "Listen, I'm really starving. Can I get something to eat?"

"Sorry. Not yet." Detective Sam Lipsky pinned Peter with a glance. "Sit tight. I'll leave the door open. You're not going anywhere just yet. Better give me the keys to your camper, or we'll just pry off the lock."

14

While the cops combed through his truck, Peter talked to other detectives who asked the same questions in different ways, over and over. Peter gave them more or less the same answers. This wasn't his first rodeo. He knew to vary his answers enough to be believable.

And all the while, his heart beat too fast, the white static buzzed and crackled in his brain, and his feet twitched for a lonely mountain. Breathe in, breathe out.

When they were finished with their questions, they left him alone to sit. He thought about the last time he had an official interview. He'd been back in the States for three days, and he sat in the small cluttered office of a Navy shrink.

It was part of the discharge process. The Pentagon wanted every soldier, sailor, airman, and Marine to have at least one session with a mental health professional before returning to civilian life. The idea was to make sure that veterans weren't emotionally or mentally disturbed, or if they were, to get them into treatment. But in reality, almost nobody admitted to problems. It was part of the culture. Man up and keep going. And you sure as hell didn't want anything on your record.

The Navy shrink was a stout, friendly lieutenant commander with soft hands but a strong grip. He asked Peter why he didn't eat in the officers' mess, why he slept outside on the wild part of the base. Was there something wrong with his quarters? A thick folder open on the desk before him. Peter's service record.

Peter said he liked the open air. It was a way to get some time to himself. He didn't mention the way his lungs got tight and the walls closed in and his heartbeat would accelerate inside a building. Especially an institutional building, like the vast office complex where the shrink sat behind his steel desk under flickering fluorescent lights. Peter could barely keep himself in the chair.

The Navy shrink looked at him with a kind smile, and Peter knew the man could see it in him, the pressure in his head, the way the sparks crackled up his brainstem.

"It's a nice day out," said the shrink. He closed the folder and set it aside. "How about we go for a walk?" And he watched Peter's breathing slow in the open air as the static subsided.

"How bad is it?" the man finally asked as they walked the manicured paths. "I'm not writing anything down. This is just you and me."

Peter told him it was fine if he stayed outside.

"That's gonna get in the way of civilian life," said the shrink. "Was it worse during fighting, during downtime, or both?"

"It didn't start until I got off the plane here," said Peter. "End of the tour."

The shrink nodded like he'd heard it a thousand times before.

Maybe he had.

"What you're experiencing is called a panic attack," he said. "It can be triggered in many different ways. For you, it shows up as an acute claustrophobia. When you were in combat, was there a lot of fighting inside, clearing buildings?"

"Yes," said Peter. "Fallujah. Twice. But now I can barely go inside the dining hall. That's not a combat zone."

"Your body is reacting to an environment that was very stressful over a relatively long period of time. It was a useful reaction in Fallujah. It helped keep you alive. But now it's too sensitive. It's overreacting to a perceived threat, and your fight-or-flight reflex goes into overdrive."

"Well," said Peter. "Shit."

"I have to ask this," the man said, watching Peter closely. "Again, this is just you and me. But I need a brutally honest answer. Do you feel like you're a danger to yourself? Or to anyone else?"

"No," said Peter. He drank in the fresh air. "I don't want to hurt myself or anyone else. I just want to solve this. Problem."

The Navy shrink nodded again.

"A lot of combat vets are changed by war," he said. "Some of them are physically changed, wounded, missing limbs. That's very difficult. But some have other effects. Stress effects, which are no less real. And for some vets, they're harder to live with, because you can't see them.

"Sometimes those effects diminish over time," he said. "Sometimes they go away entirely. Sometimes they don't. But there are things you can do to help."

"Like what?"

The shrink said it depended on the individual. "For some people," he said, "the solution is to stress yourself in a controlled manner, a little more each time, and allow your unconscious to realize that in the civilian world, nothing bad happens. Like curing fear of flying by getting on a plane.

"And sometimes," he said, "you do the opposite. You back away, reduce the stress, and allow the brain to reorganize itself to a life where people aren't shooting at you all the time. Sometimes it's a combination of the two. You work with a therapist to find the right course of treatment. That's the best way to get better."

Peter nodded, thinking that sitting in a shrink's office was going to drive him crazy all by itself.

Reading his face, the shrink kept talking. "Not everyone wants to work with a therapist," he said. "Some people can learn to just listen to themselves and pay attention. Find someone to talk to, and work it through."

"What if it doesn't go away?" asked Peter.

The shrink gave him the same kind smile. "Then that's just who you are now," he said. "If there are limitations, there are also benefits. That's your life. Learn how to live it. Find something to do. Someone to love. Get on with things."

15

Detective Sam Lipsky returned two hours later, flipping through his notebook. Peter still sat in the back of the cruiser, his legs out the open door. He couldn't get comfortable. The white static buzzed and crackled. He worried about Dinah.

"I thought you were fresh off the plane," said Lipsky. "But you got discharged over a year ago."

Peter nodded.

"So for the last year, you've been doing what?"

"Working, here and there. Hiking out West."

"Is this some kind of hippie dropout thing?"

"All due respect, Detective?" said Peter. "Fuck you."

Lipsky smiled. "You won the silver star," said the detective. "And a lot of other medals. You were a lieutenant for eight years. I didn't know that was possible. You should have been a captain, even a major. But my contact says the details are sealed. So what happened?"

"I had a problem with the chain of command."

"I can see that," said Lipsky. "You and me both."

He produced Peter's keys and wallet from his coat pocket and handed them over, stepping back so Peter could stand.

"License expired five years ago," he said. "Like I give a shit. Renew it tomorrow. Go get something to eat, find your dog. Then go home and see your parents. And stay out of neighborhoods like this one."

Peter climbed out of the cruiser and stood in the night air. He felt the wind open him up. His shoulders loosened, and his hands unclenched. Then he asked the question he'd wanted to ask for the last three hours. "So who's the dead guy?"

Lipsky's smile fell away.

"I'm more interested in the guy who killed the dead guy," he said. "One thing, he was a helluva shot. ME won't say anything for sure yet. But probably a large-caliber handgun, a .45. Between the eyes, from a distance of fifty yards or more. While getting sprayed by an AK-47? That's a shooter with some practice."

Peter had been in a few target competitions in his time. That was probably in his service record, too. He hadn't won any, but they hadn't laughed at him, either. And he'd certainly gotten used to shooting back under fire.

He didn't take the bait. "But who's the dead guy?"

Lipsky seemed amused and world-weary at the same time. Peter knew he hadn't fooled the man one bit. "Young guy, kicked out of the Army," he said. "Dishonorable discharge, which was hard to do when they were desperate for warm bodies. Maybe a gang member, although it's not on his sheet. And walking around with an assault rifle, a real model citizen. So I won't lose sleep. Guy killed him probably did the world a favor. Probably self-defense, with that AK."

"Must be a gang thing," said Peter. "Didn't I read in the paper that Milwaukee has one of the highest murder rates in the country?"

Lipsky didn't seem to have heard him. "But I gotta wonder," he mused. "Who was he shooting at? And why? And when's the next guy gonna show up? Because if he's a gangbanger, this was some kind of deliberate hit, you know those guys take this shit personally."

Peter had been thinking about that, too. Someone had tried to kill him. The kid with the AK was just the weapon. He tried to consider it progress. It meant he was getting closer to something. Maybe it would help if he knew what it was he was getting closer to.

"But you're just an innocent bystander, right?" said Lipsky. "Not your problem."

A dog barked somewhere, deep and loud.

"Sit," called out a second voice, nervous. "Stay."

The dog barked again. It was a familiar sound.

The voice called out again. "Hey, dog, sit your ugly butt down. Sit, dammit. Stay, all right? Hey, whose dog is this? Anybody know whose damn dog this is?"

"That's my dog," said Peter. "That's my dog." He pushed through the cluster of patrolmen to where Mingus stood, panting happily beside Peter's truck, long, wet tongue lolling out past the wicked serration of his teeth. Peter was surprised he hadn't brought back the Impala's rear bumper.

A patrolman had his pepper spray out, arm extended. He spoke without taking his eyes off Mingus. "Mister, take control of your dog." This wasn't the cop who'd met Peter at the tape line, but a young guy, his uniform still crisp from the box it came in. The dog probably weighed more than he did. "Put that damn dog on a leash or I'll put him down."

"He won't hurt you, but I will." Peter's anger rose like the tide, surprising him. "You spray my dog, I'll break your head." It was the aftermath of the white static, a pale fury. And Mingus was his dog.

The patrolman lifted his thumb from the trigger of the pepper spray and half turned to eyeball Peter. He had the nervous swagger of a new recruit. "Mister, that's threatening a police officer. You want to spend the night in jail?"

But Mingus saw the opening, leaped forward, and snatched the pepper spray from the young cop's hand, rupturing the pressurized metal canister with his teeth in the process. A dense cloud of aerosolized oleoresin capsicum pepper dosed the patrolman hard before dispersing into the crowd of policemen, who backed away, coughing and swearing.

Mingus just licked his chops, dropped the bleeding canister at Peter's feet, and resumed panting with what looked suspiciously like a smile.

Lipsky hooted with laughter, wiping away the pepper-induced tears. "That monster is your dog? Jesus Christ, you are a fucking jarhead." He handed over his business card. "You decide to confess, give me a call. Now get your ass and that fucking dog out of my crime scene."

Peter's truck had an archipelago of bullet holes from the driver's door to the mahogany cargo box. But the tires still held air and the engine compartment was untouched. He opened the driver's-side door and swept the broken glass from his truck seat with the flat of his hand.

Trailing the ripe smell of pepper spray, Mingus jumped up past him and settled into the passenger seat like he'd done it a thousand times. The smell of the dog was powerful in the enclosed cab, even with the broken window. Peter leaned across him and rolled the passenger window down, too.

He had things to do, but food was the first priority. Driving down Twentieth, looking for something to eat, Peter said, "You're really something, Mingus. You know that?"

The dog didn't take notice or show any sign that he'd heard the man. He just leaned out the open window, nose in the night wind, sniffing hard for a Chevy Impala with two bullet holes.

16

The Marines had rules of engagement, drawn up by military lawyers. Turns out you can't shoot just anyone.

Some of the rules were pretty basic. Don't fire at a mosque, a school, or a hospital. Don't fire at an unarmed man; don't fire into a crowd.

If a person in civilian clothes had an assault rifle in his hands and was firing it in your direction, that was pretty clear. Shoot the motherfucker. But if he was yelling at you, and his rifle was slung behind him or pointed at the ground, you were supposed to wait until he raised the rifle. He could be local police or a friendly militiaman.

Peter was no longer overseas. He could define his own rules of engagement. And one of Peter's new rules was that if somebody provoked him, he was going to respond.

He didn't know who was responsible for the shooter on Jimmy's block. If it was the man with the scars, Peter had given Lipsky the plate number, and the detective might be persuaded to share that information. And the next time that black Ford showed up, Peter would take action.

But if it was Lewis, Peter knew where to find him. Or at least where to start.

Yellow light seeped from the apartment windows of the building on MLK Drive, but the windows in Lewis's office were dark. The expensive vehicles parked outside earlier that day were nowhere to be seen.

Peter locked Mingus in the cargo box and walked around the corner to Shorty's. The front door had steel bars and a thick Plexiglas insert starred with what looked like bullet impacts. Or maybe a javelin thrower was using it for target practice. The hinges screeched when he pulled the door open.

Peter took a deep breath and walked inside.

It was Peter's kind of place, before the static had ruined him for bars. A deep, narrow room, with an exit on the side wall and another door behind the bar. Dark pine paneling lined the walls, the varnish turning a deep orange with age. A row of similar booths made against the outside wall, sparsely populated with neighborhood people, cracked red plastic cushions on the seats and high backs. At the long mahogany bar, a half-dozen older men in worn work clothes slouched on stools, knuckly hands curled protectively around their glasses, eyeballing the newcomer.

This would be a tap beer and boilermaker place, maybe some port wine or cognac for the big spenders. No goat-cheese appetizers, no weird martinis. Just a corner bar owned by a neighborhood warlord. Or whatever Lewis was.

The white static clamored for his attention, but not more than he could stand. Maybe it was the comedown from the shooting, or talking to Lipsky. Maybe it was the anticipation of seeing Lewis, and what that might entail.

Peter wondered what that Navy shrink would say. How fucked up was it that walking inside freaked Peter out, but the prospect of a fistfight or shoot-out calmed him down?

Peter went to the curved end of the bar where he could stand with the room in full view and his back to the wall. An ancient stereo played what sounded like Ray Charles. *Unchain my heart. Baby let me go.* The barman was built like a bulldog, complete with jowls. He dropped a bar napkin and lifted his eyebrows in a silent question.

Peter said, "I'm looking for Lewis."

The bartender's face was empty. "Don't know who you're talking about." But he didn't move down the bar. He had a fringe of gray on his head, but his arms and shoulders were heavy with muscle. There would be a baseball bat behind the bar within easy reach. Maybe a shotgun, too.

"Get him on the phone," said Peter. "Tell him there was an accident. The jarhead wants to see him."

"You want a drink or not?"

"Draft beer."

"Pabst?"

Peter nodded. The bartender pulled a glass, minimal foam, and set it on the napkin. "Two bucks."

Peter dropped a few singles on the bar. The bartender scooped up the cash, dropped it in the register, and disappeared through the swinging door into the back room.

The Pabst tasted better than usual.

There was definitely something wrong with him, thought Peter. He'd just been shot at, had killed a man and lied to the cops, and now he was drinking beer like nothing had happened. He thought it should bother him, but mostly it made him angry.

The Navy shrink had told him that being angry was a perfectly normal response to Peter's experience overseas. War *should* make you angry. But Peter wasn't sure how to feel about that, either.

The Marines had put a lot of effort into teaching him how to kill. They didn't fuck around, they came right out and said it. Your job is to kill the enemy using any means at your disposal. And Peter was good at it. He'd had a lot of practice. He wasn't complaining. He'd signed up for it. He'd wanted to serve his country. He was a goddamned Marine. He'd have that forever.

But it seemed strange, now that they'd all been to war, after all those years of fighting and killing and bleeding and dying, that they were just supposed to go home and get a job, or go back to school, or whatever.

Strange, definitely.

And even if you'd somehow made it home alive and relatively intact, you still carried it around with you, that powerful mix of pride and shame.

For who you were. For what you'd done.

Peter finished his beer while the static crackled in his head.

The bartender reappeared and filled a few drinks for the thirsty old guys down the way. Then he poured two fresh drafts, came back, set one in front of Peter and one on the rail for himself. "Stick around." He had a tattoo on his forearm, a big blue anchor, but faded with years.

Peter put a twenty on the bar, drank some beer. "You worked with Jimmy, right?" The bartender didn't answer. But he didn't pick up the twenty, either. "We served together," said Peter. "He was my friend."

The bartender looked at him.

"That tattoo," said Peter. "Navy, right?" The bartender nodded. "Well, you know what those survivor benefits are like, right? Not enough." Peter drank some beer. At least the bartender wasn't walking away. "Jimmy was helping his family, doing what he could. But now he's dead. I'm just trying to help, too."

The bartender said, "Talk to Lewis first."

Peter nodded. "I talked to Lewis. I talked to Nino and Ray. I know what they are. They know I'm looking. But they didn't work with Jimmy. I just want to know what he was like before he killed himself."

The bartender shrugged. "He was just a guy."

"He did the work? No fucking the dog?"

That got a little smile. "No, he did the work. I tell him to change a keg, man got right to it."

Peter nodded. Jimmy was never one to stand around when there was work to be done. "Sounds like you liked him."

Another shrug. "Sure."

"When he killed himself. Did he say anything to you, before?"

The bartender shook his head. "No." Then pushed his mouth to one side, then the other, thinking. "But we got another part-time guy, showed up for Jimmy's shift one day. Said he was covering. Said Jimmy told him he'd be gone for a while. Next thing I know, Jimmy's killed himself. Weird."

No more weird than Jimmy cleaning out his fridge, thought Peter. Or paying his landlady in advance. More evidence of the polite suicide.

Maybe he wanted the part-time guy to get the work. Or maybe just not bail on the job. Peter could see Jimmy doing that. He took his responsibilities seriously.

"Then this cop shows up," said the bartender. "Wants Jimmy's things."

"What did they take?"

The barman shook his head. "Ain't nothing to take. House rules, nobody leaves nothing. Lewis wants this place so clean it squeaks." He scratched his ear thoughtfully. "Jimmy did try to leave this ratty old suitcase here. Wanted me to lock it up in the liquor storage. Told him hell, no. Lewis would have my ass."

The suitcase got Peter's attention. He was willing to bet it was a black Samsonite. "Do you remember when that was? How long before he died?"

"Not that long."

So under Dinah's porch wasn't Jimmy's first choice.

"Did anyone else come looking for him, after he left? Maybe a big guy missing an earlobe, with scars on his face?" Peter drew the scars with his fingertips.

The bartender shook his head.

"What about before he left? Did he have visitors, maybe do a little business on the side?"

"Hell, no. Nobody runs anything out of here. Lewis owns the joint. Jimmy knew how it was."

"But he came up with Lewis, right? Maybe he had a pass."

A flat look. "Nobody gets a pass. Nobody."

Then his eyes flicked past Peter, and in a single smooth motion he plucked up his glass and walked away.

Peter turned and saw Lewis coming in the side door, a black suede jacket over his crisp white shirt, trailing Nino and Oklahoma Ray.

Watching, Peter couldn't think why Lewis needed them. The man moved with no visible effort, and in the dim light of the bar, he seemed almost to float across the floor. Stopping at the bar, his weight was balanced, his knees slightly bent. He was out of Peter's reach but ready to change that. Ready for anything.

He looked Peter up and down. Calm, quiet, his voice

just audible over the music. "You don't seem no worse for wear."

"The accident happened to somebody else."

Lewis didn't even blink. "And I give a shit why?"

"Because you're going to have to call his mama. And tell her why her boy got shot in the head."

Lewis turned to go. Over his shoulder, he said, "We'll talk about this outside." He said something to Nino, who led the way through the door, his right hand rooting in the pocket of his Packers jacket.

Peter went last, the taste of copper in his mouth, wishing he hadn't left his .45 in pieces strewn all over town.

17

As he stepped outside, Nino was already throwing a looping overhead right at his head. Brass knuckles gleamed slightly on the leading edge.

Peter smiled. The fresh air felt good in his lungs. The oxygen charged into his bloodstream and into his muscles.

Nino was very fast for a guy shaped like a beer keg.

But he was overeager, maybe overconfident, and started out too far away from his target, Peter's head. And Peter had known something was coming.

So he pulled his head back out of the way and gave Nino's arm a push as it went past, adding momentum to the weighted fist on its plotted path. This encouraged Nino's rotation, Nino having overcommitted because he was counting too much on the knucks.

And on top of it he hadn't kept his chin tucked.

Peter had no sympathy for a guy with brass knuckles.

He could feel Oklahoma Ray winding up somewhere

behind him, so he made it quick. Before Nino could unwrap himself, Peter stepped in close and hit him with a short, hard left to the side of his thick neck.

It knocked Nino back, choking and off-balance. Peter pivoted toward Oklahoma Ray, who was hard up on the toes of one foot, the other already airborne fast toward the side of Peter's head.

At least the guy had put on some shoes, thought Peter, watching the foot approach. He knew he was too late to get completely out of the way of it, but he was still willing to try. He bent his knees and turned away from the blow, catching just the toe of Ray's red boxing boot high on his cheek. The pain bloomed like a midnight rose.

But Peter had been hit before. Pain was just information. Information that should not interfere with your ability to do the job at hand.

He kept his focus on Ray, whose second foot followed faster, with more momentum.

He was fully airborne, nearly horizontal, his form perfect until Peter dropped beneath his scissoring legs and punched him hard in the crotch.

Ray landed badly, one elbow on the pavement. Peter kicked him in the head, not unkindly, saw Nino staying down with both hands clutched at his neck, then turned, all charged up, toward Lewis, who stood ten feet away with a flat black automatic pistol in a perfect two-handed marksman's pose.

Awash in adrenaline, Peter touched the forming bruise on the side of his face.

"Now you've got three mamas to call. And what have you got to show for it?"

Lewis gave Peter the same faint, tilted smile. "One dead jarhead is what I got. I'm not calling anybody's mama."

Peter held his hands away from his body.

"I'm not carrying," he said, glad of it now. "Want me to turn around so you can shoot me in the back?"

"Depends whether you want to see it coming."

The muzzle of the pistol didn't waver. Outside the circle of the bar's door light, it was almost invisible in his hand.

The night was dark, the streetlights broken and the moon in hiding.

Peter wondered if he would die outside a corner bar in Milwaukee, after everything he'd seen and done.

It didn't bother him as much as he'd expected.

At least he wouldn't die bored. Or wondering if he'd ever have a normal life.

Then he thought of Dinah.

With the paper bag of money tied up with string, and the man with the scars driving past her house. Maybe finally stopping and getting out of his big black Ford, the chrome pistol in his hand. Walking up the new porch steps and rapping on the front door.

Okay, that bothered him.

It bothered him more than almost anything.

He put down his hands. "Don't you want to know who got shot in the head?"

"Don't b'lieve I care," said Lewis. "Long as it ain't me."

"Somebody sent a shooter my way. Not you?"

Lewis shook his head. "Nah," he said. "I sent a shooter, you'd be dead six times."

Peter believed it. He angled his head at the two men trying to pick themselves up off the sidewalk. "Then why this?"

Lewis shrugged, the tilted smile wider now, showing a little of who the man was. The gun vanished into a coat pocket. "Thought it'd be fun. See what you got."

"Now you know."

Lewis nodded, thoughtful. "That I do."

Nino was clearly having trouble breathing as his throat swelled up. Ray, still blinking off the sparkles, hadn't yet risen past his hands and knees.

Peter said, "How's your health plan?"

"We vet'rans, man. Uncle Sam got our back." He turned to Nino. "Can you drive?"

Nino opened his mouth, but nothing came out. He nodded.

Lewis angled his head toward the Escalade parked across the street. "We working next week," he said. "Better go see Saint Mary. Tell 'em you got in a fight over a woman."

Which maybe wasn't too far from the truth, thought Peter. Nino and Ray were just collateral damage.

The Escalade drove away. Peter thought about their conversation earlier in the day. He said, "What about

Dinah? Will you still keep an eye on her? Discourage the guy with the scars?"

Lewis stared at him. "Told you I would," he said. "I keep my word." The tilted smile was gone. His tone was casual, but he was serious.

Peter nodded. "Good." Somehow it was the answer he knew he would get.

Lewis regarded Peter like an object of great rarity. "You get that," he said.

Peter shrugged. "What's not to get?" His cheek throbbed. He would have a nice bruise tomorrow. It was traditional to put a steak on it, but Mingus would just eat it, then lick him to death. A bag of frozen peas would be better. The dog was not a vegetarian.

Then he had a better idea. "Hang on a sec," he told Lewis. Went inside, pulled on his coat, and paid the barman for a six-pack of PBR in longneck bottles. Went back out, handed a bottle to Lewis, and opened one for himself.

Then raised it in a toast. "Semper fi, motherfucker."

"Fuck the Army," said Lewis, then drank. His shoulders touched the brick building. He appeared to lean against it, but the position was deceptive. He wasn't at rest. His weight was still balanced, his feet still directly beneath him. Like a big cat in a tree, watching what passed below. Watching Peter.

Peter rolled the bottle against his cheek. The cold felt good. He took a long drink, half the bottle. He could feel the adrenaline draining from his system. The static drifting down and away. He wanted a shower. He wanted to sleep in a bed. Not necessarily by himself.

But mostly he wanted to find out what the fuck was going on.

It was becoming a very familiar feeling.

Lewis said, “So what’s your play here?”

“There’s no play,” said Peter. “I came to fix Jimmy’s porch and found a bag of money. Dinah thought it might be yours. That guy with the scars was watching her house.”

“I meant the original play,” said Lewis. “The one that got you fixing her porch to begin with.”

Peter noticed that the man didn’t always sound like the street. It might be where he came from, but it wasn’t who he was. Peter figured there was more to Lewis than anyone knew.

He said, “The Marine Corps has a program—”

“There is no program,” said Lewis. “I made some calls. The Marines aren’t paying you to fix anything. You got your discharge sixteen months ago. So why the fuck are you here?”

Peter sighed.

“Jimmy was my best friend,” he said. “He got wounded on my watch, and got sent home. Then I heard he killed himself, and I hadn’t gone to see him. I let him down. That’s how it is. So I came to help his family. Fixing the porch was a place to start. And I didn’t think Dinah would let me help unless I told her it was on Uncle Sam.”

"And Jimmy's widow gonna show her gratitude?"

"It's not like that, Lewis. She doesn't show it, but she's drowning. She's going to lose her house. She needs to refinance, but the banks aren't lending to anyone, let alone a single mother whose house is worth half what she paid for it."

Lewis just looked at him without expression. Peter didn't figure him for a guy who was following the foreclosure crisis, but he didn't look confused, either.

"Dinah's a strong woman," Peter said quietly. "She's not going to do anything she doesn't want to do. She doesn't owe me anything. I'm the one paying the debt here."

Lewis shook his head. "You some piece of work, jarhead. Buying into all that shit about honor and obligation."

Peter looked back at Lewis. "I'm not the only one," he said.

Something passed between them then. Some acknowledgment of Dinah. Of debts owed to the past, before the future could be recognized or imagined.

"Maybe not," said Lewis. He looked into the darkness. "Shit."

They drank some beer. The November wind whistled in the trees. A car alarm sounded on the next block.

"So you were Army," said Peter. Lewis nodded. "How long were you in?"

"Just the one tour. Early on. Didn't like taking orders."

"What, you expected different? It's the Army."

Lewis gave another eloquent shrug. "Had my reasons. Learned what I wanted and got the fuck out. Put myself to work." He looked at Peter. "Could put some your way, too, you want. Man with your skills."

"I'm working this right now," said Peter.

"Yeah, but you're flat broke," said Lewis. "I can tell just looking at you. Wearing the same clothes two or three days. You ain't had a shower in longer than that." He looked at Peter steadily. "Pay's good. Just a few hours' work. Your kind of work."

"I'm done with that, Lewis."

"Riiiiight," said Lewis, the tilted smile wide now in genuine amusement. "Tonight you shoot a guy trying to kill you. You take out a pair of skilled operators looking to give you a beatdown, and do it in about fifteen seconds. When I pull a gun, you don't even blink. You not done with nothing, jarhead. You just a goddamn soldier of fortune like the rest of us."

"I'm going to finish this thing here," said Peter. "After that I don't know." He shrugged. "Go home, maybe. Get a job."

Lewis snorted. "Get a job? Swing a hammer? Be a damn citizen? That's not a life. Might as well be laid out in a bag. No, you got a taste of the real life over there, a real solid taste. And now you can't live without it."

Peter shook his head. "That's you," he said. "Not me."

Lewis looked at him with a certain uncharacteristic kindness. "I saw your face when Nino came at you with those knucks. You lit up like it was your birthday. Like you was alive for real." He pointed his bottle at Peter. "We not that damn different, troop. You may think you done, but I know better. You best figure that shit out."

Peter drained his beer. "That reminds me," he said. "You know where I can buy a weapon? I had to get rid of mine earlier."

Lewis laughed out loud. "Oh, you one solid fuckin' citizen, all right."

Later that night, Peter sat in his truck and looked through his windshield at the Riverside Veterans' Center. He'd gotten the address from the business card he'd found with Jimmy's things.

Mingus lay on the passenger seat, his stink sharp enough to cut.

The vet center was in the front corner of a big old building, a repurposed warehouse that had seen better days. It was after eleven, but a warm yellow light spilled through the big windows. He saw shadows moving inside, shadows that must be people.

He wondered if anyone in there had the white static.

If they'd managed to do anything about it.

He'd come back tomorrow and see if anyone knew Jimmy.

A woman came out, a backpack slung over one shoulder, holding the door open with her foot, still talking to someone inside. She moved her hands a lot when she talked. She finally waved good-bye, shrugged into the backpack, and walked up the sidewalk.

She had dark curly hair in an unruly ponytail, and she wore a fleece jacket zipped to the neck. In paint-spattered jeans and hiking boots, she had a long, purposeful stride, like she could walk forever.

But she watched her surroundings. She saw Peter sitting in his truck across the street, his missing driver's-side window maybe looking like the window was rolled down. Her face creased in a smile, but he noticed she didn't come too close to the truck. Definitely careful.

"Hey," she said. Her voice carried in the dark. "You waiting for somebody?"

"Nope," said Peter. "Just hanging out." Mingus perked up and came to the window, stepping on Peter's crotch as he did. "Ow. Shit." He struggled to adjust.

"Oh, you have a dog." She came closer then. "Okay if I pet him?"

"He doesn't like everybody," said Peter, but the dog was already grinning at her, tongue hanging out over the picket fence of his teeth, tail wagging hard enough to knock the rearview mirror out of whack.

"Hi, puppy." She showed Mingus her hand, then rubbed him behind the ears, releasing a wave of pepper spray and dog funk. "Whoa. He must have rolled in something pretty gnarly."

"Yeah, he's overdue for a bath," said Peter.

But she wasn't looking at the dog, she was looking at Peter. "We have showers in the center," she said. The bruise left by Ray's shoe was on the far side of his face, hidden by the dog. But still aching. "I think there's some chili left, too, if you're hungry."

"I'm good," said Peter, wondering how she knew he was a veteran. "I've got something to do, anyway."

"Suit yourself." She gave Mingus one last rub. "Bye, puppy."

And she walked away with that long, purposeful stride, scanning the street ahead and not looking back.

Peter didn't have anything else to do. Unless you counted four more beers and an ice pack for his bruised face.

And a parking spot in front of Dinah's house.

Because if Lewis hadn't sent the shooter, then the scarred man did.

And the scarred man knew where Dinah lived.

The Man in the Black Canvas Chore Coat

The campfire guttered low in the cold wind. The man in the black canvas chore coat leaned over to pick up another log and set it in place. The wind blew the coals bright orange, and the flames soon caught the new log.

The van driver sat on a tree stump, hands out to catch some heat. He wore a camouflage hunting jacket over his plumber's sweatshirt, with the hood pulled up. A scatter of beer cans lay at his feet. "Shit, put on another, Mid. It's colder'n hell out here."

Midden, the man in the black chore coat, shook his head. "We're keeping a low profile, remember? We don't want some local boy to see the light out in the woods and wonder who we are."

The van driver took the last pull from a pint bottle of tequila, then threw the bottle on the fire, where it shattered and flared briefly as the alcohol burned. "Shit, nobody's lookin' for us, Mid. We're fuckin' ghosts, man. We're gonna change fuckin' history, show those fuckin' bankers that the *people* run this country. C'mon, put on another log. It's the last run. Might as well party, right?"

Midden looked at his watch. He was tired. And tired of this. "Sure," he said. Then reached inside his black canvas chore coat, pulled out a target pistol, and shot the van driver twice in the chest.

The van driver fell off his stump, two dark red spots barely showing through his camouflage jacket.

He made a gurgling sound and turned his head from side to side. His hands wandered across the fallen leaves, reaching for something that wasn't there.

Midden stood over him, pistol at his side. He wanted to tell the man to hold still, but it didn't seem right to ask.

Then the van driver looked right up at him, eyes trying to focus. Aware or unaware that he was dying. Midden shot him once in the forehead. He stared down at the other man for a moment, watching as the light went out of him. He wondered what it was like.

Then went to get the new shovel from the back of the old Ford.

He'd burn the truck long after midnight, when the flames were least likely to be seen. The plume of black smoke would dissipate before dawn.

He'd be sorry to see the old Ford go. It had carried him many miles without complaint. But it had been seen by too many people. It had to burn.

PART 2

18

A tapping sound, and Peter was fully awake in his sleeping bag, hand reaching for the new .45 Lewis had sold him. It was just starting to get light out.

"Peter?" Dinah's voice, quiet and almost in his ear. As if he'd dreamed it.

He looked up and saw her framed like a shadow in the broken driver's-side window. "Everything okay?"

"It's fine," she said. "Listen, I'm working extra shifts, so I'm sleeping at the hospital tonight. The boys will spend the night at my grandmother's. This is my work number."

She laid a scrap of paper on the dashboard. If she saw the bruise on his face or the beer bottles, she didn't mention them. Then she was gone.

He looked up through the windshield as the brightening sky illuminated the bare branches of the street trees. It was colder than before. It was the first day he could really taste winter in the air.

One thing about living outside, you really develop a relationship with the weather.

If he was in the mountains, up above the tree line, he'd climb out of his bag in his wool socks and his fleece and shiver while he made coffee and watched the sunlight rise up the valley walls, seeing their color shift from black to purple to blue to green. Then he'd load his pack and lace up his boots and set out on the trail again. The movement would warm him for the rest of the day, while the snow-capped peaks kept him company in silent perfection.

When you woke on a clifftop in a granite cathedral, it was easy to think you'd chosen that life on purpose.

But when you woke in your perforated truck on a city street as autumn slid downhill toward winter, things weren't always so clear. You tended to wonder, for example, what the fuck you were going to do with the rest of your life.

When you had a mission, Peter told himself, nothing else mattered.

He pictured Dinah in that old house, waking before first light. Before he could stop himself, he was picturing what she wore to bed.

He tried to shut it down, she was Jimmy's wife, but she was already there in his imagination, wearing an old T-shirt, shrunk slightly from the wash, and soft and thin from years of wear. Perhaps turning translucent in places. And smelling slightly of soap.

Eight years in the Marines and another in the mountains made the smell of soap one of the sexiest things Peter could imagine.

He told himself that Jimmy was like his brother. Which made Dinah like Peter's sister. That made it easier to put her out of his mind. But it had been a very long time since he'd spent this much time with an actual woman.

The dog whined in the back. His face hurt where Oklahoma Ray had kicked him. He sat up and checked it in the rearview. The top of his cheek was swollen and had turned purple, with a little green around the edges. Nothing broken. The ice pack lay melted on the floor mat, and the truck smelled like stale beer. Not frozen beer, not yet. It was only November.

Would he still be sleeping in the truck when it snowed?

It was the kind of thing that might limit a guy's female relationships.

He wondered again how long he would live like this. Or if he even minded.

Peter got himself dressed, which wasn't easy in the cab of a pickup truck, then let Mingus out, amazed again at the dog's evolving stench. The pepper spray added a certain eye-watering richness, like snorting habañero sauce deep into your sinuses. He had to do something about that. But washing the dog was further down the list.

Finding the scarred man was at the top.

If he was the one who'd sent the shooter, he'd know by now that things had not gone as planned. Peter figured he'd give the scarred man another shot at it.

And use himself as bait.

But first, breakfast. He unfolded his chair on the parking strip, started the little backpacking stove, and filled his battered tin percolator. Coffee before work, whenever possible.

Halfway through his first cup, twelve-year-old Charlie and eight-year-old Miles came out the front door. They stomped around on the new porch deck for a few minutes, testing its strength against their school shoes. Then they saw the dog roaming off the leash, without the stick tied up in its mouth.

The dog grinned at them, tongue lolling to one side through the murderous gate of its teeth.

"Dang! What are you doin'?" Charlie pushed his little brother back inside the house. Then came out with his baseball bat held at the ready, like an impossibly skinny Barry Bonds, and called out to Peter from the top of the steps. "You set that dog loose? What are you, some kinda crazy?"

"Probably," said Peter. "Charlie, who are you named for?"

The boy straightened up. "Charlie Parker, alto sax."

"And your brother?"

"Miles Davis. Trumpet."

Peter nodded. "Well, yesterday I found out this dog's name is Charles Mingus. Named after a bass player.

Turns out he's your father's dog. Come on down, you can give him something to eat. Make friends."

"No dang way." Charlie caught himself. "I mean no, sir. I'll stay right here."

"How are you going to get your little brother to school?"

Charlie considered for a minute. He still stood on the porch steps. "Go out the back, sir, and run like heck through the alley."

"You think I'd let that dog hurt you?" Peter took the coffeepot off the stove and put on the big frying pan, set some butter to melt.

"No offense, sir, but you're still sitting down and that dog's got four-wheel drive. And he looks real hungry."

"He is hungry," said Peter, assembling supplies from his cooler and laying them out in the pan. "I haven't fed him anything yet. What about you? You hungry?"

"I already had my cereal this morning, sir."

The bread sizzled in the hot butter. The dog sniffed the air and came over. Peter pushed the dog away. "You mean you don't want a grilled ham-and-cheese sandwich? Nice and hot? I might have a few doughnuts in the cooler, too."

Charlie crept down the steps, bat held at the ready. "Sir, you are a mean bastard, sir."

Peter grinned. "Courage, Charlie." He flipped the sandwiches. "Courage is doing something that scares the hell out of you. But you do it anyway. Your dad taught me that."

Mingus stuck his nose in the pan. When Peter whacked it with the spatula, Charlie's eyes got even wider, if that was possible. The dog backed away, focused on the pan, just the tip of his tongue showing now, and the white serration of his teeth. A string of drool hung from one jowl.

Charlie choked up on the bat so he could hold it with one hand, and tiptoed closer. Mingus ignored him, his gaze locked on the food. Then Charlie glanced at Peter's face and saw the bruise.

"Sir? What happened to you?"

"A misunderstanding," said Peter. "Don't worry about it."

He wanted to say that the other two guys went to the hospital. But that probably wasn't the right message to send to the boy.

Instead he laid out the four sandwiches on the wide cedar plank he used as a cutting board, and chopped each sandwich into quarters. Charlie stood with the chair and stove between him and the dog, still poised to flee. Peter handed him a section of sandwich. Mingus's massive head turned as if on a swivel, following the sandwich. The string of drool hung longer.

"Hold it on the palm of your hand," said Peter. "Like this."

He held another section on his own hand, fingers fully open and outstretched. Mingus took it with surprising delicacy, like a little old lady nibbling a cucumber sandwich, except for the slick of saliva left behind. Mingus licked his chops, the white teeth flashing, then went over to Charlie and nosed his elbow as if to say, "You gonna eat that?"

Charlie blinked at high speed, and a slight but rapid vibration ran through his entire body. But he lowered his hand, fingers carefully spread.

Mingus took the food with just the tips of his teeth and wolfed it down without seeming to chew. Then sniffed the hand thoroughly and licked the remaining butter off with several swipes of his huge tongue.

Charlie smiled so wide Peter thought his face would split. "Can I do it again?"

"Sure," said Peter. "But get your brother first, so he can meet Mingus, too." Peter busied himself making more sandwiches, wishing with everything he had that Big Jimmy was there to see his boys growing up.

In the end, he wrapped up a hot sandwich and a pair of doughnuts in a paper towel for each boy to eat on the way to school.

"Sir," said Charlie, "Mingus really smells bad."

"I know," said Peter. "It's on my list."

He drove back to the lumberyard, keeping one eye on his rearview, and bought new steel entry doors and locks for Dinah's house. The work would take him a good chunk of the day, and he'd be outside where anyone could see him.

Anyone at all.

Peter wasn't quite sure what to think of the scarred

man. The confident swagger was real enough, but he didn't set off Peter's radar like Lewis did, or Nino, or Oklahoma Ray. Still, Peter didn't fool himself into thinking the scarred man wasn't dangerous.

He set up his tools in Dinah's narrow side yard. The nearby houses protected his flank, and the tall wooden fence at the alley shielded him somewhat from the rear. If they came from the front and back, he could always duck through the house.

He wondered how many there would be. Probably more than one.

The yard was a few steps above the street, so he could see over the parked cars up and down the block. High ground, somewhat protected. He'd had worse positions. And the dog was on sentry duty, pacing the sidewalk, trailing a plume of stink so powerful you could practically see it coming off him. A walking gas grenade with four legs and a tail.

A car came down the street. A red Kia. It didn't stop.

Now a blue pickup. It didn't stop, either. This could take all day.

He kept the new Sig Sauer in his jacket pocket, spare clip on the other side. He'd paid Lewis twice what it would have cost in any gun shop, but the serial number was ground down, and the gun was clearly otherwise unused, with traces of the heavy packing oil still in the checkered handgrip.

Peter didn't mind the cost. He thought of it as health insurance.

Another car, a silver Toyota sedan. A big old Buick. A woman pushing a stroller, who crossed the street to avoid the dog. His awareness was raised to a watchful hum. Then a tan GMC Yukon with an elaborate tubular bumper. He couldn't see the driver, but he figured it was Lewis, keeping his word to keep an eye out for Dinah.

He bounced on his toes. He might as well get some work done.

He started with the back door, the worst one, damaged in the break-in. The hundred-year-old glue had basically given up, and the jamb stops were so flimsy that little Miles could have kicked his way through. Peter pulled off the trim with a flat bar, used the Sawzall to cut the nails holding the jamb in place, and the whole assembly came out in one piece. It was a challenge getting the new door into the crooked old opening, especially with one eye on the dog and one hand on the .45, stopping to eyeball the street whenever a car drove by. A white minivan. A rusted-out Mustang.

He'd done harder work under more difficult conditions.

When he had the new doorknob and deadbolt in place, it was time for lunch. Cheese and crackers, a blueberry yogurt, and cold coffee.

Six cars drove by while he ate. No scarred man. No assault rifles.

Then the tan Yukon swung by again, and Peter was off the steps and into the street.

Lewis wore his suede jacket and starched white shirt and tilted smile.

Peter walked to the driver's side. The window hummed down and a puff of heated air escaped. He said, "See anything?"

Lewis shook his head. "No guy with scars, no black Ford SUV. But I'll keep driving. Give you another day, maybe two. After that I got paid work."

"Thanks," said Peter.

"Not doin' it for you, jarhead."

Peter nodded. "I know. But thanks, anyway."

The window hummed back up and the Yukon rumbled away.

Peter gulped down his coffee and moved his tools to the new porch and took out the old front door. This one was a sixties retrofit with a rotten sill and a funky glass insert patched with tape. This replacement door went in more quickly than the last, and with no shots fired.

The last part a disappointment, really.

He put away his tools and went to buy a phone.

He'd gotten rid of all electronics when he went to the mountains. Cut up his credit card, too. It seemed symbolic at the time. But now it was just a pain in the ass.

He found a Best Buy store, where he broke the world's record for fastest purchase of a prepaid phone and a cheap laptop, making it out before the white sparks flared too badly.

He didn't have much cash left. Not after the Sig Sauer

and Best Buy. He didn't want to dip into Jimmy's money unless he had to.

Best Buy needed a few hours to configure the laptop, so he sat in the suburban parking lot with the uncharged phone plugged into the cigarette lighter and called Dinah at work. The woman he spoke to at the nursing station told him Dinah was with a patient and she'd call him back, but it would probably be a while.

The wind blew cold through the broken window of his truck. He went into the cargo box and brought out the box of Jimmy's things he'd gotten from Dinah. He found the yellow flier for the missing Marine, tapped in the grandmother's number, and took out the stainless-steel Lake Capital Funds pen to take notes.

The phone rang six times before voicemail picked up.

A young man's voice.

"Hello, you've reached Mrs. Aurelia Castellano, but she's not home at the moment. Please leave a message and she will call you back."

It was a good voice, quiet but confident. Peter looked at the flier, wondering if that was Felix Castellano's voice. It probably was.

He wondered if the grandmother called her own number just to hear his voice. If she thought of her grandson every time she played her messages.

Peter thought of his own mother. He hadn't spoken to her or his dad since he'd gotten off the plane.

At the beep, Peter opened his mouth to speak, but nothing came out.

He looked at the Lake Capital Funds pen in his hand. It was a nice pen. An expensive pen.

Then he knew what the next step was.

He walked back into the store to use one of their demo computers as the white static flared and his shoulders cramped up. He needed to get online, just for a minute.

19

Peter pushed the truck hard toward downtown, the city roads rough with potholes, trying to get to Lake Capital before they closed the doors for the day.

One eye on the rearview, watching for the black Ford. But it would be easy to miss in heavy traffic. And Peter's truck would be easy to follow. Unless he was willing to rent a beige sedan, he couldn't do anything about it.

He didn't have a plan for Lake Capital. But the principle wasn't complicated. It was the same principle he'd operated under for years.

Poke a stick into something and see what happened.

The hedge fund's headquarters was in the U.S. Bank building at the edge of downtown, overlooking Lake Michigan and the art museum. The tall, rectangular tower's white aluminum cladding over the steel structural grid glowed in the pale autumn light. Peter remembered taking a tour of the building as part of a high school field trip, and the profound surprise that something like an office building could be beautiful. Designed in the late 1960s by Chicago's Skidmore, Owings & Merrill, it stood forty-plus stories and was still, he was fairly sure, the tallest building in the state.

It seemed about a million miles from Dinah's little house.

He parked at a meter and walked in through the high glass atrium that was transparent to the outside. He felt it again walking past the broad window panels that went directly to the ceiling. That sense of expansion, like anything might be possible.

A twin row of twenty-foot-tall trees in giant marble planters led to escalators running to the second-floor lobby, with more big plants and wide glass window panels and long views on three sides. The white-clad structure was visible as he passed from the exterior to the interior, which added to the feeling of transparency. It was enough to make you want to believe in something.

He watched the constant flow of men and women in suits and business casual, with access badges on cords around their necks or clipped to lapels. Peter automatically checked for the exits, but the feeling of openness, the remains of the daylight, and the outside views kept the white static down for the moment.

There were placards for the building's bigger tenants, including U.S. Bank and several big national financial companies and a large law firm. But nothing for Lake Capital.

Peter walked up to the security desk. “What floor is Lake Capital on?”

The security man in his neat blue uniform checked his computer. “Fifth floor,” he said, and pointed Peter to a bank of elevators.

The static didn’t like elevators.

“Are there any stairs?” The static didn’t like stairs, either, but they were better than an elevator. Peter could run up and down.

The security man shook his head. “Fire stairs only. Not for the public.”

Shit.

But it was just three floors up, and the elevator was nearly empty. Peter closed his eyes and focused on his breathing to keep the static down. It took only a minute, but by the time the doors opened, his neck was tight and his shoulders were starting to clamp up.

Lake Capital was smaller than Peter expected, sharing the floor with three other companies. Its reception area was all glass and stainless steel done in sleek, streamlined curves, but no windows. Expensive conceptual art on the walls, bright plastic machined into corporate abstraction.

Sort of like what high finance had turned out to be, thought Peter, after the bubble burst in 2008. An expensive abstraction that made other people’s money disappear.

The woman at the desk wore a severe gray suit of some synthetic fiber that fit snugly over sculpted curves, her long fingernails polished to a high gloss. Her makeup was a thin sheen over flawless skin, her hair a lacquered black helmet. She looked so sleek that reality would slide right off her.

She kept her access badge on the desk to avoid ruining the effect of the suit, Peter was sure. The room smelled of acetone, hair spray, and carpet-cleaning chemicals. The white static climbed higher, began to fizz and pop. He could feel his heart beating faster, and he was starting to sweat. He wouldn't last long at this rate.

"Can I help you?"

There was no rising inflection in her voice, as if the question were rhetorical. As if she knew in advance that the man standing before her with the purple bruise on his face and sawdust on his work clothes was in a category beyond her ability to help, and she was making no secret of it.

"I'd like to see Jonathan Skinner," he said. The CEO, and the only name that was on the website.

She scanned him with an appraiser's eye. A hint of what she might be like without the severe gray suit to constrain her. There was a quick gleam of interest, maybe from the width of his shoulders or the size of his hands. But not enough to be transactional, not with his substandard wardrobe and clearly inadequate income. She would sleep only above her level.

"You lack," she said, "an appointment."

"Well," said Peter, breathing slow and deep to dampen his heart rate, "I'd like to make an appointment."

"Hm," she said. "And what is this regarding?" She made no move to write anything down.

"I'd like to engage the services of this firm."

"Who referred you?"

The door opened silently behind her, pushed by a man walking out. Peter caught a glimpse of plush carpet, vacant cubicles, and empty chairs. There was no sound of conversation or business being done.

The man appeared to be near Peter's age, with an aristocrat's bloodless good looks and white-blond hair spilling carelessly down to his shoulders. He wore an elegant suit in a pale green that was the exact color of money. It fit like it was made for him, and it probably had been. He wore it with an elegant disregard, as if he didn't particularly care for it, or someone else had paid for it, or he had a dozen more like it in his closet. Or all of the above.

Peter found himself disliking the man intensely. The white static flared higher. Peter pushed it down again. Breathe in, breathe out.

The man in the pale green suit didn't appear to realize that anyone else was in the room. He walked past the desk without looking at Peter or the lacquered receptionist. He carried no briefcase or other evidence that he'd done any work that day. He pushed open the door to the elevator lobby, then half turned, as if just noticing Peter, a cocky, handsome grin showing brilliant white teeth.

"Gretchen, do we have an unscheduled repair?"

The receptionist opened her lips in a smile, and Peter knew she was sleeping with the man in the money-colored suit.

"Not at all," she said. "Nothing to concern you. Remember, you have a squash date at seven tomorrow."

The man nodded and turned, lifting a hand in a wave, and walked toward the elevator, the lobby door easing silently shut behind him.

Peter looked at the receptionist, who still looked at the closed lobby door. There was a slackness on her face as she reviewed a memory of the man or imagined something yet to come. Then Peter knew.

"That was Skinner, wasn't it?"

The receptionist opened her mouth to deny it, but Peter was already pushing through the door to the elevator lobby. The elevator doors were just closing, too late for Peter to get a hand or a foot between them.

He turned to the stairwell, but the door was locked. An electronic reader on the wall beside it. He thought of the desk man in the lobby. *Fire stairs only. Not for the public.*

He ducked back into reception and plucked the woman's access badge from her desk.

"Hey, you jerk," she said, launching into further sophisticated language that went mercifully silent as the door closed behind him and he put the badge to the reader and the lock opened with a clack.

He dropped the badge in the lobby and took the steps three at a time, his boots slapping hard on the concrete. The sound echoed behind him, the static submerged by the adrenaline of action. Through the door to the main lobby, he turned the corner to the elevators and the lights over the door. He'd arrived right on time. But the elevator didn't stop. The down arrow simply blinked and the number changed to LL.

Skinner was headed farther down. Probably to get his car.

The desk man looked at him and reached for the phone. Peter ducked back to the stairs, thankfully unlocked on a public level, and down two more short flights to the rear exit. People streamed out of the elevators in all directions, but he couldn't see the white-blond hair or the money-green suit. There had to be ten parking garages within a few blocks.

A man who ran a billion-dollar hedge fund wouldn't walk far.

Peter turned to the exit and through the doors. He was in a low covered area, for taxis and deliveries and drive-through banking. A security guard looked at him but made no move. People were walking up a long, shallow foot ramp to the street. He jogged past them into the relief of the high, darkening sky and the cold lake wind, looking left, then right.

A big parking structure with the U.S. Bank logo was at the end of the block across the street. Peter ran.

A long, dark sedan appeared at the mouth of the structure, coasting into the road, turning away. Under a streetlight Peter saw a flash of pale skin and white-blond hair through the driver's window. Peter didn't recognize the model of the car. He didn't even recognize the logo on the trunk.

Then the engine gave a noisy blatt. *Look at me,* it said. *See how special.* As the car leaped down the block and out of reach. What the hell kind of car was that? The rich didn't even buy the same cars as everyone else.

As the taillights disappeared around the corner, Peter wondered if Skinner was always this elusive, or if his secretary just had an attitude. Because the only thing that got Peter here in the first place was a stainless-steel pen with the name of a hedge fund on it.

Maybe it was just another dead end.

Peter's stomach rumbled. He stretched his shoulders. Exercise would loosen him up. Mingus could use a run, too. He turned and walked up the hill toward his truck. At the top of a loading zone, past a car with a Zaffiro's Pizza sign and a big telecom truck, nearly invisible in the lowering dark, stood a big black Ford SUV idling at a hydrant.

Before he could do anything, the Ford pulled into traffic with its lights off and rolled down the hill and around the corner, down the same street Skinner had taken.

"Shit." Peter sprinted around the corner for his truck. Cars thick on the main drag at five o'clock, four lanes waiting for the signal to turn green. He couldn't even get out of his parking spot with people in a hurry to get home.

By the time he'd cut off twenty people and nearly wrecked a city bus to get into traffic, Mingus barking like a hellhound in the back, the black Ford was gone.

20

He drove through downtown, the white spotlit U.S. Bank tower bright behind him, disappearing then reappearing in his mirrors over the heads of smaller buildings.

He slipped through the traffic, took the open side streets when he could. He dodged the lights, coasted through stop signs, and generally tried to drive how the scarred man would drive, looking for the fastest routes away.

Had the scarred man followed Peter, or was he there to follow Skinner?

After a twenty-minute tour through the small downtown without another glimpse of the black Ford, he turned toward the old neighborhoods and Dinah's house.

The narrow streets were crowded with cars, and he drove on automatic pilot. He saw the veterans' center building, and his foot rose off the gas as he pictured the woman with the ponytail and the paint-spattered jeans. He'd meant to stop back anyway. To ask about Jimmy.

His new phone buzzed. Only one person had the number. He swung the truck over and pulled the phone out of his pocket. It was a text message.

Too busy to talk today. Let's catch up tomorrow. -Dinah.

Peter texted a reply. *Your new doors are installed, keys under flower pot on picnic table.*

Thanks! How much do I owe you?

Nothing. USMC still picking up tab. He didn't like that he was still lying about the repairs, but there was no way he'd let her pay for it. *Talk to you tomorrow.*

Across the street, the veterans' center door opened. Someone came out and looked at him. She waited for a break in the traffic, then angled across the street. It was the woman with the ponytail and the paint-spattered jeans. Different jeans today, but these were also flecked with paint. She wore a Brewers hat with her hair pulled through the opening in the back. It was a look Peter had always liked.

"Hey," she said. "I thought I recognized that truck. You're about on time for dinner. Three-bean soup tonight."

"Sorry," he said. "I have plans." What those plans were, he wasn't quite sure.

She cocked her head at him. "So. What are you doing here?"

"I got a text, so I pulled over."

"Aren't you the responsible one," she said. "Do me a

favor and come inside for a few minutes. We're getting this place into shape and we need help. You're a carpenter or something, right?"

Peter opened his mouth, then closed it again. Drawn by this woman, but not wanting to go inside. He was conscious of the bruise on his face. He already had a headache from his time indoors that day. She saw the hesitation. "Or not," she said. "Hey, whatever."

"No, I'll come." He turned off the engine and the lights. "But I only have a few minutes."

"Sure," she said. "I'm Josie."

"Peter."

She stepped into the flow of traffic so he could open the door. Cars slowed and diverted around her without honking, as if she were a boulder fallen in the road or some other force of nature. Her eyes flicked across the bruise on his face. "Just to let you know," Josie said. "House rules. No drugs, no weapons, no fighting, and no assholes."

"Who decides on the assholes?"

She put her hands on her hips and faced him squarely, chin out. "I do," she said. Standing in the street, backlit by the headlights of waiting cars. "Problem with that, Hoss?"

"No, ma'am," said Peter, smiling. He liked her toughness and her ponytail and the faint smear of paint on the corner of her jaw. "No problem at all."

She nodded, turned into the traffic, and led him through. By the time Peter crossed the street, she was holding the door open for him.

But when he got to the threshold, the white static began to fizz and pop. Sparks flew the length of his nervous system. His fingers drummed anxiously on his jeans. The iron band around his chest began to tighten, making it harder to draw a full breath. The need to do something, anything, was urgent and real. Fight or flight.

He was stuck in the doorway. His legs wouldn't let him inside.

It was a big room, the full width of the storefront, with fresh paint on the dented walls and mismatched carpet remnants laid over the bare concrete floor. At one end, three ancient steel desks stood in a line, their legs rusting from the bottom up as if they'd survived a flood. The nearest held a desktop computer and a potted plant and a broken-handled mug filled with pens. At the far desk, a skinny young guy with a buzz cut and a gigantic black beard poked experimentally at a vintage laptop while he muttered to himself.

Arrayed near the big front windows were a long homemade plywood table and a dozen cheap folding chairs. In the middle of the room stood an assortment of ratty plaid couches, where another man lay sleeping with his arm over his eyes and his coat for a pillow. At the back was a raw plywood wall, rough-nailed in place, with a framed opening that led to a dim plywood hallway.

It was the bare plywood that stopped him, thought Peter. It looked like the combat outpost they had carved out of that Afghan hilltop. Unfinished plywood walls and ceilings, plywood bunks, even a makeshift plywood command center. Everything reinforced with Hescos and sandbags to keep out the RPGs and contain the mortar blasts.

"It's not much," said Josie. "Not yet, anyway. Go in. I'll show you what we need." She still held the door behind him, still waiting for Peter to walk inside. He liked the lines around her mouth, the bright intensity of her eyes.

He reminded himself that he'd wanted to ask about Jimmy. It was a big open room with big windows. He'd be okay for a few minutes. He took a deep breath and stepped inside.

"A friend of mine used to come here," he said. "Maybe you knew him, James Johnson, usually went by Jimmy. He was here maybe three or four weeks ago?"

"What's he look like?"

"Black guy, big." Peter held his hand six inches above his own head. "Real friendly, big smile, great sense of humor. The kind of guy who liked everybody, or tried to."

She nodded in recognition. "Yeah, I think he was here a few days. We're not much for recordkeeping, so I couldn't swear to it. I haven't seen him since. How's he doing?"

"The police said he killed himself. That's why I'm here. Trying to understand."

She closed her eyes. "I'm sorry," she said. "Fuck." Angry now. "What a *fucking* waste."

The skinny man with the gigantic beard said, loudly, "On behalf of the American people!"

Josie sighed. "Cas, keep it down, okay?"

The skinny man's eyes were wide. He stood abruptly, knocking his chair over backward. "The American people! We shall rise!"

"Cas," said Josie, slightly louder now. "Have you taken your meds today?"

The skinny man closed his mouth with an audible click, eyes flicking from side to side. Then hurriedly bent to pick up his chair and sat down.

Peter looked at the skinny man more closely. The beard was big and bushy, hiding the lower half of the man's face. With the buzz-cut hair, what you saw was the shape of the skull. But there was something familiar around the eyes.

"Sorry," said Josie, turning back to Peter. She lowered her voice. "Cas is our special case. The shelters are full of the people that got foreclosed on or dumped on the street when the mental hospitals got closed down. Even veterans are on waiting lists, and there are a lot of us who are homeless. Someone figured out Cas was a Marine, and he ended up with us. Harmless, but a little excitable. Just don't talk about the financial crisis or the economy. Or politics."

"He's sleeping here?"

She nodded. "Don't tell the city, 'cause we're not legal. But yeah, we've got people sleeping here. Where else are they supposed to go?"

"Semper fi," said Peter.

"Absofuckinglutely." The woman was fierce. "If you

served your country, you deserve help. It's not easy getting back to the world. The skills we learned overseas don't tend to apply to the civilian world. Veterans have *double* the rate of unemployment and homelessness as similar nonveterans. Then there's bomb-blast brain injuries and PTSD, a lot of it undiagnosed. And the suicide rates are through the roof. The VA isn't helping much. So we've got to help ourselves."

"And my friend Jimmy, was he here to get help?"

"I hope so," she said. "I really do. I only talked to him once or twice." She made a face. "But clearly we didn't help enough. Not if he killed himself."

The white sparks clamored in his head. "I've got to leave soon," he said. "You wanted to show me something?"

"Right." She turned toward the opening in the plywood partition. "This way. We want to expand the bunkroom and add more bathrooms. Maybe you could help."

The hallway was dim, lit only by a hanging string of construction lights in yellow plastic cages, which shed no light into the darkened openings of other rooms. Stacks of cardboard boxes only made the hall more narrow. There was a giant black metal door at the end.

The grain of the plywood whorled and looped. Peter felt dizzy, and his legs wouldn't carry him forward. The iron band around his chest drew tighter. He couldn't catch his breath.

"I can't." Sparks rose up in him like white starbursts. His head felt like it would split. "I need to go."

She looked at him then, just long enough for him to notice the disconcerting way she seemed to see him, clearly and in entirety. Her expression held neither pity nor disappointment.

"No problem, Hoss. I'll walk you out."

He stepped away from her and out the front door into the open canopy of night. He leaned against the spalled brick façade and let the clean, cold autumn wind blow through him. The street was busy with cars, and the trees on the parking strip were naked of leaves. But the wind filled his chest with oxygen and he could begin to breathe again.

Josie stood a few paces away, hands in her pockets, watching the traffic.

Eventually she said, "You were boots on the ground, right?"

He nodded.

"Iraq or Afghanistan?"

"Both," he said. "Marines."

"Ah." A smile ghosted across her face. She was still watching rush hour crawl by. "I flew Black Hawks," she said. "Air cav. Three tours and tons of fun until I got shot down. By some asshole with a Kalashnikov." She shook her head. "A twenty-five-million-dollar helicopter taken out by an illiterate tribesman with a stamped-metal Russian hand-me-down piece of shit. Somehow managed to hit a hydraulic line and down I went. Broke both my legs and cracked three ribs. I crawled out of the wreck and saw those Talib assholes coming for me in a hurry. Figured they'll lock me in a hole and rape me for a while, then make a movie while they chop off my head. I wasn't looking forward to it."

She turned to look at him. "But a squad of Marines was set up on the next hill, and they got to me first. They saved me. I was never so glad to see a jarhead in my life."

Peter smiled gently, his breathing coming under control now. "Marines are always bailing out the Army."

Josie smiled back. "Those jarheads tried to sell me that same line. I didn't argue at the time."

"Is that why you're not flying now?"

She shook her head. "Too many pilots, not enough birds. Besides, can you see me as the Eye in the Sky for Channel Twelve, doing the traffic?"

He could see her doing whatever she set her mind to. "What about the cops?" he said. "Or a commercial pilot?"

She raised her eyebrows. "Flying some rich shitbird to his mansion in the Hamptons? While Cas is living on the street?"

"I see your point."

"Besides," she said. "I like the mission, being a part of something bigger. It's good to be needed."

Peter rolled his shoulders to work out the cramps and felt the stiffness of Jimmy's photo in his shirt pocket. He was ashamed that he'd forgotten about it, even for a few minutes.

"I'm sorry," he said. "It's been nice talking to you. But there's really someplace I need to be right now."

She lifted one hand in a wave as he walked toward his truck.

But of course, after he drove back to Dinah's house and parked on the street, the house was dark.

He'd forgotten.

Dinah was at work. Charlie and Miles were at her grandmother's.

They didn't need him that night.

21

Raindrops dotted his windshield and dampened his shirtsleeve at the broken window.

Closer to the freeway, the neighborhood was sprinkled with vacant lots, sometimes half a dozen to a block. The city had taken foreclosed and derelict homes for back taxes, sold what it could, and torn down the ones past saving. They'd filled in the foundations and planted grass, hoping the economy would change and the lots would be worth something again. Maybe they would.

He chose a lot on a relatively full block, a narrow gap in the cityscape that stood out like a missing tooth. The ground sloped uphill from the sidewalk, and from the rear of the lot he'd be able to see over the parked cars. The demolition crew had left a driveway in place, probably because it was nearly new. A sign in the middle of the grass read NO PARKING, NO DUMPING, NO DOGS, NO FIRES. BY ORDER OF THE CITY OF MILWAUKEE.

Peter backed his truck to the end of the drive, let Mingus out to wander, then walked the perimeter of the property until he'd found enough stones and broken bricks to make a decent fire ring. Once his kindling was alight, he laid on deadfall sticks and scrap lumber from Dinah's porch to get a good base of coals. He'd picked up surprisingly little garbage. He figured some neighbor had adopted the lot, mowing the grass and cleaning up. He wondered how long he'd have before someone called the cops.

The rain was worse now, slanting down in small, hard drops, so he unfolded his silver poly tarp and stretched it from hooks at the top of the cargo box to wooden stakes he pushed into the wet ground, trying to keep his cook-fire mostly dry without setting the tarp alight. He found an empty garbage bag and closed one end of it at the top of the truck door and let the other end hang down over the broken window. It might keep most of the rain out of his sleeping quarters.

He needed to get that window fixed.

Then, with his campsite otherwise in order, he unfolded his chair, snagged a beer from the cooler, and fed the fire while he thought about Dinah and Jimmy and the scarred man. Jimmy's money and the C-4 in the suitcase. Lewis and Skinner and the missing Marine and the Riverside Veterans' Center and Josie with the ponytail.

He thought about what he knew, which wasn't much, and what he didn't know, which was a lot.

Starting with why Jimmy had put the money under

Dinah's porch. He hadn't been able to leave it at the bar where he worked. Why hadn't he just left it under his own bed?

Then Peter thought about the shooter with the AK-47, who showed up when Peter was leaving. And the three guys passing the joint on the corner, one of them on his phone. Maybe the scarred man had been trying to find Jimmy's place. Maybe, like Peter, he knew the block but not the house. Maybe he found the house by following Peter. It would have been easy enough to track his truck.

All that thinking made him hungry. He'd stopped for groceries earlier in the day, which included a long piece of flank steak. When he got up for his second beer, he dropped the steak into a plastic bag to marinate in some lime juice and soy sauce and garlic chunks, then set his grill grate over the flames. Camping out is no reason to eat bad food.

As always, he thought about scraping the previously burned meat off the grill and decided against it with the irrefutable logic that the heat would kill off the germs.

When the coals were orange and white and several inches thick, he dug the flank steak out of the marinade and draped it gently on the grate to char while he dug out the tortillas and salsa and a pot of black beans. The beans were genuine refrieds, meaning that he'd cooked them several days before, and now he was cooking them again. He set the pot on the grate and poured in some beer to help the beans rehydrate, thinking that there were benefits to city living. He couldn't cook flank steak over a fire above the tree line. Not unless it was from the flank of a trout.

Maybe he could be an urban camper. Buy one of these vacant lots and sleep outside. Maybe rig up an outdoor shower. That would work, right?

Until winter came.

Mingus came back from his explorations, wet and stinking worse than ever. He shook himself, then came to the fire to sniff at the steak. His fur steamed in the heat as he leaned against Peter's legs, soaking his jeans. Aside from the parked truck and the silver tarp, the flickering orange light made the modern world recede until Peter and Mingus could have been any hunting pair from the last ten thousand years.

Hungry and wet, waiting for the meat to cook.

When the flank steak was charred but still pink inside, Peter forked it off the grill onto his cedar plank and sliced it thin with his knife, elbowing the dog away with each slice. "Bad dog, Mingus. Wait your damn turn."

He warmed the corn tortillas briefly on the grate and assembled a giant plate of world-class steak tacos. Laid on some beans and salsa and folded one into a tight roll and offered it to Mingus. He swallowed without appearing to chew, as was his right as a dog. Peter figured Mingus wouldn't mind the salsa, given that he'd basically inhaled a whole canister of pepper spray the day before.

He needed to wash the dog. With some kind of serious soap.

"Ahoy the fire."

A voice out of the night, filtered through the rain.

Peter was so focused on dinner that he hadn't noticed the figure approaching from the sidewalk. Some Marine. The rain on the tarp damped the sound, and the firelight wrecked his night vision. But he didn't feel too bad. The dog hadn't noticed, either.

Anyway, he figured anyone out to hurt him wouldn't have made an announcement. So he wasn't going to stand up. If he abandoned the cutting board, the dog would eat everything, including the cutting board.

"Come on in," he said.

The figure came closer, still hidden by the night. The raspy voice of an older man raised up over the sound of the rain. "This here's city prop'ty. Like a park. Ain't no camping on city prop'ty."

Mingus woofed and bumped past Peter in his chair, a hundred and fifty pounds of wet, stinking dog. "Mingus, stay."

"Hold your dog, mister," said the raspy voice. "I don't want to shoot no man's dog."

"Hang on." Peter scrambled to his knees on the wet grass to grab Mingus by the rope collar. "Don't shoot."

At the edge of the circle of firelight was a black man maybe eighty years old in an oilcloth slicker and a black fedora with rain streaming from the brim. His face was sunken and rubbery, like maybe he didn't have his teeth in. But he stood broad and strong for all his years, and he held a gleaming bolt-action rifle like he knew what to do with it.

He tilted his chin at the bullet holes in Peter's truck and cargo box. "You been shot at enough from the look of things," he said. "And I wouldn't put a dog out in this weather. So I give you 'til nine ayem tomorrah 'fore I call the police. But do me the courtesy of cleanin' up before you go."

"Yessir," said Peter. "I will."

The old man half turned to go, then turned back. "You gon' be warm enough out here?"

"Yessir," said Peter. "I'm fine, thanks. In fact, I can offer you a cold beer if you'd care to sit by the fire."

The old man shook his head. "I got to be home direc'ly or catch hell from the missus. But you stay dry and take care, hear?"

Peter smiled. "Yessir."

The Man in the Black Canvas Chore Coat

Midden could hear the bar band out in the parking lot.

It was Friday night, and a steady stream of pickup trucks and battered old American cars pulled off the highway onto the flat stretch of gravel, then emptied themselves of singles and groups and couples already starting to dance as they headed toward the front door.

Midden sat in the white Dodge van, watching.

Beside him, a big man with scars on his face, missing one earlobe, shifted restlessly on his seat. "Come on, motherfucker," he growled. "Where the fuck are you?"

"Calm down, Boomer," said Midden. "Don't spook this guy. He's going to be nervous as it is."

The man with the scars glared at him. "Remember who you're talking to. I'm the king of cool."

"I can tell," said Midden.

"Listen, motherfucker—"

"There he is," said Midden, nodding at a man walking alone across the gravel. "Keep it relaxed, okay?"

"I know what I'm doing," said the man with the scars. Then he opened the door and stepped out into the parking lot, calling out, "Hey, Kevin. Kevin, my man!"

Midden followed, staying three steps behind to reduce the appearance of threat, watching Boomer calm himself. It was, Midden thought, a little unnerving how the man went from cocky asshole to cool customer in a dozen steps. But he knew that Boomer had practiced this discipline each time he'd put on the bulky blast suit, breathing deep, bringing his pulse down, preparing to defuse whatever jury-rigged device the patrols had found. You can't have shaking hands when you hold the wire cutters.

Kevin took a step back when he saw Boomer striding toward him. Boomer slapped a hand on the man's thick shoulder, smiling and nodding. "Hey, how you doin', man? Gettin' ready to tear it up on a Friday night?"

Kevin said, "Hey. Uh, I thought we were meeting inside."

The quarryman was built wide and strong and close to the ground. Pale limestone dust drifted lightly across the legs of his work jeans and the tails of his quilted flannel shirt. But he looked nervous, thought Midden. Nervous wasn't good.

"It's so damn loud inside, hard to have a real conversation, you know?" said Boomer with a wide grin, the man's best friend. "You got what we asked for, right? I got your money right here." Boomer patted his coat pocket. "Where's the stuff?"

"Uh, yeah," said Kevin, his eyes flicking to Midden, then back to Boomer. "Over here." He led them reluctantly over to his muddy Dodge pickup and opened the hatch on the cap. "This is all I could get," he said, handing over a wrinkled brown paper grocery bag.

Boomer unrolled the top and pulled out a handful of newspaper-wrapped cylinders. He unwrapped one to expose a gleaming silver tube, a little smaller than a cigarette, with wires coming out of one end.

"Kevin," he said. "I certainly do need the blasting caps. But I can buy those at any gun show. What I need," he said, his voice rising, "what I fuckin' need, is a dozen full sticks. We talked about this."

"The sticks are a lot harder to fake the paperwork," said the quarryman. "Especially the amount you need. This is serious shit, you know."

"But can you get them?" said Boomer. His smile flickered on and off like a bad lightbulb. "You told me two weeks ago you could get them."

Kevin shifted on his feet. The leather was worn away from the steel toes of his boots, the exposed metal polished from the stone dust and shining in the sodium lights of the parking lot. "What do you need this for, anyway?"

Boomer's smile flickered on again. "I told you already. I want to divert a creek on my land up north. Got some big boulders to break up."

"Yeah, that's what you said." The quarryman looked from Boomer to Midden, standing a few paces away, then back to Boomer. His heavy hands were curled into loose fists at his sides. "I can't do it," he said. "The risk is too big. They're paying too close attention."

"Man, I already paid you," said Boomer. "Is this about money? You need more?"

"No," said Kevin. "It's not the money. I just can't do it. The money you gave me, it's in the bag. Take the caps and we'll call it even."

"We're not even," said Boomer. "We need the sticks."

The quarryman closed the cap's rear hatch with a slam. "Can't help you. And I'm leaving, so get the hell out of my way."

Boomer opened his coat to show the man the chrome pistol tucked into his waistband. "You're not leaving yet."

The man took another step back, one hand slowly rising into the air. But the other hand was a little slower, seemed to get caught on his shirttail for a moment.

Then his hand came up holding a giant Magnum revolver, a real Dirty Harry hogleg, and pointed it right at

Boomer's face, Kevin's eyes bright under the pole lights. "Asshole, I said I'm *leaving*."

Midden sighed. Everyone's a gun nut, he thought, as he took a half-step behind Boomer's bulk. He raised the .22 and put a single round past Boomer's shoulder into the quarryman's forehead.

The shot made a flat slapping sound that was lost in the noise of the bar band, which was deep into some drum-heavy oldies number. Kevin went over like a tipped tombstone.

Boomer spun, one hand cupped over his ear. "Motherfucker, we *needed* him!"

Midden shook his head and tucked the pistol away. "He was done. One way or the other. He had a gun. And he saw us both."

"Fuck," said Boomer. "Fuck!" He kicked the body hard, and air went out of the dead lungs with a whoof.

"Keep it down," said Midden, bending to pick up the quarryman's feet. "Get his hands."

Boomer examined the fallen Magnum. "Where's the fucking safety on this thing?"

Midden stood patiently, holding the dead man's heels. "Boomer, get his hands. We can't leave him here."

They carried the body toward the van. Boomer said, "And I don't appreciate your using me as cover."

"It was just to hide my gun hand," said Midden. "Those Magnum rounds would punch through both of us without slowing down."

They lifted the body into the back of the van. The

bowels let go and the distinct odor of shit and death filled the cargo space.

"Jesus Christ," said Boomer. "We're gonna have to smell that?"

"Until we find a place to bury him."

They climbed into the van and Midden started the engine. Boomer rolled down his window, still complaining as the cold November air flooded in.

"That goddamn Kevin. We're runnin' out of time, and we need that starter charge. It's gonna be hard to find another quarryman. Fuck, it's cold in here."

He rolled up the window, sniffed experimentally, then swore and rolled it down again.

"None of this would have happened if that fucker hadn't run off with my plastic."

"Tell me again why you can't just make a new batch."

Boomer glared at him, all riled up again. "It's not that goddamn easy, all right? You can't make the real deal on a hot plate out of bleach and salt substitute. These are seriously volatile chemicals. The batch we lost took me two goddamn months to get right. I searched that whole damn house top to bottom and didn't come up with anything. And that fuckin' dog about chewed my ass off as I was leaving."

"What about the new guy?"

"That carpenter, says he's a Marine? Turns out he's harder to kill than the last guy. But I'll get him."

"You hired it out," said Midden. "Should have done it yourself."

"Good thing I didn't," said Boomer. "Motherfucker would have killed me instead."

It was a bad plan to begin with, thought Midden. He should have told Boomer to wait. It wasn't his skill set. Midden should have taken care of it. But it didn't matter. As it turned out, the plan might evolve. To include the Marine.

Midden kept his eyes on the twin cones of light illuminating the road ahead. He was starting to have trouble maintaining focus on the task at hand. On the end goal. He didn't know how much more of this he could manage.

The autumn wind roared in his ears and cut through his coat as the van picked up speed. He didn't mind the cold. It helped him keep going.

"He has what you lost," said Midden over the noise. "We need it. We'll find it. And get it back."

PART 3

22

The phone rang and rang, and finally went to voicemail. Again Peter heard the young man's voice, quiet but confident, and was convinced it was the voice of the missing young Marine, Felix Castellano.

"Hello, you've reached Mrs. Aurelia Castellano, but she's not home at the moment. Please leave a message and she will call you back."

Sitting in his truck, Peter held the yellow flier in his lap, looking down at the face badly reproduced there. Clean-shaven, dark hair combed down, a shy smile. But it was hard to see much more than that. Copy paper wasn't photo paper, and it looked like it had been out in the weather awhile before Jimmy pulled it off a telephone pole. Not to mention that the young man in the neat new uniform might not bear any resemblance to the man he had become during the war. He thought of the Marines he had lost over there. He thought of Jimmy, who he had failed.

When the beep came, this time he left a message.

"Hi, my name is Peter Ash. I saw your flier about Felix, and wanted to talk with you for a few minutes." He left his number. "Please call me back, I'd like to help."

He got dressed and made coffee and a grilled cheese sandwich on the little backpacking stove, glad to have something warm in his stomach. The day was cold and damp. His breath made a dense fog, and the cloud cover hung low enough to hide the treetops. When he folded the gray tarp, he had to shake off a thin rime of ice that had formed overnight.

Before he left the vacant lot, he scattered the stones and broken bricks of the fire ring to the far corners, not wanting to damage the old man's lawnmower in the spring. The wind had already taken the ashes. Other than the charred circle at the end of the driveway and the dry spot where his truck had stood, he left no sign that he was ever there.

At Best Buy, the clerk stared at the bruise on Peter's cheek, which was evolving into an ugly greenish yellow, but he didn't have long to look. Peter was in and out in under two minutes.

He could find free Wi-Fi outside any chain coffee shop, but it was too windy for an outdoor table, and it would be awkward to sort through the box of Jimmy's things from the seat of his truck, even if the Wi-Fi made it to his parking spot. But the university library might work.

He parked on Kenwood near the Union, checking the street for the scarred man's Ford, but didn't see it. He got out of the truck and closed the door before Mingus could jump out after him. The dog cocked his head for a puzzled moment, then jumped gracefully through the empty window frame. Not an easy feat for a hundred-and-fifty-pound dog.

He really needed to get that window fixed. Especially if he was still here when it snowed. He opened the door again. "Get back up there, Mingus. I need you to guard the truck."

Mingus jumped up on the seat. Peter closed the door. Mingus jumped out the window again, then looked up at him with that serrated grin, tongue lolling.

Peter sighed. "Okay, buddy. But I don't think they're going to let you in the library. Especially not with that stink you've got going."

Peter wondered if they'd keep him out, too. After four days without a shower, he didn't smell so good himself.

He opened the back and collected the cardboard box with Jimmy's personal effects. He added the bag of papers he'd taken from Jimmy's apartment and went to find the library. He needed a place with decent windows to spread out and think.

Mingus ranged ahead to terrify the coeds, trailing the stench of pepper spray and dog funk like a plume of tear gas.

Peter had always liked big universities. He liked the young undergrads, the scruffy grad students, and the even scruffier professors. He liked the idealistic vibe, the fliers posted everywhere for meetings and talks and galleries and concerts. He liked the coffee shops and cheap restaurants at the perimeter. Maybe one of these days he'd be a student again. Maybe.

The University of Wisconsin at Milwaukee wasn't beautiful. Most of the unruly jumble of buildings seemed to date from architecture's uglier periods. Now that the sun had come out, the sky a high, clear blue, the air crisp and cold, Peter's legs twitched for a long run.

He found a glass-walled addition to the student union that connected to the library. He looked around for the dog, but Mingus had disappeared. Peter shrugged and pulled open the door. The dog could clearly take care of himself. He knew where the truck was.

Inside, the white static rose up, but less than Peter had anticipated. Maybe it was all the windows, the natural light. Maybe because it was a university, it didn't set him off like an office building or a cheap motel.

He wondered, could the static tell the difference?

He bought himself a cup of coffee and an accordion folder at the bookstore, then headed into the library.

The girl at the information desk wore red lip gloss, rectangular glasses, and a form-fitting red blouse. She had her hair up in an unraveling bun, trying for that hot-librarian look. Usually Peter went for that kind of thing, and he was sure the undergraduates were eating it up. But next to Dinah or Josie, this girl looked like a spoiled child.

She raised her eyebrows at him as he strode past, the cardboard box tucked under his arm. "May I help you?"

she asked, wrinkling her nose and staring at the bruise on his cheek.

"No, thanks," Peter said, and kept walking.

"There's no sleeping in the library," she called after him.

Peter looked down at his work clothes, now worn for four days running. Clearly this girl thought he was a homeless person. She wasn't exactly wrong.

He had to find a shower, and soon.

He walked through a bright open room until he found an unoccupied table by a window with a view of a broad courtyard. His shoulders were tight, the white static making itself known, but he pushed it down as he thought about why Jimmy would have a suitcase full of hundreds and enough plastic explosive to blow up a car.

Peter couldn't see Jimmy as a mad bomber, no matter how bad his PTSD was. Couldn't see him as a mercenary, either, blowing shit up for money. And he couldn't see Jimmy planning something, then killing himself from remorse before he did it. None of it made sense.

He opened the box of Jimmy's things and began to lay them out on the table. It was a pitifully small collection of objects to represent a man's life.

On the left, he set out the things from Dinah's cardboard box of memories. Jimmy's medals. The photos of Jimmy and Dinah, and Jimmy with his kids, Charlie and Miles looking younger in each picture.

On the right, he put the papers he took from the apartment. The yellow flier about the missing Marine. The folders with his VA paperwork and discharge papers.

In the middle, Peter laid out the things Jimmy had with him when he died. The Lake Capital pen from Jimmy's coat pocket, and the little notebook with the front pages torn out. The belt with the hidden compartment that had held five crisp new hundreds, the same yellow flier about Felix Castellano, the missing Marine, and the business card for the Riverside Veterans' Center with the phone number written in spidery black handwriting on the back. And Jimmy's wallet with only a few dollars, a grocery receipt, a library card, and a driver's license with his wife's address.

Last was the torn scrap of paper with Jimmy's same confident scrawl, but this one written more clearly: *worth more dead than alive*. The police told Dinah it was Jimmy's suicide note.

Somehow, though, it didn't look like the handwriting of a man who would kill himself.

The odd chord that had rung the first time Peter had read the note at Dinah's house began to chime again. Something Jimmy had said. But what? Where?

Peter closed his eyes and took himself back to the battered city of Baghdad during the insurgency. He remembered standing with Jimmy in the corner of a briefing room, while some major told them about the psychology of suicide bombers.

Jimmy had raised his hand. "Excuse me, sir? I just

want to know something. What kind of motherfucker would convince these dumb bastards that they were worth more to their cause dead than they are alive? What kind of motherfucker would do that?" Jimmy was polite, but he was also profane as all hell.

The major had told Jimmy to shut up, but nobody heard him because the rest of the enlisted men were all laughing. But Jimmy was serious and genuinely pissed off. What kind of motherfucker would do something like that?

Then another memory, this time of Jimmy standing at the gunner's post of a neighborhood outpost after a car bomb had exploded while trying to ram the blast barrier. "These poor dumb bastards. Some asshole convinced them they were worth more dead than alive."

The slip of paper wasn't Jimmy's suicide note.

It was a kind of invocation. Kept in the man's wallet to remind himself.

A refusal to believe that a single life had no other use than to be wasted.

And a reminder of the reasons to live.

Because nobody was worth more dead than alive.

Peter looked at the slip of paper again. It was torn on two sides. Someone had torn off the first part of that note, whatever it was.

To make it look like suicide.

Son of a bitch.

* * *

Peter thought back through what he'd learned.

Jimmy had paid his rent in advance and told his landlady he was traveling.

He'd cleaned his apartment, even emptied the fridge.

He'd covered his shifts at work and told the bartender he would be out of town.

Jimmy got a damn dog, for chrissake. Would a man contemplating suicide go out and get a dog?

Peter had thought Jimmy had killed himself because the man was *polite*?

It was just another way Peter had failed his friend. Failed to keep him safe in the war. Failed to support him at home. And failed to believe in him after he was dead.

He said it aloud.

"Jimmy didn't kill himself."

Which meant somebody else did.

Now Peter looked back at Jimmy's things with new eyes.

These weren't keys to understanding a suicide.

They were clues to a killer.

A killer Peter was going to find.

Peter swept his eyes across the table. What stood out?

The yellow fliers, obviously. Peter needed to talk to the missing Marine's grandmother.

The business card for the veterans' center. He needed to go back there again.

He picked up the pen. It was heavy in his hand. *Lake Capital Funds.*

Dinah told him they didn't have any investments. They were barely holding on to their house, so why would Jimmy be talking to an investment adviser?

That suitcase full of money.

Although if he was going to invest it, why was it hidden in a Samsonite suitcase under a rotting porch? And why was the dog there?

He thought now about what else was under that porch when he'd cleaned it out, aside from a few decades' worth of trash. The money, the dog. And an old dog bed—wasn't there an old dog bed under there?

When he put it together like that, the answer was clear.

Jimmy had hidden the suitcase full of money and explosives under the porch and left his dog there to guard it. With the dog's bed, so Mingus would know where home was.

Which was why the dog had stayed so long.

After his master was dead.

Peter needed to talk to the hedge-fund guy, Jonathan Skinner.

He brought out the accordion file he'd bought at the bookstore. It had divided sections to keep things organized, and a cover flap that tied in place. It was more compact than the box, and felt somehow more respectful. He put Jimmy's things away, then opened up his new laptop and got online.

Lake Capital wasn't a financial-planning outfit, a place for normal people to put their retirement money. Lake Capital was a hedge fund, an investment vehicle for the very wealthy, or for large financial institutions like employee pension funds, looking to balance the risk in their portfolios. Hedge fund, as in *hedge your bets.*

Hedge funds were a great racket. The fund manager—in this case, Jonathan Skinner—got paid twice. He was paid a small percentage of the base value of the fund, usually two percent each year. He also took a percentage of the profits, usually twenty percent. Hedge funds were considered risky but could be highly profitable. Especially for the hedge-fund managers, who always made something, even if their clients lost a lot. And in the big market crash, most funds had lost a huge amount of their value. But a few had made billions.

The Lake Capital website was clean and elegantly designed, but thin on details. The main page featured a beautiful photo of a big luxury sailboat moving fast in high winds, and another of attractive people arranged in a family group. Crisp graphics showed the hedge fund's performance at more than three times the rate of the market as a whole for six years running. But not much detail about how that was achieved. And no data from the last three years. So either they hadn't updated their website or they hadn't done so well since the crash.

He searched the *Milwaukee Journal Sentinel*'s site and found many articles featuring Lake Capital, a prominent corporate citizen. Skinner and his wife, Martha, were mentioned often in connection with local charities, with Martha a particular favorite of the paper, even after her death. When she was killed in a home invasion in 2007, there was a long and glowing obituary. But after the market collapse in late 2008, Lake Capital went downhill.

Returns were in the negatives, and many Lake Capital investors had pulled out their money. The Securities and Exchange Commission was also investigating. Lake Capital was down to bare bones, with only a few employees left. And although Skinner had built up a great deal of personal wealth, he had invested much of his own and his wife's money in the fund, so when Lake Capital closed its doors—and a recent newspaper article speculated that it was only a matter of time—Skinner would be reduced from extravagantly wealthy to merely rich.

Which made $400K in hard cash much more relevant to the conversation.

This time he'd call ahead and make an appointment. He took out his new phone.

"Lake Capital. How may we help you?"

The receptionist was much nicer on the phone than she was in person. Maybe because she couldn't see Peter's worn work clothes and unshaven face.

"Skinner in?" Peter tried to sound like an Army captain he'd known in Afghanistan, whose family fortune dated back to the Civil War. The captain talked like the world existed to do his bidding. "Need to see him."

"I'm so sorry, he's in meetings all day," said the

receptionist with practiced sincerity. "May I take your information so he can reach you later?"

Her name, Peter remembered, was Gretchen.

"Listen, Gretchen, tell Skinner that I know his recent numbers are shit. But my attorney tells me the man's on his way up again. So I need to meet him, and soon. Need to park this money before the fucking IRS gets it."

Gretchen was practically purring. "His meeting is ending just now," she said. "I think I can grab him. Can you hold for just one moment?"

23

As Peter put away his phone, a campus security guard approached. Maybe in his early twenties, with a soft face. The uniform fit him as if made for a different person. "Um, sir? Are you a student here?"

The girl at the information desk must have ratted him out. Peter gathered up his things. He said, "This is a public library. I don't need to be a student to come in here."

"Well, um, no, sir?" said the guard. "But we do want to make sure the library is used for, um, appropriate activities?"

Everything was a question with this kid. Peter was glad the guard didn't have a sidearm. He imagined the kid saying, *Um, stop? Or I'll shoot?*

But it wasn't worth the argument. "I was just leaving," said Peter.

He handed the guard the empty box, tucked the accordion file under his arm, and began to thread his way through the tables toward the exit. "You have a public gym, right?" This was his plan to get a shower and change his clothes before meeting Dinah.

The guard, trailing behind Peter, looked relieved at the lack of confrontation. Peter was six inches taller and twenty pounds heavier, even with the guard's spongy bulk. "Um, I'd have to send you to the campus rec department? I think you need a membership? Or maybe a day pass?"

Peter pushed the door open. The crisp fall air washed through him. "So which way to the campus rec department?"

Then he saw Mingus racing toward him across the brown grass. An uneaten hamburger wedged in his mouth, he was pursued by a campus cop in a golf cart and another cruising behind on foot. The security guard from the library had a walkie-talkie on his belt. It crackled, and a garbled voice said, "Rogue animal, rogue animal. All officers respond."

Then Peter saw that the cop in the golf cart had his sidearm in his hand. While driving.

This could go wrong six different ways. Peter stepped into the center of the paved area, waved his arms, and raised his voice. "Mingus!"

The dog saw Peter and cranked around in a tight turn. He galloped over, wolfing down the burger on the way, then came to a leisurely stop. His tongue hung out of the side of his mouth as he panted happily. The golf cart almost tipped over as it tried to follow.

"Sir, is this your dog?"

The cop in the cart had his finger inside the trigger guard. He was in late middle age, with the pale and fleshy look of a boneless chicken breast, except for his face, which was bright red with righteous indignation.

"He's his own dog," said Peter. "I just clean up after him. Put that gun away, will you?"

The running cop was barely breathing hard. He was young, clean-shaven, and his uniform shirt was pressed. He wore sneakers, and he couldn't hide his grin. "A couple of girls tried to adopt him, let him into their dorm. He raided the lunch buffet pretty bad."

"Shit." Peter didn't know whether to be proud or embarrassed.

The cop with the gun spoke loudly as he levered himself out of the golf cart. "Dogs are not permitted in the residence halls," he said, glaring at the younger man. "And this animal does not have a license. I have notified animal control." He hadn't put the gun away. Maybe he just liked to have it in his hand.

"We'll just go," said Peter. "Sorry for the mess."

"Oh, no," said the cop with the gun. It was something fancy, bright, shiny chrome with mother-of-pearl grips. "You're staying right here, pal. There's a lot of paperwork for this, and the police are coming. You may face charges yourself."

Peter looked at the young cop. "Seriously?"

The young cop shrugged, his face artfully blank. "Marv's the senior officer."

"Yes, I am," said Marv, still louder than he needed to

be. "Take hold of your animal." He still had his finger inside the trigger guard. Peter could see the red dot on the safety, meaning the safety was off. The barrel was pointing all over the place.

"Sure," said Peter. He stepped between Marv and Mingus, facing the dog. Then he pivoted and took hold of the pistol, one finger jammed behind the trigger so it wouldn't go off, and twisted the gun from Marv's grip.

"Hey!" said Marv, eyes wide.

The younger cop put his hand to his own sidearm.

"Wait," said Peter, eyes on the younger man. He held up the gun by the barrel. "The safety was off. His finger was on the trigger." He found the magazine release and dropped it into his waiting palm, and handed it to the other man. Then he racked the slide to eject the round from the chamber, caught it in the air, and held it up between thumb and forefinger for the younger man to see. "Is this how you were trained?"

The younger cop shook his head. "Christ, Marv," he said. "We talked about this, remember? Somebody's gonna get hurt."

"Goddamn you little shits." Marv was pulling a black-jack from his pocket.

"Marv," said the younger cop, stepping in close. "We talked about this. Get back in the cart."

Peter dropped the pistol into a campus mailbox. "I'm leaving now," he said. "Sorry about the lunch buffet."

The security guard from the library said, "Um, sir? I'll just see you off campus?"

He was writing Peter's license number down in his notebook as Mingus jumped into the cab of the truck.

As Peter climbed in after him, the dog slurped him in the face. His breath smelled like hamburgers. The rest of him smelled like ten gallons of hot sauce at the city dump.

Peter shook his head. "Mingus, you are a bad goddamn dog. Now I'm never going to get my shower."

The cold November wind came through the broken window as he drove. He kept one eye on his mirrors, hoping to see a black Ford SUV. But no luck.

He had some time before his meeting with Skinner. He needed to get showered and changed if he wanted the guy to talk to him. And Dinah, he had to talk to Dinah.

He pulled out his phone and called the number she'd given him, which was the nurse's station on her floor. It took them five minutes to get her to the phone.

"I'm sorry to bother you," he said. "Can we meet after your shift?"

"That's fine with me," she said. "I'll be home about six."

He wanted to ask if he could use her shower. Maybe run a load of laundry through the wash. But he'd just spent an hour in the library, his head was aching, and bathrooms were definitely indoors. He was used to splashing himself in a glacial stream under the vast dome of the sky. The last time he'd showered was at that motel, which hadn't gone well. He didn't ask.

"Okay," he said. "I'll see you at six."

He broke the connection and cruised, watching the traffic. Waiting for the black Ford. Feeling the cold wind on his face. He caught sight of his face in the rearview, the bruise turning truly interesting colors now. Purple, yellow, green. He sure looked like a solid citizen.

He passed an old Pathfinder with a crumpled front passenger side, the glass missing, plastic sheeting taped up in its place. That was a great look. No bullet holes, though. You needed bullet holes for the truly custom effect.

Peter knew he should be making some kind of plan. Some kind of plan for his life. Find some new glass for his truck. That wouldn't be easy, with a forty-year-old truck. Then fix the sheet metal, fix whatever other damage the bullets had done to the truck he'd taken hundreds of hours to restore. Figure out what to do next. With the rest of his life.

After he figured out Jimmy, he told himself.

After he saved Dinah and the boys.

After that, he'd do the next thing, whatever it was.

The bruise would heal itself in time. A shower and a change of clothes would make all the difference. Maybe he could shower at the Y.

Mingus leaned up against him, tongue hanging, stinking up the cab. Weren't dogs supposed to have a fantastic sense of smell? Peter didn't know how the animal could stand himself.

Maybe the stink was like canine cologne. And all the bitches thought Mingus smelled like an investment banker.

He passed a car wash and had an idea. He circled around and parked facing out, mostly hidden from the street, with a straight line to the exit.

It was a self-serve place. Eight chrome washing bays, each with a coin-op control and a spray wand. But you could wash more than a truck in a place like that.

Peter plugged in a dozen quarters and turned the setting to plain warm water.

"C'mere, Mingus."

He got a good grip on the dog's rope collar and dragged him over. It wasn't easy to drag a hundred-and-fifty-pound dog somewhere he didn't want to go. But Peter made it happen, straddled the dog, grabbed the spray wand, dialed down the pressure to the lowest level, and got to work, using his hand to minimize the force of the water.

It wasn't a lot of fun.

When Mingus got wet, the stink got worse. As if the water somehow rehydrated the stench.

Shit and death and pepper spray mixed with a deep animal funk, worse than anything Peter had ever smelled. It was unspeakable.

Peter tried to breathe through his mouth.

Mingus, of course, couldn't care less about the smell. It was the bath he didn't like. He whined and flattened his ears and hunkered down close to the pavement while

Peter worked his way around, closing his pitiful dog eyes when the water got close to his face. When the time came to wash his chest and belly, Peter had to roll him over by main force, kneeling on him again and talking in the same calm voice as he had under the porch, when the dog had been trying to rip off his face. Mingus whined louder.

Peter didn't blame him. The day hadn't warmed up any, and having some guy you just met wash your belly was bad for a tough dog's image.

The soap was listed as nontoxic, so he figured that would be okay. He'd skip the wax setting, though. When the bubbles came out, the stench improved, but Mingus tried to bolt. Peter had a good grip on the collar and almost got pulled into traffic. Soaked through himself, he had to tie the dog's rope collar to the coin-op machine.

The soap smelled like plastic strawberries, but that was a definite improvement over the original stench. Mingus tucked his tail and cowered on the wet concrete as Peter used his own hairbrush on the dog's matted fur. Maybe a haircut was the best solution. For both of them. He'd have to buy some clippers. He sure wouldn't be using that hairbrush again.

Then back to the warm water, rinsing away the strawberry-smelling soap, talking gently. They were both shivering in the late-autumn air. When Mingus growled, Peter said, "Watch your manners, dog. I'd rather be somewhere else, too, but this has got to get done."

The dog growled again. This time it was the tank-engine rumble, the sound that meant business.

Peter looked up to see a black Chevy Caprice roll slowly into the car wash. It had no city seal on the door, no light bar on the roof, but the tan municipal plates and folded spotlights by the side mirrors clearly marked it as a police car.

The driver parked in a way that would appear casual to someone who hadn't run tactical missions in three countries. But the Caprice now blocked Peter's truck from an easy exit. Unless he was willing to jump a high curb and crash through a fence in a restored forty-year-old truck with a custom mahogany cargo box. Which he wasn't. Even with the bullet holes.

The cruiser door opened and Detective Lipsky unfolded his lean marathoner's frame, surveying the scene. Peter remained crouched over Mingus. Hairbrush in one hand, collar in the other. Man and dog both soaked to the skin.

Lipsky looked down at him, those X-ray eyes surprisingly pale in the daylight. "I guess you really are a dog lover," he said. "That's illegal in fifty states, but I keep an open mind. You two need a little more private time?"

It didn't look good, Peter had to admit. He said, "The dog didn't mind the pepper spray, but I did."

Lipsky wore a chocolate-colored topcoat over a moss-green blazer and dark blue dress pants, no tie. "Yeah, I took a nice long shower myself," he said, crossing his arms comfortably. "In my own house. Where I happen to live. Suit's already at the dry cleaner's." He glanced at Peter's jeans and shirt, the same he'd worn two days before. "You do have more than one change of clothes, right?"

Lipsky was trying to get into his head again. This wasn't the direction Peter wanted the conversation to go. "Any news on those license plates from the other day?"

Lipsky ignored the question. He gave Peter a steady stare, apparently done with the banter. "It wasn't hard to find you," he said. "I can tell that truck of yours from a mile away. You are still a suspect in that killing. And apparently a nuisance at UWM, you and that dog both. Your truck plate came in with a request for information."

"I'm not hiding," said Peter. "I have work to do. What about those license plates?"

Lipsky shook his head and watched the traffic. "The Impala turned up stolen, owned by a white kid lives on the south side. His dad called it in that afternoon. They found it in a parking lot at Mayfair Mall, with a couple of bullet holes in the rear end." He said, "The other plate, the Ford SUV, I think you got the number wrong. The number you gave me is for a BMW sedan, not a Ford SUV. Owned by a dry cleaner in Brookfield, seventy years old. No record. I talked to the guy, said he hasn't been downtown in years."

Peter knew he hadn't gotten it wrong. His face must have showed something.

Lipsky put a curious look on his face. Maybe it was even genuine. "What do you care about that Ford?"

Mingus whined. Peter went back to work with the hairbrush. "I told you the guy in that Ford almost ran me over, right? What really happened was he almost hit my dog. That's why Mingus ran off that night. That guy was driving like a complete asshole. I wanted to have a talk with him about civic responsibility."

"Mm," said Lipsky, clearly not buying a word of it. He looked at Peter as if measuring him for a suit he knew wouldn't fit. "Is that where you got that beautiful shiner? In a conversation about civic responsibility?"

"What, this?" said Peter, touching the multicolored bruise on his cheek. "Just a misunderstanding. Could happen to anyone."

"A misunderstanding," said Lipsky. "With a couple of ex-Army tough guys who got patched up at Saint Mary's night before last, am I right? They gave the ER doc a line she didn't believe."

Again, not how Peter wanted the conversation to go.

The detective smiled. "I like to check the hospitals after a shooting," he said. "See what might connect up."

Mingus abruptly ducked his head and backed out of the wet rope collar, then dashed gleefully to the far side of the parking lot. After shaking himself thoroughly, he looked at Peter, tongue out in a canine grin.

"Shit," said Peter.

Lipsky measured up the bruise with his X-ray eyes. "What happened, they call you a jarhead?"

"Something like that," Peter admitted.

Lipsky nodded. "Let's take a little inventory here," he said, ticking off each item on his fingers. "One, you're sleeping in your truck. Which has a broken window, and some bullet holes, let me add, so its usefulness as a homeless shelter is dropping fast. Two, you're doing pickup carpentry in a shit neighborhood, so I know you're going broke if you're not there already. Three, you're getting into fights with strangers, although at least you seem to be winning. Then there's number four, the personal-hygiene thing. Generally a problem when you're homeless. Can I ask how long has it been since you had a shower? And walking through a car wash doesn't count."

Peter could see Lipsky's point. But Lipsky didn't have the whole story, and Peter wasn't about to tell it. Lipsky could think what he wanted.

Peter opened the back of his truck and climbed up for his duffel. "I do have a change of clothes," he said, peeling off his wet shirt and pants. Not sure why he felt the need to explain himself. The photo of Jimmy in his pocket had gotten damp, too. He dried it gently and laid it down where he wouldn't forget it.

"That's good," said Lipsky, peering past him into the box. Peter could practically feel him cataloging the contents. "Otherwise you'd freeze to death. Which reminds me. I think I found you a new driver's-side window. At some car graveyard in Mobile, Alabama."

Peter turned to look at him, halfway into his last pair of clean pants.

Lipsky shrugged. "A guy I know runs a salvage yard," he said. "All this shit's on the Web now, it took him about five minutes. I'm getting it at cost. It'll be here in a couple days."

Peter stared at him. "Why would you do that? You don't know anything about me."

"Here's the thing," said Lipsky. "Maybe I do. Just a little."

While Peter put on a clean white shirt, and tucked the photo into his breast pocket, Lipsky turned away to lean on Peter's truck. Looking out at the parking lot, he took a pack of gum out of his pocket, selected a stick, and stripped off the wrapper.

"When I got my discharge from the Rangers—this was '93—I was seriously fucked up," he said, as if to nobody in particular. "Somalia killed about a dozen of my closest friends. Then Iraq—I got there months before Desert Storm. My unit was on foot in the desert, spotting targets. The Republican Guard I met didn't have their hands up."

Lipsky shook his head. "They teach you to kill, but they don't teach you to forget. That's what bourbon's for, right? I saw some bad shit over there. Hell, I *did* some bad shit. When I got home, I was lost. Couldn't sleep. Drinking with both hands. Ready to do some damage, if only to myself."

He sighed. "Anyway, my stepdad was a cop. A real hard-ass bastard. But he got me into the academy. I don't know what I would have done otherwise. It gave me something to do, something to focus on. Something useful. I can't say it plainer, the man saved me."

Lipsky watched the dog poke his nose into the bushes, then turned to Peter with his pale X-ray eyes. "Now you," he said. "You're the only suspect I have in that killing on Sixteenth Street. I can't prove you did it, but hey, I know you did. Personally, I don't give a shit one way or another. I figure you had a good reason. Guy with an assault rifle hosing down a residential street. Somebody had to stop him. That's reason enough for me. He lost his right to due process the minute he pulled the trigger."

What do you say to that? A police detective telling you he knows you killed a man and doesn't care? Peter didn't know what to say.

So he kept his mouth shut.

"But here's the damn thing, kid. You can't just kill people," said Lipsky, seeing right through him. "You can't. That's not a way to behave, back in the world. I don't know what you're into, or what happened over there, but it has to stop. You need a new mission. So I can put you in jail. Or I can put you to work. Your choice."

Mingus wandered the parking lot, watering the light posts. Lipsky kept talking.

"I know a group works with returning veterans." He scratched his chin. "It's kind of raggedy-ass, no money to speak of. They have a building not far from here. I don't know what they've got to offer, maybe some job training, basic construction skills, stuff like that. But I'm thinking you could maybe teach some of those classes. Talk to some of those guys. And they have showers, a kitchen, some bunks set up for guys who don't have anywhere to stay. Some good guys," he said. "Even some jarheads."

"Okay," said Peter.

"Okay?" said Lipsky. "You're not just blowing smoke up my ass?"

Peter shrugged. "I'll check it out," he said.

"Sure you will. Here's the deal." Lipsky stared at Peter. "If you want your new driver's-side window, you're going to have to meet me at this place to pick it up. I don't work there, but I've met a few people. I'll introduce you around. You can see what we're trying to do there. You can even use the showers. No strings attached."

Clearly, Lipsky thought Peter needed saving. Peter couldn't imagine why. He was living in his truck and had just done his personal grooming at a car wash, but that was a temporary thing. Operational necessity.

Still, when Lipsky reached out to him, offering a business card between two fingers, Peter took it.

It was cream-colored, with olive-green lettering. The Riverside Veterans' Center.

He'd seen this card before.

Jimmy had one just like it folded into his stash belt when he died.

"Okay," said Peter. "I'll call you tomorrow."

"I wrote my cell number on the back," said Lipsky over his shoulder as he strode toward his cruiser. "So you don't have any excuses."

"Hey," said Peter. "Thanks for finding that window."

"I'm a highly trained officer of the law," said Lipsky. "I can tell when a guy needs a kick in the ass to get him going."

Mingus met the detective at his car and sniffed at the pocket of his chocolate-colored coat. "Ah, you caught me. You want one?" He pulled out a small plastic package of dog treats, fished one out, and held his hand with the treat mostly hidden in his fingers. Mingus stuck his nose close and tried to nibble it out, without luck. Then sat and wagged his tail.

"Shake," said Lipsky, and Mingus put out a paw. "Good boy." Lipsky tossed the treat up, and the dog snapped it out of the air, teeth flashing white. "Good boy."

Lipsky waved, climbed into his car, and roared out of the parking lot, tires chirping. Peter looked reproachfully at the dog.

"I thought you were better than that."

Mingus butted his head into Peter's thigh.

Peter scratched the dog's heavy strawberry-smelling ruff. "Maybe you're just hungry."

24

Skinner suggested they connect at an East Side coffee shop. Peter agreed only because he wanted to talk to the man face-to-face and it was too cold for any sane person to meet outside. He parked his truck on the street, locked Mingus in the back of the truck to avoid another hamburger rampage, and left his gun tucked into his toolbox.

Alterra Coffee was a quirky local place in a repurposed industrial building, now filled with laptop-toting hipsters, businesspeople meeting out of the office, and a few street people getting out of the weather. There was a warm buzz of conversation, but the open feel and tall glass roll-up door and skylights helped keep the white static from driving Peter out immediately.

He was deliberately late but still had time to get coffee and find a table by the glass roll-up door before Skinner strolled in. The same white-blond hair and pale, aristocratic face. No coat, no briefcase, just a midnight-blue suit worn with the same elegant disregard Peter remembered from the man's office. Peter wondered if finding investors was like getting a date, where the secret was in appearing not to need one.

Skinner surveyed the room. Peter caught his eye and lifted a hand.

"Peter Ash?" Skinner walked over and flashed his easy, careless smile, almost shocking in its warmth and charm. Peter could see how the man had managed to talk so many wealthy, intelligent people out of their money. It was the smile that built Lake Capital.

You'd never know the SEC was investigating his company.

They shook hands, Skinner's grip harder than expected under the pampered skin. "Great to meet you, Peter," he said, taking in Peter's faded blue jeans and white shirt. "Boy, I wish I could dress like you every day. Better or worse, finance is still a suit-and-tie business."

His eyes lingered on the multicolored bruise on Peter's cheek.

Peter was counting on the bruise to get Skinner wondering. He was pretty sure Skinner wouldn't recognize him from his first visit to Lake Capital. He might have noticed the bruise, but it had turned a deep shade of purple. Regardless, Skinner probably didn't have many meetings with guys who looked like they'd been in a fight.

"Anyway," said Skinner as he sprawled comfortably in the skeletal metal chair. "I appreciate your interest in

Lake Capital. Somehow I haven't heard your name before. What business are you in, Peter?"

There was also a trace of an accent in Skinner's vowels, but Peter couldn't pin it down. As if he'd come from a foreign country just around the corner. Or maybe it was just private school, in the land of money.

"Oh, you know," said Peter. "A little of this, a little of that."

"Give me a hint," said Skinner, that smile flashing on and off like a beacon. "What's the most fun? What makes the most money?"

"Salvage," said Peter. "Finding opportunities others have missed."

"Oooh," said Skinner. "What kinds of opportunities?"

Peter leaned forward. Skinner leaned in to meet him. It was a salesman's trick, Peter knew, to mirror your customer. People were more likely to trust someone they thought was like them. But Peter could do that, too.

"If I told you," he said, "they wouldn't be opportunities."

"Hah! Well, it sounds like you know what you're doing," said Skinner, the smile broad now. "And you've worked hard and taken risks and now you've got some liquidity to invest. Tell me, how did you come to find us? We're not exactly Edward Jones."

"A friend of mine gave me your card," said Peter. "James Johnson. He used to work for me. Maybe you remember him."

Skinner seemed to think for a moment, then shook

his head pleasantly. "No," he said. "I don't believe I do. Is he an investor of ours?" If he was lying, he was a very good liar. Although he was in finance, so that was part of the skill set.

"He's dead now," said Peter, watching the other man closely. "He was killed."

"Oh, what a terrible shame," said Skinner, with every appearance of thoughtful sorrow. "I'm so sorry."

"Me, too," said Peter. "This business can be dangerous. Before he died, he told me he wanted to invest with you. And James often had excellent ideas."

Skinner's warm, understanding smile returned, his teeth gleaming with saliva. "How much of an investment are we talking about?"

Peter wondered if the amount would mean anything to the man. "Four hundred thousand dollars."

Something flickered across Skinner's pale face, like the shadow of a bird flying overhead.

But it was gone too quickly to identify, and the salesman was back. "Oh, dear," said Skinner. "Unfortunately, our current fund is only open to investments of a half-million or more."

"The money's in cash," said Peter. "In a suitcase. Banded stacks of hundred-dollar bills." He smiled pleasantly.

Peter was a blind man groping in the dark, but he seemed to have found something. Skinner's easy smile stiffened. His face became all hard planes, lean and muscular, and his voice went flat. "Who are you?"

Peter kept his own smile in place. “I haven’t talked to the authorities yet. I thought I’d hear your side of the story first. About where the four hundred thousand came from.”

Skinner’s face had gotten more pale, if that was possible. The warmth and charm were gone. He stared at Peter with cold, reptilian eyes.

“If you are truly an investor,” he said, “I apologize, because Lake Capital is unable to help you.” Without the engaging warmth, his eyes bulged slightly from his head. His teeth seemed somehow more prominent. “If you are something else—”

“Don’t you want to know how I got this?” Peter interrupted. He tilted his head so the other man could get a clear look at the multicolored bruise that had taken over a third of his face.

Skinner didn’t answer.

“First I killed a man,” said Peter in a calm, even voice. “Then I put two more men in the hospital with my bare hands. Trying to get a fourth man to answer my questions. So you had better answer mine now. Before things go very badly for you.”

Skinner’s pale face seemed to belong to another man entirely. He stood, trembling, teeth bared in a kind of grimace. But not in fear. This was aggression.

Skinner glared at Peter as if memorizing him. “Whatever you are, the next time we talk, I’ll ask the questions.”

He turned and stalked out of the coffee shop.

Peter shook his head. It was an odd conversation.

He'd thought he would intimidate Skinner, scare him a little. But something else had happened. He'd peeled back the charming veneer and seen what lay underneath. Something very different indeed.

No, Peter wasn't done with Jonathan Skinner.

But when he walked out of the coffee shop into the relief of the open air, he saw the black Ford SUV parked on the far side of the busy street. The man with the scars looking right at him.

25

The black Ford was parked on the far side of the one-way street, right at the corner, half a block upstream to traffic. Not obvious unless you were looking for him, but Peter was looking. Not a bad position, either, with a good line of sight through the windshield and side window. A wider view, and a wider field of fire. So the man wasn't dumb and maybe had some training.

Or maybe he got lucky with the parking.

Traffic was heavy and fast, two lanes, a city artery. Peter's truck was half a block away on this side of the street, in full view of the black Ford.

Buying time, Peter looked up and raised a palm to the sky, as if checking for raindrops. He was acutely aware of the chrome .32 the man had shown before, and Peter's own lack of ordnance.

Lewis's .45 was locked in the cargo box with the dog.

The adrenaline surged in his blood, giving rash

advice. Peter felt a powerful urge to sprint across the street and pull the scarred man out of his truck.

What he didn't want to do was get shot on the way over. Alone and on foot, he wouldn't be in any position to control the play.

He weighed his options in a hurry.

He could walk toward his truck, which was probably what the scarred man expected him to do. This way, Peter would find out what the man had planned and do his best to defend against it. He'd always been pretty good at that.

Maybe the guy would just follow Peter, as he had before, keeping him in sight.

But maybe he'd open up with an automatic weapon, in which case a lot of other people might get hurt. And Mingus was in the back of the truck. That mahogany plywood wasn't stopping any bullets.

If the man really wanted to kill Peter, though, wouldn't he have set up outside the coffee shop door? It would have been a simple thing to shoot Peter at close range when he walked outside.

So walk in the opposite direction, against the traffic, and maybe get the man out of his vehicle. If he stuck in his SUV watching Peter's truck, Peter could circle behind him. Find something to hit him with. Then have a conversation.

Which actually sounded like a plan.

Peter turned and started walking. At a decent clip, as if he had a destination in mind.

He came even with the black Ford but kept his face turned away, watching the scarred man's reflection in a shop's plate-glass window. The man tracked Peter's path with his head but didn't get out of his Ford. He wore the same black leather coat and Kangol cap.

Peter kept walking, turned the corner, left the man behind. Picked up his stride to a higher gear.

It was a decent city neighborhood, sidewalks and midsized residential buildings, but not exactly an upscale commercial area, although it was trying. He passed a couple of bars, a loading dock, a chain pizza place, and an all-night restaurant. Nobody behind him as he rounded the next corner, circling to come back on the scarred man.

He walked past a skateboard shop, a hairdresser's, and an old movie theater, looking for a piece of pipe or scrap lumber but finding nothing to hit the man with but a trash can. That would not qualify as a concealed weapon.

Moving faster still, he turned the third corner by an upscale sports bar, then a short dead-end alley, and he wasted twenty seconds scouting for a piece of chain or an unbroken bottle, anything, but there was nothing but windblown trash, beer cans, and fast-food wrappers. Then a boarded-up building, yet another fatality of the shitty economy.

Before the last corner, he stopped and took off his jacket. Turned it inside out to change its color, then balled it up under his arm to change the shape of his body from a distance. Hunched over, he walked slowly into view of the black Ford, letting the traffic slow to flow around him as he made his way across the street. The SUV still parked, the window still down, the shape of a man still visible inside almost a block away.

But now Peter was on the same side of the street, and unobserved.

He angled past a fast-food Mexican place to head into the big parking lot that took up most of the block. It wasn't full, but there were enough cars to provide decent cover. Still nothing to use as a weapon.

He put his coat on again. He was even with the Ford now. It was about forty yards away, across the parking lot and sidewalk. The scarred man indistinct through the passenger window.

Then Peter was past. No longer visible from the driver's seat. He cut across the lot toward the Ford, staying out of the side mirror's view. Objects may be closer than they appear. No weapon but his hands.

Then an old bike, shackled to a railing. A heavy cable lock, nothing he could get open without tools. But the seat. The seat post was quick-release. Peter flipped the lever and lifted it free from the bike. Which gave him a metal tube sixteen inches long. With a bicycle seat at one end. It had some weight. Gave him some reach.

Not much against a .32.

Better than nothing.

Still careful of the passenger-side mirror, he walked calmly toward the Ford. Coming at an angle from the rear. He could open the passenger door, but he'd have to attack through the vehicle. His improvised weapon wouldn't help inside that small space. And the passenger door was likely locked, anyway.

So he crossed behind. Down low to keep out of the rearview. Holding the seat post like a medieval weapon in his left hand. The arm outstretched. The Ford's engine running.

He peeked out for a gap in the traffic and almost got his head removed by a minivan. But he slipped into the stream behind it. Three quick steps up the driver's side. And he swung the seat post around in a wide sidearm loop, the scarred man registering his movement in the side mirror too late to do much but begin to raise his arm.

The bicycle seat smashed into the side of the scarred man's face, knocking him farther into the SUV. Peter swung twice more, quickly, hitting him on the temple and then on his blocking arm. The seat post was not an ideal weapon in a close environment. Peter dropped it on the road and went through the open window, the scarred man leaning over and scrabbling on the passenger seat for something under a newspaper. Peter had no target, just the man's shoulder and side protected by the thick leather car coat. Peter grabbed for the man's collar to pull him into range, but there was nothing to take hold of, so he pounded at the man's neck and face with short chopping punches, turning out to be harder to beat a man inside his own car than Peter would have thought.

The scarred man turned, showing his teeth, with the

chrome .32 in his right fist coming up to bear. Peter reached a long left arm in and put his own hand atop the slide, forcing the nose of the gun down toward the door, jamming two fingers into the trigger guard and pulling hard. The gun went off with a loud bang and the scarred man shoved the gearshift into drive and stomped on the gas, swerving into traffic. Peter kept hold of the .32 but unhinged his elbows from the window frame to let the arc of the Ford's momentum shed him onto the street with the gun still reversed in his hand. With a shriek of sheet metal, the Ford bounced off a delivery truck, tore the fender from a taxicab, ran a red light to a chorus of horns, and disappeared into the city.

Peter put a steadying hand on the hood of a stopped Honda. Then dropped the .32 into his coat pocket and threaded his way across the street to the sidewalk, where the parked cars helped hide him from view. Then he unlocked the door of his truck, started the engine, turned on his signal, and calmly pulled into the street.

He wouldn't wait around for Lipsky to show up for this one.

He smiled.

It felt good to do a little damage.

26

He still had a few hours before meeting Dinah, and he was starving. So he stopped at Café Corazón, a little Mexican place in an old triangular building around the corner from the lumberyard. He ordered to go and sat outside under a picnic shelter to eat his burrito. It was a very good burrito. Top ten, for sure. Maybe top five.

Then he took out his phone and tried Aurelia Castellano, the missing Marine's grandmother. Again he got the woman's voicemail.

He was leaving his number when he was interrupted. "Hello? Hello?" A strong voice, but with the patina of years. "Are you still there?"

"Yes, ma'am, I'm here," said Peter, strangely relieved. Part of him was afraid she'd vanished, too.

"Praise the Lord, I was afraid I'd lost you," she said. Then, "Do you know anything about my grandson

Felix?" Her voice was full of hope, absurdly. Her grandson had been missing for months.

"I'm sorry, ma'am, I don't," said Peter. "But I wonder if I could come talk to you?"

When she didn't respond, Peter said, "I'm not a reporter or a policeman. I'm a Marine, like your grandson. I think you met a friend of mine. James Johnson."

"Oh, yes," she said. He could hear the smile in her voice. People almost always smiled when they talked about Jimmy. "I met Mr. Johnson," she said. "Just over a month ago. What a *nice* man. He was looking for my Felix. But I haven't heard from him. Not for quite some time."

Peter said, "Ma'am? When could I come see you?"

She was home, just cleaning up. He could come by right now if he wanted to.

She met him at the door of a 1920s bungalow on the North Side.

The paint was old but touched up, the yard was neat, and he could see a kid's play structure in the back. The houses on either side of hers were bigger, but they were boarded up, with a blue tarp over one roof that would not last the next storm, let alone the winter. Four other houses on the block had yellow notices taped up to their front doors.

This had been a nice neighborhood once, he thought. Now it was being gutted by the recession. Families foreclosed on, bank-owned homes standing empty and rotting.

"You must be Mr. Ash," she said, holding the door open, smiling as if a stranger asking about her vanished grandson was the best part of her day. Maybe it was.

Mrs. Aurelia Castellano looked to be in her late sixties, with steel in her hair. Her skin was the color of burnished bronze. She wore half-glasses, a man's dress shirt untucked with the sleeves rolled up, and immaculate blue jeans. She looked like a high school principal on her day off.

Which made Peter wish he had showered somewhere other than a car wash. And shaved. And gotten a haircut.

"Won't you come in?"

He stood at the open door. The smell of mothballs and air freshener wafted out. He felt the static rise and his chest grow tight just with the idea of entering the house. "Ah—ma'am—"

She measured him with her eyes.

"Is there something wrong with my house, Mr. Ash?"

Peter shook his head. "No, ma'am."

"Then why are you out here in the cold? Come in, young man, come in."

And she took him by the arm and led him inside.

"Perhaps in the sunroom," she said, and sat him in a white wicker chair in a bright room with leaded-glass windows on three sides and a broad view of the street. "I put on a fresh pot of coffee," she said. "You'll have some."

It was not a question. He nodded and sat, breathing deeply, while she brought him a cup of coffee and set out a plate of cookies. Then she perched herself on the edge of the couch, hands on her knees, leaning toward Peter. She took a deep breath, then let it out.

"Now, then," she said. "Why are you here?"

"I hoped you would tell me a little bit about your grandson," said Peter.

The bright smile faded into the distance. "Felix was a nice boy. Polite, never in trouble. And a hard worker."

"He grew up with you?"

"Yes, he lived in this very house, from the age of four. Several of my grandchildren lived with me at one time or another. But Felix stayed the longest. He graduated high school, stayed away from bad influences." The smile turned sad. "My hopes were on him more than the others."

"He went overseas?" Peter asked.

Mrs. Castellano nodded. "It was my own fault," she said. "He was such a kind, quiet boy. I suggested he join the Navy or the Air Force. He was good with his hands, always fixing things around the house. I hoped he would learn a trade and get money for college." She shook her head. "He was always a skinny boy. I didn't ever imagine he would join the Marines and get sent to the fighting. Maybe he thought he was proving something. Four years they kept him. He was always quiet before. But he came home hardly talking at all. Like he had ghosts inside him."

Peter knew what that felt like. He felt it still, with the static sparking up inside him, even in that quiet, sunny room in Milwaukee. He rolled his shoulders to ease the tension, but it didn't help the tightness in his chest.

"Where did Felix live, after he came home?"

"He came home to his nana." She patted her palm on the couch cushion beside her. "I was not going to have him spending his back pay on a place of his own, not until he got a good job." She pierced him with a glance. "Veterans Day is on Monday. We're supposed to honor our veterans. You'd think a decorated veteran could get a job. But there were no jobs to be had. He did enroll in college, I made sure of that."

Peter nodded. He wouldn't have been able to resist her, either.

She shook her head. "But Felix didn't fit there, either. He was a war veteran sitting in a classroom with children just out of high school. They had no idea of what he'd been through. And the school had no idea what to do with him."

Peter had heard this story before, too. "Then he disappeared?"

"Months later," she said. "He started going to a veterans' group. I thought he might be getting better. But I arrived home one day and he was gone. He left a note."

Mrs. Castellano reached into her shirt pocket and pulled out a piece of lined notepaper, softened from handling. The creases where it had been folded were worn. After another few months they would wear through the paper entirely. Peter imagined her carrying it with her every day, and setting it on a table beside her bed before she went to sleep.

She unfolded the note with exquisite care.

"'Dear Nana,'" she read. "'I have something important to do. Please don't try to find me. If you hear anything about me, please know that I love my country, I will always love you, and I always have done what I thought was right. With love, your Felix.'"

She turned to look at Peter, eyes bright with tears. "What can he be doing?" she asked. "What can he possibly be doing?"

Peter didn't have an answer for her.

But he was afraid it involved a large sum of money and some plastic explosive. And a disturbed young man who was good with his hands.

"Ma'am," he said, "I wish I knew. I really do." He wasn't sure how to say the next thing, so he just said it. "Do you remember my asking you about another man who came to talk to you? My friend James Johnson?"

She wiped her eyes with a white handkerchief. "Yes," she said. "He said a Marine never leaves another Marine behind. He wanted to help find my Felix."

Then she seemed to catch herself, and stared fiercely at Peter. It was like the light of the sun focused down through a magnifying glass, but in a good way. Peter felt what it must have been like to be under this woman's care.

"Your friend," she said. "We spoke several times. He said he would tell me what he found. But I didn't hear from him again. That's why you're here, isn't it? Something happened to him."

"Ma'am?" said Peter. "Where did you suggest Jimmy start looking for your grandson?"

* * *

Mrs. Castellano gave Peter a short list of Felix's friends and their phone numbers. She'd given Jimmy the same list.

Felix didn't go to taverns, she said. He belonged to the YMCA on Forty-sixth Street, he took care of himself. She had convinced the staff to post fliers and review their records. Felix hadn't been to the Y since before he left her home.

Peter felt the static rise higher even before he asked his next question. The pricking of sweat on the back of his neck. He knew it would be bad.

"May I see his room?"

The stairwell was steep and narrow and tucked tightly under the eaves, and Peter had to hunch over and turn sideways to get up the stairs as the static crackled behind his ears and the steel band tightened around his chest. The bedroom wasn't much bigger than the stairwell. Peter kept breathing, in and out, in and out. He was sweating freely now. He would last only so long. He'd better make the best of it.

The narrow bed was neatly made, waiting for Felix to come home. But the closet and a leaning particleboard dresser were nearly empty. The bulletin board over the dresser was bare. Pinholes and uneven fading showed where papers had been tacked up.

"He took all his medals with him," she said. There was no space for two in the bedroom, so she stood in the doorway, looking in. "His discharge papers. His dress uniform. What would he need his dress uniform for?"

Peter felt it in his stomach. Something bad.

He thought of Jimmy's little apartment, the rent three months in advance, the fridge cleaned out for a long absence.

"Ma'am, I'd like to search the room. Is that all right? I'll put everything back the way I found it."

Mrs. Castellano nodded.

There wasn't much there. He would work fast.

He shoved the narrow bed away from the wall, pulled off the cheap linens, lifted the mattress from the box spring, then the box spring from the floor. Nothing.

He took the drawers from the dresser. A few torn T-shirts and worn-out socks, some old car magazines. He flipped through the magazines and saw only cars. Nothing taped on the undersides of the drawers.

He went through the closet, item by item. It didn't take long. Two faded dress shirts, a plastic belt with a broken buckle. A thrift-shop suit with tickets to the North Division High School prom in the breast pocket and a dried boutonniere on the lapel. The flower, once a white rose, had thinned to pale parchment as fine as ash.

Mrs. Castellano stood in the doorway, watching him make a mess of her grandson's room. "I'm sorry," he said. "I'll put it all back now."

"No, no," she said, wiping her eyes. "I should have done this myself when he left. But I just couldn't."

Peter remade the bed, put the clothes on their hangers, and picked up the drawers and went to return them to the dresser. On the floor in the open bottom of the dresser, maybe where it had fallen from the bulletin board, lay a business card.

A cream-colored card. With green lettering.

The Riverside Veterans' Center.

Peter picked up the card and turned it over. On the back was the same spidery black handwriting and the same phone number as the card that Jimmy had hidden in his money belt.

Peter took out his own wallet. Not much in there.

He removed the cream-colored card with the green lettering that Lipsky had given him.

The same card.

He turned it over.

The same phone number.

Standing outside on her stoop, Peter thanked Mrs. Castellano very much for her time. He told her that he would call her to let her know what he found out. He reminded her of the number for his cell phone.

"I'm so glad you called now," she said. "I'll have a new number this time next week. You never would have found me." She pulled out a pen and wrote it down for him.

Peter looked at her.

She smiled brightly. "I'm moving into my sister's house," she said. "I worked at a bank for forty years, but when the FDIC took them over, my pension lost most of its value. My retirement savings dropped with the market. I haven't been able to find a new job. I refinanced my house five years ago when my sister needed surgery, and now the bank is calling in the note." She shrugged gracefully. "They're taking the house."

"I'm so sorry."

She waved a hand. "Oh, it's been a year coming," she said. "I've come to terms with it. Although it certainly made Felix quite furious when he came home. That horrible bank putting his nana out of her house."

"Is there something else you can do?"

"No." She put her hand on his arm. "At least I have a place to go," she said. "And I can get Social Security. Think of all those people without jobs, without savings, without any place to call home." She shook her head. "My husband would roll over in his grave with all these bank bailouts, these executives getting their bonuses, while hardworking people lose their homes and children go hungry."

"Do you need help moving?" Peter asked.

"Oh, no," she said. "I have family for that." Her grip was fierce. "You just find my Felix."

27

Lewis's tan Yukon with its tubular steel bumper was parked up the street from Dinah's place, with a clear view of the house. The Yukon was shut off, and the windows were cracked open a half-inch. Someone sitting in a car was easy to miss, but tailpipe exhaust or fogged windows would get noticed by anyone watching Dinah's house for more than a few minutes. This wasn't Lewis's first rodeo.

Peter stopped, leaned across the seat, and rolled down his passenger window. "Anything?" he said.

Lewis wore a thick down coat and a black watch cap. "Nothing." His breath steamed in the cold. "No dude with scars, no black SUV. I'm starting to think you made this motherfucker up."

"He didn't get past you, did he?"

Lewis gave him a look.

Peter grinned. "What about the alley?"

"Nino's there now. We trade off."

"Does Dinah know you're here?"

Lewis shook his head. It didn't seem to make him happy.

"I'm picking her up now," said Peter. "You can go home, get warm. Come back in the morning. I'll be parked out here all night."

"You owe me, motherfucker."

"Hey," said Peter. "I just stepped into this. It's not my fault you got pulled in."

"Uh-huh," said Lewis. "I know what you doing. But that ain't what I mean. Nino all banged up, and Ray out with a ruptured fucking testicle, thanks to you. And I got something going in four days. So if Ray not good to go by then, you gonna get drafted."

"We'll see," said Peter. "And thanks for this."

"Don't thank me yet, motherfucker."

When Peter pulled up, Dinah came down the steps of the new front porch. She wore her good wool coat with a yellow scarf. He hadn't really talked to her in a day and a half, and a lot had happened since then.

He got out to open the door for her. She stopped him on the curb.

"What happened to you?" She leaned in to examine the bruise on his face and touched it with cool, professional fingertips. Her breath was warm on his skin. It smelled like peppermint.

"A misunderstanding," said Peter.

She gave him a look, still leaning in close. "How does the other guy look?"

"Two of them, actually," said Peter, suppressing a smile. "We have a lot to talk about. But I have something to show you first. Should we go?"

She got in the truck and they drove toward Jimmy's apartment. Dinah rubbed her hands together. "I'm cold. Do you mind rolling your window up?"

"I can't," said Peter. He cranked up the heat. "The window's broken."

"I am so sorry." She shook her head. "This neighborhood is just sad. I have got to get out of here. Did they steal anything?"

"That's not it," he said. "Somebody shot at me."

"What?" Dinah was horrified. "Where? How?"

"It's okay," said Peter. "I've been shot at before." He didn't want to tell her he'd killed the man who'd shot at him. He didn't want to tell her about his latest meeting with the scarred man, either. "But I think I got someone's attention."

"Was it the man with the scars who shot at you?"

Peter shook his head. "No. But that's probably who sent the guy. I'm working on it."

He turned at Jimmy's block and found a parking spot. He pointed at the duplex house. "That's where Jimmy was staying. The keys from his pocket fit the door to the upstairs apartment."

Dinah watched the house through the glass. She didn't speak.

Peter watched the line of her jaw, the curve of her neck. The pulse of the vein beneath her skin. "We could go in if you want," he said. "I met his landlady. Jimmy told her he was going on a trip. He paid his rent three months in advance. He was looking for a Marine veteran who had gone missing."

Dinah put her hand to her mouth and turned to Peter.

For a brief moment, it was the face of a child who had been told a terrible truth of the grown-up world. But Dinah was an adult. She knew what it meant.

Peter said it anyway. "It wasn't suicide."

He saw the muscles in her jaw clench and knot. She grabbed the edges of the seat with her fists and pressed her feet to the floor as if she were setting herself against the waters of a flood. She closed her eyes, turned inward, and took a deep, shuddering breath.

Then she turned and looked Peter hard in the face. "Tell me everything you know."

He told her about meeting Miss Rosetta Phelps, about Mingus being Jimmy's dog, about searching Jimmy's apartment. He told her about the kid with the assault rifle and being grilled by Lipsky. He told her about going back to Lewis's building, and the fight with Nino and Ray, and how Lewis had promised he would watch her house.

"I don't believe it. Lewis said that?"

Peter nodded. "When you're a guy like Lewis, all you have is your word. Your own sense of honor."

"Lewis is a criminal," she said. "A criminal and a killer."

Jimmy was a killer. It was part of his job description. Peter was a killer, too, and now a criminal. He didn't bring that up. "Doesn't matter," he said. "Lewis will keep his word."

"Lewis will keep his word? You believe that?"

Peter nodded. "I do. In an uncertain world, honor is very important. Lewis knows that."

She looked skeptical.

"Lewis lives by a code," said Peter. "You remember how he wouldn't let Nino and Ray take your money? That's part of his code. He's been parked on your street, watching for the man with the scars. Even though I basically twisted his arm to get him there. That's part of his code, too."

Dinah shook her head. She was having trouble with the thought that Lewis might not be entirely bad.

Peter said, "It's an old idea, from a time before police and lawyers and contracts. When violence was an everyday occurrence. Living by your word was both a promise and a threat." He shrugged. "It still works for a certain kind of honorable criminal. And for soldiers." He gave her a small smile. "Marines, especially."

"Like Jimmy," she said, maybe beginning to understand. "Is that why he moved out?"

"I think so," said Peter. "He needed to stand on his own. I think that's why he started looking for this missing Marine, too."

He told her about sorting through Jimmy's things,

about finding the same yellow flier on the wall that was tucked into Jimmy's belt when he died, and about Felix Castellano and his grandmother.

"The Riverside Veterans' Center," she said. "How many of these cards do you have now?"

"Three," he said. "One from Jimmy's belt compartment. One from behind Felix's dresser. One that Lipsky gave me. And they all had the same phone number on the back. The same handwriting."

"And what does all this have to do with the man with the scars, and that money?"

"I don't know yet," he said. "But I'll find out."

"Oh, hell, yes," she said.

They climbed the steep, narrow steps to the apartment.

Peter stood just inside the door, the static jolting his brainstem, while Dinah prowled the room from corner to corner, trying to capture the last faint traces of her murdered husband.

She looked at the clean dishes neatly set out to dry, at the books arranged on their shelf, at the sagging chair where he had sat. She looked at the frayed rug and the cracked plaster walls and the narrow bed where he had slept. And the shell of anger and ferocity she had built slowly peeled away. What remained was utter sorrow.

She sat carefully on the bed, put her face in her hands, and cried.

Peter tried to make himself stand and watch. He had

already cried for his dead friend. He knew how much it hurt. It still hurt.

Finally he couldn't help himself. He sat on the bed beside her and put his hand on her shoulder. She folded herself into him. He put his arms around her. She buried her face in his chest. Her shoulders heaved.

She cried for her dead husband, and for doubting him.

She cried because she had thrown him out, and because he had gone without a fight.

She cried because she had believed he'd killed himself, and because he hadn't.

Her sobs were wrenching and violent, as if she could barely gather breath between them, as if something were dying, or being born.

After she was done, she wiped her eyes with a tissue taken from her shirtsleeve. She sighed and shook her head. "You got a lot more than you bargained for."

Peter didn't say anything. She tilted her head then and looked at him sideways. "Peter," she said. "Don't take this the wrong way, but how long has it been since you've showered?"

Peter looked at his hands. "It's been a few days," he said. "I've been busy. That's mostly the dog, by the way." It was embarrassing to blame his own stink on Mingus.

"Why have you been sleeping in your truck?"

He didn't want to explain it to her. "I'm not sleeping

in my truck," he said. "I'm sleeping in front of your house."

Her face held an expression he couldn't decipher. Her voice was gentle. "Why are you sleeping in front of my house?"

"To protect you," he said. "Because Jimmy can't."

There was a moment when neither of them said anything. He filled the silence. "I was planning to get a hotel room today," he said. "To shower. But I didn't have time. I need to do laundry, too."

The corners of her mouth twitched. She said, "If James were still alive, would you stay with him?"

No, he thought. Because I can't stay inside for more than twenty minutes before starting to scream. And I'm nearing my limit.

"Sure," he said.

"Well," said Dinah, "this is his apartment. James wouldn't mind. The rent is paid up, right? I think you should stay here. You can use his bathroom."

"Okay." Peter nodded again. "I will."

"No," Dinah said. "I mean right now. Really. Go take a shower."

She stood up and took Jimmy's bathrobe from the hook by the door, and held it out. It was far too big. Peter took it anyway.

The bathroom was cold, and it felt odd to take his clothes off. Like he was removing his second skin. His protection. He was naked and Dinah was in the next room, behind the thin veneer of a hollow-core door. It was disturbing and exhilarating at the same time.

But the water of the shower was delicious. It sluiced over his shoulders and down his back, as hot as it would go, relaxing the knotted muscles and driving the white static down to a hum. He felt his pores opening up, releasing the dirt and dried sweat and the smell of dog.

He rubbed the ancient dried-out bar of soap on his chest, down his legs and the crack of his ass. He wanted to be clean. The noise of the falling water was loud in the cheap fiberglass shower stall. It sounded just like the shower his father had installed in the basement when Peter was a kid. The memory eased the static.

He closed his eyes to wash his hair and stubbled beard with the cheap shampoo. He wanted to sit on the floor and wash his feet, between his toes. He wanted to lean back and fall asleep in there.

He couldn't help wondering what Dinah was doing in the other room.

He wondered if she thought about him, too.

Peter was not proud of himself.

But that wasn't the same as being able to stop himself.

He imagined her stepping into the bathroom and standing on the other side of the shower curtain. The water coming down, the steam rising.

He imagined her slipping out of her clothes. How she might part the shower curtain with her fingers and step inside. With him. Under the water.

He imagined how she would look, the sheen of her skin, the water beading up. The slope of her breasts, the gentle mound of her belly. The softness of hair, the slickness between her legs.

The taste of her lips.

He imagined how he would pick her up. He would lift her legs and raise her up and set her slickness down on him. Gently at first, up and down. Up and down, again and again, the strength of his arms made for this, for nothing else, not made for war or fighting in the street, no, not anything else but this, only this.

The heat in the water faded to cold. He opened his eyes. He must have nearly emptied the tank. The hot was gone.

He stepped out of the shower and toweled off, put on Jimmy's enormous bathrobe. His clothes were missing from the floor.

When he opened the bathroom door, she was gone.

His jeans were neatly folded on the bed, with his keys, wallet, and new phone. The folded shirt lay beside them.

Atop the shirt was the picture he'd been carrying in his pocket.

The picture of Jimmy.

28

The light was on at Lewis's place. Walking to the door, Peter looked up at the security camera. The door opened before he got there.

Lewis wore the same tilted smile, the world and its inhabitants a source of endless amusement. "You come to sign your ass up? Could make you some serious money. I know you need it."

"Come outside and we'll talk about it."

"Man, what I want to come out there for? It fucking November in fucking Wisconsin."

"Put on a coat."

Lewis looked at Peter a little closer. "Why don't you want to come in here? I know you ain't scared of me." The tilted smile grew wider and reached his eyes. "Oh, I get it. You don't like to be inside. Maybe you had too many of those door-knocks over there. Little too much house-to-house." He shook his head with genuine amusement. "This just get better and better. How bad?"

Peter wasn't going to talk about it. "Listen, how much would you make on this job you've got coming up?"

Lewis let it go. "Anywhere from fifty to three-fifty. 'Less we get real lucky."

"And what are the odds you make nothing?"

Lewis looked at him. As if to say, Man, who you think you talking to?

"Come on," said Peter. "If you don't even know what the payday is, your intel is incomplete. What if there's more resistance than you expect? Or some teller trips the silent alarm?"

Lewis smiled at that, too. "Robbing banks is for chumps."

Peter smiled back. "Isn't that where they keep the money?"

"Oh, there money all over, you know where to look," said Lewis. "I don't steal from nobody in a position to call the police. Takes all the fun out of it. But I do need another body. Ray's hurtin' bad. You in for a share?"

"I have a better idea. Let me buy you a beer and explain it to you."

"Have a beer right here." Lewis angled his head at the bar next door. "Ain't nobody listening."

"Outside is better," said Peter. He turned to get in his truck. "Come on."

Lewis shook his head. "Ain't riding in that damn antique," he said. "I be right behind you." The locks chirped on the Yukon.

* * *

Getting out at Kern Park off Humboldt, Lewis looked around at the empty parking area; the long, curving walkway; the big old trees looming skeletal and dark. He stood easily, unconcerned, the mountain lion ready for anything.

"You not gonna try and shoot me, are you? This be a nice quiet place for it."

Peter took two beers out of the little cooler he kept behind his seat. "Not right now," he said, popping the caps with the handle of his knife and handing Lewis a bottle. "Right now, I want to hire you."

Lewis raised his eyebrows and took a sip. Then tilted the bottle to look at the label. "This pretty good."

"Goose Island," said Peter. "Chicago."

Lewis nodded. "First place," he said, "I ain't for hire." He took another sip of beer. "Might discuss a limited partnership, though."

"Call it what you want," said Peter. "I don't care."

Lewis nodded again. "Tell me."

"It's a little hard to explain," said Peter. "But the pay is an eighty-twenty split after expenses. And it doesn't count the money I found at Dinah's, that's hers regardless."

"Twenty percent ain't enough for a guy with my résumé."

Peter snorted. "You don't have a résumé. But your end is eighty. Twenty goes to Dinah and the boys."

Lewis drank more beer without expression. "So what's your end?"

"Jimmy," said Peter. "I get the guy who killed Jimmy. And Dinah stays safe."

That was the most important part. Dinah. Dinah and the boys.

Lewis pointed the bottle at him. "You an idealist. I don't like idealists. They dangerous."

Peter shrugged. "Jimmy was my friend."

Lewis looked at him steadily. "You don't want money?"

"Past putting gas in that truck, I don't much care. Most of what I want, money can't buy."

Lewis watched Peter's face for another moment. Then nodded. "How much is the payout?"

Peter shook his head. "I don't know yet. So far, it's all on spec. I have all these pieces, but I don't know what they add up to. It already turned up serious money at Dinah's. Maybe that's all there is. But there could be more. A lot more."

"But I might be workin' for nothin'."

Peter looked at him. He figured Lewis for a career criminal who made his living with his brain, his nerve, and a shotgun. The only paycheck Lewis had ever gotten was from his time in the Army, and that was for killing people. He'd probably never had a straight job in his life.

Peter said, "Think of it as pro bono, with a possible upside. Good for your image. You can put it on your résumé."

Lewis snorted and stared out into the darkness of the park. But he didn't say no.

Peter let him think. The wind came up, whispering

through the tree branches and underbrush. It carried the fermented smell of the river and the cold flavor of the coming winter. Beer always tasted better in the wind.

Lewis turned to face him. His tilted smile wide. "What the hell," he said. "I'm in. Where we start?"

"Nothing heavy," said Peter. "At least not yet. Right now, we need to find a guy. All I have is a license plate. You know any cops?"

"I know a guy can run me a plate."

Peter told him the number. "I got a pen in the truck, you want to write it down."

"Don't need to," said Lewis.

Peter nodded. He hadn't needed to write it down, either.

"It's the Ford Excursion," he said. "The guy with the scars."

"That same guy from outside Dinah's house? Followed you to my place?"

"Same guy. Black, late thirties to mid-forties. Big but not huge. Scars on his cheeks, here." Peter put his fingers on his face. "Missing his right earlobe. Wears a Kangol cap and a black leather car coat, thinks he's Samuel L. Jackson."

"That ain't right, man. I'm Samuel L. Jackson."

"In your dreams. Anyway, the Ford's all torn up on the driver's side now. You might check the body shops."

"Why we want him?"

"I think he's the one who sent that kid to shoot me. And I think he's probably an explosives guy."

Lewis raised his eyebrows. "And why the fuck is that?"

"The scars, for one thing. And with the money under Dinah's porch? I found four chunks of C-4."

The tilted smile got as wide as Peter had yet seen it. "This ain't gonna be boring, I can tell already."

Peter clapped him on the shoulder. "That's why I need a guy with your résumé."

"Yeah, yeah. So tell me the rest of it."

"Jimmy didn't kill himself."

"No shit?"

"No shit. I think Jimmy took the money and the C-4 and hid it under Dinah's porch, and someone killed him for it. Made it look like suicide. Jimmy was looking for a young Marine gone missing. There's our explosives guy with the scars. And also the head of a hedge fund, but I don't know how he connects to anything."

"You just making this up as you go," said Lewis.

"Absolutely," said Peter. "But the scarred man keeps showing up. Somebody already tried to kill me once. I'm getting closer. Maybe someone else will take a run at me and we'll find a crack in this thing."

"You know that a seriously fucked-up thing to say, right?"

"Like you're so goddamn normal," said Peter. "Anyway, I'm hoping you can find this guy with the scars. Maybe he can help us connect the dots."

* * *

Peter went to the cooler for two more beers, then broached the next topic of conversation. "What about Nino and Ray? Are they gunning for me?"

Lewis shook his head. "They won't sign on to this thing, if that what you asking. Especially not for no pro fucking bono. But I don't think you got anything to worry about. Neither one of them got an ass-whipping in five years of crime like they got from you the other night, and they still hurting. Ray's balls are swollen up like grapefruit to hear him tell it, and Nino probably gonna need surgery on his trachea."

"I didn't start that fight, remember."

"I know it, and they know it, too. Anyway, they not so bad off. They been making noises about getting out for a while, but now I think they serious. I made them too damn much money. Nino got his eye on some land up north, spend the rest of his days drinking beer and fishing. Ray going back to Tulsa, he got a girl down there."

"But not you," said Peter.

Lewis moved his shoulders. "My number a little bigger than theirs."

"I can't see you retired," said Peter. "What would you do? Buy some apartment buildings and collect the rent every month? Drink yourself to death?"

Lewis looked off into the trees. "Build a house. On the water. In the islands."

"That's a much bigger number."

"Well," said Lewis. The tilted smile came back. "I got a new business partner. Just might win the jackpot."

The Man in the Black Canvas Chore Coat

"You don't want me in the basement?" said the tank truck driver, talking loud over the gravelly rattle of the big diesel. He had a bushy black beard that hung down over his oil-stained coveralls, and a green-and-gold-striped winter hat with the Packers G front and center.

"The tank is fine," said Midden. He stood on the parking strip in front of the house, illuminated by a single streetlight and the work lights of the tanker.

"It's a safety check," said the driver, tapping his clipboard. "I gotta do it. To make sure your oil tank is sound. The company requires it once a year for all tanks, and for new customers I really gotta. It's free."

Nothing is easy, thought Midden. "It's a new tank," he said. "We just had it installed." He reached for his wallet and began counting out bills. "It's two hundred gallons. I don't need a receipt. What's that, about a thousand bucks?"

The driver shook his head. "Sorry, man. Company rules. We had a tank with a rusted bottom three years ago; the driver pumped eight hundred gallons into the basement. That house had to be torn down. Your money isn't worth my job." He turned to walk back to his tanker.

Midden was very tired. “Please,” he said. “Hang on a minute. What will it take to make this work?”

The man with the clipboard had one foot on the running board. “It takes me inspecting that fuel tank in your basement. I seen too many bad installs and rusted bottoms and cracked fuel lines to take any man’s word for it.” He looked through the pale glow of the streetlights at the dark house with the siding falling off, the yard littered with fallen roof shingles. “And I’m starting to wonder what you’re doing that you don’t want me down there.”

Midden sighed. This was not the way he wanted this to go. He liked the guy. He liked the way the guy knew his job, the way he refused the money. Nobody refused the money. Plus Midden had never run the controls on one of those big tanker trucks. But he could figure it out.

“Okay,” said Midden. “Tell you what. The basement’s a mess. We’re renovating, and there are some structural problems. We just want some heat so we can stay warm while we work. But why don’t you get your hose run, and I’ll make a path to the tank. Before you start pumping, I’ll walk you down for a look.”

The man with the clipboard nodded. “Fair enough,” he said. “I appreciate it. It’ll only take a minute.” He unclipped the fill nozzle and walked slowly backward toward the house as the hose began to unspool from its reel.

Midden went through the splintered side door and

down the rotting basement stairs into the yellow light of a kerosene lantern. It hadn't seemed worth the effort getting the power turned on. He had just found the vacant house the day before. There were a great many to choose from.

There was no new oil tank.

Instead there were ten white plastic drums that had once held fifty gallons of pickles in their brine. Each drum would hold twenty gallons of fuel oil and get filled the rest of the way with fertilizer.

It would be easiest to steal a tanker from the company yard, but stealing an oil truck would definitely get noticed. Even the UPS trucks had GPS trackers on them now. And nobody sold bulk fuel oil anymore, not to a walk-in customer. You couldn't just show up with ten pickle barrels.

Boomer had wanted racing fuel originally, which was what McVeigh had used, but that was impossible now, too. And gas stations all had cameras. He'd considered kerosene or paint thinner, bought a gallon at a time, but that would have taken forever. Midden had used up his patience buying ten thousand pounds of fertilizer in fifty-pound bags. And time was getting short. Veterans Day was only two days away.

He saw the legs of the driver through the high foundation windows. It was hard work to pull that hose all the way to the back of the house. He wasn't quite there yet.

In truth, thought Midden, this way would make

things easier. He could put the empty drums in the van again and fill them right there, straight from the tanker. No heavy lifting.

But standing in the basement in the light of a lantern, thinking through each step as he always did, it weighed on him. It was almost too much to carry now.

It was one thing to kill a man in combat, to protect yourself. Or to kill a man who you knew would be a threat because of incompetence, like the man who had driven the van. He had proven himself unreliable. A danger.

But it was another thing entirely to kill an innocent man in cold blood. A man whose only fault was that he kept an evening appointment to fill an oil tank, and had the principles to do his job well. To not take the money.

It was wrong, Midden knew that. Midden had thought he'd done so many wrong things that it didn't matter anymore. That nothing mattered.

He wasn't sure that was true anymore.

He thought he might be starting to unravel.

He looked around the basement. The concrete blocks were cracked and buckling inward with the pressure of the soil. It smelled musty and damp. That basement leaked every time it rained, and had for years. Black mold climbed the walls. How anyone had lived in that house was beyond him. But it hadn't started out such a ruin. It had been like any other house once. Someone's pride and joy. Now it was at the edge of collapse, and its owners had fled.

Midden had killed more people than he could remember. More than he could count.

So what was one more? Just one more, he told himself.

Of course, it would be more than one, before they were done.

His path was laid long ago. He was committed to this course. He already knew what the end would be.

He took the target pistol from under his jacket and looked at it.

It was light in his hand, an assassin's weapon. The .22 had no stopping power, not unless the bullet went into the skull. Then it would bounce around inside like a Ping-Pong ball, turning the brain into scrambled eggs. It was a very efficient weapon. Little blood. Almost no mess.

He held the grip in his fist and put the barrel to his temple.

Just to see.

There were other ways, of course. He hadn't decided yet.

And he had work yet to finish.

He would not be unreliable.

He moved to the bottom of the stairs and waited for the driver.

PART 4

29

The next morning, Peter decided to risk the library to read the newspaper accounts about the murder of Skinner's wife.

It was a high-profile killing with a great deal of press but not, as it turned out, much information. Most of the discussion revolved around Martha Skinner herself, who was widely considered to be a saint and had used much of her considerable family fortune to fund her charitable works in the city.

The early articles were detailed and intent. It seemed as though every quote came from a friend of the deceased or the department spokesperson, who gave a thin account of the killing and repeated that the Milwaukee police were sparing no effort to find the killer. There was discussion of a task force to combat home invasions, but it turned out that home invasions were not such an epidemic, and perhaps a special team of investigators would be enough.

After the first few days, the articles moved off the front page, and the sparsity of information became more apparent. The MPD spokesperson continued to repeat that all possible leads would be followed, but that there were few clues, no apparent motive, and random killings were the most difficult to solve.

As the weeks passed, the articles became sparser yet, until they were just short status reports noting the lack of progress in the investigation. The final article was a few paragraphs noting the disbanding of the special team of investigators. The case was still officially open but unsolved.

On his second time through, Peter found something.

At the very end of an early article, there was a single statement, probably unauthorized, by a Detective Frank Zolot, who told the reporter that it was standard police procedure to consider members of the family as potential suspects until cleared.

But nothing else from Detective Zolot in the articles that followed.

Peter went to the Milwaukee police website, found the Criminal Investigations Division, and called the number.

"Hi, I'm trying to reach Detective Frank Zolot. Can you give me a phone number?"

"Hold, please."

The vague hush of electronic limbo. Then, "Zolot."

"Hi," said Peter. "I want to ask you about Martha Skinner."

"I can't comment on an open investigation. Call the

press office." Zolot's voice was flat and fading out toward the end, the receiver already headed back to the cradle.

"Wait," said Peter. "I'm not a reporter. My name is Peter. I have some information. I'd like to talk."

"I can't comment on an open investigation," Detective Zolot said again. But there was a different quality to the statement, a kind of attentive caution.

"Actually," said Peter, "I'm not really calling about Martha Skinner. It's about someone else. A friend of mine."

A pause. Peter could hear the noise of a busy office on the other end of the phone. People talking, the sound of hard-soled shoes on a wood floor. The distinctive sound of an old file cabinet drawer as it opened and closed.

"You know Sobelman's? Burger joint by Marquette?"

"No."

"Nineteenth and Saint Paul. Just south of the freeway, west of the river. Fifteen minutes."

"I'll find it," said Peter.

But the phone was already dead.

Sobelman's was in a restored corner building just south and west of downtown, between a packinghouse and a dry ice warehouse.

Peter could tell from the outside that the white static wasn't going to like it. Not enough windows. So he stood on the sidewalk, drinking in the smell of hamburgers that seeped through the closed door.

Good thing Mingus was locked in the back of the truck.

He turned to peer through the glass, wondering if the cop had beat him there. Then he heard a voice behind him, almost in his ear.

"You must be Peter." Detective Zolot's voice.

Peter moved to turn, but a meaty hand landed on his shoulder, and another encircled his elbow in a practiced grip. "Inside, pal. Past the bar."

The hand pushed him through the swinging door and kept him moving forward. Peter didn't resist. The voice in his ear said, "Don't worry, pal, I'm a police detective. We're just going someplace quiet."

It smelled even better inside. The place was full of happy eaters chowing on giant burgers, drinking Bloody Marys and beer. The clamor of conversation and the clatter of tableware were friendly and loud, the kind of place Peter used to like. Now he felt the walls close in, too many people and too few exits, with no sight lines to outside. He felt the clamps on his chest and sweat popping on his forehead.

"Someplace quiet" turned out to be the men's room. Zolot was a head taller than Peter, with the barely suppressed violence of an offensive lineman retired too early. Hair uncombed, jowls unshaven, a grizzly bear in the small space. But he moved with surprising grace as he frisked Peter expertly, missing nothing, all without a word. He glanced through Peter's wallet, noted Peter's flushed skin and shallow breath, then seamlessly turned Peter out of the men's room and down the hall to a service exit and out into the cold.

"Fuck's the matter with you?" he asked.

"I'm fine," said Peter. "I'd just rather be outside."

"We're outside," said Zolot, heading west on Saint Paul, the hand back on Peter's elbow. "So talk already."

Peter shook off the hand. "Tell me what you had on Jonathan Skinner and why you gave up."

It was a guess, but it felt right. And Zolot's silence confirmed it. They kept walking as Zolot stewed. Peter could feel the contained heat coming off the man, even in the crisp November air.

Finally Zolot spoke. "You said this was about someone else, pal. Tell me about the someone else."

"A friend of mine got killed," said Peter. "He had one of Skinner's company pens in his things. My friend was no investor, he worked as a part-time bartender. But it turned out that he had serious money hidden away, in cash. I can't find any other source for that money. Skinner's the only connection to it I can think of. I had a meeting with him—"

Zolot stopped walking. "You met with Skinner?"

"I told him I was an investor," said Peter. "I mentioned the cash and he got very strange. I'm guessing Skinner had something to do with my friend's death. And I'm looking for something to grab hold of."

Zolot stared into Peter's face. "What was he like, when things got strange?" The force of his attention was intense. Peter wouldn't want to be a suspect of any crime Zolot was investigating.

"You met him," asked Peter. "Charming as hell, right?

A million-dollar smile. Like you're his favorite person in the world. But when I mentioned the money it all fell away, just for a few seconds. Like a snake trying to decide if you were food. Then he threatened me and left as fast as he could."

Zolot grunted and kicked at a rock on the sidewalk. Turned and started walking again. Peter walked beside him.

"How was your friend killed?" asked Zolot.

"They said it was a suicide. They said he shot himself, once under the jaw. His wallet was still in his pocket. But he didn't do it, I know that. I know it. He had a lot to live for."

"What was your friend's name?"

"James Johnson. Jimmy. He died in Riverwest less than a month ago."

"I'll look him up." Zolot looked at Peter sideways, from the corner of his eye. "And who the fuck are you, pal?"

"Peter Ash. I was a Marine lieutenant. Jimmy was my sergeant."

They walked. The open sky felt good, calming the white static. Zolot's contained rage burned like an oil-field fire, fueled by something deep beneath the surface.

"I never could fucking stand those money guys," said Zolot. "It's like you're working for them personally, and they're in charge. Like they run the whole fucking world. And maybe they do, sort of, until they fuck the whole thing up and bring it all down around our ears. Even then it's not their fault. Nothing is ever their fucking fault. Even when they kill their wives. Because he killed her, pal. Skinner was the only one with any motive."

Peter didn't say anything. He didn't want to interrupt.

Zolot kept talking. "It was mostly her money, you know," he said. "Lake Capital? She was the heir to some Chicago meatpacking fortune. I met her once, at a first responders' widows and orphans benefit. She looked like the daughter of a meatpacker, I'll tell you. One of those square Polack faces, and she didn't starve herself. But there was something really lovely about her, you know? She really looked at you. She listened. And no pushover. There was some talk about her shutting down the fund back in 2006, at the height of the bubble."

"She could do that?"

"I'm telling you, it was her fucking seed money. A lot of people respected her. She was on the board of her family's company. If she pulled out, everyone else would follow." Zolot made a face. "We looked into all this at the time, my partner and I. But there was nothing substantial to tie Skinner to the murder. There was no hard evidence at all."

"So how do you know it was Skinner?"

"Lot of things pointed to random violence, burglary gone wrong." Zolot ticked the points off on his fingers. "She was killed in the house. The mailman and the cleaning lady both said the door was never locked during the day. She was killed with a butcher knife from the kitchen like a crime of opportunity, like maybe she walked in on the guy. The envelope of petty cash they kept in a kitchen drawer was gone."

Then he flicked his hand, dismissing those points as if shaking water off his fingers. "All bullshit designed to point us toward a random killing. The most important information is what we didn't find. No defensive wounds on the victim, so it was likely someone she knew. The knife was left on the scene, but it had no prints, nothing, like it was scrubbed clean. In fact, no unknown prints anywhere in the house. Just a few smears where prints had been wiped, or maybe he wore gloves. Footprints in the blood; there was a lot of blood. But the tread was new, the shoes probably never worn before, cheap-ass sneakers you could find anywhere. No other clues of any kind. Just this perfectly nice woman stabbed twenty-one times.

"That's what got my attention right there. A thief looking for a quick payday might stab someone once or twice, out of panic, maybe misplaced aggression. But twenty-one times? That's a fucking crime of passion. That's a killer who knows his victim, pal. Or a killer who really fucking likes it."

Peter thought of the reptilian look that had flashed across Skinner's face. But he didn't want to interrupt. Zolot kept talking like he'd been waiting to get this off his chest for years.

"So we went deeper on the husband," he said. "Standard practice, anyway. The killer's almost always known to the victim, a family member or friend. We talked to Skinner's secretary. She said he was in the office all day, meetings and calls. He didn't even go to lunch. I saw the call logs, I talked to the people in the meetings. The man was alibied up the ass, like he'd done it on purpose. I even went through his closet, looking for blood traces on his clothes. Nothing. I have no idea how he did it."

"He's sleeping with his secretary," said Peter. "She might have lied for him."

"My old partner interviewed her," said Zolot. "So I don't know. He could have had time. But it doesn't matter, he killed her, I know it. I fucking know it. I knew it even before the captain called me to shut it down. My last conversation with Skinner, he shook my hand and he thanked me for my time. Said I know it isn't personal, I know you have to exhaust all avenues, et cetera, et cetera, with that charming fucking charm of his. And I could tell that he knew that I knew. He just smiled at me, and it was like he'd told me himself, that shit-eating grin was his fucking confession."

Zolot shook his head. "A lot of cops have a hobby case, something you couldn't solve, something you can't quite shake. This was going to be my hobby case. I was going to catch that cocksucker. But the captain called me in and told me word had come down, the case was over. Officially open but forever unsolved."

"And that's it? You let it go?" Peter couldn't see Zolot, this furious bear of a cop, letting anything go.

"Hey, listen, I'm no fucking angel. Twenty years on the job, I've crossed the line a few times. I get results so they let things go. But this time the captain told me to sit down and shut up or my past would come back to haunt me. I'd lose my pension, everything. As it is, they transferred me to fucking District Five. The shitheap."

Peter could practically hear the man grinding his teeth.

"My old partner liked financial crimes. He was made for that rarefied air. Very smooth, no ruffled feathers, he knew how to finesse those high-fliers. Nobody had to tell him to lay off the bigwigs. I always figured he'd retire early and go into corporate security, where the money is." He shook his head. "Not me, though. No way. Give me a good hatchet murder any day. I can't stand those fucking money guys. Some sociologist did a study, did you hear about this? There are four times as many psychopaths in finance as in the general population. About the same percentage as in prisons. And these are supposed to be the fucking bastions of our society, the bankers and financiers."

Zolot had taken them in a loop. They were back at Sobelman's, walking up to Peter's truck.

"I don't know how Skinner did it. It was the perfect fucking crime, except he never managed to get anyone else arrested for it. The best way to get away with murder, if you want to know, is find some other poor son of a bitch to take the rap. But the man killed his wife. Personally. And I'm pretty sure he's done a lot more than that. The fucking thing of it is, he made money when his wife died. You know what selling short is?"

Peter did, but he wanted to hear Zolot tell it. "No."

"Selling short is like a bet that the value of something

will drop. My old partner could explain the details, I'm just a working cop. But basically that fucker used some proxy buyers with a bullshit derivative product to sell her family company short. Legal but barely. Derivatives weren't regulated. Apparently there was some expectation that she'd take over as chairman. When she died, the stock dropped, and Skinner made another hundred million."

"I thought you weren't supposed to do that."

Zolot gave him a look. "Are you supposed to? No. Can you? In about a hundred different ways. And did I mention he inherited a big chunk of her wealth?"

Jesus, thought Peter. "So, any advice?"

"Yeah. Don't let him come up behind you with something pointy. I would guess he's capable of anything, but you'll never catch him at it."

"Shoot first, is what you're telling me."

Zolot flashed a ferocious grin. "Who, me? I never said that."

The truck shifted on its springs as the dog moved in the back, hearing Peter's voice.

Zolot peered speculatively at Peter's rocking Chevy. "What you got in there, a fucking water buffalo?"

"Listen," said Peter. "Two questions. One, if I get close to something, you want in?"

The heat of rage and violence came off the man in a wave. The grin got wider.

"I thought you'd never ask. What's your second question?"

Peter said, "Who's your old partner?"

30

The Riverside Veterans' Center looked different in the daylight. The masonry shell of the building was badly damaged. The cream-colored brick was cracked and bulging in lumpy waves as it slowly separated from the structure beneath. Chalky white stains cascaded down from the parapets, signs of water leaking through the caps or the roof. Someone would have to take the veneer apart brick by brick to get it right. Do that or tear the whole building down.

But the paint was fresh on the veterans' center's windows, and Josie, the helicopter pilot with the ponytail and a different pair of paint-spattered jeans, was cleaning the glass with a mop and a squeegee. Bare wet hands on a cold November day, and intent on her work.

Peter said, "Can I give you a hand with that?"

She looked over her shoulder. "Just like the Marines," she said. "Showing up when the tough job is done. This is my last window."

"What about lunch?" he asked. "Have you eaten yet? I'm buying."

She smiled. "Let me buy you lunch. There's a pot of chili on the stove inside." She watched his eyes. "We can haul some chairs out here if you like. Have a picnic."

Peter took a breath. "Thanks. But I'll come inside. You were going to give me the tour."

"Yes, I was." She picked up her bucket and tossed the dirty wash water into the street. "By the way, the lunch won't be free," she said. "I'll be demanding some work hours out of you down the road."

Peter opened the door for her. "I'll do what I can."

Inside, Peter saw the man with the shaved head and long beard she called Cas sitting at the same desk, typing furiously into his laptop. "Is he always here?"

"He lives here," Josie said. "I'm not here all the time, but I don't think he's left the building for more than a few hours since he showed up a few months ago."

"What's he writing, a book?"

"I asked him." She smiled. "He called it a manifesto."

"That doesn't sound good. What's it about?"

She shook her head. "I've never seen it. He's pissed off about the financial crisis, how the banks broke the economy. He's hard to follow. I gave up talking to him about it. I wouldn't worry about him. I think his meds are pretty strong."

Walking toward the back hall, Peter's eyes caught the swirling grain of the unfinished plywood. His chest began to tighten immediately.

She must have seen something in his face. "Why don't you go sit by the front windows?" she said. "The afternoon light is really great. And I'll get us some chili. You want jalapeños and cheese?"

"Yes, ma'am."

She was right, it was better by the windows, although he could still hear the clacking of the keys on Cas's laptop. The chili was spicy, full of flavor, and Josie had a way of looking at him that made him feel like she could see something inside of him. Maybe something not quite evident to Peter himself.

He really wanted for her not to be involved with this thing.

"You coming to the march tomorrow?" She had a smear of chili on the corner of her mouth. He wanted to reach out and wipe it off, but he didn't.

"What march?"

"Duh," she said. "Veterans Day. There's a march to the War Memorial. We're all going. The center will be closed up for the day. We start at Veterans Park at ten, it goes until two. There's gonna be a polka band and bratwurst and everything." Her grin made her look fifteen years old. "You should come. It'll be awesome."

"Tomorrow's busy," he said. "But I'll do my best. Gosh. Polka music and bratwurst."

"And everything." She punched him in the arm. "Don't make fun."

"Never," he said, rubbing his biceps. "Listen, I wanted

to ask you something. You remember about my friend Jimmy?"

"Who killed himself." She nodded, serious now.

"Yeah. Well. I think he was hanging around with another guy. A black guy, with scars on his face, missing one earlobe. Does that ring a bell?"

"That sounds like Boomer. Kind of a loudmouth. He was friends with Cas, they used to sit and talk."

"Was? He doesn't come around anymore?"

She shook her head. "Boomer claimed somebody stole something out of our lockers. He ran around yelling at people, starting fights. But he never would tell me what was taken. I had to kick him out. He was being an asshole."

"You have lockers?"

"Sure," she said. "Some of our guys are homeless, and they need a place to keep their stuff. I roughed some boxes together out of scrap lumber and cheap padlocks. Not super-secure."

He stood up. "I think I'm ready for that tour."

"Well, don't get your hopes up," she said. "It's not much."

The white static roiled up when Peter came to the plywood wall, but he pushed it down and focused on his breathing. The plywood hall opened into a makeshift living space. There was an improvised kitchen on one side, a dented fridge, an old electric stove, and a few secondhand cabinets. Then two rows of bunks and footlockers, made of plywood and two-by-fours, and at the far end of the room two doors. On the side wall was a cheap hollow-core door. On the back wall was a giant iron door, much older and heavier, crusted with rust flakes.

Josie waved at the cheap door. "Bathrooms through there, again, not much, we could really use some help with those. You know anything about plumbing?"

"Enough," he said. "What about that door? That big iron monster?"

"No idea," she said cheerfully. "Although we might have to get it open one of these days. I think we're going to need to expand."

"How are you funding this place?"

"Funding?" she said. "What funding? I walk around and knock on doors and ask for donations. We found the couches on the curb. I talked an appliance repairman out of the fridge and stove. Sometimes I buy food with my combat pay. But when the cold weather comes we'll get a lot more guys. We'll be stacking them like cordwood."

"What about rent? Construction, permits, all that."

She laughed at him. "You don't get it. There are no permits. We're completely under the radar. The building's owner walked away from it, I can't even find who owns the place. The Health Department doesn't even know we're here."

"It's a squat? The whole place is a squat?" Although occupying an abandoned building was definitely one way to keep the rent down.

She shrugged. "Fuck 'em. We're doing real work here.

Besides, it's always better to beg forgiveness than ask permission."

He could picture her behind the stick in a flight suit and helmet, eyes hidden behind dark glasses, cutting the hard contours of the Afghan mountains. He thought she must have been very good at her job.

"What about the neighbors? Nobody wondered who you guys were?"

"That resale shop across the street called the cops on us about four months ago. We hadn't gotten all that organized yet. The city sent some guy who came in and looked around. He was pretty nice, actually. He said not to worry about permits and permissions. Said if I was serious about helping veterans, just put up a sign outside, start doing the job. Fix the place up like we were the real thing. If the building's owner came forward, deal with that when it happened. He even came back a week later with business cards for us."

"He bought you business cards?"

She shrugged. "Someone left them by the door, I figured it was him. He seemed to want to help. Like I said, he was a nice guy."

"Do you remember his name?"

"I only met him once. Dan? Dan something, from the city."

Or maybe Sam, thought Peter.

"Tall and skinny?" he asked. "Wearing a really nice suit?"

"I guess," she said. "Clothes aren't really what I look for in a guy."

Either she wasn't part of this, thought Peter, or she was a really good actress.

She said, "Hey, after the march tomorrow? Some of us are going to the Landmark. Shoot some pool, have some beers, tell some stories. You want to come?"

"I'd love to. Really. But I have kind of a busy day tomorrow. Can I let you know?"

31

Crossing the street from the veterans' center, he saw the tan Yukon parked at the curb, Lewis in the shadows, leaning against Peter's truck. Leaning without leaning, ready to move at any time, but looking as still and patient as if he'd spent a week waiting, and was ready to spend a month more.

"Time to make the doughnuts." Lewis wore his black suede jacket, but no hat. If he felt the cold of the wind, it didn't show. "Found your black Ford. An Excursion, all chewed up on the driver's side. Put a GPS beacon under the back bumper. Find it again whenever you want."

Peter raised his eyebrows. "GPS beacon?"

"Had it lying around," said Lewis. "Syncs to my phone."

"Tell me."

"Called in a favor and had a guy look up the plate. Registered to a black Ford Excursion owned by some guy in West Bend. Bernard Sands, retired dentist, never even had a parking ticket. Living in Florida, planning to put the house on the market in the spring."

"You talked to him?"

"Yep. Told ol' Bernie I was an insurance broker, trying to save him a few bucks. He won't do business with a brother, though. Anyway, I drove to West Bend. House closed up tighter than a frog's ass, that Ford locked in the garage. But there's a different plate on Bernie's bumper. That plate registered to James R. Bond, in Milwaukee."

"James R. Bond?"

Lewis nodded. "Not his real name. Doesn't exist anywhere else. Got no credit cards, owns no property, no Social Security number. No criminal record. No James R. Bond with that date of birth found in any open state or federal database."

Peter looked at him. "I thought you were some kind of armed robber or something."

Lewis smiled his tilted smile and put a little extra street in his voice. "Maybe I is, maybe I ain't. But a man can't make no kind of living these days without a computer."

"So how'd you find that Ford?"

"Drove around. Kept my eyes open. Finally got lucky and found it parked. Stuck my GPS on it. Haven't laid eyes on Mr. James R. Bond. But that Ford ain't moved since I found it."

"So where is it?"

Lewis's eyes gleamed. He was clearly enjoying himself. "You want to know where it is?"

"Yes, Lewis, I do. Where's the fucking Ford?"

"Parked around the corner."

"Jesus H. Christ."

"So you gonna sit on it, or am I?"

Peter looked at his watch. He had something else he wanted to do, and the timing was important. "How good is that GPS?"

"Good enough. My phone'll let me know if that Ford starts moving. And where it goes."

"Okay." Peter nodded at Lewis's Yukon with its elaborate tubular steel bumper. "Are you legally connected to that truck?"

Lewis eyed Peter suspiciously. "It's my damn truck," he said. "Why you asking?"

"I'm asking if the plate and registration have your name on them. If it could be traced back to you if something happened."

"Nothing gonna happen to that truck," said Lewis. "That's a police special, bought at auction. Cop engine, cop suspension, cop tires. I love that damn truck."

"You've seen my truck," said Peter. "It's a classic, but not exactly tactical."

"No shit, jarhead. But you ain't driving my truck."

"Hey, that's fine," said Peter. "You can drive if you want. All you had to do was ask."

Lewis gave him a look.

"It'll be fine," said Peter. "Really. But first I need someone to take care of the dog."

"What, you got one of those little toy poodles? Won't it fit in your purse?"

"You'll like him." Peter walked around to the mahogany cargo box, taking out his keys. "You're not carrying a hamburger in your pocket, are you?"

"Man, I don't like dogs."

Peter turned the key and unlatched the cargo box door. Lewis backed away the whole time. Mingus punched the door open with his nose and launched himself out of the box like a guided missile. He landed four feet from Lewis at full stop, crouched, growling.

"What the fuck!" Lewis had bent his knees and brought up his hands automatically.

The growl ramped up past tank-engine levels as Mingus showed the serrations of his teeth. He had a lot of teeth.

Lewis slowly reached behind him for the Glock tucked into his belt.

"Better not," said Peter, enjoying the moment. "He's a lot faster than you."

Lewis stilled his hands, eyeing the animal. "What the fuck kind of dog is this?"

Peter smiled. "His name is Mingus. He was Jimmy's dog. I kind of inherited him. But he doesn't listen to me. He pretty much does what he wants."

"You jarheads are fucking crazy." Lewis was pinned in place by that growl.

"Mingus?" The dog cocked an ear back, willing to listen, but kept his focus totally on Lewis. "You ready for some dinner?"

Mingus came out of his crouch, licked his chops, then

yawned, showing fangs like a maniac's knife collection, bright with saliva under the streetlight. He stretched, then trotted around and jumped effortlessly through the open window of Peter's truck.

Lewis had his breathing under control. "This is why I don't fucking like dogs."

"Why don't you follow me to Dinah's house. But stay in your truck when we get there," Peter said. "She's going to be mad enough at me without her seeing your ugly ass."

"You want me to what?"

Dinah stood in her open doorway, blocking access to the house, a look of horror on her face.

Mingus sat on Peter's foot, panting happily, his teeth gleaming in the dim porch light. Peter realized that this was the first time Dinah had seen the dog without the rope-and-stick contraption. The dog looked less ridiculous without it. And more dangerous.

"It's just for one night," said Peter. "Maybe two. I brought his food."

"Peter, that dog terrorized this neighborhood for weeks."

"I think he was just hungry," said Peter. "He's actually a nice dog. Very protective."

"Peter, if you think for one minute—"

"Mom, who is it?" Charlie came to his mom at the open door. Then he saw Peter and the dog. "Mingus!"

He pushed past his mother, who grabbed for his arm and missed. The boy dropped to his knees and hugged the dog, who washed the boy's face thoroughly with his wet slab of a tongue.

"He smells like strawberries," said Charlie. "You gave him a bath."

Dinah's glare could have started a fire. "Peter."

Little Miles wandered over. "Hello, Mr. Mingus," he said, and put out a hand to the dog, knuckles up like Peter had shown him. The dog licked his way up the boy's arm, cleaning off what looked like spaghetti sauce. Miles giggled. Dogs always liked little kids. They tasted like sweat and table scraps.

Dinah sighed. It was the sound of a mother who knows when to give in.

"You better be the one to feed him," said Peter. "So he knows you're in charge."

She gave him the stinkeye. "It didn't work with you."

Peter gave her his most winning smile. "One more thing," he said. And held out the chrome .32 he'd taken off the scarred man.

"No, no." She took a step away.

"The safety is here." He showed her. "On, off. Point and shoot." He held it out again. "Take it, Dinah. Just in case."

She shook her head but opened her hand. Peter put the gun in her palm.

She held it out from her body like it might explode. "Lieutenant Ash." The muscles worked in her jaw.

"I'll be back," he said. "I promise."

She looked at the boys, who were busy with the dog, then at Peter. She reached across the space between them and tapped him hard on the chest with a pointing finger.

"You had damn well better."

32

The thin November light was fading, night coming earlier as winter came on. Peter and Lewis sat in the Yukon, waiting.

Through yet another Web search, Peter had found a newspaper article about Skinner's house in Fox Point, three suburbs north of the city. It had forested lots, narrow curving roads, and a distinct lack of streetlights. The most expensive area was between Lake Drive and Lake Michigan.

Skinner's place was on the lake.

They were parked on the verge, where they could watch both the road and the house through the thin screen of leafless trees. Although "house" didn't quite describe the place. It had wings, like a museum. Dinah's little cottage would fit inside it ten times. Maybe twenty. From the road, it was hard to know how big the place really was.

It looked like some kind of castle. Not a storybook castle with towers and turrets, but more like a Norman keep, high stone walls with tall, narrow windows and minimal plantings. It looked like a fortress with a six-car garage.

But Peter knew from the article the house was only a few years old. New construction being what it was, the stone likely was a thin veneer over particleboard and drywall. Even if he didn't want to break a window or pry open a door, he could get inside with just a crowbar and hand sledge. Most people would be appalled at how easy it was to break into a house. Especially if you didn't care about making noise.

Lewis said, "You think he's gonna tell you anything?"

Peter shrugged. "This guy faced down the cops over killing his wife, and the SEC over securities fraud. He's not going to get scared by a couple of guys knocking on his door. But if we get up his nose we might break something loose, get something in motion."

"We not just a couple of guys," said Lewis. He smiled his tilted smile and put some street in his voice. "We sho 'nuff not the po-lice. An' we def'ny not the SEC." The smile got wider. "We can apply leverage they can't."

Even sitting still, he conveyed the impression of contained power, the mountain lion not quite at rest.

Peter still wasn't quite sure what to make of Lewis. He'd been a soldier but was now a successful criminal. He knew his way around computers well enough to search state and federal databases. And with his mention of the SEC, Peter thought maybe he knew something about finance, too.

"You know what the SEC is, don't you?" asked Peter.

"Securities and Exchange Commission," said Lewis. "I gotta explain why the repeal of the Glass-Steagall Act led to the banking crisis of 2008?"

"Please, don't," said Peter, who had followed the financial crisis and its aftermath from a war zone and was now thoroughly sick of the whole thing. "But why are you interested?"

"Modern criminal needs to know. The financial system's designed to favor established capital. Investment banks, hedge funds. Corporations. They in business to hoover money out of the pockets of small investors like me. You want to keep your hard-earned green, you better know how this shit work."

"That doesn't explain your interest in Glass-Steagall," said Peter.

Lewis smiled his tilted smile. "You want to be good at your work, you study up, right? Some of these finance guys are the biggest fucking thieves out there." He shrugged. "So it's educational."

Peter looked at him. "You're not who I expected you to be."

"Nobody is," said Lewis. His face was unreadable in the dim light. "Anyway, I get interested in shit. Man can't have a hobby?"

Peter grinned at that. "Well," he said. "We can definitely apply some leverage."

Lewis tilted his chin at the road ahead. "Here comes your guy. Home from the salt mines." He shifted the Yukon into drive.

Skinner's deep blue sedan coasted toward them on the smooth asphalt road. Its engine carried just the hint of a growl.

"You know what kind of car that is?" asked Peter.

Lewis leaned forward and raised his eyebrows. "I believe that a Bentley," he said. "Nice ride. About three fifty new."

"Three hundred and fifty thousand?"

"Yup. And the steering wheel ain't even solid gold."

The deep blue sedan turned up the long driveway.

"Get up behind him," said Peter. "Give him a good bump before he gets up to the house."

Lewis goosed the gas and the Yukon leaped forward. "Bumping a Bentley like punching the *Mona Lisa*, man. Maybe I just rev the engine up loud and scare him."

"Pussy," said Peter, one hand on the oh-shit handle and the other clamped to his armrest. The needle was at fifty and climbing fast.

They made the turn into Skinner's driveway at speed, the Yukon's police suspension gobbling up the bumps on the curve. Grinning widely, Lewis kept his foot down and the deep blue sedan got closer and closer until the Yukon hit with a crunch that Peter felt in his bones.

The sedan lurched forward and the whole back end accordioned up into scrap metal and waste plastic. Lewis stood on the brake and the Yukon stopped like it was nailed to the asphalt.

Peter popped his seat belt, stepped out, and walked behind the sedan to the driver's side, aware of Lewis a few steps to his left, consciously or not keeping some distance between them to present a smaller target, as if this was a checkpoint stop.

Through the sedan windows, Peter could see the cloud of deployed air bags collapsing now as the driver pushed them down and away.

Then the sedan door opened and Skinner levered himself out, shaking and white.

"Sorry, the gas pedal stuck," said Peter. "We need to talk. Remember me?"

Skinner glared at him, mouth a red slash in the pale, aristocratic face. Peter thought the man was in shock, maybe banged up a little, but that wasn't it. He was furious.

"I know who the fuck you are," said Skinner. His thin lips parted, showing bright white teeth. Something ancient and reptilian peering through his eyes. "I know exactly who you are."

Peter wanted to hit him in the face as hard as he could. Instead he said, "You need to tell me about the cash. Four hundred thousand dollars. Where did it come from?"

"You came to my house," said Skinner. The last word was a grunt. "My *house*. I'm going to erase you. Take everything you are. Your woman. The children."

Peter took a step and slapped Skinner on the face. His hand was open, but it was still hard enough to rock the man back.

"Where did the money come from? Why was James Johnson killed?"

Skinner's smile was as cold as death. The red mark of Peter's hand slowly emerged on his pale face. "I'm so glad you did that," he said.

He was quick. He reached under his suit coat like a striking snake, brought out a flat automatic pistol, and lifted his other hand to cup the butt in his palm.

He looked like he knew what he was doing.

Peter felt the adrenaline surge, the taste of copper in his mouth. But he didn't react. Hoping Skinner would say something he shouldn't.

Skinner's hands were steady. "I have four acres here," he said. His voice was conversational, but his tongue was flicking the edges of his lips. "I could bury you in my backyard. Under the garden. I just had it tilled. The ground is nice and soft."

"But you'd rather use a knife, right?" said Peter. "Like you killed your wife? It's so much more personal that way. And you enjoyed it, didn't you?"

Skinner's face flushed pink. But he didn't answer.

"Why don't you tell me about the four hundred thousand? Did you kill James Johnson, or was it the man with the scars?"

Skinner's smile was genuine and full of pleasure. "You really have no idea about anything, do you? You're merely a tool. Put to use by those farther up the evolutionary ladder."

"Educate me," said Peter. "Tell me how smart you are."

"I honestly don't think you'd understand," said

Skinner. "This is so far above your level." His eyes shifted to Lewis, then back to Peter. In the distance, the faint, thin sound of a siren lifted above the cold wind. Skinner's knuckle whitened as he increased pressure on the trigger.

Lewis moved so fast he was just a flicker, reaching in to pluck the flat automatic pistol from Skinner's hands. There was a soft crunch as Skinner's finger broke, caught for a moment in the trigger guard.

Then Lewis was two steps away again, the gun held negligently down at his side.

"Time to go," he said. "Cops are coming. Either your man here dialed nine-one-one or the Bentley called in the accident."

Skinner was pale with rage, a peculiar glitter in his eye. He didn't even seem to notice his broken finger. Again Peter felt that powerful urge to do him permanent damage. There was something primitive about it, like the urge to kill a snake. Snakes had a certain *wrongness* to them, the flickering tongue, that sinuous slither. Skinner had a different kind of wrongness. An emptiness in the eyes. An utter lack of regard for anyone other than himself. In ordinary moments he could hide it, could put on his charming act. But not now.

Lewis climbed into the Yukon. The tubular steel bumper wore deep blue paint on its edges but was otherwise unharmed.

"Get in the truck," he said, leaning across to push open the passenger door. "I'm not waiting."

Peter took four long strides and reached for the door. Before he was fully in his seat, Lewis had the pedal down.

They took the first curve fast, but Lewis eased off as soon as he found a side road. Once they were heading away from Skinner's house on a leisurely trajectory designed not to intersect with main roads or police cars, Lewis took out a handkerchief and wiped down the gun. Then threw it out the window and into the trees.

"I don't like that he mentioned a woman," said Peter. "And children."

"Your woman," said Lewis, eyes carefully on the road. "Is what he said."

"She's not my woman," said Peter. "We've had this conversation."

"Whatever," said Lewis. "But we got to get them out of that house, somewhere away."

"We will," said Peter. Then, "I don't like how he didn't threaten us with his lawyer."

"Yeah," said Lewis. "He got something going on. You want me in on this, you gotta tell me the whole thing."

"We need to get to that black Ford. I'll buy you a burger on the way. This might be a long night."

Peter kept talking as the Yukon wove a crooked path through the suburbs, back toward the city.

The Man in the Black Canvas Chore Coat

Midden backed the white Dodge van to within a few feet of the loading dock. The van wasn't tall enough to mate with the dock directly. They would have to use a plank ramp to get the drums inside.

The new truck would be the right height, thought Midden. Loading it would be much easier on the back.

Although not on the mind.

Midden couldn't rid himself of what they had planned. It was bothering him.

He reminded himself that he was committed.

Boomer's Ford was parked by the main entrance, all scraped up on the driver's side, the front bumper torn loose and hanging. Midden didn't want to know how it happened. Boomer would surely have an excuse. The man was getting less reliable. And now he was late.

Midden got out of the van and walked the few steps to the street, looking for pedestrians. Looking for Boomer in the new truck. There was nobody out in the cold and the wind.

He looked up through the bare tree branches. He'd never noticed before how the big old trunks stayed still while the tips of the branches whipped around in the weather. It could make you dizzy, watching. He'd forgotten how beautiful November could be in the Midwest.

He walked back to the loading dock. Fallen leaves crunched under his boots. He reached behind the broken brick for the key to the padlock. It was a good lock. He might take it with him when this was done.

Jesus, Midden thought. When this was done, he could buy as many locks as he would ever need.

Part of him would always be the farm kid in secondhand clothes, up to his elbows in thirdhand farming equipment, just trying to keep things running. Setting aside old parts against the day he might need them again. How his father had been. It wasn't a bad way to view the world.

That wasn't what he was doing now, though. Fixing things.

He was doing the opposite.

He looked at his watch. Boomer was late. Midden didn't want to roll up the door until he got here. Boomer was supposed to get the hand truck. Twenty gallons of fuel oil sloshing around in a fifty-gallon plastic pickle barrel was no picnic to move, even on a level surface. Midden doubted Boomer had remembered.

It bothered him. You had to be able to count on your team.

Midden told himself that he wasn't having second thoughts. He'd done many things he wasn't proud of. A few things that haunted him. This would be just one more. The paycheck would let him get out of this life forever.

Only the memories would remain.

There wasn't much he could do about that.

He was ready for it to be over.

He'd go away somewhere. Somewhere out in the country, in the middle of nowhere. Mountains. Trees. No unreliable people.

Maybe that would end the dreams, the thoughts he couldn't escape. But he doubted it. Even now, all he had to do was close his eyes to imagine it. The rising ball of black smoke and orange flame. The smell of burning bodies.

He heard engine noise, getting louder. He turned back toward the street and saw a Mitsubishi box truck coming up the block. The kind with the windshield right up front, easy to maneuver through these old neighborhoods. Boomer looked at him through the glass, his face like a punching bag.

Definitely less reliable.

Midden walked over as the truck came to a stop. "What happened?"

"That fucking jarhead blindsided me." He sounded like he had a mouthful of marbles. Maybe his jaw was broken.

"Tell me you didn't kill the man. Or put him in the hospital. We can use him."

Boomer's ruined face twisted with anger. "I was just trying to keep an eye on him. But I was lucky to make it out of there. I wrecked my rig doing it."

Midden found that he wanted to meet the Marine. Point of fact, he might need to, if this thing was going to get done at all.

"You got the hand truck?"

"Yeah. Let's get this shit moved."

They had the fertilizer. They had the fuel oil. They had the blasting caps. But they still needed the plastic. Everything pointed to the Marine.

But Midden would make sure it worked.

He needed to be done with all of this.

He wasn't sure he could make it much longer.

He was tired of those dreams.

33

Peter saw the black Ford SUV. It was still parked on the block behind the veterans' center, in front of an ancient crumbling brick warehouse complete with a loading dock for trucks and its own railroad siding for freight car access. Heavy goods had gone in and out of that building for years. But now the steel rails were gone, maybe stolen for salvage, leaving the creosoted timbers loose in their gravel beds and rotting from the inside out. Urban renewal in this part of town was clearly a hit-or-miss thing.

A plain white Mitsubishi box truck was parked at the loading dock, the kind with the engine under the driver's compartment and the big windshield out front. It was big enough for cargo but small enough to thread through the narrow city streets. There was no logo on the truck or the cargo box.

Lewis parked the Yukon at a hydrant with a view of the Ford. The Yukon's idle was so quiet that the truck might not even have been running, but for a subtle vibration that carried though the frame into the seats. Not like Peter's truck. Peter's seats weren't heated, either.

For two hours they watched as the light faded to twilight, then full night. Peter looked up and down the narrow street. On one side was the four-story brick warehouse built almost right up to the sidewalk. It had rusting security grates over the windows to discourage thieves and squatters. The other side was packed with narrow old houses, with no driveways in sight. Cars lined both curbs.

Lewis checked the GPS on his phone when they arrived. The Ford hadn't moved since he'd found it earlier that day. Despite all the activity from the houses, the warehouse remained quiet and dark.

"This could just be a convenient place to park," said Peter. They'd talked this through several times already. "Our guy could be anywhere in a couple of blocks. The parking's bad all around here."

Lewis had been on his laptop since they'd gotten there, looking up the owners of the houses. Most of them were owned by small companies, probably landlords, so that didn't tell them anything. The scarred man could be renting any one of them. Lewis shut his computer and looked at Peter. "That big ol' warehouse is owned by a giant holding company stuck in court for the last three and a half years," he said. "Our guy could be living there, too, 'cause nobody paying attention."

Peter was impressed. "Data skills, too," he said. "Man,

I'd hate to see your hourly rate. Good thing you're working pro bono on this."

"This ain't pro bono, jarhead. This eighty percent less expenses."

"I'm glad you're keeping a positive attitude."

"That glass always half full."

"So what's next, partner? We going to sit here all night or what?"

Lewis smiled his tilted smile. "I figure we break into that warehouse. See what we can find."

"He was a tricky bastard with that license plate, wasn't he?" said Peter. "Two layers of slippery. He'd like someplace empty."

"Gotta start somewhere," said Lewis, turning off the Yukon. "What do you like for ordnance?"

"What, there's a selection?"

The tilted smile got wider. "Step around back, son."

Under the rear cargo deck, where the spare tire and jack should have been, lay a folded Mexican blanket. Lewis unfolded the blanket with a slight flourish.

Peter blinked. "Tell me exactly," he said, "what is it you do for a living."

"If I told you," said Lewis, "I'd have to kill you."

Gleaming under the rear dome light was an Ithaca combat shotgun with the big magazine, along with a sawed-off Mossberg street-sweeper, an ugly, alien-looking Steyr automatic rifle with a folding stock, and a selection of handguns ranging from a big chrome Dirty Harry .44 to an Army-issue Beretta to a pair of flat black Glock .45s. And the enormous 10-gauge shotgun that Lewis had been cleaning on the day Peter and Dinah had walked into the storefront. It made every other weapon look a little bit like a toy.

"Where's the Thompson?" said Peter. "It's not a real collection without a tommy gun."

Lewis shook his head sadly. "Can't get 'em. Illegal as all hell. However, these here fine specimens all legally purchased by a nice old lady on the North Side."

"And you're just holding on to them for her."

"She don't like to clean 'em. I find it calms my mind."

"I imagine it does," said Peter. "You're kinda freaky, you know that."

"Naw," said Lewis. "I don't sleep with 'em or nothing. They just tools. Get the job done."

Peter still had the Sig Sauer he'd bought from Lewis three days before. He took one of the Glocks to supplement and tucked it into the pocket of his Carhartt. An extra clip went into his hip pocket, in case they ran into zombies or bears or other dangerous wildlife.

Lewis propped the 10-gauge over a shoulder like a man carrying lumber. "What's our primary objective?"

He watched the warehouse as he spoke, the lazy drawl fading for a moment as he focused on the work ahead. Peter thought Lewis had probably been a pretty good soldier.

"Just a sneak and peek," said Peter. "I want an idea of who this guy is and what he's doing."

"What if he's there? Making a pipe bomb or some damn thing?"

"Then we grab him, find out from the man himself. Shoot him in the leg if you have to. No, you'd cut him in half with that cannon. Let me shoot him in the leg."

Lewis pointed to a black tool bag. "Take that, too."

It was heavy, and clanked when Peter picked it up. "How many sledgehammers do we need?"

"How else you think we gonna get in?" asked Lewis. "Just say please?"

They walked the street in the dark, Lewis carrying the 10-gauge down along his leg. The wind was up, whistling across the rooftops, and tree branches clacked overhead. The single functional streetlight had a halo around it from the damp in the air.

They bypassed the main entrance and the truck loading dock and stepped into the shelter of the rail siding, where the rusting steel-framed roof and a screen of tall weeds helped hide them from prying eyes. The cracked concrete loading platform would have been the same height as the boxcar doors.

In another neighborhood, the building would have been renovated. Peter imagined loft apartments on the upper floors and a decent restaurant on the main with tables set up under this shelter in nicer weather. He hoped the old building would be brought back to life. Although at the current rate of decay, there might be little left to restore.

The big sliding forklift doors had been boarded up

years before, and a man-door was cobbed into one of the bays. The key was broken off in the rusty deadbolt, and two heavy padlocked hasps held the door shut at top and bottom.

Peter opened the tool bag and took a penlight from his pocket to peer inside. Vertical compartments lined the interior for easy organization, with a central well for the heavy gear. "Your tools, you decide," he said in a low voice. "Sledgehammer or crowbar?"

Lewis clucked his tongue softly. "Finesse, jarhead, finesse." Reaching in, he plucked an orange-handled tool from a padded interior pocket. It looked like a cheap electric screwdriver, but with a cap covering two slender tangs of bent metal where the driver head would be.

"Lock pick," he explained quietly, plugging the twin wires into a padlock's keyhole and pulling the trigger. "If they don't know you got in, they don't know to look for you."

Usually Peter had gotten into a building by using two large Marines with a steel battering ram. That or C-4. "So you're a burglar," he said as the first padlock popped open.

"Do I look like a guy sneaks around for a living?"

"You're sneaking around right now."

Lewis's teeth gleamed in the dim glow of the penlight. "You're just dying to know, aren't you?"

The pick hummed again and the second lock opened. Lewis stowed the tool in the bag and removed two tactical flashlights, bright but small enough to hold along the barrel of a pistol. Handed one to Peter and picked up his shotgun again, holding his own light along the shotgun's slide to point where the barrel pointed. Looked at Peter and nodded.

Peter took the Sig Sauer from his pocket, opened the door a crack, and listened. No sound, no light. He turned on his flashlight and stepped inside, rising white static making a frictive buzz in the back of his head. His chest tightened immediately.

Breathe in, breathe out.

It was stale and musty. His flashlight beam picked out the corners of a big, empty chamber with walls of stained yellow brick and sixteen-foot ceilings. The floor above them was held up by giant oak timbers that had twisted and cracked as the green lumber dried. They stood on worn wood planks designed to support draft horses and the freight they had once moved.

Dust covered everything. Several sets of footprints walked away from them toward the dark gap in the wall opening to the next chamber. They followed the footprints. Everything silent but for the soft sound of their feet and the roar of the static in his head.

There would be a basement below, as well as a freight elevator to the floors above that was probably broken. Peter was not looking forward to the stairs. To do this right, Peter would have wanted at least a squad, if not the whole platoon.

The second chamber was as empty as the first. The dust equally undisturbed, save the footprints that led them forward. But the smell was changing, a low chemical funk that got more intense as they moved deeper into the warehouse.

The white static flared higher. This was too much like the industrial buildings they had searched in Iraq, where the Baathists would pop up and fire on them from cover before scuttling deeper into the maze. Peter felt the sweat begin to pop on his forehead and neck, despite the deep cold of this place. In another few minutes he'd be sweating through his shirt.

He pushed it down and kept walking.

The third chamber wasn't empty. It held a neat row of ten big white plastic drums beside the roll-up door to the truck loading dock. The door was brown with rust, but the rollers and tracks gleamed with fresh grease.

Peter walked to the plastic drums. With his bright flashlight shining behind the drums, they became translucent. A liquid darkness filled the bottom third of each drum. The drum covers were threaded, and screwed off like a jar lid. Peter found a cover that would move and spun it counterclockwise.

When he cracked the seal, a petroleum stink rose like poison perfume.

He bumped the drum with his toe and watched the languid ripples in the heavy black liquid. "Fuel oil," he said. "Ten drums of fuel oil."

He thought of several reasons somebody would stockpile partial drums of fuel oil in an abandoned warehouse.

None of those reasons were good.

Lewis had his light pointing down. "Look at the floor," he said, his voice pitched low but still carrying in the hush of the room. Peter shifted his own light.

The trail of footprints joined with many more, following the twin trails of what could only be a hand truck, through the roll-up door to the plastic drums and back again. And another traffic pattern, footprints and the same twin trails. But a lot more of them.

A scattering of fine white pellets, half ground to powder underfoot, led from the roll-up door to a fourth chamber. But this one was closed off with a plank partition, curved at the top to fit the arched brick opening. Peter could tell by the dimensions of the planks and the rough saw marks that the work was at least thirty to forty years old. But the heavy commercial security door set into the partition was new. With a steel jamb and a serious lock.

Lewis put the light on Peter's face and leaned in.

"Hey. You okay?"

Peter held up a hand to keep the light from his eyes. "I'm fine. We need to get into that next room."

"You not fine. It forty degrees in here and you sweating like a pig."

"Don't worry about it." His chest felt wrapped in metal, and his breath came hard. The static wanted to fill his head, but he kept it down, pushed it down. There was work to do now. Breathe in, breathe out.

Lewis looked at him for a moment. "Okay," he said. "Calm your shit. Gonna go get the tools."

Peter closed his eyes. Breathe in. Breathe out. It helped. He listened to the silence of Lewis walking away, then the silence of his return. The soft clank of the tool bag set on the hard plank floor. When Peter opened his eyes, Lewis was bent, examining the deadbolt.

He gave a low whistle. "That one serious. Can't open that with the electric pick. Time for the sledgehammer."

Peter shook his head. "They can't know we were here," he said. "Let me look in that bag. I have an idea."

"They gonna know we here, anyway," said Lewis, nodding at their bootprints in the dust. "Might as well get it done."

"You think they're Indian scouts, can tell a man by his bootprints?"

"You saying you wouldn't notice the extra prints?"

"Of course I'd notice," said Peter. "So would you. But I think there's a few of these guys, and they're not all brain surgeons. Now let me see that bag."

"No chain saw, if that what you looking for."

"Shut up and hold the light."

Lewis kept his tool bag neat and orderly, and Peter quickly found what he wanted.

There were certain conventions when installing doors. Usually, the hinges went on the inside, the side you were trying to protect, because the hinges were a weak point. Remove the pins, and the hinge side of the door was no longer connected to the jamb.

But whoever had installed this security door had put the hinges on the side where Peter and Lewis stood.

Which meant either the installer was trying to keep someone on the other side from getting out, or he didn't really know what he was doing. Either one was fine with Peter, as long as the guy hadn't used NRP hinges. NRPs had a threaded steel insert that kept the pins from being removed when the door was closed. But they weren't standard with every security door.

So Peter took a claw hammer and a punch and tapped on the hinge pins from below, trying to get them to lift.

They did. First the bottom, then the middle, then the top. The work helped him keep the static down. Breathe in, breathe out.

"Here," he said, holding out the slightly greasy pins. Lewis took them.

Then, with a small cat's paw on the bottom of the door, Peter slowly and carefully levered the hinge side of the door outward. The deadbolt stayed put, but when the hinge side was completely free, Peter just lifted the door away from the jamb.

Lewis stepped past him, the 10-gauge at the ready.

There was nobody in the room. It was another big chamber, maybe forty feet on a side, with the same spalling brick walls and timbered ceiling.

The floor had been swept, and a cheap folding banquet table and two plastic chairs were set up in the far corner.

Neatly stacked on four wooden pallets were large white bags in heavy-duty plastic.

Bag after bag after bag.

Lewis stepped closer and read the label.

"Fertilizer," he said. Then looked at Peter. "Ammonium nitrate. Fifty-pound bags."

Peter scanned a pallet. Breathe in, breathe out.

Counted the bags.

Did the math.

Looked back up at Lewis.

"Ten thousand pounds," he said.

The white static screamed. Peter felt himself begin to shake in the cold, dark space.

Lewis's air of detached amusement was gone. "How big was Oklahoma City? The federal building?"

"Five thousand pounds of fertilizer," said Peter. "And two drums of racing fuel. But fuel oil does the job just fine. And those ten partial drums out there probably add up to four full ones."

"Twice the size," said Lewis. "Twice the size of Oklahoma City." His eyebrows climbed his forehead. "That's a big fucking bomb."

Peter had learned about ANFO bombs in Iraq, named for their two major components, ammonium nitrate fertilizer and fuel oil. They were used by miners and farmers and guerilla fighters in asymmetric warfare. And domestic terrorists like Timothy McVeigh, who blew up the federal building in Oklahoma City in 1995.

Clearly, thought Peter, someone had big plans.

"What's the target?" he said. "If you were going to blow something up, something big, what would it be?"

Lewis shook his head. "I can't think of anything you'd

blow up for money. If you set this off at a bank, you'd vaporize the vault. Hell, the whole block."

"Unless you were going to hold something ransom."

"Like what?" said Lewis. "Lambeau Field? Threaten to blow up the stadium in Green Bay, you'd have every Packer fan in the state on your ass. And who the hell would pay?"

"This doesn't feel rational," said Peter. "Or at least not profit-driven, not how I can figure it. Timothy McVeigh didn't make a nickel, he just wanted to make a point."

"Lot of good it did him," said Lewis. "Lethal injection. But what about all that cash you found? That don't seem too ideological to me."

"Me neither," said Peter. "They didn't need it to pay for materials, the shit's already here. Unless the ideology is a diversion. Hiding some other motive. Like money."

"Always comes back to money," said Lewis. "Who we got on this thing that we know about? Who are the players?"

Something clicked. "Skinner," Peter said. "That's gotta be it. If you blow up the right thing, something happens in the markets."

Lewis shook his head. "Shit. Whatever happened to armed robbery?"

But Peter was looking around. "Wait a minute," he said. "There's gotta be a starter charge. You can't just light a match under this stuff."

Lewis nodded. "You need dynamite or Tramex or something like that."

Neither component would blow up by itself. You needed another material to create a starter blast, something to get the temperature up. Create the conditions for the big bang.

But Peter knew what they had planned to use. He looked at Lewis, and saw that Lewis knew, too.

Four beige rectangles, pliable as modeling clay, would do nicely.

Currently stashed in the secret panel under Peter's truck.

"We need to get the cops here."

Peter didn't answer. He was walking through the rest of the room, looking at what had been left. The folding table and chairs were cheap and could have been bought at any home store. But there was nothing personal, no papers. Not even fast-food wrappers. These people were not amateurs. Their only mistake was losing the C-4, and that was probably because Jimmy had taken it from a locker at the veterans' center.

At the back of the room, Peter saw an old cast-iron door set into the brick wall. It was heavy with rust, probably the same age as the building itself. There were rust flakes on the floor, too. The giant strap hinges shone with new oil, and tool marks on the door showed where someone had worked to get that door open.

Peter reviewed his mental map of the building. This wall was the end of this building.

But it wasn't an outside wall.

He had another mental map. This one of the block and the buildings on it.

He was pretty sure he knew what was on the other side of that old cast-iron door.

"Peter." Lewis didn't raise his voice, but it carried an urgency that Peter hadn't heard before. "We need to call the cops. You listening to me?"

"I hear you," said Peter. "But calling the cops is no guarantee. And just getting rid of this stuff won't get the guy who killed Jimmy. We might lose Dinah's payday. And we'd probably lose yours, too."

Lewis looked at him. "I've done my share of shit," he said. "But I can't let this thing go for some payday. Not for your revenge, neither."

"It's not just that," said Peter. "If we call the cops right now, we won't know who put this together, or how. They'll just start over. We need to get deeper into this."

"That's what the goddamn cops are for."

"Lewis, it's not even a bomb yet. Right now it's just supplies and suspicion. It'll take them hours just to mix it up and get it in the truck."

"Or we get sidetracked and come back and it's gone. You ever think of that?"

"What I think," said Peter, "is that under that slick mercenary veneer is a guy who actually gives a shit."

"Yeah, yeah." Lewis looked at his watch. "You got four hours. Then I'm calling the cops."

"I have a better idea," said Peter. "Is there a Radio Shack or something around here?"

34

Peter left Lewis to keep an eye on the warehouse, with a pocketful of shotgun shells and the Glock in his belt.

Peter had rung the doorbell only once, but Mingus's barking would wake the dead. Dinah wore thick flannel pajama bottoms and a UWM sweatshirt. Not what Peter had imagined when he pictured her sleeping.

Dinah glared at him with those glacier-blue eyes. "Peter, do you have any idea what time it is?"

Mingus poked his nose past her hip, tail wagging happily. Dinah shoved the dog back with her foot. Peter was glad to see the chrome .32 in her hand. She looked more comfortable with the weapon than he expected.

"I know it's late, and I'm sorry," said Peter. "Get your boys out of bed and pack a bag. One night, maybe two. Bring that gun. Five minutes. You're getting out of this house."

"I will not," she said. With that regal bearing, her

spine straight as an iron rod. "I have a double shift tomorrow. It's a school night. Charlie has a math test."

Of course Dinah would require an explanation.

Peter figured Mingus had woken the boys. He lowered his voice so they wouldn't hear. "You remember that suitcase I found under your porch?"

Dinah nodded.

"Well, there was more in that bag than money. There was also a decent amount of explosives." Her eyebrows shot up. "And Lewis and I just found a stash of bomb-making supplies. Enough to make a very big boom."

"You and Lewis?" She looked confused.

"He's helping me. Dinah. Something ugly is going to happen soon and I need to get you and the boys out of here now."

That finally got her attention. But she still didn't want to believe him. "Why on earth would they come here?"

Peter didn't want to tell her, but he saw no other way to get her moving in a hurry. So he said it.

"Someone threatened me. And mentioned you and the boys specifically. He was pretty convincing."

Dinah closed her eyes. He saw her bend then, just for a moment. She looked smaller, softer. Her voice was quieter, too. "The man with the scars?"

Peter nodded. "He's one of them. It's their money, and their explosives. They were watching the house, they know where it is. They might be out there right now."

She opened her eyes and forced her spine straight, the

iron rod in place again. He knew she was strong. He saw then that her perfect posture was part of her strength, the armor she wore to survive the challenges of her life. Though that was nothing compared to what they faced now.

She stepped back to let him inside. Mingus wagged his tail so hard it gave him a whole-body wiggle as Peter closed and locked the new door he'd installed just the other day. He was glad he'd bought the reinforced steel.

She asked, "Was James involved in this?"

Peter let Mingus jump up on him, then rubbed behind his ears. The dog still smelled like strawberries.

"I think Jimmy took it from them," said Peter. "He must have figured out what they were planning. They still need those explosives. They're pretty sure either you or I still have them. I imagine they'd like their money back, too. So they have more than one reason to come here."

"They can have the money. I don't care about that."

"Where did you put it?"

"It's in the attic. Over behind the boxes, still in that paper bag."

He figured it was as good a place as any. He didn't have any better ideas. There wasn't room for it in the hidden stash spot under his truck.

Dinah didn't waste any more time. She walked to the bedrooms and got the boys up and moving with a few whispered words. Then shoved clothes and toiletries into a bag. Peter walked from window to window, looking out at the night. Just because he hadn't seen anyone didn't mean they weren't there.

Charlie came out and filled a backpack with a half-gallon of milk, a box of cereal, and a few plastic containers of what Peter assumed were leftovers. Threw in a few granola bars and paper cups and some silverware. Smart kid. The Army traveling on its stomach.

Peter didn't think they would need much food. He had a feeling things were going to happen pretty fast after this.

He stood at the open door, scanning the street, when Dinah came out with a duffel slung over her shoulder, holding a sleepy-eyed Miles by the hand. Her face was set. Charlie shrugged into the backpack with the food and picked up his baseball bat.

"Leave that behind," said Dinah.

"I'm the man of the house," said Charlie. "I'm taking the bat."

Dinah opened her mouth to respond, but Peter said, "Charlie's right. Bring the bat." He already had the Sig Sauer in his hand.

They went down the walk to Peter's truck. He said, "Charlie, we don't have much room in the front. I need you to get in the back with Mingus, just for a few minutes. It's going to be pretty dark. You okay with that?"

Charlie paused for only a moment. "Yes, sir," he said. "Mingus won't be so scared with me there."

Twelve years old. Jesus Christ.

Peter saw Dinah wipe her eyes as she climbed into the passenger seat after little Miles.

This whole thing was fucked.

The first minutes, they drove in silence. But when Dinah realized where they were going, she said, "No."

Peter said, "It's not my first choice, either. But where else do you suggest? Your grandmother's house?"

She let her breath out in a thin, bitter stream.

"Dinah," he said. "I need to tell you something. The Marine Corps home-repair program. It's not real. I made it up."

She looked at him. "I know," she said. "I called the VA yesterday. We'll have a conversation about it. But not right now." She pointed her chin at Miles, half asleep on the seat between them.

"I let Jimmy down. I should have visited. I was trying to help."

Dinah nodded. "You did help," she said. "It's not your fault that it's come to this. So thank you."

He pulled the truck up in front of Lewis's building and got out. Nino and Ray were waiting outside, standing like sentinels in the cold.

Dinah closed her eyes again at the sight of them, just for a moment. Then opened her eyes, popped the latch on her door, and got out. Peter knew she didn't want to be there, but she had no choice and she knew it. So she kept going.

Peter nodded at Nino and Ray. They nodded back. He didn't know what arrangement Lewis had made with them, and he didn't care. Lewis said they'd stick and that was good enough. Dinah scooped Miles up onto her hip, where he put his arms around her neck and his face into her shoulder. He must have weighed eighty pounds, like a sack of ready-mix concrete. She carried him like he weighed nothing at all.

She looked right at Peter, her blue eyes shining clear in the dim glow of the streetlight. "We'll talk when it's over," she said. Then walked toward the building without a backward glance. Peter went to let out Charlie and the dog.

As he was locking up again, his phone rang. He pulled it from his pocket. It was the number he'd last seen in spidery handwriting on three business cards. He pushed the button. "Hello."

"Peter, sorry to call so late." Lipsky's voice was so clear he might have been standing right there, talking quietly into Peter's ear. "But I figured you'd still be up. I wanted to tell you that replacement glass for your truck window came in today. Are we still meeting at the Riverside Veterans' Center in the morning?"

"I'm looking forward to it," said Peter.

"Me, too," said Lipsky. "See you about eleven. I'll buy lunch."

"Hey, thanks for this," said Peter. "I really appreciate it."

"Just an old soldier, trying to help," said Lipsky. "See you tomorrow."

The phone dead in his hand, Peter turned to Lewis's building. But everyone had already gone inside.

He didn't figure Dinah needed any help managing Nino and Ray.

So he put the truck in gear. Picked up his phone again and punched in Detective Zolot's number.

"Who the fuck is this?"

The man even woke up angry.

"You said you wanted in," said Peter. "I'm getting close. And there's a new wrinkle."

The Man in the Black Canvas Chore Coat

From the dark interior of a rusting brown Mazda, Midden set the night-vision gear on the passenger seat and watched the old green Chevy pickup rumble away. It had been a simple thing to follow the Marine from the woman's house.

He could see why the Marine was causing so much trouble. It was a risk, what they had planned. Even from a distance, he could tell the man was the real thing.

The others were asking a lot. Involving the woman and the kids. This wasn't what Midden had signed up for.

He told himself that he was committed. He was reliable.

One last time.

Then out of it for good.

He reached into the footwell and took hold of the M4 assault rifle. Laid a chamois cloth in his lap and began to field-strip the weapon in the dark as he had done so many times before.

The series of familiar movements was like an old friend in a world where he had none.

All his other friends were dead.

VETERANS DAY

35

Peter

Peter woke early on full alert.

His truck was on a dead-end street on the south side of town, tucked in with other parked cars. Hard to find by accident.

It was still dark, his breath steaming in the cold air coming through the missing window of his truck. He stretched his ears out for whatever had gotten his sleeping mind's attention. The hush of a passing car on the next block. The faint clatter of the last leaves falling to the pavement. But nothing else, no warning sound. So he lay in his bag and thought about what he had to do that day.

"Stay right there. Don't move a muscle." The voice was calm and quiet, and coming through the missing window, right above Peter's head.

Peter's whole body tensed, but the sleeping bag was zipped up to his chin. He'd spent an hour doubling back, checking his tail to make sure he had a safe place to sleep.

He'd even looked for a GPS tracker like the one Lewis had put on the black Ford, and had found nothing.

He should have kept Mingus with him. Mingus would have warned him.

"Put your hands out." Peter knew the voice. "Slowly. Don't make me shoot you."

"How did you find me?"

A snort of derision. "I could follow this truck with my eyes closed. That cargo box is like a radar beacon. Now show me your hands. Slowly. And don't even think about the gun on the floor."

"Okay," said Peter, working his hands free of the bag and raising them past his head, resting them on the sill of the window. He should have slept in his boots. He should have slept away from the truck. He should have done a lot of things. "You're a piece of shit, you know that?"

The latch clicked as the door opened at his head. "Slide yourself out of the sleeping bag and onto the ground. Hands stay out and away."

The man wasn't going to be provoked. He was too cool, too experienced. So Peter did as he was told, scootching awkwardly out in his T-shirt and jeans to stand barefoot on the cold cracked asphalt amid skittering leaves. Peter could feel the man behind him, angling just out of reach.

A second man stood in front of him, a thoughtful five steps away, holding a gun, which took away any significant options an unarmed and barefoot man might have.

Peter had never seen him before. He wore a black canvas barn coat that made him fade into the darkness of the early morning. The only parts of him that were truly visible were his face, weatherworn and empty as a crater, and a pale hand holding a long-barreled target pistol like it was machined for the task.

"Now what?" asked Peter.

A long arm flashed fast as a whip around his neck from behind and clamped tight over his windpipe. The static flared.

"Just relax, Peter. This won't take long."

Lipsky's voice was warm in his ear as the tall detective pulled Peter close, the fist of the choking arm locked tight inside the crook of the opposing elbow. The old illegal police choke hold blocked the blood flow to the brain and would knock you out in as little as ten seconds. Two or three minutes and it could kill you.

Peter fought back, the white sparks arcing high. He stomped Lipsky's foot hard, then thrashed to the side to get the other man off-balance. He twisted and kicked and bucked, but Lipsky was fit and well trained and stronger than he looked. The former Ranger had the hold locked in place.

Peter fought, but his time was running out. He fought until the white sparks rose up to fill him completely.

He fought until the world turned to black.

36

Peter

He woke sitting in a chair. He kept his eyes closed, trying to learn whatever else he could.

His wrists were bound tight to the chair's arms, his ankles tied to the chair's legs. His bare feet were cold on a hard, dusty floor. He had a headache and a nasty taste in his mouth, his neck and throat were sore as hell, and he was absurdly glad to be alive.

He smelled the deep chemical funk of the fuel oil and knew he was in the warehouse. He had to believe that Lewis was still out there, watching. The plan wouldn't change for Lewis. The fail-safe would still be in place. That made it slightly easier to be tied to a chair.

He heard a man talking to himself in a singsong voice. "On behalf of the American people. We the people. We shall rise." The voice was familiar.

Then the same voice, softer, tinny, and distant, maybe coming from a small speaker. "We the people are making a statement with our actions today. A statement that the

American people are still the rulers of our own nation. Not the elites who would pervert our laws for their own ends." He knew that voice.

Then a different voice. "I know you're awake, Peter." Lipsky.

Peter opened his eyes.

He was in the big warehouse room with the swept floors behind the locked security door. The big iron door to the veterans' center was closed. Peter was relieved to see the bags of fertilizer still stacked on their pallets.

His chair sat behind the long folding banquet table. The table held a plastic bin with a jumble of electrical parts and long coils of flexible plastic electrical conduit joined to plastic electrical boxes, with pairs of wires showing at each end. Peter didn't need to count them. He knew there were ten, one for each white plastic drum of oil. Lipsky stood on the far side of the table.

Beside Lipsky was a small portable video camera on a tripod staring at him with its dark unblinking lens.

The white static rose up abruptly then, his chest tight, all those brick walls closing in, wrists and ankles tied with yellow plastic cuffs that kept him trapped here, inside. Peter closed his eyes again and shoved down the static. He pulled in one shallow, ragged breath, let it out. Then another, and another, breathe in, breathe out, trying to keep his heart from climbing into his throat, the white static from rising up until his mind held only the frantic need to run, to escape, to stand free under the open sky.

"I thought you were tougher than this, Peter."

Lipsky's voice was calm. "It was just a choke hold. And a little something from the police evidence locker to keep you out for a few hours."

Breathe in. Breathe out. Push it down. Think about that Navy shrink who saw the automatic panic, who walked him out to that park bench. Who told him to develop a relationship with the static. This was his life. It was up to him how he would live it.

Make friends with the static. Breathe in, breathe out.

Hello, old friend. Hello. Now fuck off, would you? I have work to do.

Lipsky's calm, kind voice, coming closer. "Maybe it's the confined space? I could see it when you sat in the back of that police car, the day we met. Must be pretty rough."

Breathe in, breathe out. Peter opened his eyes to see Lipsky standing beside him now. He thought again of Lewis, somewhere outside. Waiting.

"Does this mean I'm not getting the new glass for my truck?"

An explosion of pain to the ribs, Lipsky hitting him hard.

"Ow, shit," said Peter, coughing.

"Where's my C-4?" Lipsky's voice still calm and kind.

Peter heard the singsong voice again. "We the people. The American people."

He opened his eyes. A skinny young man in a Marine's dress blues sat on a folding chair in the far corner, tapping at the keys of an old laptop. The soft, tinny voice came next, from the laptop's speakers.

"Some within law enforcement may consider our actions to be criminal. But we are not criminals. We are veterans of the United States Armed Forces. We have fought for this great country in the past. And we fight again now to wrest power from the financial giants that have taken control of this nation that we love. We have struck once and we will strike again."

Jimmy had found him, and Peter had, too. Cas had shaved his beard and was easier to recognize. Now Peter knew why he'd taken his dress uniform from his closet.

"Hey, Felix," said Peter. "Your nana sent me to find you. She misses you and wants you to come home."

Felix Castellano flicked his eyes toward Peter for a moment, then away.

Lipsky hit Peter again, in the same spot.

"Ow, hey, what the fuck?" The pain helped to distract him from the static. "Is that how you treat a fellow veteran?"

Lipsky's voice was patient. "Where's my C-4?"

"It's gone, okay? I threw it in the lake."

Lipsky looked down at him, hands back in the pockets of his long, dark coat. He looked different, less constrained. Not like a cop, not anymore. As if for the first time in his life he wasn't wearing clothes that were too tight for his body.

"I don't think so," said Lipsky. "You're a Marine. That's ordnance. It might be useful. You've got it hidden away."

Peter shrugged. "What do you want me to say? I threw it in the lake."

He did his best to believe it was true, but he knew Lipsky could see through him. He still had those X-ray eyes.

Lipsky's phone chimed in his hand. He glanced at the screen, then back to Peter. "Don't sweat it, Peter. You'll tell me in a few minutes. I guarantee it."

Peter pulled at the cuffs again. The plastic didn't move at all. The walls were still too close. Breathe in. Breathe out. Something would happen in a few minutes. He didn't want to imagine the possibilities. He kept talking.

"So what's with the video camera?"

Lipsky smiled. "You like our little stage set? Take a look behind you." Peter turned his head and saw a large American flag hung from the wall behind him. "You made a video, Peter. You're going to be famous. Unfortunately, by the time it becomes public, you'll be dead."

Shit.

"I'm not naked, am I?"

"You've seen these videos before," said Lipsky. "Usually it's some raghead with a Koran, making a speech. Death to the infidels, that kind of thing. A vest full of C-4 and roofing nails on display." He nodded to the wiring harnesses on the table, the bags of ammonium nitrate fertilizer on their pallets. "But not you, Peter. You're more ambitious. You and Felix will change the world."

"We the people," shouted Felix from his chair in the corner.

"I was passed out," said Peter. "I must look like I'm asleep."

"You wore sunglasses," said Lipsky. "Nobody will see your eyes. You had an assault rifle in your hands and wiring harnesses on the table in front of you." He shrugged. "Maybe you looked a little stoned. But our friend Cas sat beside you and read his speech. You'll be convincing enough."

Zolot had said that the perfect crime required someone else, a scapegoat, to take the blame. Peter had thought the scapegoat would be Felix, but apparently Lipsky wanted it to be a group effort. Maybe he thought it would be better as a conspiracy. So he'd signed Peter up for the job.

"Get to the point."

"One explosion could be a crazy man," said Lipsky. "But a conspiracy of war veterans? Complete with a video manifesto declaring war on the American financial system? The media will go apeshit. And the fear of the next attack? It will be like ten bombs, or twenty."

More than that, thought Peter. It would be another great crash. The financial system, still reeling from the last disaster, would shut down in self-defense. Maybe for only a week, maybe longer. It didn't matter. It would do a lot of damage either way, and someone who knew it was coming could make an enormous amount of money.

"You are such an asshole," said Peter.

Lipsky gave Peter a kindly smile. "It's your parents I feel the most sympathy for. Their son the Marine become a domestic terrorist."

Peter felt a surge of rage, and he strained hard at the

plastic handcuffs. The static rose up as the cuffs bit painfully into his wrists, but nothing changed.

Breathe in, breathe out. Push it down, push it down. "They won't believe it," he said.

Lipsky jerked his thumb at Felix on the laptop. "He's fine-tuning the video now. We found your old e-mail address. You really should have a better password. Before we go, Cas will use your e-mail to send a copy to your mom, as well as *The New York Times* and *The Wall Street Journal*."

Peter felt that one in his gut. He thought of his mother opening the e-mail. His parents seeing his face on the national news. His father would have a stroke right there. It would kill them both.

Breathe in. Breathe out.

"What's the point?" he said, although he knew already. "Why me?"

"Because you're perfect," said Lipsky. "Homeless vet, no job, post-traumatic stress. History of violence. Look at you. Sweaty and pale. Trying to hold in whatever demons have taken root. Practically a ghost already. You're a walking time bomb. Much better than the last guy we had."

"The last guy," said Peter. And found that he already knew that, too.

"Your friend, Mr. Johnson. He was going to be our co-conspirator, although he never made it past the planning stages."

Peter clenched his jaw. "Who killed him? You?"

"It was an accident," said Lipsky with a shrug. "There's a reason cops don't use that choke hold anymore. I was just trying to get him under control."

Now Peter understood. "The bullet under his chin was to prevent an autopsy."

"A good choke doesn't leave bruises," said Lipsky. "That's a murder investigation. But I knew the coroner wouldn't think twice about another veteran suicide." He shook his head. "As it was, him dying already screwed everything up. We lost track of the contents of that suitcase." He smiled at Peter. "Until now."

"I know what you wanted the plastic for. But what's with the money?"

"Payment," said Lipsky. "Services rendered. I worked hard for that money. It's not easy to bury a murder charge. I'm going to want that back, too, by the way. It's not much compared to what we're expecting, but it's nice to have hard cash in hand, just in case. Always have more than one exit strategy, right?"

"So it's all about the money."

Lipsky raised his eyebrows. "Ten years in the Army, fifteen as a cop. My life on the line every day. Getting paid shit. And this is it? A pension promise that might get revoked the next time the governor gets the hiccups?"

Peter ignored Lipsky's whining. You signed up for it, you knew what you were getting into. "So what's the target?" he asked. "How many people are you planning to kill?"

The phone in Lipsky's hand chimed again. Lipsky glanced down. "Right on schedule. In about two minutes, you'll tell me where to find the C-4."

The scarred man walked through the big rusted iron door from the veterans' center. He wore the same black leather car coat and Kangol cap worn backward. His face was a collection of mottled bruises, the skin split and raw at the lip and left cheek. He saw Peter cuffed behind the table and sauntered toward him with a cruel smile.

"Boomer." Lipsky's voice cracked like a whip. It made Peter want to stand at attention, and he was handcuffed to a chair.

Boomer's mouth bunched like a fist, but his step faltered. "I'm just gonna hit him once." The man's face really was a mess.

"What happened to you?" asked Peter with an innocent expression. "Fall off a bicycle?"

Boomer started toward Peter again. "I'm gonna hit you so fuckin' hard—"

"Stop," said Lipsky, his voice an edged weapon. The scarred man froze in his tracks. "You can have him later, Boomer. Right now you're still working for me. So show me."

"Fine." Boomer's mouth twisted up farther, but he turned away from Peter and pulled a phone from his pocket to show Lipsky. "We're all set up."

Lipsky looked at the screen. "You've only got one kid here. Where's the dog?"

Boomer shrugged. "There was only the one kid. And no dog."

The static flared into Peter's brain. His arms strained against the cuffs, his gut clenched, and his chest was wrapped in steel bands. Breathe in, breathe out. I hear you, old friend. Just hold off for a few minutes.

Lipsky gave Boomer a sour look.

Boomer threw his hands in the air. "Hey, trust me, we looked. I wanted to shoot that dog personally."

Lipsky shook his head, then took the phone out of Boomer's hand and held it so Peter could see the screen. "This is why you're going to give me that C-4. My guys went in and took them this morning." Dinah and Miles, wearing rags as blindfolds, bound with the same yellow plastic handcuffs, sat on a bare dusty floor with a pale brick wall at their back. They were somewhere in the warehouse, maybe even the next room.

They looked so small and helpless. This wasn't supposed to happen. And where were Charlie and the dog?

But this, he knew, changed everything.

His plan with Lewis was out the window.

37

Peter

"Go watch the woman and the kid," Lipsky told Boomer. "Don't touch them. Just keep them calm and quiet. Start prepping the drums. And send Midden back here."

Boomer scooped up the coils of conduit from the table, glared at Peter, and walked through the door to the warehouse.

Peter pulled hard at the plastic cuffs. "What did you do?"

"We took them," said Lipsky. "Your other friends are dead. Collateral damage. I believe you know the term."

"If you harm them, either one of them," said Peter, "I will kill you in the most painful way possible."

Lipsky didn't seem to notice. His X-ray eyes were focused on Peter, and his voice was calm. "Here's how it is, Peter. You and I are men of the world. We've been to war. We've killed other men to protect our friends and our own skins, and to do our job. So I'm going to be honest with you. You're going to die. There's no way around that. You can't save yourself."

Lipsky held up the phone with the picture on it. Reached out and cleared a space in the bomb parts on the table, and set the phone where Peter could stare at it.

"But you can save that woman out there, and her son. They haven't seen anyone's faces. They don't know where they are or what's going on. They won't be touched. You can save them. If you give me that C-4."

Breathe in, breathe out.

The door to the veterans' center opened again, and the man in the black canvas chore coat came through.

Peter watched him read the room in a single silent glance, including Peter cuffed to the chair behind the desk, the flag on the wall, the video camera on its tripod, and Felix working feverishly at his laptop. There was a kind of empty, coiled stillness to the man, like some purpose-built mechanism awaiting only the triggering of his function. But he looked at Peter with a kind of curiosity.

To Lipsky, Peter said, "You'd kill an innocent woman? A child?"

Midden's head swiveled to stare at Lipsky.

The detective just shrugged. "Collateral damage? That's up to you."

"Not collateral damage," said Peter. "This is taking hostages. Killing hostages. For money."

"I don't want to kill them," said Lipsky, sounding like the voice of reason. "I hope I don't *have* to kill them. But again, that's up to you. Where's the C-4?"

38

Midden

Midden looked at Lipsky, trying to gauge his seriousness. Was he bluffing?

Midden had killed many people in war, and more after. So many he'd long ago lost count. Even women, when he'd had to.

But he'd never killed a child. Not knowingly.

Was this the man he had become?

Midden knew there was a point of no return. He thought he'd gone past it long ago. That he was past any salvage, let alone redemption.

But he understood now that there were additional waypoints on the path to hell that would change him further. Beyond his own recognition of even this damaged version of himself.

Would he become a man who would kill a child?

39

Peter

Peter looked at the image on the phone on the desk in front of him. On the small screen, Dinah sat on the dusty floor with Miles on her lap, her arms wrapped protectively around him. Their torn blindfolds gave them a ragged, haunted air. He knew hostages were almost never set free.

He thought of other times when he'd needed to make a similar decision.

It was different with his own men. It was part of the job to send his Marines into the fight. Knowing that men could be injured or die. It was part of the job. Part of what he had signed up for, what they all had signed up for.

Peter wasn't a lieutenant who hung back, who directed his men from the firebase. Peter went to the fight with them. His job was accomplishing the mission, yes, but his job was also protecting his men, making their jobs as safe as he could. Which didn't include leading from behind. The risk of his own injury or death should be no less than that of his men.

And men had died at his orders. As a direct result of his orders. Of his mistakes. That was part of his life now. Living with it. Those consequences. Those sacrifices.

Dinah and Miles had been drawn into this battle despite everything he had done to prevent it. Whether they would die as a result of his decision was still undetermined. But if he handed over the C-4, the odds were good that more than two would surely die.

So the answer was no.

He wasn't going to give up those beige rectangles.

Lipsky must have seen the result on his face. Because as soon as Peter reached this final point of reasoning, Lipsky's eyebrows popped up. As if the conclusion was unexpected. His X-ray eyes hadn't been able to see as deeply as he had thought.

Or maybe Lipsky simply couldn't imagine sacrificing anything he cared about for a larger cause.

"Huh," said Lipsky. "You are full of surprises. Okay. So who should we kill first, Peter? The woman?" Peter didn't answer. Lipsky kept talking, now to himself. "No, then the kid will become uncontrollable. And Boomer will have to be a babysitter. Definitely not."

He turned to the man in the black canvas chore coat. "Midden, kill the kid."

40

Midden

"No," said Midden.

It came out before he knew he would say it.

He said it again. "No." With an odd sensation he couldn't place. An internal tug. Like his organs were trying to realign themselves.

He said, "I know where he's hidden the plastic."

41

Peter

Lipsky ground his teeth in frustration. "Why the fuck didn't you say so?"

"I just figured it out," said Midden. "He's living out of his truck, so it's got to be somewhere in that vehicle. At some point he was overseas, and probably working a checkpoint, searching cars. He knows all the best places to hide something. But I had that duty, too. And I used to have a truck like his, a '67 Chevy, although mine was a short bed. I know that truck inside and out."

He took Peter's keys from the table and headed toward the door. "Give me twenty minutes."

"You're killing me, Midden," Lipsky called after him.

Breathe in, Peter told himself. Breathe out. He tried to relax in the chair and live with himself for another day. He thought of Lewis, waiting outside. He closed his eyes and reached for another plan.

Lipsky's phone rang. He took the call, walked away, and began to talk.

Peter opened his eyes and turned to Felix, still working furiously at his laptop.

"Hey, Felix."

"They call me Cas." The skinny kid didn't look up. "I'm not Felix anymore. They call me Cas."

The missing Marine was impossibly skinny. Shoulders like a coat hanger. Damaged somehow, and exploited by Lipsky.

"Your nana is worried about you, Felix. She asked me to find you. She wants you to come home. She'll take care of you."

At the mention of his grandmother, Felix's head jerked up from the laptop. But he wouldn't look at Peter. He looked at the bare brick walls, at the heavy wood ceiling timbers, at the pallets of fertilizer.

"Your nana loves you more than anything," said Peter. "She's afraid for you. She wants you to come home."

Felix's voice was loud. "There is no more home. The bank is taking her house." Shouting now, his gaunt face contorted with pain. "The banks are taking everything."

"Your nana is moving in with her sister," said Peter. "There's room for you, too, Felix."

"I'm not Felix, I'm Cas. I'm Cas." He rocked his body back and forth, eyes fixed and staring. The kid had his own white static, and it was worse than Peter's. Maybe he was just off his meds. Or Lipsky gave him something to keep him off-balance.

"You can stop this now," said Peter. "Walk away. Close up your computer and go home. Your nana loves you. She'll forgive you. She'll forgive anything."

Lipsky walked over, phone call finished, the hard soles of his shoes scraping on the floor. "He doesn't care about you, Cas."

He stood behind Felix and put his hands on the man's impossibly skinny shoulders. He winked at Peter and kept talking in a low, soothing voice. "He doesn't understand the plan, Cas. He doesn't understand what you're about to accomplish. You're going down in history, Cas. You're going to change the world."

Peter kept pushing. "What about your nana, Felix? When this comes out it's going to be very hard for her. What's going to happen to her?"

Felix shook his head wildly and rocked in his chair, the veins in his forehead and neck standing out like snakes under the skin. "I'm already dead! Watch the video! I'm already dead!"

Lipsky bent so his lips were at the younger man's ear and talked. He spoke slowly, softly, lower than Peter could hear, and all the while working his hands gently on the younger man's shoulders, calming him, soothing him like a wild animal caught in a trap.

Peter saw Lipsky in a new light.

It wasn't only about the money.

It was also about breaking something fragile.

And burning down the world just to warm his cold, hungry hands.

* * *

Lipsky rose and clapped Felix on the back. When the younger man stood, he seemed taller than Peter remembered. Maybe it was just how very thin he was. He strode without a glance past Peter to the white bags of fertilizer on their pallets, and bent to stack the fifty-pound sacks on the hand truck. He lifted one in each hand as if they weighed nothing, and worked with a focused, manic energy. Peter knew that if he tried to talk to Felix now, the younger man wouldn't even hear him.

Lipsky watched with an odd smile on his face as Felix moved his heavy load out of the room.

"What kind of meds are you giving him?" asked Peter. "Something to really fuck him up, right?"

Lipsky's smile widened, and Peter knew he'd guessed it. Lipsky had pushed the young Marine over the brink. But Lipsky would never admit it. "Hey, the man's a patriot," said Lipsky. "That's all there is to it."

"No, he's zonked out of his gourd," said Peter. "Delusional and damaged. So what's your excuse?"

"You really should read your own manifesto," said Lipsky. "Modern banks have wrecked the economy. They've grown so large they can gamble everything on a roll of the dice, and the government has no choice but to bail them out. They're sucking money out of the middle class. They're set up now just to profit themselves, rather than facilitate production and innovation, which is the role they're designed to perform. Something has to change."

"And you're actually into this?" asked Peter. "Lipsky the revolutionary?"

Felix came in and stacked eight bags of fertilizer on the hand truck while Lipsky watched silently. After Felix walked back out, Lipsky turned to Peter.

"What I believe," said Lipsky, "is that the social contract is broken. Government has proven itself incompetent, and our elected leaders are driven only by greed for wealth and power. Corporations are no longer loyal to their employees or their customers, just their stock price. Executives no longer do what's best for their companies, just themselves. Enron, WorldCom, AIG, Countrywide, JPMorgan. The list goes on." He shrugged. "The only response for a rational person is to act in his own best interest. To take what you can get."

"Oh," said Peter. "I see. You're a thief. That's why you're working with Skinner. A prince among thieves."

The veterans' center door banged open and Midden came through, towing a stumbling bear of a man by one unnaturally angled arm. "I got sidetracked by this guy. He must have been watching the truck."

Detective Frank Zolot moved in an agonized hunch, his face a furious clench of pain. His other arm hung free like a pendulum, some essential connection no longer functional. His cheap suit was rumpled and torn.

Peter thought about Lewis, parked by the loading dock, not by the veterans' center.

Midden wasn't even sweating and there wasn't a mark on him. Although from the black specks on his face and the grime on his fingers, Peter knew he'd been under the truck. But Peter couldn't imagine how Midden had broken both of the big detective's enormous arms without any visible effort. Midden was clearly the most dangerous man in the room.

Lipsky walked over. "What the fuck? Where'd this guy come from?"

Zolot's lip lifted in a silent snarl. Midden handed Lipsky a black automatic pistol. It looked like a Glock. "He had this. He said he was a cop."

Lipsky took the gun. "Where's the plastic? Did you find it?"

"I think so," said Midden. "Give me a couple more minutes." He dropped Zolot's arm and the pain on the man's face eased. Midden fixed Lipsky with a pointed stare. "Don't kill anyone until I get back."

Midden held the stare until Lipsky nodded. Then Midden walked out.

Lipsky turned to Zolot. "Hello, Frank."

"Fuck you." Zolot's injuries had not improved the detective's mood. Although his broken arms rendered him essentially harmless, the heat of his rage still radiated like a glowing forge.

"Who else knows about this?"

"There's a SWAT team gearing up in a parking lot three blocks from here. They have orders to shoot you on sight."

Lipsky grabbed Zolot's wrist and twisted. Zolot gasped in pain.

"Who else knows, Frank?"

The big detective opened his mouth. Nothing came out but an agonized yelp.

Peter sighed. He'd wondered if Zolot could deliver the cops. If his reputation was too damaged. Now he knew. Zolot was just another man caught in Lipsky's web.

Lipsky shook his head and released the other man's wrist. "Nobody believes you, Frank. They never did. Shit, just look at you. You're in a bad way, partner."

"You're not my partner. You were never my partner. You were only out for yourself. How much did that asshole Skinner pay you to look away? What's the going rate to duck a murder?"

Four hundred grand, thought Peter, understanding now. In neatly banded stacks of hundred-dollar bills.

"Frank, we had no proof," said Lipsky. "The DA made the call, not me. Look in the record. We didn't have enough to indict, let alone convict."

"He paid the DA, too, in campaign contributions. But he killed her. You know it, I know it. We could have sweated that fucker. But we didn't. He got away with murder. And now? Now you're going to blow something up. What's the rate for that, you cocksucker?"

"You eat what you kill, Frank," said Lipsky. "You never did see it. Where the power is. Where the money is. Nobody's going to make your fortune but you. If you want to inch along on your tiny little salary for the rest of your life, you go for it. You could have taken a risk. You could have forged ahead. But you stuck to your narrow little view. And look where it's gotten you."

Zolot looked at Lipsky as if he were a different species. "It's called an oath, Sam. We swore an oath. Do you remember? To serve and protect. All the people, not just the people with money."

"You're a fucking dinosaur, Frank. Nobody cares about the people. Even the people don't care about the people, they only care about themselves." He shook his head again. "I don't know why I bother. You didn't get it then, you don't get it now. And I'm tired of listening to your sermons. Good-bye, Frank."

Lipsky raised the pistol and shot Zolot in the head.

The noise rang off the brick walls. Zolot crumpled to the dry and dusty floor, which soaked up the blood like bread under gravy. The smell of it was alive in the room.

"Jesus Christ," said Peter.

"What?" said Lipsky, taking out a handkerchief and wiping down the weapon. His face was indifferent. "You thought I was going to let him live?"

"No," said Peter. "But he used to be your partner."

Lipsky looked at him, those X-ray eyes boring through him. "Partners are overrated."

Felix returned with the hand truck to take another load of fertilizer. The stacks of bags were shrinking fast.

"Hey, Cas." Lipsky held out the pistol with his pinkie through the trigger guard. "This is for you. It's loaded and live."

Felix stood up the hand truck, then took the weapon,

his face alive with interest. He dropped the magazine, checked the load, racked the slide to eject the live round, pushed the round into the magazine, and popped the magazine into place, all in under a count of five. Then tucked the gun into his belt at the small of his back and bent to reload the hand truck.

Whatever was wrong with the guy, thought Peter, some parts of him were clearly still highly functional. The wrong parts.

Midden walked through the door with a black-plastic-wrapped rectangle in his hand. When he saw Zolot dead on the floor, he stopped. "I told you not to kill anyone."

Lipsky took the package from his hand. "You don't make those decisions, Sergeant. I do."

Something flickered across Midden's face and was gone just as quickly. But Peter saw it.

Lipsky must have, too. "Look, I'm sorry. The man was in pain," he said. "And he'd seen all of us, Midden. You killed him when you brought him in here. You know that. Hell, he killed himself when he braced you outside. I put him out of his misery, and ours, too. All right?"

He didn't wait for a response. He carried the package to the table and tore open the plastic, exposing two beige rectangles. "Only two," he said. He turned to Midden. "This is it?"

Midden shook his head. "That's all I found." He glanced at Peter. "Good hiding place, too."

"Not good enough," said Peter.

"That's only half," said Lipsky. "Where's the rest?"

"I got rid of it. And that's the truth."

Lipsky looked at Peter with his X-ray eyes and seemed to accept it.

"It's enough, anyway," he said. "Midden, thank you." Lipsky took his phone from his pocket and hit a button. "We've got it. Bring them in. You need to finish the detonator."

"Wait a minute," said Peter. Although this was what he had known would happen. "You said they hadn't seen any faces. You said you wouldn't touch them if you got the C-4."

"I said I wouldn't if you provided the plastic. And you didn't. Midden had to find it. And we're missing half our goods."

Peter was watching Midden with one eye and saw it again. That flicker across his face, a look of disgust that came and went so quickly Peter almost missed it. Then the empty coiled stillness was back. But there was something beneath it, Peter now knew. Something submerged.

Boomer, his face a mass of bruises, came through the door, towing Dinah by an elbow. Still handcuffed, Dinah had put the circle of her arms around Miles. They still wore their ragged blindfolds.

Boomer steered them into a corner. "Sit yourselves down right there," he said. "Don't move, don't talk." Then he went to the table and peeled the plastic facing off the rectangles of C-4.

Peter said, "I'm sorry, Dinah. It's my fault you're here."

"Peter?" She turned her face, trying to find the

direction of his voice. She'd pulled Miles into her lap. "Peter, where are you?"

"No talking," called Lipsky. He was on the phone again.

"I'm cuffed to a chair," said Peter. "Keep your blindfold on. It's going to be okay."

"I said don't talk." Boomer came over and backhanded Peter across the face. "You gotta learn to do what you're told."

Peter tasted blood. "Fuck you," he said. "Cut these cuffs off and hit me again. I'll have you pissing blood for a week."

"Please, Peter," said Dinah, arms wrapped tight around Miles, her face shrouded by the blindfold. "Do whatever they say. They told me they'll let us go when they have what they need. I just told them where the money is."

Lipsky turned to the scarred man. "Boomer, get that detonator finished. Midden, go keep an eye on Cas. Help him get the bags dumped into the drums." Midden nodded and walked out to the warehouse.

Dinah buried her face in Miles's neck.

Boomer took another folding chair and sat at the table across from Peter, a cruel smile playing across his ruined face. "I'm looking forward to watching you turn into pink mist."

Peter smiled pleasantly. "That's funny. I'm looking forward to tearing off your head and using your neck for a latrine. I think it'll improve your looks."

Boomer stood up again, reached under his coat, and brought out a gigantic revolver. “I think I’ll just shoot you now, fuckface.”

“Boomer.” Lipsky’s voice cracked like a whip. “We keep him alive for now, remember?”

“What is the plan, anyway?” asked Peter. “Sure seems like you’re making this up as you go along.”

Lipsky looked at Peter. “I take it back, Boomer. Go ahead and hit him. But with your hand, and not in the face.”

Boomer came around the table and drove his fist into Peter’s stomach.

“Ooogh.” Peter doubled forward as much as the plastic handcuffs would let him, and tried to sound as if all the air had gone out of him. He’d hardened his gut muscles when he’d known where the punch would hit, and it wasn’t that bad. He’d had worse during sparring.

Boomer puffed up in triumph. “Now who’s the asshole?”

Lipsky put a hand on Boomer’s shoulder, pulling him away. “Now finish the goddamned detonator.”

“All right, all right.” Boomer emptied the plastic bin onto the table and raked through the bomb parts. A twelve-volt battery. A gray plastic junction box. A cell phone. And a neatly coiled group of wires connected by a plastic wiring harness. To Peter, he said, “You ever get blown up, asshole? They say suicide bombers don’t feel a thing, but how would they know? I’m pretty sure it’s gonna hurt like hell.”

The wiring harness looked like something you'd find under the hood of a car. There were ten short wire pigtails made up of two color-coded wires, blue and white. One end of each pigtail came together in the long, narrow harness. The free ends each ended in a quick connector.

Ten pigtails, Peter thought, for ten sets of conduit. For ten plastic oil drums.

On the far end of the wiring harness, a single pair of wires came out, again blue and white, again with quick connectors. Humming happily, Boomer plugged the single blue wire to one of two blue wires soldered into the open back of the cell phone, then plugged the second blue wire from the phone to a third blue wire soldered to one terminal of the twelve-volt battery.

The cell phone would be the trigger. A remote switch that worked by connecting the phone's vibrator to a set of wires. When the vibrator was set off with a call or text, the circuit would close and the battery would send power to the detonator.

"Was this how you got blown up, making bombs?" said Peter. "Nasty scars. Lost part of an ear. And you were ugly to begin with. Must be hard to get a date with a face like that."

Boomer smiled at the wires, his hands busy with his work. "You kidding? I'm a war hero, motherfucker. I get *all* the pussy."

"But they feel sorry for you," said Peter. "That's a pity fuck. That's a hand job from your sister." Peter didn't know what he had to gain by provoking the man, but he was tied to a chair and hating it. And he wasn't built to wait.

He saw the muscles work in Boomer's jaw for a moment, but he still didn't lift his eyes from his work. "Boy, it don't matter what you say anymore." Boomer reached for the free white wire, and plugged its quick connect to a second white wire soldered to the battery's second terminal. "Because in less than an hour, I'm gonna make a phone call. This here switch gonna close, and ten blasting caps gonna pop, setting off ten beautiful chunks of plastic. The plastic will light up the fuel oil. The oil will light up the fertilizer. All in about half a second. And there will be one big-ass explosion. Take down a tall building."

He looked up at Peter, his ruined face shining with the thought of it. Seduced by the fire blossoms of Iraq.

And all the while, his busy hands were arranging the assembled device neatly in the gray plastic junction box.

Peter's shirt was wet with sweat in the cold room. His whole body was trembling, maybe with the cold. He hoped it was with the cold.

Breathe in, breathe out.

Felix came in with the hand truck for another load of fertilizer.

Come on, Lewis. Anytime now.

42

Midden

In the back of the truck, Midden slit open another fertilizer bag from the shrinking stack and dumped it into the last white plastic drum. The pellets slid beneath the dark surface of the fuel oil, raising its level slightly.

The smell was dense and cloying. It reminded him of the long fight through the Iraqi oil fields, always with the stink of the ruptured pipeline and the ferocious heat of the burning wells.

Stay focused, he thought. Although loading the drums required nothing of him other than the strength of his back and the blade of his knife. It was surreal, like before any operation. He had a pre-mission ritual in the bad old days, a system of checking his equipment that distracted him from the fact that they were about to step outside the boundaries of civilization and go kill people.

Although it was different in the war. In those days, they were fighting the enemy. People who were doing their best to kill Midden and his friends.

This was not like those days.

This was killing for money.

But it was what he had agreed to do.

No matter how he felt about it.

Stay focused.

He slit the last bag and poured it into the last drum. It disappeared below the surface of the black ooze without a trace. The drum lid with its junction box and flexible conduit screwed down snug with a slithering sound.

He left Cas to tie down the load and walked back to tell Lipsky.

One last time.

43

Peter

Lipsky took a gun out of his coat pocket and pointed it at Miles.

"Here's what's going to happen," he told Peter. "Midden is going to cut the cuffs off the arms of the chair, then cuff your hands to each other. If you sneeze, if you so much as fucking blink, I'm going to shoot the kid. Do you understand me?"

Peter nodded.

"Then he'll cut the leg cuffs and stand you up."

Peter knew that Lipsky planned to kill them all, anyway. Himself, Dinah, and little Miles, too. But he was no longer willing to allow it to start early. He was counting on Lewis. So he nodded.

It happened just like Lipsky wanted. Midden had a wicked folding knife with a serrated blade that cut through the yellow plastic cuffs like they weren't even there. Peter held out his hands to be cuffed like a good prisoner. Once the new cuffs were tight on his wrists,

Midden cut the leg cuffs from behind the chair, so Peter couldn't get him with his feet. Then he backed away while Peter stood, leaving no opportunity for a quick strike.

"Take him to the truck," said Lipsky. "Cuff him to a cargo ring."

Peter walked through the warehouse door, Midden two careful steps behind him. The loading dock door was rolled up, and the translucent roof panel gave him enough light to see the white plastic oil drums arranged in the Mitsubishi's cargo box.

They were cinched together with webbing, which was strapped to the cargo rings on the sides of the truck, so the load wouldn't shift during travel. Each drum now had a small plastic junction box stuck to its lid, with the flexible electrical conduit leading to a central point like a spider's web in the making. From the end of each piece of conduit came those blue and white wires, with a quick connector on each end.

He stepped into the back of the truck and the smell of fuel oil hit him like a wall. The space was much smaller than the warehouse room, and mostly full of bomb. The white static was tired of waiting. Peter kept breathing, in and out. But it was harder and harder, and his chest felt tighter and tighter. The static began to spark up, heating his brain. Breathe in, breathe out. He could still look through the loading dock door, though, and into the open warehouse. When that truck door rolled down, things would get very bad.

Come on, Lewis. Do it.

"Take this," said Midden, looking at him with a mild curiosity. He held out another plastic handcuff.

Breathe in, breathe out. "You're really doing this," Peter said, turning to face him. Midden backed automatically, the coiled mechanism inside him keeping Peter at an optimal distance. "A truck bomb. Hundreds of people."

"Put one end of the cuff on you," said Midden. "Run the other end through the top cargo ring, so your hands are over your head."

Peter looked the man in the eye, but it was like staring down the barrel of a sniper rifle. "Why?" he asked. "Why are you involved with these jokers? Why are you doing this?"

"Take the cuffs," said Midden. But maybe there was something else in his eyes.

"Or else you're just riding the fastest road to hell," said Peter, and took the cuffs. He wrapped one strap around the midpoint of the cuffs already on him and tightened it with his teeth. "Trying to find something, finally, that you can't live with. Is that it?"

"Shut the fuck up," said Boomer, pushing past Midden with his detonator box. "He's gettin' paid. We're all gettin' paid. Then we'll live like kings. Like captains of fuckin' industry."

"Sure," said Peter. "And you only had to murder a few hundred people to do it. Or maybe it will be a few thousand."

That same look flashed across Midden's face, clearer now. As if something hiding beneath the mechanism was peering out, just for a moment. But he just pointed at the side of the truck. "Now the cargo ring," he said.

So Peter slipped the loop through the metal ring at head level and cuffed himself to the truck. Hoping like hell that Lewis was out there somewhere and paying attention.

Boomer took ten golf-ball-sized lumps of plastic explosive and stuck one into the bottom of each junction box epoxied to the lid of each drum. Then he jammed an electric blasting cap, a silver tube like half a shiny pencil, into each lump of C-4. Out of the end of each blasting cap came two wires, one blue and one white, with quick connectors on their ends. Boomer connected the blasting cap wires to the conduit wires inside each junction box, then screwed on the box covers, his face rapt.

With the junction boxes secured, Boomer gathered the free ends of the conduit and began to attach their threaded ends to the central detonator box with plastic nuts, methodically snapping the quick connectors together, like any electrician getting the job done. The ordinariness of it made Peter's skin crawl and the harsh white sparks sizzle in his skull.

Breathe in, breathe out.

Then Boomer picked up the cover to the detonator box and screwed that on, too. He took a double syringe from his pocket and snapped off the twin tips. On the box lid he squeezed out double pools of gel, then used the syringe noses to mix the two gels together.

"There was one guy in Sadr City liked to do this," said

Boomer, and waved the double syringe. "Five-minute epoxy." He dipped the noses in the mixture and dabbed it over the screw heads on the central detonator box. "Makes this shit really hard to take apart." He reached over the spiderweb of conduit to the smaller junction boxes and dabbed more epoxy on their cover screws, too. "I always figured he wanted more time. If someone found his IED and called us to defuse, he had a few more minutes to get there. I figured he liked to watch."

"And you like to watch," said Peter.

"Oh, yeah," said Boomer, eyes gleaming. "The best is when you're close enough for the pressure wave to just about knock you on your ass."

"Oh," said Peter. "That's where your brain damage came from."

"That's enough." Lipsky stood in the loading dock door. "Midden, you're riding in the back until we get to the site." He jerked his head at Peter. "I want to make sure this guy stays put."

"What about Dinah and the boy?" said Peter, the clamps on his chest getting tighter and tighter.

"Don't worry about them," said Lipsky. "Don't worry about anything. In less than an hour you'll be dead." He nodded at Midden. "Unless you mess with this guy, in which case you'll die whenever he wants you to."

Peter heard the rumble of an expensive engine, the crunch of tires on the driveway, and the slam of a car door right beside the truck. Lipsky had his pistol out so quickly that Peter didn't even see it happen.

"Is the party still happening?" Skinner's pale, aristocratic face peered through the gap between the truck and the warehouse, his white-blond hair stylishly unkempt. "I wanted to see the device before it was too late." He put a foot on the bumper, climbed up onto the loading dock's bumper pad, and peered into the truck, his eyes wide. "Wow! That is really something, gentlemen."

His face was flushed. He wore an off-white summer-weight suit, a money-green tie, and a feverish grin. The finger that Lewis had broken when he tore the gun from Skinner's hand was set in a cheap drugstore splint. Peter hoped it hurt like hell.

"What the fuck are you doing here?" said Lipsky, truly angry for the first time that Peter had seen. "You're supposed to be on a plane."

Skinner waved him off. "Private charter, direct to the Caymans," he said. "They're on my clock." He dipped his hand in his pocket and came out with a little knife that he opened with his thumb. "But I have something to settle with this guy first." He started toward Peter.

Peter held hard to the cargo ring with both hands and prepared to kill Skinner with his feet, but Midden took a step to intercept.

"Ow! Hey," said Skinner, holding his wrist. "Give me that!"

"Jon, control yourself," said Lipsky.

"He wrecked my Bentley! That was a three-hundred-thousand-dollar car!"

Lipsky put a hand on his arm. "I'll buy you another

one. Okay? Whatever color you want. But you need to be on that plane. Now, don't touch anything else, get in your car, and go directly to the airport. When you get to the hotel, destroy your suit and shoes and replace them from the hotel shop. Do you hear me?"

"Come on, he's going to die anyway. Why can't I kill him?" Skinner sounded like a child. Something was definitely not right in there.

Peter said, "You know he's slipped his leash, right?"

"Shut your mouth, or I'll give him his knife back."

"Look at his eyes, Detective. What if he decides to stab a stewardess? Then you're really screwed."

Lipsky pivoted and swung his pistol into the side of Peter's head, which flared in a bright burst of pain. He closed his eyes against it and kept breathing, in and out. Kept the static from rising up completely.

Lipsky's voice was a little farther away now. "Keep an eye on him, Sergeant. I'll come for you when it's time. We're almost there."

"Can I hit him?" Skinner's voice was eager.

"No," said Lipsky, calm again. "You're leaving."

"What about the nigger? The one who was with him when he wrecked my Bentley?"

"Wait," said Lipsky. "There's someone else?"

Felix walked past to slip out the loading dock door. Boomer followed with Dinah and Miles.

Lipsky rolled down the truck door with a clatter. Then the clank of the latch. Peter was trapped in the back with Midden and the bomb.

Waiting for Lewis.

He heard Boomer talking faintly through the aluminum skin of the truck. Then Lipsky, and maybe Dinah.

Breathe in, breathe out. The white static rose.

Then he heard the bark of a dog.

44

TWO HOURS EARLIER

Charlie

"Run. Charlie, run!" his mother screamed. Charlie froze. He'd never heard her sound so scared before.

There was a loud noise and smoke in the room, and Lieutenant Ash's two friends raced forward with guns in their hands. But his mom shoved him through the door to the basement stairs and closed the door behind him. He stood on the step in the dark with Mingus beside him and he couldn't see anything.

He put his hand on the door and felt the thunk as she threw the deadbolt.

Mingus growled at the banging and shouting above them. People were shooting, Charlie knew. Shooting at one another. Maybe at his mother.

Then Mingus bumped Charlie with his shoulder, nudging him down the stairs. Charlie reached out to grab his rope collar. Mingus pulled him onward through the dim, musty maze of the basement to another set of stairs with a faint rectangular frame of light at the top. Charlie climbed up into the kitchen of some kind of empty old restaurant that smelled like spilled beer and old people. He locked the basement door behind him, ran past the bar and the tables with their chairs stacked on top, opened the deadbolt on the outside door, and ran across the street, the dog hard at his heels.

He watched from the shelter of overgrown bushes, Mingus crouched beside him, as two men put his mother and brother in the back of a plain white van and climbed in. Charlie felt a wave of relief seeing them alive, even if they did have what looked like old shirts over their heads. But the other two men, the friends of Lieutenant Ash, did not come out.

The dog growled.

"Mingus, quiet," said Charlie. "Just wait."

He didn't think anyone had taught the dog those commands, but Mingus seemed to understand. Charlie wished he had his baseball bat, but he knew better than to think it would help him against these men and their guns. He was angry and afraid in equal amounts. He wondered if that was how his dad had felt when he was off at war. Or back home.

The white van's engine started. Behind him in the bushes, leaning against the house, Charlie found an old ten-speed bike with curly handlebars. When the white van pulled out, Charlie hopped on and followed.

Good thing he'd run all those sprints at basketball practice. He had to pedal awfully hard to keep up with the van.

He was pretty sure that the two men had killed Lieutenant Ash's friends.

The van was pulling away from him, so Charlie pedaled harder. He was the man of the family, and he was going after his mother and his brother. Mingus was ahead of him, but the dog kept looking over his shoulder to make sure Charlie was still there.

The white van drove like every other car or truck, no crazy moves. Nobody would know there were people trapped inside, maybe tied up. Maybe hurt.

Still, the van drove faster than Charlie could ride on the old ten-speed, and he had trouble keeping up. Only three speeds worked. He felt bad about taking the bike, because stealing was definitely wrong. Not that he had much choice. But at the same time he wished he'd managed to steal a better bike, and wondered what Father Lehane would say about that.

He was lucky that there were a lot of cars on the road, because when the van got stuck in traffic or at a light, Charlie could make up lost ground. And he knew he didn't want to get too close. Even Mingus seemed to know he couldn't do anything while the van was still moving.

Eventually the van came up to a giant old falling-apart brick building. A big squat-nosed cargo truck, like the rent-to-own furniture trucks, only plain white with no markings, was backed right up against the building.

"Mingus, come." Charlie stopped in the street, breathing hard behind the shelter of a tan SUV, and got his hand on Mingus's collar. He wished again that he had his baseball bat. He wanted to hit those men with the bat, hit them hard and make them pay. Mingus pulled to get away.

"Mingus, stay," said Charlie.

He used his serious voice the way Lieutenant Ash told him to. He watched the van pull up to the building and wait.

Mingus pulled at his collar again, like he wanted Charlie to do something. But Charlie didn't know what to do. Maybe Mingus didn't, either.

Then a window hummed down in the tan SUV.

A deep voice said, "Hey, kid. Where you get that ugly dog?"

45

Lewis

The kid took a step back and looked Lewis right in the eye. "Mister, I don't know you."

The kid looked more like Jimmy than Lewis would have thought possible. Lean, not grown into it, but he would get some size on him, you could tell. Big bony shoulders, and feet like a damn yeti.

"Your dog knows me," said Lewis, putting out his hand for the animal to sniff. "Name of Mingus. Peter found him under your porch. And you one of Dinah's boys, supposed to be with your mom and Nino and Ray at my place."

The kid looked at him with a complexity of expression older than his years. "I think Nino and Ray are dead."

It hit Lewis like a stone, that crippling loss, but he made himself set it aside. Time for that later. "Tell me."

"Two other men came. My mom put me and Mingus down the basement stairs, and I made it out another way. I watched from the bushes while they put my mom and little brother in that van right there." He pointed at the white Dodge van that had pulled up right before the kid. "I took this bike, and followed them here."

Lewis looked at the boy with new respect. It was no small thing, what he'd done. But he couldn't be out on the street, not now.

Lewis said, "Put up that bike and get in here."

When the kid opened the passenger side, the damn dog jumped in first, crouched down on the center console, growling at the white van and tearing up the leather with his claws. Breathing down Lewis's neck, that big fucking dog.

Lewis didn't like dogs. He'd never liked dogs. Would never like dogs. Then again, to have a four-legged assault weapon was maybe not such a bad thing. Although he didn't think this particular dog could actually be controlled. This dog had a mind of his own.

The guy with the scarred face got out of the white van and looked around like Mr. Magoo trying to spot a tail. Very subtle. Then he walked to the rear doors and opened them up, the doors blocking the view. Lewis caught a glimpse of a blank-faced man in a black jacket, with his hand on someone's elbow, and maybe a fourth person, who must be the little brother, as they walked behind the big Mitsubishi to the loading dock and disappeared.

"Shit," said Lewis. "Shit, shit, shit."

He'd been there all night, waiting for Peter to come back. The jarhead was supposed to meet the cop at eleven and set things in motion from there. But something had gone wrong, because Peter hadn't come back and hadn't answered his phone, either.

Lewis had decided he would stay put, watch and wait. Do nothing without word from Peter, unless the big Mitsubishi tried to leave. Then he'd trigger the charge they'd rigged under the Mitsubishi's engine block overnight, and use his shotgun to take out the driver and anyone else he didn't know. Lewis was looking forward to it. The cops would come soon enough after that.

But this was new information. Dinah taken. This changed the plan. He could not just watch and wait. Hell, no, he could not.

Not once Dinah got taken inside.

Seeing her, it was like he was fifteen again.

He wanted to kick the door down and do some damage. Do it old-school.

But Dinah's oldest boy was under his care. Lewis couldn't leave him, at least not yet. He'd watch and wait a few more minutes, see what happened next.

He wondered if the kid knew how to drive. It would be a help. Twelve was old enough to learn.

But Dinah was inside. He couldn't leave her, either. He looked at his watch. He would give it fifteen minutes. Then call the cops and go in.

"Aren't you going to go get my mom?"

The kid was looking at him. Lewis couldn't get over how much he looked like Jimmy.

"Yeah," he said. "I am. But not yet."

He heard the faint tick of the second hand and kept

both eyes on the truck. He thought about what these assholes were up to. It had to be about money. It was always about money, one way or another. So how could a man make a profit by putting a big bomb together with a hedge-fund asshole?

Lewis had been thinking about it since last night. He was pretty sure he had it figured out.

He didn't think the target even mattered.

It probably didn't even matter if the bomb actually went off.

A bomb found at the Federal Reserve Bank of Chicago, or at any regional headquarters of a big commercial bank, would send the markets into the tank. If Skinner knew when that would happen and planned ahead, he would clean up.

Lewis briefly wished he could get online and make a few trades.

Instead he waited.

And counted.

He was about ready to send the kid to the Boys and Girls Club and kick in that warehouse door when Skinner showed up.

Not in the busted-up Bentley, Lewis noted. But in a very nice Audi SUV, which he parked beside the box truck like he owned the place. He walked around to the back of the truck and climbed up the loading dock and inside.

So Peter was right about the hedge-fund asshole, which meant Lewis was right about the financial part.

* * *

After a minute or two, Skinner sauntered out to his car and drove away.

Lewis had the little Radio Shack transmitter in his hand, ready to blow the charge on the truck's engine block. The 10-gauge was muzzle-down in the footwell, ready to put some holes through the driver of the truck. Then the radiator, then the tires. Better to blow it up here in a neighborhood of single-family houses, where evacuation would be relatively simple and fast, than a more dense target area. Like downtown Chicago. It was only ninety miles away.

"Okay, kid. Time for you to get out of the truck, take that dog, and get as far away from here as you can. Someplace safe."

"Sir, I'm not going anywhere."

Kid had that same stubborn look as Jimmy, too. "Listen," said Lewis. "I ain't askin', I'm tellin'. The shit is about to hit and you gotta be somewhere else. There gonna be bullets flying and God knows what. And your mom would skin me alive if something happened to you. So get out the truck and walk away from that warehouse. I want you at least two blocks away."

"Mister, that's my mom, and my little brother." The kid's mouth was set. "I'll duck down low. Nobody will see me. But I'm not leaving."

Lewis was starting to think that he wouldn't win this one. The engine would shield the kid some. It wasn't the worst idea, except for the bomb. But if the bomb went off, wouldn't none of them be left in one piece. The cold autumn wind blew through the open windows. The dog panted in his ear. He opened his mouth to reply when a skinny shave-headed guy in a Marine's dress uniform came out and climbed up into the driver's seat of the big box truck. That would be Jimmy's missing Marine, Felix.

"Get down. Now," said Lewis. He opened the door and stepped out of the Yukon. He laid the 10-gauge across the hood and flipped the power switch on the transmitter, arming the radio. He put his thumb on the little red button.

Then the guy with the scars came out holding the smaller boy by the arm, not gently.

"Shit," said Lewis, and took his thumb off the little red button. He watched as the guy with the scars pushed the kid up into the cab of the truck on the driver's side, and the missing Marine scooted over to the passenger seat to make room. Then a tall, rangy white guy with a nice coat and a cop haircut—had to be the cop Lipsky—came out with his hand hard on Dinah's arm. Lewis was stunned by the sight of her, even half a block away. He didn't think he'd ever be able to see her without that tightness in his stomach. He didn't think he wanted to.

Had she been wearing handcuffs before? She wasn't now. Lipsky hustled her up into the driver's seat, and Lewis knew he'd lost his chance to blow the engine block. It would kill Dinah, and the boy, too.

Lewis only had the 10-gauge. At that distance, he

might well kill everyone in the cab of that truck with a single pull of the trigger. And he wasn't going to do that. It paralyzed him, just the sight of her. So there he stood, one foot on the ground, one foot still in the Yukon, unable to decide. Kill Dinah and her boy, or let the truck go. Let them all go.

Then the damn dog started barking, loud enough to be heard in Chicago. Lewis saw Dinah turn her head and look right at him, eyes wide. The cop shouted to the Marine and stepped up to the running board. He reached in through the open window and started the truck with a diesel rattle. Then he spotted Lewis with his cop eyes and pulled out his pistol.

Dinah ground the truck into gear without taking her eyes off Lewis.

And Lewis still couldn't do a thing.

The cop shouted again and Dinah gunned the engine and pulled the Mitsubishi out of the loading dock and onto the street like she'd been driving a truck all her life.

She turned right, up the street and away from Lewis, and the cop Lipsky stepped off the running board, walking toward Lewis with his pistol held down at his side like Wyatt fucking Earp.

The truck was at the end of the block now and turning behind the bulk of the warehouse. Lewis reached for the 10-gauge and Lipsky raised his gun and started firing steadily.

Lewis stood behind his door, which gave him some protection, but it didn't feel like it when the slugs started punching into the Yukon, spiderwebbing the glass. The guy wasn't just emptying his clip, he was aiming. For fifty yards away and walking, the guy was accurate as hell.

Lewis wanted to step out with the 10-gauge and put some holes in the man. It's what he should have done. Put the man down. But the boy was right beside him, Dinah's boy. And the boy didn't ask for this. The boy didn't have a choice.

So he ducked into the driver's seat, threw the Yukon in reverse, and roared backward up the street, steering with his mirrors and hoping like hell he wouldn't hit anything.

Maybe everyone else would die when that bomb went off, but not this boy. Not the son of Jimmy and Dinah, the woman they had both loved.

46

Peter

The white sparks rose up in him like something alive. Peter focused instead on the pain of the plastic handcuffs biting into his wrists as the truck lurched around the corner, picking up speed. Whoever was driving wasn't fucking around.

Something was very wrong. When the big diesel started up, he expected the next sound to be the hard crack of the charge detonating on the engine block. Instead the truck rolled out and he heard the pop pop pop of pistol fire.

He had to assume Lewis was dead. He was on his own.

The white sparks grew until he thought the top of his head would come off. His lungs were barely functional, sweat running down his face. Breathe in. Breathe out.

Midden stood on the other side of the cargo box, one hand looped easily through a cargo strap, blank as an unchiseled tombstone. Was there something in there?

"You think you're going to walk away from this?"

Peter's voice sounded strangled in his throat. Breathe in. Breathe out.

Midden didn't react in any way. As if Peter was already a ghost.

"They're going to kill everyone else, you know. Felix. Me. Dinah and Miles. Boomer. And you. It's going to be Lipsky and Skinner. They need someone to blame, and you're on the list."

The truck slowed slightly, then turned again. Peter swung at the end of his handcuff tether, his muscles clamping tight as the white static filled him. Where were they going? How long did he have? The truck gathered speed again, the tires thumping on the potholes. Midden stood like his feet were bolted to the floor.

Peter said, "You think you're ever going to get out of this truck? Boomer has the detonator, and it's armed. Have you even checked to see if that roll-up is unlocked?"

Midden just stared at him, his face a barren field. The soil so toxic that nothing could grow for millennia. But there was something going on inside that implacable mechanism. Peter knew there was. He just had to get access to it.

The white static roared in him, louder, higher. Wait, friend, please wait. The bands around his chest tighter and tighter. It was all he could do to speak.

"Listen, I don't know what you've done in your life. But nothing could be worse than what is about to happen. And it doesn't have to happen."

Midden just closed his eyes, as if profoundly tired. As if to pray. Or to weep.

47

Charlie

He held on with both hands as the SUV flew around the corners. Mingus crouched between the seats, digging in with his toenails, tongue flapping.

"Do you see it?" said the driver, Lieutenant Ash's friend. He drove like he was playing a video game, but this was not a game. "Do you see the truck? With your mom and your brother."

Charlie twisted in his seat, looking all around them. "I don't see it, I don't see it." Horns blared as they slid between the cars, cutting across lanes. His mom would kill him if she saw him like this. His feet on the seat, safety belt barely on. But he had to find her first. Once he got her free she could kill him all she wanted.

After zooming backward away from the guy shooting at them, they'd circled around to catch the big truck his mom was driving, but it had somehow gone a different way. And no matter where they went now, Charlie still didn't see it.

"Keep looking," said Lieutenant Ash's friend. "Guess I head for the freeway." He roared around a Volkswagen and took a right on Locust, then slowed past the district police station. "You know where they're going?"

"No," Charlie said, shaking his head. Did the guy think he wouldn't have mentioned it? But he kept looking. "Tell me who you are again?"

"Name's Lewis. Friend of your mom and dad, from a long time ago." He looked sideways at Charlie for a moment, his face gone funny. "You look like him, you know. Like your dad." He turned back to the road. "Sorry about him dying."

It was a weird thing to say, but people had said a lot of weird things since his dad had died. But Charlie was curious about something. "So, um. Why haven't I met you before?"

"We were friends in school. We all got mad and had a big fight. It was a long time ago. You want to talk about it later, that's fine with me, but maybe right now we find that truck, all right?"

With the police station behind them, they sped up again, weaving through traffic like they were standing still.

"Charlie," said Lewis. "I need your help. So I got to tell you something hard. You ready?" He looked sideways at Charlie again. "That truck got a bomb in it."

Charlie closed his eyes. Damn. His mom. His little brother. His damn mom! "What are they going to do with it?"

"That's what I want to know," said Lewis. "What's the target? Shit, what if it's in downtown Chicago?"

Charlie thought that seemed like a long way to go with a bomb in your truck. It was like the challenge problems in math class, trying to find the right path though a complicated equation. Then he saw the path.

He said, "What's the tallest building in Milwaukee?"

48

Lewis

Lewis blinked.

It was the U.S. Bank building.

He could see it in his head, a forty-two-story tower with white geometric bars, the bank logo right at the top. It even looked a little like the World Trade Center.

He looked at Charlie. "You got it. That's the one."

Thinking now that he really knew how they were going to make money. Skinner would have shorted bank stocks in general for several months in advance, as well as the market as a whole. He could have done that for nearly nothing, with a colossal upside if he could collapse the market, even for a day.

It was a good plan. Wasn't illegal to bet against the banks.

He pulled the Yukon to the side of the road. "Okay, kid. Time for you to get out."

The kid shook his head. Looked straight out the windshield. "No, sir," he said. The dog growled.

"No?" Lewis gave him his best dead-eyed glare. "Boy, you do not want to go where I'm going. This shit is gonna get real ugly. So get the hell outta my ride and take that damn dog, too."

"Nope." The kid set his mouth, stuck his chin out, and shook his head again. He looked so much like Jimmy right then. That same fucking stubbornness.

"Don't make me hurt you, boy. Get out of the truck."

Charlie looked at Lewis then, looked him right in the eye. "No, sir," he said. Very crisp and clear. "That's my mom and my little brother in that truck. So I'm going. Sir."

Lewis looked at the boy. Could see the man he might become. Lewis thought he'd like to know him. Not that Dinah would allow it. Even if they both managed to live through the next twenty minutes.

"Okay." Lewis nodded. "Okay." Then he put the pedal down and peeled out into traffic. "But here's the deal. You pay close attention, you do what I say, the first time I say it. No bullshit, no back talk, you hear me? I'm trying to keep you alive. If you die and your mother lives, she's gonna consider that failure, and so would I. That's not the trade she would make, you hear me? So keep your damn fool head down. And I'm not givin' you a firearm, so don't ask. Now I got something stupid planned, so get in the backseat. Right behind me, hear? And put on your seat belt nice and tight."

"What about Mingus?"

Lewis shook his head. All this shit and the kid was still thinking about the damn dog.

"Get him in your lap if you can, and hold on tight. You don't want him on the passenger side."

49

Dinah

Dinah wrestled the Mitsubishi down Humboldt. The huge pit in her stomach had nothing to do with driving the truck. It was big and clumsy, but if she didn't have to make too many turns, it wasn't difficult. She looked sideways at Felix in his uniform with his spooky eyes. He had his arm around her boy's shoulder, the muzzle of the gun pressed into his side.

"Why are you doing this?"

He didn't answer her. He stared straight ahead, lips moving but no sound coming out. Like he was praying.

The road was terrible, and the Mitsubishi's suspension was not designed for comfort. She felt every crack and pothole with a jolt up her spine.

"Talk to me, please, talk to me," she said. "Tell me why my son has to die."

"Just drive," said the man. His voice was thin, but his grip on her son was still strong. "It'll be over soon."

She wanted the courage to just wreck the truck, drive it off a bridge. The river was coming up. That would be the best thing for it, to drop the bomb in the river. But she wasn't sure she could.

50

Peter

The plastic handcuffs bit into the skin of Peter's wrists with each lurch and shudder of the truck. He trembled with the effort of holding in the static.

The cargo box was closed in around him, his heart thumping in his chest, his breath trapped in his lungs. He was burning up in his sweat-soaked T-shirt even though it was cold enough to see his breath.

The dark chemical stink of fuel oil filled the truck. His muscles were tight as clamps.

Static was like a flashing thundercloud in his head, wrapped tight around his brainstem. His skull throbbed, about to explode.

Midden stood by the cargo door with his eyes closed, still holding the tie strap. The man was as lethally capable as any man Peter had ever met. Peter saw how he'd hauled Zolot in. He'd broken both of the burly policeman's arms without any apparent effort. He could surely stop Peter from doing anything, handcuffed to the wall as he was. Plus he had a wicked-looking folding knife clipped into his front pants pocket.

But Peter saw something in him. A flash of morality at Lipsky's willingness to kill Dinah and Miles. He seemed to be thinking. And he seemed to be listening.

Meanwhile, the truck kept rolling closer to its terminal destination, and Peter was sure he'd heard Dinah and Miles in the cab.

He didn't have long.

He couldn't hold back the white static forever.

He said, "I'm guessing you were overseas, like me." Midden didn't open his eyes or show in any other way that he'd heard. Peter said, "Maybe that gives us something in common, maybe not. I don't know your part in this, and I don't care. I just need to stop it."

51

Midden

Midden listened while the Marine talked. Eyes still closed.

That alone was an admission of guilt, a willingness to die, given that he was well within the reach of the Marine's feet. But the Marine made no move, not yet.

Holding on to the strap, truck bucking unpredictably under his feet, Midden thought about everything he'd done to this point in his life.

The years and lives wasted in Iraq for a bankrupt cause.

The leaders he once trusted proving themselves unworthy of his trust, unworthy of the sacrifices of his fellow soldiers.

Proving it over and over again.

He had thought by working with Lipsky and Boomer that he would serve himself for once. Be done with causes and get paid. Retire someplace quiet with his nightmares and his memories, and see how long he could keep from eating his gun. Not long, he suspected. Not long at all.

Only to discover that this Marine, who had likely had the same experiences as Midden, the same friends killed for the same wrong reasons, the same utter loss of all faith in man and God, was still fighting for a cause.

Still willing to sacrifice his own life for others.

The Marine kept talking. "You can do the right thing right now. Do nothing. And I'll forget we ever met. You just walk away. You have my word."

"No," said Midden. Eyes still closed.

There it was again, that word come unbidden.

Midden had spent the last years trying to pretend the war hadn't happened, the war and everything he'd done fighting it. But now he found that he didn't want to hide from what he'd done, in the war or in this dirty little scheme.

Like the others, he, too, had wanted to get rich. And now he would share their guilt. There was blood on his hands. He had to be accountable for this. For everything.

The Marine was silent. There was just the roar of the engine, carrying them forward.

Then it occurred to Midden that maybe the Marine didn't know what he meant.

"Yes," said Midden. "Go. Do it."

When he opened his eyes, he saw the Marine's jaw clenched, the tendons popped on his neck, every muscle standing out clearly on his arms.

52

Peter

Now, Peter told himself.

And let go.

The static rose up in him, through him, without pause or hesitation. Like a beast straining against a leash, suddenly released.

He bit down hard to keep himself from roaring aloud.

What he wasn't prepared for was how *good* it felt.

The power. The release.

The white static moved his arms. The black plastic center block that locked the handcuffs gave way and the yellow cuff flew free from his strong left hand. The white static grinned through his mouth as it whipped the end free of the cuff locked to the truck.

The man in the black canvas chore coat stared at him, eyes wide, holding on to his cargo strap like a lifeline.

Peter ignored him and let the white static focus on the bomb.

The scarred man's design was good. The layers of protection were solid. The junction-box lids were epoxied shut, so he couldn't get to the C-4 directly. The weakest point was the heavy conduit conveying the wires from the central control box. If he could break the threaded connectors, he could pull the wires and free the blasting cap from the C-4 inside.

He took hold of the closest length of armored conduit and gave a hard jerk. No quick snap of the connectors, nothing gave way. Of course it couldn't be that easy. He braced his knees on the drums, set himself, and let the white static pull until his shoulders ached. But after a moment it was clear that the connectors and conduit were too strong to break that way.

He could crack them all eventually by stressing the joints, repeatedly bending the conduit back and forth. But it would take minutes for each drum, and he'd never get them all, not in time. Not before they arrived at wherever Lipsky had chosen for his ground zero.

His mind worked hard, riding the static like some animal tamer. Running through possibilities, searching for an answer, while also trying furiously to keep himself intact inside the rush of blinding white electricity. The hardest part was the pure joy of the static, the pleasure in destruction. He hadn't remembered how good it was, how alive he felt. Part of him, a disturbingly large part, wanted to leave the bomb in place just to watch it explode. To watch the world come down.

But he ignored that urge and channeled it. He leaped up onto the plastic drums for better leverage, and crept across the ordered conduit like a fly testing a spiderweb for weaknesses, and all the while the heaving truck tried to throw him to the floor. He had to get to Boomer's ignition system, the big central control box. If he could get only one box open, it had to be that one, where the cell-phone igniter connected the twelve-volt battery to the wires for the blasting caps. That way he could essentially pull all the wires at once.

The control box was at the center of the bomb. This plastic lid also was epoxied in place, but there was a little overhang, a thin lip where Peter might get a grip. Peter caught one edge of the loosened handcuff strap under the lip, and again set himself. Using his back and legs for leverage, he put the white static to work, roaring aloud as he pulled until his muscles screamed. Then he pulled harder. But the epoxy was stronger than the handcuffs had been. Stronger than Peter.

He kicked at the plastic box with his bare foot, hoping the box would crack and he could gain purchase there, but Boomer had used exterior-rated boxes, with thicker walls and stronger corners. Peter's foot did nothing.

He looked down from his perch on the drums at Midden, who still hung on to the cargo strap while the truck leaped and lurched under his feet. Peter saw the steel clip at his front pants pocket.

"Your knife," said Peter, barely recognizing his own voice. "Give me your knife."

The man seemed lost in his head, banished to whatever purgatory or hell he was making for himself there. He didn't seem to notice that Peter had spoken.

"Hey," said Peter, the white static roaring fully through him now. "HEY! Make yourself useful. Give me your knife."

The man didn't respond for a long moment.

The chemical fumes of the fuel oil mixed with the thumping of the truck over the potholes to give everything a terrible urgency. Every moment of travel that much closer to the time when the world would turn to fire.

Then the man's dark, dead eyes rose to meet Peter's while his right hand went to his pocket and took out the knife.

He opened it with his thumb, revealing the wide, wicked blade. The serrations designed for nothing other than opening up the flesh of a man.

He looked at Peter for a long moment.

Then swung his arm and lofted the knife underhand in a gentle pitch devoid of spin, one workman tossing a tool to another.

Peter smiled as it came, plucked it easily from the air, and in the next movement plunged the knife into the lid of the central control box.

53

Dinah

Dinah crossed North Avenue at the top of the hill, looking down toward the bridge where she hoped to put the truck into the river.

Miles clutched her waist and whimpered softly in the seat beside her. She wanted to put her arms around him, but the skinny man with the spooky eyes had his own arm wrapped around her son's neck, and she needed both hands to drive anyway. She'd take her son back soon.

Halfway down and picking up speed, she realized that she'd forgotten about the rebuilt bridge with its thick concrete guardrails. If she wanted to put the truck in the river, she'd have to turn a hard right at mid-bridge and jump the curb.

But she couldn't see it working now. She couldn't see this truck breaking through the thick concrete to make it to the river, not at an angle, not already slowed by the high curb, and the river only a few dozen yards across. If she made the turn at high speed, she'd flip the truck. She could see it happening in her mind.

They wouldn't make it to the water. She'd likely just flip the truck.

With the hundreds of car accident victims she'd seen at the hospital, she could see clearly the trauma of the accident, to her and to Miles. They had their seat belts on, but Miles was only eight. The seat belts wouldn't do enough.

It would break his neck.

And the man with the scars was behind them somewhere with his triggering device.

So the truck would explode anyway, with them both still in it.

But at least the blast would be in an open area, with only a few big residential buildings around them. Hopefully, most of the people would still be at work.

Thinking all this with her foot pressing harder on the gas and the bridge getting closer and closer.

Then they were at the river and Miles was crying, "Mommy, I'm scared." And the curb and guardrail were so high. She couldn't make her arms turn the wheel, she just couldn't. For a brief moment she saw the river shimmering below them, stretching toward the business district.

Then the bridge was past and the road ran uphill again.

As if on its own, the truck slowed for the light.

"Go right here," said the man with the spooky eyes.

His gun still pressed into her son's side. "We're going downtown."

She turned right down the narrow corridor between the tall new condominiums where the tanneries had once stood, seeing the river in tantalizing steel-gray glimpses between the buildings, bounded now by concrete banks on both sides. Sometimes she drove to work this way, liking the vitality of it, the big buildings and storefronts, the way the city was always making itself new again.

Then she caught her first glimpse of the tall white tower at the edge of downtown, the tallest building in the state. She knew their destination.

And how many people would die.

She thought of the road ahead. There were four more bridges before they came to the left for the tall, white bank building. All had been repaired or rebuilt in recent years, but one bridge had a block-long approach and open space to one side. She thought she could get up some speed and put the truck through the fence, over the bank, and into the water. She pressed the gas down.

"It's okay, Miles, honey," she said. "Everything's going to be okay. I love you very much."

She pushed the truck down the hill and around the curve where the road changed to four lanes, picking up as much speed as she could handle. Four blocks ahead was the Cherry Street Bridge. She was going almost fifty. The traffic was thin on this Veterans Day afternoon.

It wouldn't snow for another month at least, she thought.

She had always loved the first snow.

The bridge came into view. She could see her path. She took her hand off the gearshift and put it across her son's body, as much to simply touch his small, vulnerable body as anything like a hope that she might protect him from what came next.

"Go straight, slow down," said the man with the spooky eyes. "Slow down and go straight or I shoot the boy!" He jabbed the gun hard into Miles's side and the boy cried out in pain.

Her foot moved instinctively to the brake.

But before she could press down, a tan SUV with a big tubular bumper came up fast on her left, pulled even, then swerved hard right into the Mitsubishi's left front tire. Right at her feet.

She couldn't see the driver, but she recognized the Yukon.

There was a crunch and something gave way, something important. The steering wheel jerked and spun in her hand. She began to fight it automatically but forced herself to let go of the wheel, pivot her foot to the gas, and stomp down.

By the time the truck began to tilt, she was turned in her seat with her strong right arm pressing her son's chest hard into the back of his seat, and her left hand on the barrel of the spooky man's pistol.

54

Peter

In the cargo box, the plastic drums shifted in their webbing as the truck lurched hard to one side. Peter dug his toes into the lines of rugged conduit to hold himself, the white static powering his muscles to lock himself in place while he hacked the plastic cover off the central control box. It came off in sharp chunks, but it came off. Inside was the cell-phone-turned-detonator and the twelve-volt battery tucked under the neat bundles of colored wires that led to the blasting caps and the C-4. It was almost beautiful in its elegance.

It was possible that Boomer had built in a false circuit to kill anyone trying to disable the bomb, but Peter didn't have time to even contemplate that. He had to take this apart now or die in the attempt. He could clearly envision the scarred man with his phone in his hand. Beginning to make the call that would complete the circuit and set off the bomb.

He traced the wires with his finger, thinking that the

battery was the key to everything. Without the battery, the blasting caps would not explode. Without the blasting caps, the C-4 wouldn't go, or the rest of it.

The truck tilted beneath him. The static flared as Peter's muscles responded. He dropped to his belly and wedged his feet farther under the conduit. Then reached into the control box, through the wires, to the big battery. Grabbed it hard and maneuvered it out from beneath the bundled wires.

Boomer had actually soldered the power wires to the battery's terminals in great greasy conductive lumps. The white static burned cold as he wrapped the wires in his fist and pulled.

Trying to free them from the big battery.

Hoping to hell there wasn't anything else he should have done instead.

55

Lewis

"Here we go, kid. Hang on to that dog. Remember, do what I tell you."

Mingus growled over the roar of the engine as Lewis turned the wheel and punched the Yukon's front end hard into the Mitsubishi's driver's-side tire. He saw Dinah's face in her window, her eyes wide. Metal shrieked and the seat belt bit into him.

The Yukon's nose dropped as the bigger truck crushed its front suspension, then pushed it hard away. But something had broken or bent at that side of the Mitsubishi, the tie rod or axle, forcing it into an abrupt turn. The right-side tires left the ground as the truck began to tilt.

"Charlie, you okay? Charlie?"

No answer from the backseat. The Yukon sputtered and died.

Lewis looked through his cracked windshield to see Dinah in the cab of the Mitsubishi, wrestling with the skinny guy in the uniform for the gun. The big truck heaved across two lanes of traffic and up a curb to smash its passenger side into a lamppost.

"Charlie, get out right now and run away as fast as you can."

Lewis slipped off his seat belt and climbed out of the ruined Yukon to help Dinah. He looked over his shoulder as he ran and saw the black Ford pull up a block away.

The scarred man had something in his hand that looked like a cell phone.

Even at that distance, Lewis could see the look of rapture on the scarred man's face as his thumb stabbed down on the keypad.

Lewis sprinted around the front of the Mitsubishi and hauled open the passenger door.

56

Peter

The detonator phone's screen flashed white as an incoming call activated the vibrator.

The circuit closed. The vibrator hummed.

But the wiring hung torn from the big battery like a broken spiderweb.

Peter remained miraculously alive.

"Go go go," he said as he pulled his feet from under the conduit and jumped to the plank floor. Midden was kicking the twisted roll-up door free of its broken latch, sheared off by the impact of the collisions.

Together they hauled up the door and saw the scarred man standing outside the Ford SUV, pressing a button on his cell phone again and again. Midden took a target pistol from his coat pocket and shot out two tires on the Ford without appearing to aim. Boomer looked up from his phone, startled.

A dog growled low and deep.

Peter knew that growl.

The growl sounded like his white static felt. Like overwhelming fury harnessed to an unrelenting will.

"Mingus, get him."

Not that the dog was waiting for permission. He bolted past the open roll-up door, all fluid muscle and flashing teeth and orange polka-dotted fur that shone somehow bright under the pale November sky.

Boomer's eyes grew wide, and he turned to run. Mingus growled happily at the sight.

Mingus wouldn't actually eat the man, would he? Although Peter hoped the dog would at least chew on him some.

Behind the big Ford, a black unmarked police car glided to a halt, a cockeyed gumball flashing red on its roof. Lipsky unfolded himself from behind the wheel with his pistol in one hand and his badge in the other.

"Nobody move!" he shouted. "You're all under arrest!"

Lipsky looked good, Peter had to admit. The detective clearly had his survival strategy worked out. He'd be the good guy. The savior of the city.

But the man in the black canvas chore coat reached out his hand, the target pistol like a pointing finger. The single report was surprisingly quiet in the still air.

A faint red hole appeared in Lipsky's forehead.

He looked vaguely surprised, just for a moment. Then he dropped like a stone.

Peter jumped to the ground and ran around to the cab of the truck. Thinking of Dinah up there with Felix.

But Peter was too late.

Felix lay curled into a ball on the median. Lewis held Miles securely in his arms, grinning wide while Charlie helped his mom out of the truck.

As it turned out, Lewis was a hero after all.

"The cop is dead, and the bomb's out of commission," said Peter.

"That's good," said Lewis, " 'cause this kid's heavy." Although the way he held the boy, hands locked tight together, face half buried in his hair, it looked like he'd never let Miles go.

Peter had wondered what Lewis would do if he had the chance. If Lewis would step into that empty space.

He felt happy for Lewis, and for Dinah. This might be the best possible result.

For himself, he felt only relief as the pressure began to ease in his head. The white static deflating like spent foam from a fire extinguisher, leaving behind it only the shakes, the beginning of a killer headache.

He went to find the man in the black barn coat.

Midden stood in the open cargo bay of the Mitsubishi, with his target pistol pressed into the soft flesh under his own chin. Finger on the trigger, knuckle gone white with pressure.

"I think you'd better give me that," said Peter, reaching out his hand.

Midden stared at him, dark eyes swimming in unwept tears. "I've done so much," he said. "You'll never know."

"I do know," said Peter gently. "Really, I do. Give me the weapon."

But he didn't wait for the other man to move. He extended his hand with infinite care and took the pistol from the other man's hand. Then looped an arm around the man's shoulder and pulled him in close.

"You're okay," he said. "It's all okay. My name's Peter."

The sound of sirens rose up around them as they stood, coming no doubt from the Veterans Day parade less than a mile away.

Peter had another thought. "Lewis," he called out. "Hey, Lewis." He stuck his head around the corner of the truck.

Lewis stood watching Dinah with a dopey grin on his face. Dinah looked deeply confused but not entirely unhappy. The boys jumped up and down like maniacs.

"Lewis, you better get out of here before the cops come," said Peter. "And take this guy with you. He's a friend of ours."

Lewis opened his mouth to talk, but Peter shook his head.

"He's a friend. And I'll deal with the cops," he said. "I'll find you in a few days. You know we're still missing one asshole. Skinner's still going to make out like a bandit on this."

Lewis nodded. Then ducked in cautiously to peck Dinah on the cheek. Dinah didn't lean in to the kiss, but she didn't move away, either. Her eyes were shining.

The sound of the sirens grew louder, and came from all directions.

"Come on," said Lewis to Midden. "We gotta skate."

As the two men jogged across the bridge to disappear into the tangled streets of Brewer's Hill, Peter turned to Dinah. "You're okay?"

"Oh, hell, no," she said, tears streaming down her face. She pulled her boys close with a ferocious smile. "But I'm good."

"I'm going to take off for a few minutes," said Peter. "Get hold of my dog. I don't want the cops to shoot him. But I'll be right back."

EPILOGUE

The British Virgin Islands were a boater's paradise, with steady winter winds, sheltered anchorages, and excellent restaurants. The sailing yacht *Skin Deep* swung on her anchor in thirty feet of turquoise water off Cooper Island. Manchioneel Bay was crowded with boats, the Christmas tourist season in full flood.

The fifty-foot cruiser was a beautiful boat, her sleek lines much admired by the charter tourists from Indiana and Missouri in their smaller rented plastic tubs. *Skin Deep*'s owner had brought her in by himself, the boat apparently rigged to sail single-handed with every modern convenience.

Like the boat, her owner was handsome with an aristocratic charm, clearly a man of means and much invited to dinner at the Cooper Island Beach Club. He flirted shamelessly with the wives and daughters and impressed the men with his broad knowledge of fine wines and the financial markets. When asked what he did for a living, he smiled broadly and said only that he was an investor whose biggest bet had paid off handsomely. Then changed the subject to various routes through the islands to South America. He planned to make Rio in time for Carnival.

After dark, the reggae grew louder in the beachside bars. Daiquiri-stunned tourists steered their buzzing dinghies uncertainly from the Beach Club to their chartered tubs. Nobody noticed the silent swimmers easing through the black water toward *Skin Deep*'s teak-trimmed stern ladder.

Three forms floated like ghosts up her side and into her salon. Footprints wet on the deck, and warm as blood.

Then came a moment when the boat rocked violently, but only for a moment. Perhaps just a rogue wave in the night, from a ship passing far out at sea.

Then *Skin Deep*'s hatches slid shut one by one. The generator started up and the air-conditioning came on, the metallic purr floating softly across the water. For a long time, no other sound could be heard.

In the morning, the charter tourists noticed that *Skin Deep*, that elegant sailing yacht, seemed to have slipped her moorings in the night and headed off to sea.

Standing behind the big chrome wheel, steering past Great Dog Island, Lewis was sorry they couldn't keep the boat.

When the news of the bomb came out, the markets

panicked. Even though the bomb didn't actually explode, Skinner's scheme paid off in a big way.

So once they had the account numbers and passwords, once the money was transferred and laundered, Lewis could buy his own boat. They all could. They could buy a damn fleet.

Although he was probably just going to go back home. He and Dinah were really talking again. And those boys. He was crazy about those boys.

He didn't know if it would work out. But he could try.

It was amazing what happened when you started doing the right thing.

He could see Midden and Peter inside the boat's salon, talking quietly with Skinner, who lay wide-eyed and duct-taped on the teak floor. Skinner's laptop was open on the chart table, waiting for the satellite connection.

The lights of Virgin Gorda were gone behind the headland when Peter came out of the salon with two cold bottles of Red Stripe.

He took a deep breath of the cool night air to settle the white static and closed the door behind him. "It's done." He handed Lewis a beer.

Lewis smiled, his tilted grin wide. "How much?"

"You won't believe it," said Peter. The breeze felt clean on his face, and the lights on the distant islands looked close enough to touch. The boat lifted on the waves and he felt his shoulders loosen and drop. "More than an honest man could make in a hundred lifetimes."

"Never said I was an honest man," said Lewis, his grin white in the dark night. "Four-way split, right?"

"Our deal was eighty-twenty, remember? Eighty for you, twenty for Dinah."

Lewis shook his head. "I invalidate that agreement, motherfucker. Make it an even split, four ways. You, me, Midden, and Dinah."

"What you do with your money is up to you," said Peter. "I wouldn't know what to do with it."

"We'll work that out," said Lewis. "I got some ideas. Midden and Josie talking about the vet center, want to get it going for real." Lewis flashed the tilted grin again. "Got some decent funding now. Do some good in the world. Could use us a jarhead."

"I can't spend the winter in Wisconsin," said Peter. "If I'm stuck inside more than twenty minutes, I start climbing the walls. It took me eight Xanax to manage the plane trip here."

"Got people you can talk to about that," said Lewis, not unkindly. "Don't have to be no permanent condition."

Josie had told Peter the same thing, before she'd kissed him good-bye. She was staying in Milwaukee. She had work to do.

"Here's the thing," said Peter, and opened his arms to the warm Caribbean wind. A smile spread across his face. "Mostly I'd just rather be outside. Someplace where the weather isn't trying to kill me."

AUTHOR'S NOTE

The plight of America's veterans is very real.

Most veterans come home and restart their lives. They go to work or school, reconnect with their families or start new ones. Thanks to improvements in battlefield medicine, more injured veterans survive their physical wounds than ever before.

But our country still doesn't put enough effort into helping those veterans settle back into civilian life. There's a great deal yet unknown about traumatic brain injury and post-traumatic stress, war wounds that are often not visible but can lead to significant challenges for those affected.

When I began researching this book in 2010, veterans had a significantly higher rate of homelessness and unemployment when compared to others of similar age and background. I'm glad to note that, according to 2013 reports by the Department of Veteran's Affairs and the Department of Housing and Urban Development, these statistics are improving. But *Stars and Stripes* reported in 2014 that veteran suicide rates were actually getting worse, not better. Clearly these challenges are still substantial for everyone involved. For a country with our wealth, history, and ideals, we can continue to do better for those who have given so much to serve their country. On the positive side, many cities are making great strides in eliminating homelessness among veterans, although this remains an ongoing issue.

I'm not an expert in veterans' affairs. My primary goal is to entertain you, my readers. But if I'm lucky, perhaps the stories I invent will also have the ring of some kind of truth, will make you feel and think.

I made a point to avoid writing about Peter's life overseas because I wasn't there.

But in the years after 9/11, as the wars and those who fought them on our behalf became a significant part of the national conversation, I began to read and watch documentaries about service members' experiences, both during war and coming home. I had friends and professional acquaintances and customers who'd been in the service, and talking with them illuminated a part of the American story that I hadn't quite understood before.

Perhaps the most meaningful conversation I had was also one of the shortest. It was seven or eight years ago, but I remember it clearly.

I was inspecting a small older home for an Army

veteran and his wife. He was at least fifteen years younger than me, back in the States for less than a month. He was smart and curious and polite.

When I learned where he'd been, I said to him, as I often did in the early years of those wars, "Thanks for your service."

"Man, don't say that." He shook his head. "Don't say 'Thanks for your service.' It drives me nuts."

"Okay." We were down in the basement. It was musty and cold. His wife was upstairs measuring for curtains. "What should I say?"

I can't begin to describe the expression on his face. Equal parts haunted and proud and relieved.

"Just say, 'Welcome home,'" he told me. "That's all."

So that's what I've said for many years, and I say it again now, to all those who have served.

Welcome home.

ACKNOWLEDGMENTS

This book was fun and challenging to write, and I didn't do it alone. I'd like to thank many people who have helped me along the way.

Thanks to Margret, sweet patootie, artist and reader and expert editor of far too many drafts, and to Duncan, my hero and role model. I can't wait to see what you both do next.

Thanks to Mom and Maryl for many years of encouraging literary criticism.

Thanks to Dad for spreadsheets and fatherly advice, some of which I actually acted on.

Thanks to Bob and Dani for a quiet space to work on Washington Island. Thanks to Taylor for her encouragement, and Robbie for his enthusiasm.

Thanks to Danny and Chuck for all those excellent conversations, diatribes, and rants.

Thanks to Aimee O'Connor for an encouraging read at a crucial time.

Thanks to Collectivo Coffee (formerly Alterra) for being my second office, where the java is strong, pastries are available, and there are voices other than the ones I hear in my head. ¡Viva la revolución!

Thanks to Brett Elver for answering my questions about finance—the liberties I've taken with reality are mine, not his.

Thanks to WFB friends for shared meals and liquid therapy and for making all those fantastic kids.

Thanks to Dale W. Davis, the first Marine I ever met, force of nature and certified piece of work, and to his wife, Jan, a strong woman and force of nature in her own right. Thanks for the great conversation and advice over the years.

Thanks to my teachers, including but definitely not limited to David Shields, Charlie D'Ambrosio, Maya Sonenberg, and David Bosworth in Seattle; Warren Hecht in Ann Arbor, who taught me to write a good sentence; and Mike Huth of SHS, gone but not forgotten. Thanks to Scott Wilson for his carpentry tutorial, and for our continued friendship since then.

Thanks also to many writers, including but not limited to Nathaniel Fick, whose book *One Bullet Away* helped illuminate one Marine lieutenant's thinking; Tim O'Brien for *The Things They Carried*, which sure cleared up one young man's idea of war as glamorous; Phil Klay for *Redeployment*, which was a personal revelation for me as both reader and writer; and David Finkel for the reporting and writing in *Thank You for Your Service*. These last three should be required reading for all aspiring architects of future wars.

Thanks especially to those men and women who shared their experiences online or in person. I still haven't talked to enough of you.

And last but definitely not least, thanks to the wonderful Barbara Poelle at Irene Goodman Literary Agency for taking time out of her third trimester sabbatical to read this book and find it a home (yes, she's that kind of agent). Also to the astounding Sara Minnich at Putnam for her extraordinary eye and ear, as well as the rest of the design and editing team at Putnam. They are the reason you're reading this today, and I am supremely grateful for their time and patience and professional expertise.

If you're reading this in a language other than English, that's due to the efforts of Heather Baror-Shapiro, of Baror International, who boggles my mind.

TURN THE PAGE FOR AN EXCERPT

In the new novel featuring war veteran Peter Ash, "an action hero of the likes of Jack Reacher or Jason Bourne" (*Lincoln Journal Star*), a woman's life is in Ash's hands—and her story is stranger than he could ever imagine. What they find leads them to an eccentric recluse, a shadowy pseudo-military organization, and an extraordinary tool that may change the modern world forever.

1

When he rounded the curve on the narrow trail and saw the bear, Peter Ash was thinking about robbing a liquor store. Or a gas station, he was weighing his options.

On foot with a pack on his back, he was as deep into old-growth redwood country as he could get. Although most of the original giants had been logged off decades before, there were still a few decent-sized protected areas along the California coast, with enough steep, tangled acreage to get truly lost. In the deep, damp drainage bottoms thick with underbrush, redwood trunks fifteen feet in diameter shot up into the mist like gnarled columns holding up the sky.

But Peter hadn't counted on the coastal fog. It had been constant for days. He couldn't see more than a hundred feet in any direction, and it made the white static crackle and spark in the back of his head.

It was the static that made him want to rob a liquor store.

The closest one was at least a few days' walk ahead of him, so the plan was still purely theoretical. But he was putting the pieces together in his mind.

He didn't want to use a weapon, because he was pretty sure armed robbery carried a longer sentence than he was willing to take. He didn't want to go to actual prison, just the local jail, and only for a few days. He'd settle for overnight. Although how he'd try to rob a liquor store without a visible weapon was a problem he hadn't yet solved.

He could put his hand inside a paper bag and pretend to be holding a gun. He'd probably have to hold something, to make it more realistic. Maybe a banana?

Hell, now he was just embarrassing himself.

Any respectable liquor store employee would just laugh at him. Hopefully they'd still call the cops, who would put him in the back of a squad car, then at least a holding cell. Maybe overnight, maybe for a few days. It was a calculated risk.

The problem was these woods. They were so dense and dark, the coastal cloud cover so thick and low, that he hadn't seen the sky for weeks. The white static wouldn't leave him alone, even out here, miles from so-called civilization. It pissed him off. He'd wanted to walk in this ancient forest for years. Now he was here in this green paradise and he couldn't enjoy it.

Peter Ash was tall and rangy, muscle and bone, nothing extra. His long face was angular, the tips of his ears slightly pointed, his dark hair an unruly shag. He had wide, knuckly hands and the thoughtful eyes of a werewolf a week before the change. Some part of him was always in motion—even now, hiking in the woods, his fingertips twitched in time to some interior metronome that never ceased.

He'd been a Marine lieutenant in Iraq and Afghanistan, eight years and more deployments than he cared to remember. Boots on the ground, tip of the spear. He'd finished with his war two years before, but the war still wasn't finished with him. It had left him with a souvenir. He called it the white static, an oddball form of post-traumatic stress that showed up as claustrophobia, an intense reaction to enclosed spaces.

It hadn't appeared until he was back home, just days from mustering out.

At first, going inside a building was merely uncomfortable. He'd feel a fine-grained sensation at the back of his neck, like electric foam, a small battery stuck under the skin. If he stayed inside, it would intensify. The foam would turn to sparks, a crackling unease in his brainstem, a profound dissonance just at the edge of hearing. His neck would tense, and his shoulders would begin to rise as his muscles tightened. He'd look for the exits as his chest clamped up, and he'd begin to have trouble catching his breath. After twenty minutes, he'd be in a full-blown panic attack, hyperventilating, the fight-or-flight mechanism cranked up all the way.

Mostly, he'd chosen flight.

He'd spent over a year backpacking in the Western mountains, trying to let himself get back to normal. But it hadn't worked. He'd finally forced himself outside his comfort zone to help some friends the year before, and it had gotten a little better. He'd thought he was making progress. But they'd gone back to their lives and Peter had gone off on his own again, and something had happened. Somehow he'd lost the ground he'd gained.

Lost so much ground that even walking through the foggy redwoods in the spring was enough to get the static sparking in his head.

Which is why he was contemplating the best way to get himself locked up. Get this shit out of his system once and for all.

He wasn't thinking it was a *good* idea.

Then he saw the bear.

It was about thirty yards ahead of him, just downslope from the narrow trail that wound along the flank of the mountain.

At first all he could see was a mottled brown form roughly the size and shape of a Volkswagen Beetle, covered with fur, attempting to roll a half-rotted log down the side of the mountain.

It took Peter a few more steps to figure out that he was seeing a bear.

The trail ran through a deep pocket of old-growth

trees in an area too steep for commercial logging. It was mid-March, and Peter assumed the bear was looking for food. There would be grubs under the log, which would provide much-needed protein in that still-lean time of the year. The bear grumbled to itself as it dug into the dirt, sounding a little like Peter's dad when he cleaned out the back of his truck. The bear was focused on its task, and hadn't yet noticed the human.

Peter stopped walking.

Black bears were plentiful in the wilder pockets of the West, but they were smaller, usually three or four hundred pounds when fully grown. Black bears could do a lot of damage if they felt threatened, but they usually avoided confrontation with humans. Peter had chased black bears out of his campsite by clapping his hands and shouting.

This was not a black bear.

This bear was a rich reddish-brown, with a pronounced hump, and very big. A grizzly. At the top of the food chain, grizzlies could be very aggressive, and were known to kill hikers. Clapping his hands wouldn't discourage the bear. It would be more like a dinner bell, alerting the bear to the possibility of a good meal.

The most dangerous time to meet a grizzly was in the fall, when they were desperately packing on fat to make it through the winter.

The second-most dangerous time was spring, with the bear right out of hibernation and extremely hungry. Like now.

Peter was lean and strong from weeks of backcountry hiking. His clothes were worn thin by rock and brush, the pack cinched tight on his back to make it easier to scramble through the heavy undergrowth. His leather boots had been resoled twice, the padded leather collars patched where mice had nibbled them for the salt while he slept wrapped in his ground cloth.

He'd walked a lot of miles in those mountains.

Now he wondered how fast he could run.

He took a slow step back, trying to be as quiet as possible, then another. Maybe he could disappear in the fog.

Peter had once met an old-timer who'd called the bears Mr. Griz, as a term of respect. The old man had recited the facts like a litany. Mr. Griz can grow to a thousand pounds or more. Mr. Griz can run forty miles an hour in short bursts. His jaws are strong enough to crush a bowling ball. Mr. Griz eats everything. He will attack a human being if he feels threatened or hungry. Mr. Griz has no natural enemies.

The bear was still focused on the rotting log. Peter took a third step back, then a fourth. A little faster now.

Call it a retreat in the face of overwhelming force. No dishonor in that, right? Even for a United States Marine.

The California grizzly was supposed to be extinct. But this bear looked big, and big males were known to travel long distances in search of mates. He was only sixty miles south of the Oregon border, and in this dark primeval forest, anything seemed possible.

Five steps, now six. Peter didn't care how much this

particular grizzly weighed, or what he felt like eating. He didn't want to find out. He was almost back to the bend in the trail. This would be a good story to tell someday.

Then he felt a slight breeze move the hairs on the back of his neck. The wind, which had been in his face, had shifted.

He was in trouble.

Grizzlies have fair eyesight and good hearing, but their sense of smell is superb. And the mountain breeze carried Peter's weeks-long hiking stink, along with the smell of his supplies, directly to the bear's brain. The supplies included a delicious trail mix made of cashews and almonds and peanuts and raisins and chocolate chips.

Much better than grubs under a log.

The bear's head popped up with a snort.

Peter stepped backward a bit faster, feeling the adrenaline sing in his blood, reminding himself of the old-timer's advice on meeting Mr. Griz.

You don't want to appear to be a threat, or to look like food. Running away is a bad idea, because bears can run faster than people. And running away is prey behavior.

What you were supposed to do, said the old-timer, was drop your pack to give the bear something to investigate, then retreat backward. If the bear charged, curl up into a ball, protecting your head, neck, and face with your arms. You might get mauled, but you'd be less likely to be killed.

Peter was not exactly the curl-into-a-ball type.

The bear stood upright on its hind legs, now a good

eight or nine feet tall, swung its enormous head toward Peter, and sniffed the air like a Silicon Valley sommelier.

Mmmm. Trail mix.

Peter took another step back. Then another.

The bear dropped to all fours and charged.

Peter shucked his pack and ran like hell.

He'd grown up with animals. Dogs in the yard, horses in the barn, chickens and cats wherever they felt like going. He'd kind of inherited a big dog the year before, or maybe the dog had inherited him, it wasn't entirely clear. In the end the dog had found a better home than Peter could provide.

But he liked animals. Hell, he liked grizzly bears, at least in theory. He certainly liked how it felt to know a big predator was out there. It made him feel more alive.

The backpack distracted the bear for only a few seconds, barely long enough for Peter to round the corner, find a climbable sapling, and jump up. The bear was right at his heels at the end. Mr. Griz chomped a chunk of rubber from the sole of Peter's boot. Peter was glad he got to keep the foot.

He scrambled higher, finding handholds in the cervices of the soft, deep bark. This was a redwood sapling, tall and straight as a flagpole. He hugged the trunk with his arms and legs while the bear roared and thumped the sapling with his forepaws, apparently uninterested in climbing up after him. The young tree rocked back and forth and Peter's heart thumped in his chest.

Alive, alive, I am alive.

Would you rather be here, or stuck behind a desk somewhere?

"Bad bear," he called down. "You are a very bad bear."

After a few minutes, Mr. Griz gave up and wandered back toward the smell of trail mix. Peter had to climb another ten feet before he found a branch that would hold his weight. He was wondering how long to wait when the bear returned, dragging Peter's backpack. It settled itself at the base of the tree and began to enthusiastically disembowel the pack.

After an hour, Peter's two-week food supply was working its way through the entrepreneurial bear's digestive system, along with his emergency phone, long underwear, and fifty feet of climbing rope.

"Mr. Griz, you give the word 'omnivore' a whole new meaning," Peter said from the safety of his high perch.

The bear then proceeded to entertain itself by shredding Peter's sleeping bag, rain gear, and spare clothing. Peter said a few bad words about the bear's mother.

Mr. Griz was tearing up Peter's new featherweight tent when it began to rain again. Big, pelting drops.

Peter sighed. He'd really liked that tent.

For one thing, it kept the rain off.

* * *

He'd slept in many strange places in his thirty-some years. His first six months, he was told that he slept in a dresser drawer. As a teenager in fairly constant and general disagreement with his father, he often preferred to sleep in the barn with the horses, even during the severe winter weather common in northern Wisconsin. He'd slept in tents, on boats, under the stars, and in the cab of his 1968 Chevy pickup. In Iraq and Afghanistan, he'd slept in a bombed-out cigarette factory, in a looted palace, in combat outposts and Humvees and MRAPs and anyplace else he could manage to catch a few Z's.

He'd never slept in a tree before.

It wasn't easy. The rain fell steadily, and soaked through his clothes. As the adrenaline faded, the static returned to fizz and spark at the back of his brain, which added to the challenge of sleep. His eyes would flutter shut and he would drift off, arms wrapped around the trunk of the sapling, serenaded by the snores of Mr. Griz below. Then he'd abruptly jerk awake to the sensation of falling and find himself scrabbling for a handhold, shivering in the cold and wet.

The night seemed to last a long time.

He spent the time awake remembering the previous winter, spent camping alone in the Utah desert. But the arid emptiness had left him with a longing for tall trees, so he made his way through the beautiful emptiness of Nevada to California's thirsty, fertile central valley and the overdeveloped mess of the northern Bay Area. It made him think, as he often did, that the world would be better off without so many people in it.

He'd parked his pickup in the driveway of a fellow Marine in Clearlake, California, and walked through housing tracts and mini-malls and vineyards and cow pastures to the southern end of the Mendocino National Forest, where he headed north. Sometimes he hiked on established routes, sometimes on game trails, sometimes wayfinding the forested ridges, trying to get above the rain and the fog and into the sun. He'd come too early in the year for summer's blue skies, but he didn't want the woods all cluttered up with people.

Instead he'd found a very large bear.

When it became light enough to see the ground, he looked down and considered his options. His gear was wrecked, his food supplies gone. Mr. Griz still down there, bigger than ever. Still snoring.

A cup of coffee would be nice, he thought. But not likely.

He was pretty sure his coffee supply was bear food, too.

He looked up. He was astride a sapling in a mature redwood forest. Although he couldn't see far in the fog, he was pretty sure the sapling went up another forty or fifty feet. The mature trees probably went up two or three hundred feet after that.

The rain had stopped sometime in the night, and although the fog was still thick, some quality of the mist had changed. It glowed faintly, green with growth and heady with the oxygen exhaled by giants. He thought maybe the sun had come out, somewhere up there. It turned the forest into something like an ancient cathedral.

He looked down. Mr. Griz, still sleeping. The contents of Peter's pack destroyed or eaten. The static fizzing and popping in his head. Peter himself cold and wet and tired.

He looked up again. The promise of sunlight, and warmth, and a view.

What, you want to live forever?

He smiled, and began to climb.

NICK PETRIE

"Lots of characters get compared to my own Jack Reacher, but [Petrie's] Peter Ash is the real deal."
—Lee Child